"Wake up," he growled, gripping the chin of the closest man and shaking him.

The slaver came to at once, grunting as he tried to yell through the cloth gag in his mouth. The sound was pitifully muffled, and he struggled with the bindings on his wrists and ankles.

"Shout all you want. No one can hear you through that," Raz spat, standing up.

The man stilled and grew silent, eyes wide, taking in Raz's towering outline against the lantern light from the road.

"If I'd wanted you dead, you'd be dead, so stop worrying. I have a message. On the other hand, if it's not delivered—well, your friends will be happy to explain the consequences to you."

He gestured to the other figures laying in the dark past the bound man, who turned to look. His muted scream was oddly satisfying, and Raz smirked humorlessly. The slaver fell over in his haste to scoot away. Blood pooled on the cobbled stone, forming black puddles where each of the rest of the patrol had had their throats slit. Every horrified gaze was wide and staring, some fixed upon the night sky above, some on the walls around them.

Raz had made sure each and every one knew they were going to die.

"Are you listening?" he asked.

The man nodded hurriedly, seeming unable to look away from the bodies of his comrades.

"Good. Then tell your employers that Raz i'Syul is coming for them next. Tell them the Monster says they'd best start running, and that they'd best start running *now*."

CHILD OF THE DAYSTAR
Book One of *The Wings of War* Series
Bryce O'Connor

ISBN: 0-9988106-1-4
ISBN-13: 978-0-9988106-1-4
Edited by Marcus Trower
Map by Bryce O'Connor

Cover art by Andreas Zafiratos
Cover design by Bryce O'Connor and Andreas Zafiratos

CHILD
OF THE DAYSTAR

BRYCE O'CONNOR

For my father,
who has only ever let me be
exactly who I wanted to be.

And my mother,
without whose drive and passion
I'd have never found my own.

Acknowledgments

There are so many to whom I owe everything and more when it comes to *Daystar*. If I had another 200 pages to fill, I might have a shot at giving them all the honors they deserve, but sadly this is not the case. Instead, I will limit myself to naming those individuals and groups without whom this book would truly have never existed, whether they are aware of their involvement or not.

My first thoughts are immediately of my family. To my sister, Sabine, for reading and giving her feedback, to my mother, Isaure, for her encouragement, and especially my father, Vincent, for his tireless patience and priceless critiquing.

To my friends and classmates who volunteered themselves as guinea pigs: Bryan Blanchette, Greg Yakimec, Tyler Kenton, Dan Moloney, Cassidy Goepel, Jenni Zelner, Cory Olivares, William Sisskind, Ethan Alderman, Heather Eastty, Chelsea France, and so many others. Thank you all.

To my good friends Patrick Anguish, David Haselden, and Debra Knickerbocker, for your golden support in my campaign toward publication.

To Professor Katharyn Howd Machan for helping me develop the only thing more important than imagination to a writer: discipline.

To Bev and Dan McCarron for helping me cinch the final knots, and Gary and Barb Kuscan for being my refuge when I needed a home away from home.

To Kate Thoene, because your friendship alone means more than any world I might be able to create.

To my incredible cover artist, Andreas Zafiratos, for working with me so patiently. See more of his work at www.facebook.com/artofalbinoz

To the numerous musical prodigies that comprise Two Steps From Hell. Thank you for almost single-handedly crafting the melodies and themes that allowed me to bring Raz and his crusade to life.

Similarly, to Todd Lockwood and Raymond Swanland. Thank you for creating art of such power it drives me to craft worlds of words that would do your pieces justice.

To Barnes & Noble for being the haven for so many of us hopeful dreamers. I wrote 99% of the words in this story seated at one of your tables.

To Brian Jacques, immortal in the memories of his readers, for making me realize the power of storytelling. To Elizabeth Hayden for my favorite fantasy novel to date. To Kristen Britain, Jennifer Roberson, Trudi Canavan, Robin Hobb, Terry Brooks, Anne Bishop, and every author who has ever enthralled and enchanted me with their characters and style.

And lastly, to two individuals whom I will never be able to thank enough for their contributions to my writing, imagination, and life:

J.K. Rowling, for lighting the spark of dreams and creativity.

And Brent Weeks, for blowing that spark into a firestorm.

CHILD
OF THE DAYSTAR

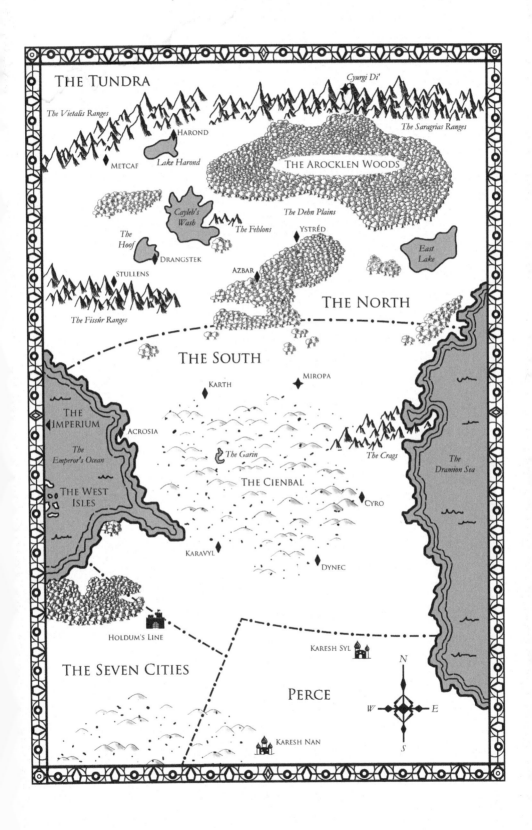

842 v.S.

Prologue

"By the Sun's grace, I grow. By the Moon's, I sleep. It is in their light that the world is, and it is by their light that I shall live."

—"The Twin's Prayer," from the libraries of Cyurgi' Di

He was at it again.

The boy's screams cracked the heavy silence of the desert air. Iron wristlets bound his clawed hands together, rusted edges lined with dried and still-drying blood. Heavy ropes kept his tail and leathery wings lashed tight around his scaled body. Just the same, despite the shackles and his small size, he still managed to hiss and snap at his captors whenever the opportunity presented itself. Like a snake the atherian bared budding fangs at anyone who got too close, the crest of steel-blue skin along the spine of his neck flaring brightly.

Vashül Tyre rubbed his temples with thumb and forefinger before rolling gray eyes to the blazing Sun above the caravan. Bedecked in pale cloth thinned by age and sand, he wiped the sweat from his nose and gave a tug on the leather reins of his gelding to keep the animal from wandering off course. They'd been on the move for two weeks already. Two weeks. By now the line was usually broken by hunger and fright, or at least by the endless heat that cast ripples like transparent ribbons across the horizon. The rest of them, the wingless lizard-kind stumbling along with the chains that kept them single file, had long since given up the fight. A few still joined the little one whenever he began his rants, squawking and screeching in unison, but it only took a few quick prods from the drivers' spears to shut them up.

There was no such treatment for the boy. Beatings only made the outbursts worse when they came.

Still... temporary satisfaction had its merits.

"Rincer!" the slavemaster snapped, tired of the atherian's endless tantrum. "Shut him up!"

Rincer Gravin, a burly former bandit with a heavy beard and three fingers missing from his left hand, dropped back to the end of the line where the babe was chained. The atherian watched him with narrowed

1

eyes, hissing at the man as the slaver drew a nine-tailed whip from his belt. Rincer leered from beneath his cowl, grinning until it was possible to see the reddish stain of ragroot in his yellowed teeth.

"You heard the master, didn't 'ya, boy?" he breathed into the child's face, bending low. "If'n you don't shut it, I'm gonna have some fun with this here toy of mine."

He rustled the nine-tails' studded straps in front of the atherian's snout for emphasis. The boy stilled, vertical pupils following the whip's motions with more caution than mutiny now.

Rincer chuckled. Turning around, he raised a hand to catch Tyre's attention.

"Reckon you just gotta know how to handle the flesh-eaters! I done put 'im in his pl—*ARGHHHHH!*"

It happened so suddenly no one had time to cry out a warning. Taking advantage of the man's turned back, the atherian pounced, heedless of the shackles that held his hands or the ropes that limited his movement. His teeth, barely a fraction of their adult size, found the back of Rincer's neck through the thin cowl and dug to the bone. The curved claws of his feet ripped and tore as the pair fell into the sand. As one the slave line faltered, the closest captives stumbling toward the fight, pulled along by the chains.

The lizard-babe attacked with weeks of pent-up savagery. Rincer screamed, writhing in the hot sand. Talons made short work of cloth and everything beneath. Blood and strips of flesh splattered the desert around them. Bones snapped and fabric ripped. The other slavers swarmed to the scene, Tyre screaming at them from the front of the line, "DON'T TOUCH HIM! HE'S WINGED! HE'S WORTH YOUR WEIGHT AGAIN IN CROWNS!"

Rincer's attempts to defend himself were pitiful. Atherian were stronger than men and faster by far. It was only superior planning that allowed Tyre's small group to do well selling them off to the Seven Cities and the gambling pits of Perce to the south. Even with that advantage it was a rare raid that went without injury.

Not that casualties, truth be told, were much less common...

"LEAVE HIM, I SAY!" the slavemaster screamed, swinging a leg over his saddle and leaping off his horse. With a flailing whip he broke through the ring of men that surrounded the pair still writhing on the ground. "Rincer was fool to turn his back on the animals! He deserves no help from the likes of—"

CRACK.

The atherian's jaws, still sunk deep around the back of the unfortunate slaver's neck, twisted suddenly. Rincer's whole body spasmed, arms and legs convulsing. Then the jerks subsided and he lay still, his head at a strange angle, his broad back flayed open. The air smelled of blood, and rivulets thick and dark dried until the sand around his corpse was dyed black. Only then, when Rincer's eyes stared sightlessly from his dust-caked face, did the boy let off his attack. Snout slick with gore, he raised his head and bared reddened fangs, the loose blue crest flaring again along the back of his neck. His wings tried to extend, but the bindings held tight, and he screamed in frustration at the slavers that surrounded him. His war cry was shrill, lacking the ferocity of an adult's, but it nevertheless rang with a defiance that had every one of the men take pause. The line was at a standstill, every eye on the boy.

"Move in slowly," Tyre ordered in a gruff hiss, taking a step forward. The blade of his saber scraped against its sheath as he drew it. "I don't want him harmed. We'll *drag* him to the Cities if we have to, but by the Sun he is coming with us."

"Ya' sure that's smart?" someone quipped from the back of the group. The slavemaster ignored them.

"Forward. Easy now..."

The drivers edged closer. The atherian in turn took a step back, off Rincer's body, hissing and struggling with his chains. Behind him the other captives in the line were spitting as well, bearing fangs at the men that threatened one of their young.

"Closer... closer..."

And then, faster than any of them could anticipate, the boy pounced again. He landed on the chest of the closest man, bearing him shrieking to the ground as a wolf might down a deer. Heavy black claws cut furrows once more, and the lizard-kind snapped at the man's throat, going for the kill.

There was a panicked howl, the flash of steel, and a blade bit into the infant's shoulder.

"NO!" Tyre yelled. The atherian screamed, but too late. Another sword landed, slicing open the boy's thigh, then another, spraying blood from nicked ribs. Mercifully, the next blow to connect was the butt of an old spear, catching the child in the side of the head. There was a second *crack* of breaking bone, and he collapsed, falling to the ground like a paper kite on dead wind.

3

"NO!" Tyre howled, laying about wildly with his whip again and scattering the men. "I said NOT TO TOUCH HIM. If he's dead, you'll pay! You'll all *PAY!*"

The line settled at once, the slavers breathing hard, all eyes on the still form of the lizard-babe. The remaining captives screeched and pined, seeing their hopes of rebellion shatter before them. One of the adults pulled forward, tugging a few of the others with her, trying to pick the infant up with her bound hands.

"Back!" Tyre roared, cracking the slave across the arms. "Get back! Damn flesh-eaters. Yssey! Check if the wretch is alive."

An older man with arms like a blacksmith's approached prudently, prodding the motionless figure with the tip of his dagger before venturing closer. Carefully he poked the body, then shook it, eventually even braving a couple of solid kicks for good measure.

"Nothin'," he concluded finally, stepping away. "Dead as dead."

A fluid string of curses leapt from Tyre's lips, and he whirled on the group.

"You, you, and you!" he raged, pointing out three haphazard men in his fury. "*You* three started this! I said you would pay. CHAIN THEM TO THE LINE! Their price should make up for part of losing a winged male."

The three men who'd been designated wailed out denials as the others pounced on them, eager to avoid the slavemaster's growing rage.

"As for *you.*" Tyre whirled on the man he did, in fact, know bore the spear that delivered the killing blow. Before the driver could protest, the whip was around his neck. With a tug Tyre dragged him forward, lifting the saber in his other hand.

Running the man through sternum to spine, he didn't so much as blink.

"Let Her have you," he breathed into the dying slaver's face.

Twisting the body away, Tyre let it slide off the blade to collapse upon the sand. When he looked up, the others were all watching him apprehensively. It took a few seconds for the slavemaster to calm himself.

"What are you all gaping at? Get the scallies back in line! We've got a ways yet! Finner, Jek. Collect what you can from the bodies. Yssey, get the animals going! Rylle...!"

Not ten minutes after the start of the commotion, the line was on the move again, driven hard, trekking out over the endless desert suddenly three members light. The group hadn't long faded into the heat before the vultures came, twisted black shapes circling above the dead, wondering if they could yet brave a descent.

The men would go first. Atherian hide was tougher to rip at by far.

I

"They are beasts who, upon first encounter, have some semblances of the compassion we pride ourselves in as men and women. Do not be led astray. They are savages, barbarians, and if it is easier to kill than barter, they will pounce."

—Stevan Ashani, head of the Ashani clan, concerning the atherian

---

Agais Arro's family had had a good year. Trade had favored them throughout the season and—despite the harsh trek across the desert plains of the Cienbal every other month—they'd profited well. New horses were purchased for the wagons whose animals had been past their prime, extra blankets and furs bought for those couples with young. Agais smiled, thanking the Sun above for their good fortune throughout the cool season, and offering up a small prayer that it might continue into the next.

The Cienbal was not generally considered a favorable place to reside. The desert was a dangerous friend at best, its perils not only limited to the flesh-stripping heat. Water was beyond scarce, river-holes and oases hard to find and unreliable by their nature. Bandits weren't so uncommon unfortunately, though they tended to bide along the outer rings of the desert, relying on the more bountiful resources of the civilized fringe cities. Still, it did happen that bands would venture into the deeper parts of the sands, braving the elements for the chance of catching the trading clans unaware.

Regardless, even more dangerous than thieves were the inhabitants of the Cienbal itself.

Sandcats and dune scorpions were the worst, a real threat in any situation, but the wild pack dogs had been known to drag more than one traveler off into the night. All manner of venomous snakes and night-spiders hid out of sight in whatever bit of shade they could find, as did a few other species of poisonous insects whose bite could leave one feverish and vomiting for days before death. Even the atherian could be trouble, though the lizard-kind tended to stay away from men apart from what little trade the two people did. When food and water were scant, though, whole families had been known to go missing mysteriously.

Man, after all, was as edible as anything else among the dunes.

Agais shivered, then smiled. The Cienbal had rarely caused his little group any grief. They were at peace with the place, and the Twins had always blessed them. The desert was their home. It would take more than the threat of thieves and a few oversized arachnids to make the Arros change the way they'd been living for generations.

Grea sat beside her husband, watching him think. Agais was a tall man, his skin tanned and his long hair and beard bleached blonde by the Sun. Nomadic tribal rings pierced his lips and ears, strung together with leather cord. A single silver chain, the sign of his position as head of the Arro family, hung from ear to ear, cutting low then up across his cheeks to pierce the bridge of his nose between his gray eyes. To some the symbols of the desert lifestyle were ugly and overdone, but to Grea they were a connection to ancestry and heritage. The fact that her husband bore the silver chain made her pride swell every time she looked at him.

As did the small kick that made her bare, swollen belly twitch outward.

Agais caught the motion, smiling at his wife as he shifted the horses' direction slightly.

"Eager to join us, isn't he?" he laughed. The woman smiled in return, gently resting a hand on the man's muscled arm.

"Or *she*," she said, shifting so that her stomach rested more comfortably. "Don't get too wrapped up in the idea of a son just yet."

"If it were a daughter we were waiting for, the Grandmother would have said so."

Grea sighed, nodding. "True enough. Still, it would be nice to give you a little girl…"

"There's always time for more," Agais murmured into her ear roguishly, and the woman laughed, accepting a happy kiss from the bearded man.

"Agais!"

A voice cut over the racket of the wheels, calling out from behind the moving cart. Looking around, Agais handed the reins to his wife and grabbed the top of his seat. With strong arms he leaned over the side, looking backwards at the line that trailed resolutely behind them, his braided hair twisting in the wind. Nine wagons in all, the Arros were amongst the largest of the clans to travel the desert trade-paths. Two-dozen people made up their family, young and old included, and at the moment Asahbet, one of Agais' younger nephews, was skirting the dune edge parallel to the caravan path, hands cupped around his mouth as he yelled.

"Agais! Hold the carts! The Grandmother says *hold the carts!*"

Agais frowned. Waving back an acknowledgement, he had Grea pull the horses to a slow halt. The sand hills were treacherous, and a hasty stop was too often the cause of a lamed animal.

"What's going on?" Grea asked him, concerned.

Agais hopped down and turned to help her off. "The Grandmother's told us to stop."

A raised brow was the only response he got, and he smiled. Grea had always been one to prefer action to pointless questioning.

Together the pair made their way across the shifting hill, the soles of their bare feet—roughened by the years—mocking the heat of the giving sand. The Grandmother's wagon was at the end of the train, its front thickly quilted with leather and furs to block out the dust and grit kicked up by the dozens of axels ahead of it. Its roughened, bare presentation, though, deceived the wonder of the rolling hut's interior.

Colorful trinkets and bits of dyed cloth hung from the timber ribs, suspended next to crystals and glass baubles the old woman had collected over long years. Jars of viscous liquids tinted all shades of color clinked in their shelves beside leather-bound books written in any of a dozen old languages. Sheets of woven animal bones clattered hollowly as they swayed from pegs on the back wall.

Taken together they gave the hut a certain mystical quality and, as Agais pulled back the leathers to let his wife into the wise-woman's motile hut, the couple couldn't help but feel it.

On the other hand, if the space itself was peculiar, the woman who sat at the small circular table at its center was utterly mundane. Grandmother Arro wore plain clothes of thin red cloth and sun-bleached hide like the rest of the clan, and her silver-black hair was pulled into a tight bun behind her head. The only symbols she wore on her face were the clan-chain, running from her right ear to her right nostril, and a small bronze ring that pierced her left eyebrow, denoting an elder, a position uniquely hers amongst the Arros. In any other situation she might have passed for an aged woman, fortunately youthful despite her years but possessing an ardor that spoke of a lifetime of amassed wisdom.

At the moment, though, Grandmother Arro looked very much like *the* Grandmother.

She sat cross-legged on the floor, the low table reaching the top of her knees, its stained surface littered with a queer selection of bird skulls, painted stones, and the dried legs of a tarantula. She was muttering under her breath, her gray eyes—so typical of the nomadic tribes—darting from one piece of the miscellany to another, tying together the signs as only the Grandmother could. Agais and Grea took a seat silently across from her, nodding to Agais' younger brother Jarden, the clan champion, leaning against the wall in a back corner of the wheeled hut.

The Grandmother's telling took several more minutes. All three waited patiently, knowing the act couldn't be rushed. Sometimes the signs made no sense, and Grandmother would finish quickly, saying to trust in the Twins for guidance. Other times the signs were clear, but it took the old woman hours to collect them and put them together.

Time we have, Agais thought to himself, reaching out to squeeze his wife's hand. *Time is on our side.*

Summer was here, and the burning season—the hottest part of the year—had started. For the next couple of months prolonged travel would be out of the question for anyone but the foolish or insane. The Arros were making for the Garin, the great desert oasis, where they and many other trading clans would stay for the next two turns or so, awaiting better climates. There was no such thing as winter in the Cienbal, nor autumn or spring. There were only the predominantly cooler months— when the heat was bearable—followed by the months of summer, when the Sun seared the eyes and practically burned flesh from bone. True seasons were a thing of the North, of the Arocklen Woods and the great mountain ranges before the tundra. Agais and Jarden's father had often told them of the snows and winds that claimed those territories for much of the year, a time the Northerners called "the freeze."

Neither brother had ever been keen on getting close enough to the border to experience it for themselves.

"Agais?"

Agais jerked out of his own thoughts, looking to the Grandmother. The telling was through, the trance broken. The woman sat, eyes clear and one finger running along the chain on the right side of her face as she pondered a moment more.

"Your son nears life under the Sun," she said at last. "But again you are warned the child will not be as you expect."

Beside him Grea blanched, drawing her hand from her husband's to place it delicately on her swollen belly.

"You, my dear," Grandmother said, looking at the woman with a smile, "have nothing to fear. Your life is safe."

"And the child?" Grea breathed with only the barest note of begging in her voice.

"Your son," Grandmother responded pointedly, looking back to Agais, "will survive, though his arrival to us will be filled with hardship for some time... Do you remember the words I spoke to you?"

Agais nodded, reciting:

> *Of blood will be born the next of score-and-four,*
> *yet twice will be the cost.*
> *The only of his kind, he will fall for a face of snow,*
> *and follow and be followed to dark depths and icy summits.*
> *Son of the Sun he is.*
> *Son of the Sun he will be named.*

Grandmother smiled in approval.

"And I'm assuming you've considered them. Carefully."

Here, Agais hesitated. Beside him Grea tensed as well. They'd whispered into the long hours of many nights since the Grandmother had first spoken to them of their child, discussing the implications of what the words could mean.

... yet twice will be the cost.

What was it telling them? A price clearly, but "twice" what? Eventually they'd given up, deciding that only time would be able to tell what sacrifices would have to be made. Besides, it was the next line that had always frightened them most:

The only of his kind...

Did that mean their child would be birthed misshapen? Perhaps deformed or cursed with some unique disease? More than once Agais had been frightened to consciousness in the black of night by vivid nightmares, dreaming of a small, twisted form with blind eyes and bloody, toothless gums, reaching tiny white hands through the dark.

No, Agais thought. His son would be healthy. The rest of the telling made that clear. If a great man was to be born amongst the Arros, then his differences would matter little.

"He is our son, born yet or not," Grea responded first. "He is our child. We will love him as any child should be loved by his parents."

The Grandmother nodded again, seeing the agreement shine in Agais' eyes.

"Then you accept what is to come, and the Twins charge you with upholding your vows. Now, Jarden, come sit."

Jarden detached himself from the wall, coming to squat by the table. Agais smirked, watching his brother's body language. The man hated sitting. It made him feel vulnerable, especially with his staff and dagger discarded at the entrance of the wagon. He looked oddly diminished with only his panpipes—ever with him—strapped to his belt.

"You will be the boy's teacher," Grandmother said, watching the man intently. "Your brother will be a great father, and will give his son much, but it is from you that the child must learn many other things."

Jarden, usually so alert and quick, looked distinctly taken aback. "Me? Wha—? B-but I've no idea how to raise a boy."

The old woman chuckled, leaning over to pinch the man's stubbled cheek fondly.

"Well it's a good thing you *won't be* then, isn't it?" she said with a laugh. "There are other things. Self-preservation. Survival. You're damn good with that big stick of yours. He may come from a people accustomed to the desert and its harshness, but only so many things can one be born knowing."

Jarden sighed, obviously relieved, before nodding. Agais, on the other hand, had heard something else in the old woman's laughter, but even as he thought this the Grandmother's eyes fell on his again. He was just about to voice his question when the hut flap was pulled away abruptly, filling the room with a blazing light. There was a cough, and Asahbet poked his head in.

"I'm sorry, Grandmother," he whispered shrilly, "but Agais and Jarden are needed. My father claims to have seen something from the top of the sand ridge."

"Ishmal claims to have seen *something?*" Jarden repeated, annoyed. Military efficiency wasn't the strongest trait amongst the nomads. Asahbet merely nodded. Agais and his brother excused themselves to follow the boy, leaving Grea to speak with the Grandmother. Outside, Jarden retrieved his staff from the side of the wagon, tucking his long-dagger into his belt.

The winds had picked up again, lifting clouds of sand to spin through the air in stunted whirlwinds. Covering their eyes with lifted hands, the three men pulled the loose cloth around their necks up over their mouths, making for easier breathing. Slowly they made their way to the upper edge of the dune. Ishmal was waiting for them, facing southward, cupping his face to give himself a clearer view of the great expanse of sand that seemed to stretch on and on with no end.

"What is it?" Agais asked, coming to stand behind the man and raising his voice to beat the rush of the wind. Ishmal had been husband to Agais and Jarden's older sister, Bryâ. Sickness had claimed her four years ago, leaving the man a widower, but not before the couple bore four sons to the world.

"There." Ishmal pointed with a finger before covering his eyes again. "Just below the horizon. Something's moving."

The brothers squinted, trying to make out whatever it was the older man could see. After a time the shape manifested, fading in and out through the waves of heat that fractured their vision. A long thin line, most likely another caravan of some kind, heading south, away from the Arros.

"Well if they're bandits we should be safe," Jarden muttered. "Our wagons are hidden by the hill, and they're not heading this way. Have Tolman roll the wagon line farther down just in case, but—"

"Wait," Agais cut in before Asahbet could move to follow the order. The clanmaster continued to watch the horizon. He could have sworn he'd seen something else. It looked for a moment as though the line was moving away from another, smaller group. After a few seconds he saw them again. Two or three people, unmoving.

Corpses.

Agais cursed under his breath. Easy meat so close to the trade routes was a dangerous thing, especially when so many would be making their way toward the Garin. Sandcats would swarm within the day, taking whatever the vultures left behind.

And there were certainly vultures, Agais realized, glancing up at the sky above the distant forms.

"We stay," he ordered, dropping his hands. "Set up camp along the bottom of the dune. Ishmal, mark a line of sight. I want to be able to find that place tonight. Jarden, have a watch set up. Tell them to keep an eye out for cats."

As one the three nodded, knowing better than to question. After Asahbet and Ishmal had turned back to tell the wagons to move on, though, Jarden nudged his brother with an elbow in silent query.

"Bodies," Agais told him quietly, eyes on the distant spot he knew the still forms lay. "Unburied. Either bandits too lazy to get the shovels out, or slavers in too much of a rush to bother. Tonight you and I will take care of it. No need to trouble the others."

Jarden cursed too, then nodded.

II

Night was sudden in its coming, as was typical of a desert twilight. For less than an hour the sky—usually a solid canvas of pale blue arranged around a single splash of blinding light—turned into a painting of oranges and yellows and greens, arching in heavy strokes across the heavens. Then, like a black tide washing away the colors, darkness slunk out to chase the Sun over the western edge of the world.

After that there was nothing left but the Moon and Her Stars and the silent expanse of rolling sands in every direction.

The line of sight Ishmal had set up was a simple mechanism. Two rods about an arm's length in height were pounded into the desert a body length apart, a leather string pulled tight across the top. The line acted as a measure for the eye, guiding one's vision across the Cienbal expanse. It was a useful tool, especially when it came to navigating new watering holes or likely shelter. The Stars did the rest.

Wrapped in sewn fur coats to ward off the freezing twilight, Agais and Jarden slipped out of camp, dodging through the shadows cast by the large bonfire in the center of the wagon ring. Evening was the time of gathering and play, and the brothers hoped the festive noises and music from the rest of the clan would drown out their momentary escape. Only the Grandmother, Grea, and Jarden's wife Surah knew of their departure.

Agais shivered when they reached the horse enclosure. It wasn't the cold that bothered him, but rather the look the Grandmother had given him as he'd left her wagon-hut. Again he'd felt as though she were trying to tell him something, fighting the bindings of some celestial decree not to voice it aloud.

Clicking his tongue, Agais called two of the horses to them. Gale and Sandrider, his and Jarden's companions, trotted over without a moment's hesitation. Gale nickered softly, and Agais hushed her, stroking her nose and whispering quiet words in her ear. The mare seemed to understand the need for silence. She calmed and dipped her head to munch on the handful of saltgrass he'd brought her.

The enclosure was a crude thing, little more than a circle of dropped stones the horses had been trained not to step over. The two men made quick work of freeing them, closing the ring again once their mounts were clear. Without a word they leapt atop the animals, gently grasping fistfuls of mane for reins before nudging them into a trot. It was only when they were a ways away from camp that the pair pressed the horses into a full gallop, heading for the southern star that would guide them directly over the dead.

The ride was longer than most might believe. In the Cienbal, where only dunes and dry mountains marred the endless sands, one could usually see for leagues in all directions. The heat could trick the eyes, bending the light so that oftentimes things that seemed so distant one moment looked close the next. More than once Agais had been fooled into believing a town or oasis was minutes away, only to arrive a half hour later.

At night, though, the Cienbal stilled, and the sensation was akin to sailing out of a storm into calm sea. The world became serene, hushed, glowing an evening-blue as the Moon lit the desert just enough to travel by. The only sound was a rare wind and the muffled pounding of hooves across the sand. Nothing moved. It was Agais' favorite time, and he could often be found forgoing the evening celebrations to sit outside the light, taking in the landscape.

Jarden whistled suddenly. He was pointing southeast, slowing to turn. Agais mimicked him, peering in the direction his brother was indicating. It was only a few seconds before he, too, made them out. Three still forms, lying only slightly apart from each other, sprawled over the sand. Dark shapes hopped and hovered around them, black wings spread wide, fighting for meat.

The brothers didn't slow when they finally reached the corpses, driving right between them and scattering the vultures. The birds screeched and cawed, hopping awkwardly away from their meal. A few fled skyward at once, startled by the arrival. It took another two passes to run the rest away, Jarden swinging his bleached-wood staff around his head and yelling *"Hyah! Hyah!"* as they rode.

When the last of the buzzards had disappeared into the night, Agais pulled Gale to a steady halt. Dismounting, he approached the bodies with his cloth mask pressed against his face. It couldn't have even been half a day, but the ravages of the Sun and the desert's occupants had left the closest two putrid and barely recognizable. Human, the pair of them, the clanmaster could tell. Likely males, based on the size of the leather boots still clinging to what was left of their legs. Whoever they'd been, though, they were now little more than a mess of bloody rags and exposed bone. Most of the flesh had been stripped away from their skeletons, leaving leering skulls specked with slips of skin and sinew as the only reminders of what must have been full, healthy faces just hours before.

Still, what was left was more than enough to attract the cats…

The third body was an anomaly. Atherian, Agais had no problem identifying, and a young one at that. The size of the infant—just under four feet tall—pointed at the child being somewhere between two and four summers old, the latter only likely if he was a runt.

"What the hell is a lizard-babe doing in a place like this?" Agais muttered to himself, perplexed and moving closer to examine the creature.

Lizard-kind hide was thick, explaining why the birds seemed to have gotten to the infant least of all three. Lying on its back in the sand, the babe's major injuries—three long gashes across its shoulder, thigh, and chest—looked more like sword wounds than anything the birds could have done. Windblown sand covered half its body, mounding in odd piles around it. New scars crisscrossed the atherian's chest and the arm that Agais could see, and its wrist bore a ring of missing scales and raw flesh the vultures seemed to have managed a few good picks at.

Shackle marks…

"Slavers," Agais sighed, looking back at the mutilated corpses that Jarden was already digging graves for, scraping away a pit of sand with one of the two shovels they'd brought.

At the word, his brother paused to look up.

"You sure?" He stepped out of the shallow hole and came to stand on the other side of the dead babe. Agais nodded, pointing to the raw ring on the atherian's wrist.

"Only chains could have done that." He kneeled beside the creature's serpentine head. "Can't even guess as to what happened, but it must have been bloody to end up with these three dead. They got stripped of anything useful and left behind. The others probably took the irons with them."

Jarden nodded, respect in his eyes as he looked down at the infant.

"I know his kind can be vicious, but Sun's praise goes to this little one. Probably got to both these brutes before the others overwhelmed him."

Agais nodded, standing up. "Praise goes to him," he muttered out of habit.

He was about to turn away, thinking to help Jarden with the graves, when something else caught his eye.

The child's face was cut up and picked at, but otherwise left whole by the birds. There was one spot, though, just below the torn membrane of its webbed ear, that was crusted over with blood. In the dark it was hard to be sure, but it looked like the infant's jaw was askew, broken by some blow to the head or face.

It would be difficult to kill an atherian, even a young one like this, with blunt force. Their skin was tougher than hide, their bones twice as strong as man's. Trouble was, while the gashes the child had sustained were bad, none were life threatening. A quick examination told Agais there were no other visible wounds. Perhaps hidden under the sand that partially covered it? Or on its back?

"Jarden..." Agais began, intent on recruiting his brother's help in rolling the lizard-babe over. Before he could say another word, though, he took a step to the side, around the child's head, and put his weight down on one of the curious mounds of sand that surrounded the body.

There was a sharp *crunch*, and the desert exploded.

The atherian came to life in a whirlwind of teeth and claws, screeching in pain and anger. Wide wings, hidden under the scattered sand, shot upwards in a shower of loose earth. Agais felt the ground pulled out from under him like a rug as the wing he'd been standing on was tugged free, and he tumbled backwards. The infant was on its feet in an instant, and the clanmaster's throat clenched. The babe's right wing, its membrane an aquamarine blue, hung loose just above the shoulder, and Agais was looking up from his back into sunset eyes that burned with agony, fear, and hunger.

"Agais! Get BACK!" Jarden yelled, leaping between his brother and the pain-crazed atherian, wielding the shovel he'd been digging with, his body free of the heavy furs. On his rear, Agais scrambled away across the sand, heeding the warning. He watched as Jarden danced around the lizard-kind, shouting taunts to draw its attention, prodding the babe with the blade of the shovel whenever he got the chance.

And then it fought back.

With a throaty hiss the atherian leapt clear into the air, claws outstretched and fangs bared despite its broken jaw. Jarden had just enough time to block, throwing the shovel up before him, but it made little difference. A swipe of its arm connected with the thin wooden shaft, snapping it in two, and in the same motion the clawed fingers of a scaly hand nicked his cheek. Both feet planted directly into Jarden's broad chest, kicking him back and drawing blood yet again. He stumbled and fell into the sand, still holding both halves of the shovel.

The atherian landed heavily, spitting, mouth agape and eyes fixed on

Jarden. It was about to attack again when Agais did the most foolish thing he'd ever done in his life. Completely unarmed, he dashed forward, howling like a madman and swinging his arms frantically. The infant's attention shifted only a second, but for Jarden it was enough. With all the speed he could muster, the man rolled to his feet and leapt forward, swinging the bladed end of his shovel. The flat surface of the spade connected sharply with the side of the lizard-babe's broken jaw, and a sound like a bell toll rang through the night. Jarden's swing carried through, knocking the creature to the ground in a heap of claws and wings where it lay, finally still.

For a long moment Agais and Jarden stood at the ready, breathing hard, anticipating another surprise attack. It was only when nothing happened for almost a full minute that they finally relaxed.

"Her Stars!" Jarden cursed, dropping to his knees in the sand. The two halves of the shovel that had saved his life fell limply from his hands. "The damned thing is *winged*, Agais! A winged male! I've never seen one!"

"That makes two of us," the clanmaster agreed, not taking his eyes off the prone form.

Atherian in general were a flightless species, wingless. They typically kept to the Crags, the arid mountain range that looped down into the Cienbal from the east. Agais himself had done little trading with the lizard-folk, but he knew merchants who had. To a one, they all said the same thing:

Stay away from the males.

Male atherian were a rarity as it was. Hatchlings were one in twenty at best, and the natural instincts of preserving their gender within the lizard-kind's crude society led them to be far more unpredictable than their female counterparts. Atherian culture—it was generally agreed—was a primitive, animalistic one. One male could mate with over a score of females in his lifetime but never stay with any of them. The males were nomadic loners, moving from place to place while doing their utmost to avoid each other. But those were the flightless males.

Winged males, on the other hand…

Agais had only ever heard little about them, much less seen one with his own eyes. A winged atherian was said to be—lacking a better description—a feral, vicious creature. They were territorial and savage, even from a young age, and kept harems of females rather than traveling from place to place. Anyone who came too near their land or mates, they slaughtered.

Lizard-kind or not.

"What are we going to do with him?" Jarden hissed, voicing the question just as it rose in Agais' head as well. "Kill him?"

"No."

That answer was easy, and glancing over Agais knew his brother was thinking the same thing. Murder was unacceptable amongst nomads outside of self-defense. Like burying your dead, it was unwritten desert code.

And, despite their brutal nature, the atherian were a people like any other.

"Well, if we're not going to kill him, then what?"

"Sun only knows," Agais muttered under his breath.

Killing the lizard-babe was out of the question, but just as much was leaving it to die when day came and the heat returned. Abandoning a living person to the sands was an incomparable cruelty.

"Are you badly hurt?" Agais asked, giving himself time to think. Jarden wiped blood and sand off his face, tracing the shallow cuts that ran along his cheek with a finger. He winced, but shook his head.

"Just a few scratches," he shrugged, getting to his feet and tearing open his shirt. His chest was much the same, though it bled a little more from where the infant's talons had caught him.

"Good," Agais breathed, feeling things fall back into place. The last few minutes had been a storm of action and disjointed thought. "Get back to the caravan and fetch the Grandmother. Once you've been patched up, bring her here, along with any of the men that are still awake. And bring bindings, but no ropes or chains. This poor child has had enough of both, I think."

Jarden nodded. Tossing aside his useless shirt, he picked up his fur coat, shaking it clean before moving to stand beside Sandrider. There he paused, bending over, and pulled something large out of the sand. He smiled and threw it to Agais, who caught it barely.

It was the other shovel.

"In case he wakes up before we get back," Jarden explained, leaping atop the horse and turning to face his brother. "Seems to keep him in check."

Agais snorted, watching the man galloping off toward the wagons, pale braided hair whipping behind him. When he was gone, the clanmaster shrugged off his own furs and got to digging, too wound up from the evening's events to pass the time calmly waiting.

18

Unknown to him, three pairs of golden eyes watched through the dark, blinking just out of sight.

Jarden returned within the hour, heading a small party. They raced across the desert, pulling up when the dark shapes that were Agais, his horse, and the unconscious atherian bloomed out of the night. Agais—just finishing the second of the two graves—stood up and waved when he heard them, making sure they didn't ride past him in the dark.

"Any change?"

Jarden drew Sandrider to a halt. Agais shook his head, looking down at the prone boy. He'd carefully thrown one of his fur coats over the still form, unsure of how well lizard-kind dealt with the cold, but even when the soft pelts fell over him like a blanket, the creature remained still.

"He's alive. I checked just a few minutes ago. I'm not surprised the slavers left him. Probably thought he was dead, the way he's barely breathing. You didn't hold back…"

Jarden dismounted and shrugged as he moved to meet the other three riders that followed. He was bandaged up hastily, the wounds on his face cleaned but uncovered, a smudge of blood seeping through the rough white linens wrapped around his chest.

"If I'd hit him any lighter, there's a good chance neither of us would be here to argue about it."

"If you'd hit him any harder, you'd probably have dented the shovel," Agais muttered, watching the Grandmother hurriedly let their cousin Kosen help her off her horse.

"Is he hurt?" she demanded, rushing forward. "Let me see him!"

Catching sight of the child, she fell to her knees beside him and pulled out a small leather healer's kit from the folds of the thick skins she wore.

"Achtel, come help," she snapped, surprising everyone, setting the kit on the ground and opening it. Achtel, a friend who had taken on the family name years ago, hurried to obey. Together the two of them gently lifted Agais' coat from the child, revealing the battered body once again. Agais felt a rush of fear and relief when the lizard-babe twitched, cawing softly from the depths of stupor at the cold night air washing over his skin.

19

"Shh," the Grandmother murmured into its torn ear, stroking the child's scaly cheek fearlessly with one hand. From the leather case beside her she pulled out a hooked needle. "Shh, my child. Sleep. You're in the company of friends now. Sleep."

The old woman worked with a fervor that surprised every one of the men around her. She labored over the atherian babe as though it were one of the family, cleaning raw flesh and open wounds, gluing together the tissue that had been split by steel. All the while she muttered prayers to the Twins, the words too soft to make out. The four clansmen stood behind her, watching the miracle unfold before their eyes. The Grandmother's talents for preserving life were unmatched even by the trained physicians that held offices in Miropa, the Gem of the South, the largest of the fringe cities.

After what seemed like hours of meticulous work, the Grandmother asked Agais to retrieve the broken shovel for her. Jarden must have told her the events in detail, he decided, scrounging the area for the pieces. He found them together, right where his brother had dropped them.

Handing them over, Agais looked on in amazement. The Grandmother clipped the shattered wooden edges away with a small, whisper-thin silver surgeon's knife. Twisting the two parts of the haft free, one from the handle and one from the blade, she held up two similarly long bars of strong wood. Still praying, she quickly slit three small cuts straight through the lizard-kind's membranous wing just below the two halves of the bone Agais had mistakenly broken.

The atherian twitched when the knife pierced skin, and again when the Grandmother set his wing, but otherwise remained dead to the world. Even as Achtel splinted the break with the wooden shafts, slipping horse-gut twine through the cuts in the membrane, the child didn't move.

"That's all that can be done for now," the Grandmother said finally, closing her kit and getting to her feet. "There's no sense is setting that jaw until we're back at the caravan, but I'll need to work on it as soon as possible. If he wakes in pain, it will mean trouble for all of us."

"You mean to bring him back with us?" Agais asked, stepping forward. He might be master of their clan, but when the Grandmother spoke, the Arros listened. Even him.

The old woman, for her part, stared at him blankly. "Do you see another option?"

None of the men had a response to that. Even so, neither were any of them too keen on the idea of having a winged atherian tagging along to the Garin, no matter how young he might be.

"If he comes to…" Kosen began, but trailed off, leaving the obvious dangers unspoken. He was the oldest of the Arros apart from the Grandmother herself, an aging man with a cropped, bristly beard peppered white and gray, and he was rarely known to speak foolishly.

"He won't," the Grandmother assured them. "Bring him back, and have a cot made up in my wagon. Make sure that wing of his is extended, or it won't heal properly."

Unanimously all four men nodded. The order was given, and there was no arguing. How the Grandmother was going to keep the babe sedated none of them could guess, but she seemed confident enough to dispel any lingering concern.

Gently Agais and Jarden picked the child out of the sand, careful not to jostle the broken bones. Behind them, Achtel and Kosen were already setting up the blanket of leather skins that would serve as a stretcher. When it was securely rigged to the necks of the horses, the two men moved to help the brothers, placing the boy carefully on the mat. Before long the group was heading for the wagon ring once more, cutting a slower pace through the sand, doing their utmost to keep the stretcher steady as it left a long flattened trail through the pale night.

It was only once the dark had almost swallowed the party completely that three shapes lifted themselves from their places of hiding, darting after the horses and following the clear path back to the camp. When they saw the winged hatchling lifted gently into one of the wagons and placed into a soft bed, the scouts finally abandoned their pursuit. As one they crept back, away from the dancing pools of light spilling through the wagons, and shrank soundlessly into the dark.

The atherian trusted in the winds to cover their tracks.

They were leagues away when the three stopped, halting just along the crest of the highest dune within a half day's walk. The tallest among them fumbled through her pouch, pulling out a short tube of thick reed sealed with wax while the others began striking flint over a handful of dry grass. Within moments the grass caught, and the first of the females stripped the wax away from the reed gingerly, covering her snout with a clawed hand as the reek of the sulfur mix sealed inside escaped. Holding the tube high above her head, she let one of the others reach up with the flaming plant tendrils.

BANG.

With a crack as loud as a thunderclap, the higher half of the container erupted in a small explosion. She'd been expecting it, but still the atherian dropped the instrument at once and jumped away.

But not before the ignited sulfur flashed bright as the Daystar, illuminating the night for a fraction of a second before acrid smoke filled the air.

They were on the move again at once, and so were too far down the sandy hill to see the lights that flared momentarily far ahead of them, like distant lightning, passing the message along in great leaps through the dark.

III

"The writings of the Gone tell us that this land—our land—was once far more than the charred, twisted sea of sand and wind it is today. The desert is a new happening, a curse left upon the heads of the living for displeasing the First-Born, the Daystar. What the Children of old did to earn this wrath, none know, but it is said the Last-Born, the Night's Eye, took pity on us, and so every time the First-Born sleeps, She gives us shadow and coolness to ease our burning hide."

—Sian-Lazzara Rhan, Third-Queen

"I beg your forgiveness, my Queen, but this is the extent of what my informants have managed to procure for us thus far," Sassyl Gal hissed from his place at the foot of the stone dais, finishing his recounting. "I hope it's brought you some ease of mind."

The royal advisor was aging, his once-bright eyes no longer so sharp as in years past, but his mind seemed never to wear. The throne's delicate webs of scouts and spies were as strong as ever in the old male's weaving hands, and more atherian slaves had been freed since his rise to the position than in the hundred previous years. He was a rarity, to say the least.

Most males of their kind were useless brutes of little value aside from mating fodder.

It had been days since first word had reached the Under-Caves, but here at last was the whole story. Shas-hana Rhan sighed in relief, relaxing against the back of her stone throne. For the first time in what seemed like a small eternity, she breathed easy.

Her hatchling had been taken in by the trading clans. Her son was safe.

"You've done well," the Queen said, waving him away with a clawed hand. "Go. Rest your tired bones. I will summon you if I've need. And send Uhsula to me."

Sassyl bowed again, shuffling off, his body permanently rent crooked by the years. After he'd exited the audience chamber, the Queen let the relief wash over her in full. Her body shook, and she rested a scaled cheek in the palm of her hand, closing her golden eyes.

So even the First-Born had mercy.

Her child lived, despite his encounter with the slavers. The seer would have paid in blood if the boy hadn't made it through but, as always, Uhsula proved right yet again.

Opening her eyes, Shas-hana rose to her feet, casting away the staff of black ash and ivory that was one of the few symbols of her position. She kept the crystal crown of obsidian glass, accustomed to its weight against her ridged brow. Tall and lithe like most younger females, she was ill at ease underground. It was her family's blessing and curse, however, to be secluded here beneath the mountains humans called the Crags, hidden from the world.

Half of her own people, scattered across the desert, didn't believe in Shas-hana's existence. Some didn't know she might even exist at all...

The Queen of the Under-Caves hissed in frustration. They were hiding. They had *always* been hiding. Most of mankind refused to accept her people *as* a people. "Lizards" they called them in their tongue. Common animals. Humans were unwilling to see the intelligence that lurked behind the eyes of the atherian, and as such had reduced them to savages and slaves. They couldn't see the promise that dwelled in the Children.

Even so, showing herself to the world would do no good, Shas-hana knew. No atherian knew the language of man well enough to prove useful. There were still those amongst her followers eager to risk their lives and freedom to attempt assimilation, but the Queen was unwilling to let them. That hand had been played before, and to no avail. Even good-hearted men were turned against them, their opinions twisted by rooted misunderstandings and years of necessity driving her people to acts often below their intelligence. Eating flesh was in their nature. Man had once been prey like any other animal, and willpower was hard-pressed to win the battle over instinct when starvation was thrown into the mix.

No. The acceptance of the atherian into the world of man would take time, and would have to come from an angle unfamiliar to both sides. Uhsula, along with Shas-hana's hatching of a winged male—a line most thought lost with the death of the Queen's grand-sire—had provided an opportunity.

At that moment the seer herself arrived, leaning heavily on the knotted oak staff she always carried. While Sassyl was old, he was spry and youthful compared to Uhsula of the Other Worlds. Her eyes were nearly completely opaque, blinded by a combination of long years and a lifetime of living in the darkness of the mountain caverns. She moved at a snail's pace, her left foot dragging uselessly along, much like her tail. The membranes of her ears—sky blue in an atherian's youth, then sunset orange, then black and red—were now mottled gray. Her jaw hung agape, revealing worn teeth that were little good except for gnawing at old bones and chewing the thin strips of softened meat her acolytes readied for her meals.

"You sent for me, my Queen?" the elder rasped, eyes following the pacing of her sovereign despite being unable to see her.

"Uhsula. Come. Sit with me."

Shas-hana took the ancient female's arm carefully, leading her to the steps of the stone dais. The seer felt around for a moment before easing herself down, bones creaking so audibly that the young queen winced.

Uhsula smiled. "I hope one day you see the long days of my age, child," she chuckled, slipping into a less formal tone. "By then you'll have realized that aching joints and rotting claws are only some of life's most insignificant troubles."

Shas-hana nodded, her thoughts elsewhere again. She sat beside the seer, and Uhsula's brow wrinkled.

"You are troubled, Hana?" she asked with her incomprehensible gift of making any question a clear statement.

The Queen nodded again. "My... the boy," she said. "He's been taken in. Moving men. After he killed one of the slavers he was beaten nearly to death. The scouts were able to do little more than keep the flesh-birds from tearing him apart. I ordered them never to touch him..."

Uhsula nodded, but remained silent.

"A merchant tribe found him. One of their elders cared for his wounds as best she could, but their language is a strange one. We don't know what they're planning to do."

"Did they bind the child?"

The Queen shook her head. She had asked the same question of Sassyl already.

"No. They'd brought bindings, leather and cloth, but never used them."

"Leather and cloth are good signs. I doubt anyone planning on selling the boy back to the slavers would risk comfortable restraints."

Shas-hana nodded, feeling some of the residual tension trickle out of her system.

"Thank you," she breathed, getting to her feet and pacing again. "Just one last thing..."

"Again?"

Shas-hana nodded. Despite her blindness, the old seer chuckled.

Then she began reciting, as she had every day for the last few weeks, ever since the Queen's child had been taken from the base of the Crags:

Of one kind, and yet of another,
wings and wind bear him forth.
From chains comes his second birth
and never shall he stand for them.
Child of the Daystar, he will speak the language
and be the speaker of his people.
To leave and then return,
bearing a woman of ice and snow on his arm.

IV

"There is little interaction between the territories of North and South. While this is partially due to bubbling diplomatic and criminal issues that plague the desert plains, it would likely be more accurate to blame the climates for our social distancing. Drastic spikes in heat make lengthy travel almost impossible in the South during the summer season, whereas those same months are the only limited time in which the harsh freeze of the North abates enough to move cross-land easily. These conflicting weathers force border traders and travelers into one of two choices: either move quickly in the few weeks at the beginning and end of the summer season, or be willing to seek shelter for most of a year until those brief periods of travel open up again."

—from the libraries of Cyurgi' Di, concerning trade

In the days that followed the rescue, the atherian was kept isolated in the Grandmother's hut, away from the curious glances of the children and prying questions of the adults. The Arros were a strong-headed breed, however, and being kept at bay hadn't done much to ease the tension amongst the most concerned. The commotion it had caused was slight, but for Agais it was amongst the most frustrating ordeals he'd had to deal with since his father's passing left him head of the family two years prior.

It took several hours to calm the men and women enough to begin their trek anew. Most trusted outright in Agais and the Grandmother, and when both spoke out against leaving the lizard-kind to die, citing the nomadic code, they nodded their understanding and returned to the wagons. A few, though—namely the ones with young children—were less agreeable. None of them were open to the idea of willingly harboring what they saw as nothing short of a rabid animal all the way to the shores of the Garin.

"If the beast can do that to Jarden, what could it do to the other men?" Iriso, Achtel's wife, demanded of Agais after he'd revealed the unconscious atherian to the rest of the Arros. "And the women? And the *children?* That thing is dangerous. It cannot be allowed to stay among us!"

Jarden, who was now swathed in proper bandages, making his injuries appear far worse than they were, stepped forward to defend his brother.

Agais' raised hand held him up.

"Let me make this clear, Iriso." Agais' voice was firm and strong, ensuring that every other person standing around him could hear the

27

finality in the statement. "I will not stand for murder in my clan. Lizard-kind or not, that creature is as alive and aware as you and far younger than even your own children. You want to taste the blood of an infant, you go somewhere else to find it."

He'd stared her down then, the woman glaring angrily, gray eyes shining through her bangs of bleached hair. Finally, she'd looked away, conceding, and stepped back. Achtel put an arm around her shoulders to comfort her.

"And that goes for all of you!" Agais announced, looking around into the group. "Jarden and I were the only ones attacked. If anyone has the right to claim a voice in what happens to the babe, it is us. My vote is cast—"

"As is mine," Jarden offered up, crossing his arms decisively and standing tall beside his brother.

"—and so the discussion is closed," Agais finished. "The Grandmother has assured us that the boy will not leave her wagon, and as you all claim to trust in her voice, I hope you will consider this matter settled."

There was a mixed murmur of disgruntled agreements, but ultimately the Arros let the subject go. They dispersed, some less content than others, to ready their wagons for departure.

"Think we'll have any trouble from them?" Agais asked Jarden over his shoulder after all the men and women had returned to their own business.

His brother snorted. "From them? No. Tolman is the only one who could pose a problem if he wanted, but he's sided with us."

Agais nodded, still concerned. Jarden noticed the withdrawal.

"I could run a sentry to stay with the Grandmother," he offered with a shrug. "Tolman, Ishmal, Kosen, and myself could easily cover the nights it would take to reach the Garin. We're only two weeks out at this point."

Agais shook his head. "Putting up a guard would only imply that we don't trust our own. While I'll not stand for murder, I'm even less inclined to allow this lizard-boy to create a rift in my family. He will heal, and once the Grandmother says he is fit to be on his own we can turn him over to the next atherian tribe we come across. There's bound to be a few traveling through the oasis, and the damn child is winged. They should have no qualms taking him in."

"So if we can hold off Iriso for another two weeks, we'll be rid of him."

The clanmaster chuckled, then nodded.

A week later travel was steady, if a little rough. The family got bogged down for a day by a sandstorm that half buried the caravan, but otherwise they'd encountered no trouble. Once, when Gale nickered nervously, tugging along with their other draft horses, Agais caught sight of a large black shape scuttling along the top of the dune to their left. Almost immediately it disappeared, burying itself into the sands. The scorpion didn't surface within sight, thankfully, and after a few hours Agais relaxed, confident the thing wouldn't show up again.

The atherian's progress was even better. Grea visited him daily, aiding the Grandmother whenever she was able. The young woman seemed to have taken to the infant as only a pending mother could, cooing over his slumbering form much as the Grandmother herself did. They'd managed to feed him cut strips of dried meat over time—it was fascinating to watch the child instinctively swallow them whole—and getting him to drink was much the same. Once, Agais had even walked in on Grea speaking to the boy, telling him about the baby in her stomach and how it kicked so fiercely sometimes. When she noticed her husband, she'd stopped and smiled.

"Watch," she told him, and ran the tips of her fingers over the ridge of the atherian's snout and small head. As she did, the lizard-babe's torn ears, healing at last, spread slightly. The sapphire crest along the back of his neck flickered, and his mouth cracked opened in what was unmistakably some small expression of pleasure. Though those golden eyes remained closed, trapped in the stupor of Grandmother's herbs, the child called out in a quiet tone much like the low cry of a baby bird.

Even Agais couldn't help but smile, though his measured amusement was far gone from his wife's.

What deceptive innocence for such a dangerous creature.

They were less than four days out when the Grandmother made her decision. The babe healed at a remarkable rate. Already the gashes along his ribs, thigh, and shoulder had sealed completely, rapidly grown over by new, shiny black and olive-green scales. His jaw was mending, and the gash beside his left eye where he'd been struck twice—once by some blunt object and again by Jarden's shovel—was little more than a dark bruise visible beneath a few broken scales. His wing was still fragile, though she'd been able to remove the splint a few days earlier, and she hoped her plan wouldn't cause the brittle new bone to crack again. The slices she'd had to cut through the membrane had sealed over in a matter of hours and, now, less than three days later, there was no trace left of them except for three pale lines she doubted would be visible through the night.

"It's time, child," she murmured, stroking the infant's smooth cheek gently. "Rise now."

The ritual was a private one, something the Grandmother knew most of the other Arros wouldn't approve of without deliberation. Still, it had to be done. Carefully, muttering her prayers to the Twins, the old woman tipped a thin stream of eastern sea-salts from a glass vial into the bowl of hot water she'd laid beside the babe's head. It dissolved instantly, and quickly she followed it with a few drops of oil pressed from the redgrass leaves they could find around most watering holes. At first the fluid refused to mix, clinging to the water's surface. Then slowly it sank, spreading out to hang like a thin layer of broken red silk along the notched bottom of the bowl.

Her concoction ready, the Grandmother drew a long silver needle from one of the many small chests she had spread around the room. Heating it over a candle, she waited until the metal burned white-hot before slipping it into the fluid.

There was a hiss of boiling liquid. A tiny puff of steam wafted from the bowl, dissipating beside the atherian's face. The Grandmother held her breath until the haze dispersed completely, carefully avoiding the wafts. The opiate mixture had its uses, good for bringing some small bit of strength back into the limbs of the old or ailing, but to the healthy it could be addicting, even deadly. She had to be careful not to inhale it or she'd find herself so pent full of energy she'd be unable to sleep for days.

The process was repeated again, then again, and each time the old woman watched the babe. At last, as she slid the heated needle in for a fourth time, he stirred suddenly, yellow-gold eyes flickering.

Going through the motions one last time, her prayers stronger now as the potion hissed, the Grandmother checked to make sure the cloth bindings around the atherian's wrists, ankles, and wings were secure. The restraints were more for the boy's safety than her own. He would be extremely weak rising out of the herbs' influences, and the woman wasn't sure she'd be able to convey to him that he needed to keep still. Getting up to throw the rest of the mixture out into the desert night, she returned and scooted her chair just a little closer.

No need for the child to wake up thinking he was tied down *and* alone.

It took another quarter hour before his eyes opened again. All the while the boy stirred and twisted, subconsciously fighting the cloth wrappings that held him to the L-shaped bed, his injured right wing extended to one side, the other pinned under his body. There was little room left in the small hut, and the Grandmother realized with a twist of her stomach that if she'd miscalculated the boy's strength, even in stupor, she would have nowhere to go.

Still, the bindings were designed to comfortably hold down a full-grown man. She had her doubts the babe couldn't have broken out of them uninhibited, but the old woman had been careful to dose him only enough to partially awaken. He just needed to be aware of his surroundings, needed to understand that he was being taken care of. She hoped that, when he was ready, the boy would realize that he was among friends.

At last the creature opened his eyes once again, and this time they stayed open, though only barely. He was scarcely conscious, just alert enough to roll his head and look around from below heavy lids. He squawked feebly when he caught sight of the woman beside him. His mouth drooped open, revealing the lines of needlelike teeth inside, and he tried to hiss.

"Shh-sh-sh," the Grandmother hushed him in soothing tones, grasping his wrists lightly as the boy tried to fight the restraints again. "Rest, my child. Rest. You're in good hands."

She smiled at him, hoping that this universal sign of friendship amongst humans might just cross between species, and it seemed to work somewhat. The child quieted, his mouth fluttering soundlessly and split tongue lolling to one side, but he continued to struggle against the linen cuffs. Against her better judgment the Grandmother loosened each one slightly, careful to make sure the boy watched her do it.

"Shh," she said again, sitting back down and turning her gray eyes to meet his. "You see? You are safe, child. You are safe here."

The freeing of his wrists and ankles, if only marginally, seemed to do the trick. The atherian finally stilled, only occasionally tugging weakly at his wing. He looked at his caretaker expectantly, but the old healer shook her head sadly.

"No, my darling," she whispered. "No. You're hurt there. I can't risk you doing more harm to yourself."

It became clear right then how profound the lost words between the two of them were. The boy had obviously not understood a thing. He began to pull at his wing more fiercely, rolling his head to look at the long straps of leather holding it down. The Grandmother was prepared for this, though, and from her pocket she pulled two short wooden sticks, twigs she'd collected from the stocked kindling the clan used for its fire every night. Stowing one into her sleeve while the lizard-babe wasn't looking, she touched his shoulder cautiously, waiting for him to turn his head to her. When he did, she pointed at the stick in her hand, then reached out to lightly prod the recently healed upper bone of his wing. She didn't press hard, but pushed just enough for the child to feel the pressure and wince, opening his mouth again to try and nip at her hand. She shook her head, indicating the stick again, and snapped it in two pieces. Then, sure she had the child's attention, she pointed at herself, stuck the two pieces back together, and began wrapping them in a spare bit of cloth bandage. It was a small trick to switch the broken halves with the whole stick in her sleeve, and when she was through with the wrapping she smiled, pointed at herself again, and began unraveling the cloth. All the while the atherian watched, intrigued, tired eyes tinged with childish curiosity. When the last of the wrappings fell away, the Grandmother held up the "healed" stick.

The effect was unexpected. The child's mouth tugged back as it did when Grea stroked his head, and he made a sound somewhere between a series of hiccups and snarls.

The Grandmother smiled when she realized he was laughing.

Satisfied that her point was made, she was about to throw the sticks out into the night when the boy whined, straining against his bindings, eyes on the wooden bits.

"Again?" the Grandmother asked him with a laugh, returning to her seat and holding up the twigs. He whined again, and the old woman couldn't help but chuckle.

"All right," she said, turning her back to him so he wouldn't see her push the broken halves back together and hide the whole one once more, "but at some point, Raz, you're going to have to let this old bag of bones get some sleep."

32

V

"He's awake."

Agais raised a brow in surprise. He turned to his wife, forgetting the pelt blankets he was tucking away in preparation for their departure beneath the golden glow of an early morning. Grea was breathing hard, laboring under the weight of her eight-month swell. She must have run to his wagon in all her excitement, and Agais was about to scold her when she shot him a look.

"I think, as the mother, I'm fully capable of judging what I can and cannot do. Come though! It's amazing."

Rebuked, Agais tossed the folded blankets to the wagon floor and jumped down, following Grea across the caravan ring. They passed the ashes and coals of the previous night's fire, making for the Grandmother's cart. When they were close, Grea held up a finger for silence, and Agais nodded. Together they crept to the side of the hut and, her smile bright with excitement, Grea pulled back the goatskin entrance flap just enough for him to see around.

Peering inside, Agais did a full double take.

There was the Grandmother, looking haggard but happy, seated beside the atherian's bed. She was watching the lizard-babe play with a thick copper hoop, something she'd probably conjured from her eclectic collection of trinkets. With a jolt Agais realized the boy's hands were no longer tied to the bed. His clawed fingers toyed with the hoop curiously, amber eyes—looking almost wholly awake—not straying from the shiny bauble. He didn't look away from it even when the Grandmother got up to retrieve a wooden cup from the back wall, nor when she returned with a sewn-leather water pouch.

"Here, child," Agais heard the woman say quietly. "Drink now. Here."

She poured a bit of water into the cup before holding it over the creature's mouth. With her free hand she helped the boy grab it awkwardly in his long fingers, then sat back and watched the atherian lift his head and tip the contents down his throat. The motion was awkward, as though he had only just learned it, and a good portion of the water splashed over the linens.

"Tell me he's still drugged," Agais whispered to his wife without looking away. Beside him he felt Grea jerk in alarm, but too late.

Despite the discreet volume of Agais' voice, the atherian's barely healed ears flicked immediately to attention. With a cry somewhere between a hiss and a scream the boy flung the wooden cup away and tried to lift his body from the bed. Fortunately the leather straps still bound his wing and chest, so instead he thrashed, arms flailing as he tried to rise from his vulnerable position.

"Now look what you've done," Grea huffed, annoyed, pulling the flap aside completely to reveal them. Carefully she clambered up the hanging steps into the wagon, glaring at Agais over her shoulder. "It took us most of the morning to get him to trust *me*, and now you've probably gone and undone all the progress we made."

"He could *hear* me?" Agais demanded, astonished, following his wife up into the hut.

The Grandmother was trying hard to calm the child, her hands struggling to push his arms down with little result. He ignored her completely. In fact, Agais realized with another shock as he stood up, the boy seemed more interested in getting between the Grandmother and the newcomers than anything else. His eyes—only a shade or two lighter than the rising Sun outside—darted between the two Arros, lingering on Agais.

"Hush, Raz! Hush, foolish boy!" Grandmother panted, struggling hard to quell the outburst. "You've already met Grea, and I very much doubt Agais is here to bring you any harm!"

The words obviously meant nothing to the child. He continued to struggle, at one point even grabbing the Grandmother's arm and nearly unbalancing her as he tried to pull her back. There was a *snap*, and the cloth loop that tied his left ankle to the bed broke, adding another limb to the melee.

Agais was about to move forward to help, but Grea held him up with a hand to his chest.

"Do. Not. Move," she hissed. "You're male, human, and unfamiliar. I'd have thought you understood what that represents to him right now."

Agais froze, eyeing the sky-blue membranes of the atherian's pinned wing. Slender red veins cut patterns through the leathered skin, and the limb flexed and stretched as much as it could beneath its bindings. He trusted it was well secured, but regardless Agais found it hard not to imagine those wings spreading out to swallow him.

He kept very still. Instead, Grea edged forward, hands up and fingers spread. She was smiling, trying to make her face bright and trustworthy. As she got closer, the babe seemed to recognize her fully, and he relaxed the slightest bit. He stopped writhing, focusing instead on threatening

Agais with spread ears and exposed fangs as he switched between hisses and juvenile squawks that were a clear attempt at the intimidating roar he might one day develop. His head, awkwardly raised from his position on the bed, seemed to grow and shrink with the extension and folding of the blue crest.

"Quiet, Raz, quiet," Grea hushed, stepping closer. "Friend… Frieeeeend. See?" She pointed at herself, then at Agais. "Friend. No need to be scared."

Who is more scared, him or us? Agais thought, mimicking his wife and slowly raising his open hands. Grea moved around the bed carefully, still smiling, until she was standing behind the boy's head. There she knelt, mindful of her pregnant belly, to rest with both knees on the ground. The lizard-babe—Raz, as she and the Grandmother had apparently named him—flinched when she touched the top of his head, but the woman only paused. Smoothly she ran the tips of her fingers down the apex of the scaled snout and between his ears, whispering as she did. Raz remained tense, his golden eyes never leaving Agais, but his noises stopped. Instead his bluish ears continued to fold and spread, twitching this way and that.

"Make no sudden movements," the Grandmother said quietly. She'd seated herself slightly back and to the side of Grea, nursing the part of her arm the atherian had grabbed. "But come closer. *Slowly.*"

Even as Agais took his first step, Raz became agitated again. His eyes widened and mouth opened to let out a low hiss. Grea shushed him, stroking the crest of his head, nodding for Agais to continue.

It took the man almost a full minute to approach the side of the bed, not wanting to take any chances. He steered clear of the babe's free leg, all too aware of what those wicked claws were capable of, and came to stand beside the Grandmother out of reach of Raz's unrestrained arms.

"Give me your hand," the old woman said without looking over her shoulder at him, a smile plastered on her face. Hesitating, Agais held it out. The Grandmother took a hold of his arm and pulled him nearer to the bed. She didn't say anything, inching the man's fingers closer and closer to the atherian's all-too-visible teeth. Agais turned his head away, helplessly anticipating the chomp and crunch of crushing bone.

It never came.

Instead, there was nothing. Then, after a few seconds, he was aware of something rough brushing against the surface of his palm. Dry breath rushed over his hand. He looked and watched in astonishment as Raz sniffed at his open hand and fingers, snakelike tongue flicking out to taste the calloused skin. The boy's nose traveled up Agais' arm a ways, then back down, then nudged the bottom of his wrist. The Grandmother turned Agais' hand over, and the process was repeated.

After a minute or so Raz seemed to have had his fill. He let his head fall back to the bed so Grea could continue stroking it, half closing his eyes. Still the atherian's gaze didn't leave Agais, but threat and suspicion seemed now replaced by the much more tempered glint of mild curiosity.

Agais himself, feeling his heart dropping to a normal rhythm for the first time since entering the tent, sighed. "How is he?" he asked, watching the child's webbed ears twitch at the sound of his voice.

"Very well." The Grandmother was watching Raz fondly. "I'm not familiar with his kind so much as to know if his recuperation is race-related or a gift he's uniquely blessed with, but he should be fit to walk by the time we reach the Garin. I'd like to have him familiarized with all the rest of the family by that point so as to avoid another scene like today's. Jarden first. His introduction may pose the greatest problem."

"You'd be upset, too, if you'd been cracked across the face with a shovel," Agais muttered. "You think it's necessary that he get to know everyone? I don't know how much longer he'll be staying with us. The oasis crosses atherian land, and there's usually a tribe or two holed up nearby. The only reason they stand for us living around their watering hole for a few months a year is because they know they can't stop it."

"For now we must assume we won't be handing him over to his kind anytime soon," the Grandmother said, and once again Agais heard something layered behind the tone of her voice. "It's only speculation on our part that the atherian will want to take him back. They could just as easily kill him."

She's planting doubts, Agais realized, astounded, watching the head of the bed where sudden concern had leapt across Grea's face. Why, though, he had no idea.

But she also had a point. Raz was a winged male, and while to men that meant only a faster, stronger, and more dangerous atherian, the lizard-kind were a strange race. They might not want the anomaly of a more powerful male in their society. Perhaps the child had even been sold into slavery by his own people, the whole species unwilling to deal with his existence themselves.

There was no way of knowing. Still, Agais had to put his foot down somewhere.

"We've sheltered him, fed him, and treated him as best we could. Unless *you* wish to raise the beast, Grandmother, I suggest you figure out how to tell him we will be handing him over to his kind soon enough."

The Grandmother said nothing. Instead she watched Raz yawn, fully revealing the mottled black and pink inside of his serpentine mouth as he gave in once again to the remnant drugs in his system. Grea, for her part, looked sad, but didn't argue. As the boy fell asleep she got up and followed Agais out of the tent.

After the flap had fallen closed behind them, the Grandmother got to her feet. Bending down, she picked up the copper toy Raz had been so infatuated with before the commotion and placed it gently back in the child's hands. She smiled as his clawed fingers curled over it in his sleep.

For the two days that followed, the wagon train approaching its goal with every passing hour, Agais felt as though conversation with his wife was oddly forced. It had happened before, these periods of silence, but they'd generally accompanied her times of moonblood, which had obviously stopped since the conception of their child. Frequently he watched her, trying to discern what was bothering the woman, though he thought he had a good notion. As noon of the third day passed and Grea still showed no signs of rising from her sulk, he sighed, sick of it, and gave in.

"What else would you have me do?" he grumbled, twitching the reins so that Gale and Haron picked up a little speed along the bottom of a dune. "I was willing to give leeway to the Grandmother while the child was unhealthy, but we can't *keep* the babe, Grea."

"Maybe through the summer, at least?" his wife asked, looking at him fully for the first time all day.

I hate when I'm right, Agais thought bitterly.

"And to what end?" he asked, forcing himself to keep a steady tone. "After the summer is over, what would we do with him? Abandon him in the first fringe city we pass through and hope he survives? He's a *child*, despite whatever intelligence he shows. He'd die or, worse, get sold right back into the chains he nearly killed himself to be free of."

Grea was silent, watching the passing desert again.

"The best thing we can do is get him to his own kind," Agais pressed, eyes on the distant, twisted line of the hilly horizon. "It's a risk, I admit, but a small one, at least compared to the other choices we have on hand. Males are rare amongst the atherian. A winged one could provide some backbone to their survival."

"And if they kill him?" his wife asked without looking at him, resting her head against the side of the cart. "What would you do then?"

Sun burn you, Grandmother.

"There's nothing I can do. We've treated him to the best of our abilities. Now we can only hope the lizard-kind around the Garin will be willing to take him in."

Grea had the look of someone biting back an argument, twisting away to make herself more comfortable. Agais glanced down in time to see a bump appear momentarily in the side of her swollen belly, and he smiled.

"Besides, if you adopted him, we'd have to worry about *two* new mouths to feed, and I'm not quite sure I'm ready to handle the one we're expecting already."

The woman smiled unwillingly, but still refused to look around. After a few minutes of silence Agais decided to try again, though this time he was unsure of whether he wanted to hear the answer to his question.

"So... you named the boy?" he asked. Grea nodded but didn't respond. After a while, though, she seemed to tire of the silence herself, straightening in her seat.

"Raz i'Syul," she explained. "The Grandmother said in the old desert tongue it means 'Child of the Sun.' It's what a lot of people think the atherian believe themselves to be: Children of the Sun and Moon. Children of the Twins."

Agais stiffened. Grea didn't notice.

"I didn't know she knew old desert," he said casually, straightening the horses from a distracted course once more.

Grea shrugged. "She knows enough." She shifted in the seat again. The child must really have been bothering her. "We weren't about to give him a name in the Common Tongue. They do that to slaves. And obviously no one knows the atherian language, so that didn't leave us with much. So: Raz i'Syul."

"Not what you expect," Agais quoted under his breath, feeling his temper touch surface.

"Sorry?" his wife asked, looking at him curiously.

"Nothing."

38

Sun burn you, Grandmother. Sun burn you.

VI

"I don't understand the game you're playing."

The Grandmother looked up at Agais from where she sat cross-legged on the floor of her hut, the lines of her face a picture of innocence. Night was falling once more and, though they usually rode until the dark claimed every foot of the desert, the clanmaster had called an early halt.

When Grea had asked him why, his silence was so sullen she hadn't braved voicing the question again.

"And what game is that?"

Agais glared at the Grandmother, caught between respect for his elder and exercising his role as head of the Arros.

And as a father-to-be.

"You can't manipulate the signs, Grandmother," he forced through gritted teeth. His eyes passed to the once again unconscious form of Raz, still held to the bed. "I don't know if you had visions of this creature and made up the fortune, or if you're trying to bend fortune around him, but you can't manipulate prophecy."

"The telling is real," Grandmother said quietly.

"Then stop trying to entwine it around this boy!" Agais snapped, pointing at the child. "Raz i'Syul? Did you think I wouldn't notice, or that Grea wouldn't tell me? 'Child of the Sun'? *'Son of the Sun'?* You're trying to match the words to an *atherian*, Grandmother!"

"There are scholars who believe lizard-kind consider themselves to be Children of the—"

"I DON'T GIVE A MOON'S *FUCK* WHAT THEY CONSIDER THEMSELVES TO BE!"

The old woman jumped at Agais' roar, eyes wide. Beside her, Raz stirred but did not wake. The man, for one, took a deep breath.

"I'm sorry," he said after a moment, seating himself on the floor and leaning an elbow against the short table in its center. "But you frustrate me. You've given Grea reason to fear for that boy's life,"—he motioned toward Raz—"and as an expecting mother she's taken to the idea of keeping him with the clan."

"Agais…"

"If she realizes you think this atherian is the one the signs are pointing to, she'll be twice as upset. You told us it was *our* son who would bear the burden, not some castaway we crossed paths with in the desert."

"Agais."

"Even if you *aren't* wrong and this boy is the one of whom the Sun speaks to you, it wouldn't be up to us to raise him. It can't work. We can't even be sure the boy is capable of developing normally around men. Could he learn our language? Our culture? Could he—"

"AGAIS!"

It was the Grandmother's turn to yell, and this time Raz woke abruptly, jerking in the bed. Every one of his limbs except for his wing had been freed, and the child clambered to straighten, looking around and hissing. The old woman went to him immediately, and he calmed at the sight of her. She soothed him, placing a hand on his scaled arm and stroking his face with the other. When he was quiet, she turned back to the clanmaster.

"Agais," she said in almost a whisper, forcing herself to look him in the eye. "I-I was not intending to tell you..."

She faltered, and in that breadth of silence Agais felt some invisible steel hand grab at his throat. Cold crushed over him, watching the emotions that flit across the old woman's eyes. Fear, pain, frustration, grief... For a face usually so calm and understanding, it was frightening.

"Agais... your child won't... your daughter... she won't..."

And then the cold was gone. Numbness replaced it absolutely, draining his skin of feeling before rushing inward. The only sensation the man could make out was the deep, drowning pound of his own heart. For a moment he sat, oblivious to all except the wordless facts that were painted out in the Grandmother's gray eyes. She opened her mouth to try and explain further, but he raised a hand to stop her.

For a full minute Agais sat in silence, letting the realizations weigh on him, letting them catch hold in the frenzied jumble of his thoughts. When at last he could speak again, it was only barely.

"Grea... Grea cannot... Grea will not hear of this," he stammered, feeling the heavy stone of grief drop from his throat into the pit of his stomach. "Is that understood? You will never tell her what you... what you mean to tell me."

The Grandmother swallowed, eyes wet, but nodded, and Agais got to his feet. His sight was oddly blunt, as though he were looking at the world through dirty glass. Horrible thoughts snaked into his reality, like some tangible nightmare. For a time he stood, one hand on the wall of the cart for support, alone and trapped in his own cruel mind. The Grandmother stood by, silent, hands clasped in front of her chest to keep them from shaking.

Finally Agais blinked and looked around. Then, slowly, he made his way to the hut's entrance.

"Grandmother..." He stopped before pulling the flap open. His voice was hoarse and dead, barely his own, and his eyes looked out into the pale night unseeing. "As a father, I can hope. As a father, I have to hope..."

Only a soft sob responded from behind him, and with that Agais felt the stone sink a little deeper. Stepping out into the cold, he let the hides fall behind him and turned right to head for his favorite spot outside the wagon ring. He felt unwilling, just then, to return to his wife and unborn daughter.

His fated daughter...

Back in the hut, the Grandmother grasped for the edge of the bed and eased herself to her knees as she continued to cry wordlessly. With one wrinkled hand covering her face she let her body shake, hating the truths that had finally fought their way free. After a few minutes something heavy pressed against her hair, lifted, then pressed again. Looking up, the woman realized that Raz had shifted in his bed enough to reach her with a clawed hand, and was attempting to stroke her head in the same way he enjoyed so much. Despite herself, the Grandmother smiled a sad smile, daring even to gently grab hold of the infant's slim fingers, finding comfort in the alien grasp.

Over the last days of the journey, Agais did as the Grandmother had suggested, and a slow trickle of visitors flowed through the old woman's hut as the rest of the clan were introduced to Raz. Jarden, with some prodding from his lovable—if slightly rebellious—younger wife Surah, went first. The man, brave as he was, was not so anxious to come face-to-face with the atherian again now that the babe was awake. He approached the Grandmother's wagon with the same caution one typically took when trying to get close enough to a dog to see if it was rabid. Surah, losing patience, had threatened the withholding of certain nighttime comforts if the man didn't enter, which proved enough to spark Jarden's usual courage back to life.

The encounter had initially gone about as well as could be expected, despite the Grandmother's and Grea's attempts to warn Raz of Jarden's arrival. They admitted later that Agais' suggestion of temporarily replacing the restraints on the boy's arms and legs had been a good one, but too late. It took almost ten minutes to calm the atherian sufficiently to let Jarden approach and offer his hand to be sniffed. Surprisingly, potential for a promising bond took seed when Raz finished his sensory inspection of the offered limb and proceeded to nip it playfully. Jarden yelped and leapt back, examining the appendage only to find that it was barely scratched. The child, meanwhile, erupted into his series of harsh sounds that everyone had rapidly realized to be laughter. Jarden, hearing this and satisfied that all five fingers of his hand were still attached and moving, began to chuckle as well, until both of them were laughing uproariously.

After that the introductions went smoothly. Or at least relatively so. All the adults went first, Tolman—a dark-skinned, dark-eyed Percian friend—leading the way. After him came Ishmal, Kosen and his wife Delfry, Ovan and Hannas—another married couple and friends of the true Arros—Trina, the widowed wife of Surah's brother, and finally Achtel and the ever-skeptical Iriso. The woman appeared as unconvinced as ever, even after Raz had accepted her with his childishly alien smile, and she stormed out of the hut as soon as possible.

The next day came the younger members of the family, one at a time. Kosen and Delfry's older daughters, Eara and Zadi, went first, both a shade nervous, but left the Grandmother's wagon with no qualms. Prida, a young runaway the clan had accepted two years ago at the tender age of sixteen, entered closely followed by a guarding and watchful Tolman. Some of the older members of the clan disapproved of the man's interest in the girl. He was eight years her senior, true, but Agais had looked into the situation and found nothing but patient affection, and so had let the matter drop.

The youngest children were more hesitant, skittishly eyeing the hut until Izan—Achtel's oldest of four sons at fifteen—stuck out his chest and marched in. He came out wide-eyed, staring at the hand the lizard-kind had examined like it had grown a mouth and learned to speak.

After that the other children had had to be forced into a line to keep them from all rushing in at once.

Asahbet was next, followed by his younger brothers Ryler and Sasham. Trina led her daughter Kâtyn in a minute later, and Ovan tailed off the main group, escorting his little twins—brother and sister—into the hut. Foeli and Barna, both six, had eyes the size of their small fists when their father coaxed them into offering hands to Raz. After all, despite being at least three summers younger, the babe was a half head taller than either of them and covered in scales.

It was then that the day's only difficulties arose. Iriso flat-out refused to let her children Mychal, an energetic boy of seven, and Anges, a shy little girl of five, near the atherian despite even her husband's encouragement. The Grandmother herself had grave words for the woman, saying Iriso was counter-intuitively endangering the two youngsters by *not* familiarizing them with Raz. What might happen if the boy ever got loose, she'd asked darkly. What would happen if he didn't recognize them?

Iriso had retorted that having the "beast" amongst them to begin with was a danger in and of itself, but with the entire clan introduced to Raz and finding little to fear, she finally gave in. Still, the woman somehow negotiated that Jarden, Tolman, Agais, *and* her husband all be in the hut while her children were being familiarized with the boy, and so the quarters were more than a little cramped. Mychal went bravely, smiling at Raz's searching nose, and Anges giggled when the babe's forked tongue flicked over the skin of her small arm. Scowling, Iriso hurried them out of the hut, muttering under her breath about "flesh-eaters" and "oversized reptiles."

Both the Grandmother and Grea had had to cover snorts of derisive amusement. The happy sound added a drop of darkness to Agais' quickly blackening mood.

For days now Agais had watched his wife. Silently he judged her movement and actions. She looked healthy enough, and there were no signs of trouble with the pregnancy. In fact, several times she'd gasped in momentary shock as the baby kicked or punched lively, smiling and catching her breath.

And yet, each time this happened, Agais felt dread grab at his throat like some wicked spirit of terror.

The Grandmother had never been wrong about a birthing. Or any other similar event for that matter. The Sun had blessed her with clear voices, visions that struck her at odd times, giving her a glimpse of what would come to pass. As it was with the telling, as it was with her vision of Agais' child.

His daughter, he thought with a sick mix of thrill and grief.

Still, it was possible that the woman could be wrong. There had to be a first mistake somewhere in these glimpses the Grandmother had.

Agais, against his will, allowed himself to hope, if only a little. He needed to hope. He needed to have that glimmer of light to hold on to if he wanted a prayer of keeping what he'd seen in the Grandmother's eyes from Grea. She was a few days into her ninth month now. The birth was near, proven by the baby's increased agitation, and hopefully within the next few weeks the nightmare would end. Agais would hold his crying daughter—or son, even—up before the Grandmother.

He would prove her wrong.

At that moment, shortly after Iriso had ushered her children out of the cramped hut, Agais caught his wife's eye. The woman smiled at him from beneath loose strands of long bleached hair, winking affectionately. He felt his stomach turn, but forced a smile back at her, pretending that he, too, was pleased with the day's work. In truth, Agais had watched from the depth of his own thoughts for most of the time, too preoccupied to bother being in the room with body *and* mind.

The lovely Grea. His soul's better half in every way.

He would prove the Grandmother wrong. He had to.

VII

The Garin was a sight no matter how many times one might have witnessed it before. Surrounded by a wall of high dunes, it bloomed from the sands as travelers crested the hills from any direction. The desert lake, it was called, and not lightly. The Garin was a little piece of paradise in the middle of the barren wastes that were the Cienbal. It had everything—clean water, shade provided by the numerous copses of palm and weeping trees that patched its shores, slim silver fish flickering just under the lake's surface. The only reason a town hadn't developed around the oasis was that it was a hundred leagues too far from anywhere, making routine trade nearly impossible. It did, however, form the Garin into an ideal resting spot for the weary traveler, as well as the perfect place to spend the broiling months of the summer season. A twisted double crescent of sparkling water against an endless canvas of dusty tan, the lake had wide shores more than large enough to house a hundred families with room to spare.

Despite the delays they'd had, the Arros still arrived fairly early in the season. Only a dozen or so clans were already camped at the edge of the oasis. Their timing was fortunate, giving the family a good choice of where to settle for the next two months, and they needed the selection. Grea's coming labor would require quick water from the lake, and almost as important was the need to keep Raz's presence quiet. It might be weeks, but until the atherian tribes came from the Crags to the east, there was too much risk in letting the other families find out the Arros were keeping the babe.

One Iriso was manageable. A hundred, on the other hand…

"There."

Agais, Jarden, and Tolman were debating by the clanmaster's wagon, looking out over the Garin from their place atop the northern dunes. Agais was pointing to a spot at the near edge of the lake just below them.

"In the nook of the west shore, beside the palm groves. We can set up by the trees, near the shallows. We'll have shade, spare wood to burn or sell, and a safe place to collect water and bathe. And, worst come to worst, the trees will provide plenty of cover if the ath—if Raz needs it."

Or we need it, he thought humorlessly after the two men had nodded and left to spread the word.

The Garin was a clear diamond against the scoured face of the desert, but it was a flawed gem. Danger was present as much as comfort, and it paid to be ready. Marsh crocodiles and their smaller caiman cousins were locals of the lake, making washing, fishing, and collecting drinking water safe only in the extreme shallows along the shore. Besides that, where large amounts of living creatures amassed, so too came the predators. Man-flesh might not be the most reliable source of food, but sandcat attacks happened repeatedly over the summer months regardless, though few were ever successful. Even the dune scorpions braved an occasional assault at some of the smaller families, striking and dragging their prey off into the dunes before any widespread alarm could be raised. It was the reason why, once most of the clans arrived, they tended to form little pockets of massed settlements to dot the oasis rather than spread thin around its edge. It was a habit that had proven useful often, and sometimes in unexpected ways.

Seven years ago, long before Agais and Jarden's father's death, the Garin had fallen prey to raiders. Or fallen under attack, at least. The raiders in question had either severely underestimated the number of clansmen they were up against, or had somehow lost a vast part of their force to the summer heat. The result was just under fifty lightly armored marauders charging down the hill in the middle of the night, bearing torches and swinging sabers. The element of surprise had been on their side, granted, but they'd made the mistake of attacking one of the largest mini-settlements around the lake. Likely they'd thought it would yield the largest take in a quick smash-and-grab.

It was about the only thing they got right.

Twenty-five families awoke to several burning homes, each caravan with at least four capable men and women among them and some with more than ten. Rather than the easy victory they'd anticipated, the raiders had found themselves surrounded by almost two-hundred very angry nomads, not a few among them skilled with a bow, blade, or staff.

While thirty clansmen died that night, only half-a-dozen bandits managed to escape up the hill without an arrow in their back or steel between their ribs. The Arros had been in the midst of the conflict, but thankfully all made it out with their lives.

Sometimes, though, when he'd indulged in too many spirits, Jarden still liked to show off the scar on his left thigh he'd received from a "lucky" saber slash.

Chuckling at the thought, Agais heaved himself onto the front of the wagon where Grea waited as usual, gray eyes wide with excitement, looking out over the Garin. Grabbing the draft horses' reins, Agais gave them a snap, and the train began moving again. A quarter of an hour later the carts circled in, forming the practiced ring just at the edge of the shadows cast by the palms.

The next few hours were spent making camp, a much larger endeavor than the usual nightly fire and stone ring to keep in the horses. One at a time, starting with the Grandmother's wagon at the back and moving forward, patched canvas tents were pitched, backed up against the carts for support and extra room. The entrances faced inward, leaving the inside ring an open circle just big enough to fit all twenty-four Arros comfortably around an evening bonfire. Afterwards, the men worked together to unload the lengths of crafted wood that made up the more permanent horse pen—stowed away in Tolman's relatively empty wagon—and set about digging pits in the sand deep enough that the vertical posts would hold firm. Meanwhile, the women and younger children began setting up the camp in more detail, covering the hut floors with large cloth carpets and reed mats, wide enough to ensure that little sand could escape into the living areas, even with the wind. Thin bedrolls—the same ones the families used during the cooler months— were laid out alongside each other, sheltered by the tents and leaving the wagons with much more room to spare.

The smell of cooking soon drove the men to finish the horse pen. Once Gale, Haron, Sandrider, and the other animals were cleaned, fed, and driven into the wooden confines of the enclosure, everyone returned to their women, sweaty but pleased at the conclusion of the day's chores. By agreement the large portions of leftover dried meat would be consumed first so as to avoid wasting food. Tomorrow they would fish, keeping to the shallow depths with nets and spears but casting lines into the dark blue of the deeper waters. Carp was good and not hard to dry, so the Arros would easily amass ample rations to last them the summer. Reserves they would gather over the last few weeks, ensuring sufficient food on the way to their trade route's starting cities.

All in all the afternoon passed comfortably. When the Sun started to fade behind the high dunes to the west, Agais began to feel some of his trepidations slip away with it. For the first time in days he'd let his mind focus on other things apart from his wife and daughter. It felt good to be able to stop worrying, if only for a few hours. Sadly, though, even as this warm thought caught him, the Grandmother ducked out of her tent and looked around. It didn't take her long to notice him relaxing in the sand by the cooking fire.

"Raz has recovered completely," the old woman told him quietly, coming to sit by Agais while he watched the flames. Now that they'd reached the oasis, they would use the rest of the driftwood stores they'd bought and kept. The kindling, soaked with salts and hardened after drying, burned with a myriad of colors for hours on end. Whisping tongues of blue, green, and red licked the bottom of the wide iron cauldron in which Grea and Delfry were boiling fresh water. Beside them, Surah and Iriso were slicing up narrow strips of dried meat. The other women had taken the children into the palms, searching out whatever edible plants they could find in the fading light.

Agais sat silent. He'd forgotten about the damn lizard, too, for once, and was hesitant to speak his mind as the Grandmother watched him levelly.

"Release him," she insisted. "I will take responsibility for Raz if you are unwilling to do so, but he's been bedridden for over two weeks and doesn't understand *why*. I've had to keep him a little under the entire time, just to make sure he doesn't let himself loose. He's unconscious now. He's unconscious every time I leave him."

Still Agais didn't speak. His eyes took in the fire, dark in the light as he contemplated the decision.

Soon the Garin would be overrun with other families. The Kahnts, the Eamons, the Asani, and five-score more. Because of their placement, the Arros would likely be at the very edge of any settlement that sprouted around them, but other clans would still pen them in. Agais was starting to regret not figuring out some way to get rid of the boy sooner. It would probably be impossible to hide him even *if* he was kept tied to the bed until the atherian came from the east.

A cruel thought to say the least.

"We'll discuss it over the meal," he said finally, giving in. "I will tell you I believe Raz can be controlled. I've seen it. But a decision such as this is not mine to make alone. Iriso will undoubtedly have something to say. Others, too. Some might be content enough to bear the child's presence while he is secluded to your hut, but I doubt they'll all be as open to having him move free amongst them and their children. No matter how tame he might seem."

The Grandmother opened her mouth to speak, perhaps to argue that Raz was of no danger so long as he was watched, but Agais held his hand up. Wearily he leaned back on one elbow in the sand.

"You know as well as I do, Grandmother, that if you should decide to release the boy on your own, I won't be able to stop you. You hold the only voice stronger than mine. It is out of respect, therefore, that I ask that you be patient, at least until we have discussed it as a family. By giving the others a say in what is done with the child from here on out, I hope to show them that I trust them wholly, no matter what."

The old woman shut her mouth and said nothing. Then she nodded. For the next half hour the two sat quietly, content in their silence, watching the foragers return with decent findings and listening to the women chatting incessantly over the smell of rich meat soup.

The Grandmother was true to her word, and so before dinner began and under the excited hum of discussion about the coming months of comfort, Agais got to his feet. Conversations ended quickly, all eyes turning to the clanmaster.

"There is something to be discussed," Agais began, his gray eyes circling the ring of people, "before we can eat."

He hesitated, gaze lingering on the Grandmother, who nodded encouragingly from her spot beside Grea.

"The lizard-child,"—he saw Iriso roll her eyes—"is no longer ailing. He's recovered fully from his injuries. It is the Grandmother's opinion that Raz should be released and allowed some limited movement around the camp."

There was a moment's stunned silence.

And then Iriso leapt to her feet.

"Release him?" she demanded shrilly, gaping at Agais. "You want to let that *monster* run loose around our children? Has the Moon cursed you with insanity, Agais, or are you purposefully acting like a fool? I'm starting to question your abilities as head of this family!"

The silence that followed was more profound, but kept even shorter by Jarden's angry voice.

"It's you who are the fool, Iriso!" he spat at her, still seated on the ground, but eyes blazing. "Twice already you've challenged my brother on this matter, and twice you've been proven wrong! Agais has never shown anything but the utmost capability to lead us true, even through hard times. It is your prejudice against a child who has shown no ill will to anyone in the last week that has you floundering! Well I tell you this: I hold faith in my brother, I hold faith in the Grandmother, and I hold faith in Raz's ability to continue being nothing but a well-behaved boy. He tries to *protect* those who have cared for him when anything he conceives as a threat approaches. With that I remind you that you, too, have been cared for. You bear the name Arro, but you are not blood. Our father accepted you into this family before his death with no qualms, and I've no qualms with you as a sister. BUT ONLY IF YOU STOP QUESTIONING THOSE WHO HAVE BEEN NOTHING BUT GIVING TOWARD YOU!"

Jarden's last statement reverberated, and Agais was silently grateful they'd made camp so far away from the other clusters of tents around the lake. Iriso, for one, looked shocked and on the verge of tears, though whether they were tears of anger or hurt the man couldn't tell. On the other hand, Jarden's lecture had done the trick. She grew silent and sat back down heavily, leaning into the cradling arms of her husband. Still, the woman's retreat did nothing to quell the fire in Jarden's voice.

"I stand by the Grandmother," he said, looking around with a bit more threat in his eyes than Agais might have thought necessary. "She has never led us wrong."

"And I," Tolman said in his deep Percian voice, lifting a hand and nodding.

"I too," young Prida said shyly from beside the dark-skinned man, smiling up at him. Though she was barely of age to have a say, the girl's vote triggered the other women to nod or shake their heads, murmuring yays or nays, and the rest of the men soon followed. By the end, Agais was relieved to find that his vote would have little effect on the decision. Grea, the Grandmother, Kosen and Delfry, and Ovan all voted for Raz's release. Eara and Zadi, the sisters, were split, Eara, the older, voting yes as Zadi shook her head. Not surprisingly, the other younger mothers, Trina and Hannas, voted against Raz's release, as did Ishmal, shrugging apologetically and glancing nervously at Sasham, his youngest. Achtel, always a clever man, knew a positive vote would do little to change the outcome, so he cast nay, supporting the wife he still held to his chest. Iriso remained silent, but Agais was kind enough to place her voice where her heart was.

"With my choice that makes a count of ten to six eligible voices in favor of releasing Raz," he said aloud, double-checking his math so as to avoid sparking any angry voices. "However, as that's not the majority I would like, let me offer a compromise. The boy will be released, but he will be limited to the Grandmother's tent and wagon for the time being, along with some time outside after dark. That should give him room to spread his wings and for all of us to develop our opinion of him further."

His eyes found Iriso. The woman was looking up at him in surprise.

"Does that satisfy all of you?" Agais asked pointedly, not looking away.

As one the clan nodded, even the scorned woman, and Agais sighed inwardly as the matter finally closed. Dinner got underway at once, and when he'd sat down Agais leaned close to the Grandmother.

"I want him sedated when we untie him, just enough so that it doesn't cause a commotion. And Jarden, Tolman, and I are to be with you."

The Grandmother nodded, intent on her bowl of soup.

"And Grea?" she asked quietly.

Agais glanced around the woman to his wife. She was happily playing with Foeli and Barna, the twin brother and sister, tickling them and smiling when they rolled and giggled. He felt a pang of fear seeing the deep pleasure she took in the children, but battled it back.

"No. I'll discuss it with her, but while I trust that Raz will behave, I side with Iriso in the fact that we can't be absolutely sure. I'm unwilling to endanger my wife and child after the... discussion you and I had recently."

The Grandmother shrugged in an understanding fashion.

"A fair concern," she said, finishing her meal and getting to her feet. "Come to my tent after you've convinced Grea."

Agais nodded, watching her walk away.

I thought I asked you to wait for us," Agais groaned, rubbing his temples in frustration. Seated on the stool she'd carried down from her wagon, the Grandmother smiled mischievously.

"I've already held one promise to you today," she said, her eyes twinkling. "You should only expect so much patience from an old crone like me."

Agais snorted, watching Jarden and Tolman playing with Raz, cross-legged on the reed mats. The boy was heavily sedated—at least the Grandmother had fulfilled that part of the bargain—and his attempts to grab the copper ring from the two grown men's outstretched hands were weak. When they let him get it, however, he laughed, emitting the series of hiccups and caws that were his unique manifestation of childish merriment.

As a creature, the babe was a magnificent beast. Despite his slurred motions he stood strong, far come from the beaten and ragged thing they'd found abandoned to the sands. His leathery wings almost glowed blue in the oil-fed lamplight of the tent whenever he stretched them, contrasting the black-green tinge of his skin. The paired joints outside his shoulders allowed Raz to fold the wings tight and low against his back, almost completely hiding them from view. Nothing but faint scars remained from the three sword wounds, and the side of his head, just below his webbed ears, was only a little bare where new scales were still growing to replace the broken ones. His wrists, on the other hand, were marked with twin rings of pale, smooth skin. Agais had seen older atherian slaves with the same markings.

He doubted those scales would ever grow back.

"Get him something to cover the scars," he said. "I won't have people thinking we're keeping slaves on the off chance they find out he's here. And has he eaten today? There's leftover soup that's going to go to waste if it doesn't get finished."

The Grandmother smirked at Agais' concern, but said nothing. Instead she climbed into her wagon through the open entrance as Tolman left to fetch food for the boy. She returned a minute later with a handful of slim silver bands and a carved oak bracelet.

"Put these on him." She handed them to Jarden, on the floor still playing with Raz. Letting the boy toy with the copper ring with one hand, the man slipped the silver jewelry over his left wrist with little effort.

"These aren't going to stay on easy," he told the Grandmother, switching hands and pushing the wooden armlet onto the child's other wrist. "They're too loose."

"He'll grow into them," the old woman responded dismissively. Agais gave her a sharp look. It was fortunate Tolman chose that moment to return, steaming bowl in hand.

While Raz ate—sticking his reptilian snout into the soup and lapping it up noisily, spilling much of it on the floor—the adults sat and talked. All of them were in agreement that the boy wasn't making any moves to harm anyone, though Jarden fairly pointed out that the sedatives could be affecting him. They'd have to pass through the night and see how he was in the morning, and Agais gave the Grandmother permission to stop drugging him, granted Raz remained behaved.

"If he'd wanted to hurt us, he would have tried to by now," he conceded, watching Raz finish licking his bowl clean and toss it away, taking an interest in the shiny new bangles on his wrist. "Even so, it'll settle the minds of the others if we keep him in here for a few more days at least. We'll take him outside at night, but briefly."

They all agreed, watching the child, who was hiccupping as he flicked the bracelets and listened to them jingle. As small as he was, Raz would have looked harmless had he been human. Instead, though, the folded wings on his back, his sharp sunset eyes, and his scales, claws, and tail gave him a distinctly predatory air. Agais remembered the first time he'd seen the boy move, a blur of limbs and teeth, and he shivered.

"Just a few days," he said again, hoping Raz wouldn't get tired of being cooped up. "After that it won't be long before the lizard-kind come from the mountains, and he can be someone else's problem."

Jarden and Tolman nodded, but it was the Grandmother Agais' eyes flicked to. The old woman didn't move. Instead she watched Raz yawn, showing off his dozens of narrow teeth before curling up into a ball on the floor, tail looped around him. One wing unfurled to cover his body like a blanket, and almost at once the boy's breathing was long and deep.

Finally the Grandmother glanced at Agais, and the look in her eyes spelled the mutiny of her thoughts out so clearly she might as well have screamed it to the heavens.

VIII

The next day proved utterly uneventful, as did the following. Steadily more families were trickling over the dunes, and within a week the number of caravans and tents pitched around the desert lake swelled from a dozen to four times that. More would arrive in the coming days, others probably sporadically after that, but regardless their little settlements would grow quickly. It was a mere stroke of luck that none of the clans had chosen to circle in too near the Arros, allowing Raz's presence to remain concealed.

That would change soon enough, Agais forced himself to acknowledge.

Still, he had bigger things to worry about. Grea had been confined to their tent for over a day now—too uncomfortable to walk as the baby shifted ceaselessly in her womb—and while she was still capable of eating, sleep had been difficult the last few nights.

For her and her husband both.

Agais' original sense of wonder at his wife's pregnancy was fading with every passing hour. Now he felt her pain, felt her discomfort whenever she flinched or let out an involuntary groan, and felt much more than that. His mind was a muddled mess of thoughts and images, a splintering display of questions and concerns that resulted from this clashing anxiety between finally being a father and his black fear of the Grandmother's silent warning. He was at once thinking of what he would do when his child learned to walk, and what he would do if his child didn't survive. Or if Grea didn't survive. Or if they both didn't survive…

In the end, though, the hope he had formed for himself held solid. He clung to it like a single lit candle in the dark, trusting the light to keep the shadows at bay. The child—son or daughter, it didn't matter—would be strong and healthy. They would grow to laugh and play with the older boys and girls and would one day marry and bear him grandchildren to bounce on his lap. All else faded as Agais drove that image to the forefront of his mind, and soon he was even able to let go of the Grandmother's irksome belief that Raz i'Syul was the answer to the telling the Twins had granted her.

Not that Raz would grow up poorly, though. Agais felt funny admitting it to himself, but the babe—had he been born to man—could have been any mother's dream. After the effects of the herbs wore off, Raz had emerged an intelligent, well-behaved, and pleasant boy. Fully aware for the first time in weeks, the child only complained about his confined space in the tent and wagon, squawking unhappily until the Grandmother had finally figured out how to convey to him that he had to be quiet or he would be in danger. When, astonishingly, he listened, the old woman convinced Agais to let Raz out a little earlier every night. The other caravans were still some distance away and usually kept to themselves in the evenings, and the clanmaster took amusement in watching the lizard-babe emerge from his tent for the couple of hours of sunset and twilight that followed. For the first two nights the infant had examined everything with expected curiosity, split eyes wide when he saw the wagons and fire and horses for the first time. By the third, though, he'd lost interest, and instead somehow managed to coax Jarden and Tolman into playing in the sand with him.

But Raz, as childish as he seemed, was still the beast at heart. Night noises pricked his ears, and more than once he abandoned what he was doing to bare small fangs at the empty darkness outside the camp. It was impossible to aptly explain the occurrence of breaking branches and loud neighbors, so Agais, the Grandmother, Jarden, and Tolman could only wait until these spouts of defensiveness passed. Raz instinctively didn't leave the ring—though whether this was because he felt it was home or because he was scared of the world outside remained unknown—and after several long seconds he would relax, sniff the air, and return to whatever game he was about.

Another day passed, then the next, and with every rising Sun Agais' nervousness redoubled. Sleeping had become next to impossible for Grea, despite being confined to her bed, propped up by pillows against the wheel of the wagon. Her pain had subsided somewhat, her anxiety the only cause of restless nights now, but Agais couldn't help but feel that it was the calm before the storm. Sure enough, after the clan's tenth day at the edge of the Garin, the Grandmother appeared from their tent looking haggard, approaching the edgy husband who'd waited outside during her inspection.

"Tomorrow," she told him quietly, placing a hand on his arm. "The day after at the latest. Agais, I know we agreed not to tell her, but please—"

"You can't be sure," he said flatly, not looking away from the tent. He pictured his child again, holding his son or daughter in his arms, and the light held. The Grandmother's words barely grated him. "At this point I doubt I would tell her even if you could be. She's too fragile."

The woman sighed, unhooking a lock of silvery hair that had gotten caught in her tribal chain and looping it behind her ear. "Fine. But if you aren't going to tell her, at least prepare yourself. The vision was clear, Agais, the girl won't—"

"You. Can't. Be. Sure," he hissed, closing his mind to the words he imagined she would finish with. Moving around her, he nearly ripped off the leathered hides stepping inside.

Grea was sitting up again, her sweet face bright and enlivened. Reaching out to take his hand, the woman pulled her husband down suddenly, wrapping her free arm around his neck to kiss him.

"Tomorrow," she breathed after she released his lips from her own, closing her eyes and resting her forehead on his. "Agais, tomorrow you will be a father."

"She said maybe the day after," he whispered, hoping silently, not moving her arm from around his shoulders as he kneeled beside her. Before his knees even hit the mats, the man felt something sharp and cold wrench into his stomach and twist.

Her Stars, he cursed silently. He was *hoping* for a delay of the moment he'd been anticipating for the past seven months of his life, ever since Grea had told him she was pregnant. He could feel his candle dimming and scrambled to hold onto it, trying to conjure his happy images.

They wouldn't come.

Instead, all he could do was look into his wife's face—his beautiful, loving wife—and imagine it twisted with pain, confusion, and immeasurable grief.

What if? What if the Grandmother was right? What if the child didn't survive? Could Grea, who so wanted to be the mother of the baby she bore in her womb, live past that tragedy? The idea of losing a daughter hurt Agais enough, but at the thought of losing his wife as well...

"Grea..."

But she wouldn't let him speak. Instead she kissed him again, misunderstanding the building tears in his eyes for tears of joy. By the time she was done wordlessly telling her husband of her love for him, Agais' strength was gone completely. He sat in silence for the next hour, holding his wife and rocking her gently until she mercifully dozed off.

Morning dawned faster than any Agais could remember. The night had seemed fleeting, despite his own lack of sleep this time, and to the clanmaster the Sun rose so quickly he swore the day would pass like an hour. He stood outside the caravan, toeing the shallows of the Garin and watching morning come. Soon Grea would wake from her rare moment of rest, and then he wouldn't leave her side again. He'd forgotten all about Raz for once, his entire being revolving around his wife, trying to feed the dying ember that was all that was left of his hope.

The Grandmother had never been wrong before…

From somewhere off to his left, amidst the palm grove, quiet music played on the wind, whispering its way into camp. Jarden was having an early morning as well, apparently, and Agais stood at the edge of the lake listening to his brother play a melody on his panpipes, praising the new day.

And hopefully praying to the Moon that she would not have need to visit them tonight.

By noon her water had broken, and within a few hours Grea's labor was in full swing. The Grandmother and Agais hadn't left the tent since late in the morning, and every other member of the clan knew better than to go in unless called. Even then only Delfry—with her own two daughters and her experience assisting in the birth of a half-dozen others—was asked to fetch water and aid with the tasks.

Everyone else, for their part, went about their business as best they could, ignoring Grea's pained keens. Kosen, the oldest member of the clan apart from the Grandmother, took over Agais' responsibilities, delegating tasks to the rest of the family. When the Sun began to dip toward the western hills, Trina, Iriso, and Hannas started on making dinner as the rest of the women set up fishing lines baited with bits of meat. Izan and his brothers were sent with a few copper barons to buy dried fruit from the other clans along the lake border, then to fetch wood from the grove. Jarden took it upon himself to watch over Raz, distracting the confused boy by letting him play with the panpipes, amused as the infant tried to imitate him, blowing awkwardly down the wrong end of the tubes.

Even so, eventually the birth became impossible to ignore, and some of the smaller children grew increasingly frightened by Grea's building groans and cries. In an attempt to occupy them, Ovan shepherded the group out of the wagon rings and into the oasis shallows. Tolman, armed with a staff and the long dagger he'd always worn before joining the Arros, stood guard, watching the waters for dark shapes. Stripped naked, the little ones shouted and played, splashing left and right.

It wasn't long before Delfry appeared once again, looking drained and weighed down with a heavy pan filled to the brim. Tolman got up to help her, wrinkling his nose at the mix of water and sick inside.

"Any news?" he asked quietly. Together they carried the heavy basin away from the playing children, pouring its putrid contents out deep in the trees and kicking sand over the spot. The Garin fed off an underground river, but it was common agreement that waste and other such things be given over to the desert rather than the lake. "How is she?"

The exhausted woman glanced around quickly, making sure the happy exclamations were still a ways away before speaking.

"She's a good bit paler than we'd like, but the Grandmother isn't worried about Grea," Delfry told him, bending down to scrub the pan with sand. "The baby though... It hasn't tried to emerge fully yet, but we saw its feet. She had to turn it around so that it will come out headfirst."

Tolman looked at her blankly in response. Getting to her feet, Delfry explained.

"The baby has to come out head first or there's a chance its neck will get caught. From there, freeing it can be... difficult."

"Ah," Tolman said simply, nodding, and together the pair made their way back to the water's edge.

"There shouldn't be a problem, though," Delfry continued hopefully, filling the pan with clean water. "The Grandmother managed to turn the child around. Now all we can do is wait for it to come. Grea is doing her best to coax it, but it's a stubborn thing. She's exhausted, and the Grandmother's already gotten her permission to trigger the delivery if it hasn't started by nightfall. She has the plants necessary."

Tolman nodded, watching her go. Then, turning west, he grimaced, seeing the Sun's lowest tip sink below the dunes in the distance. Returning to his place by the water, he sat down, hard pressed to watch the tiring children as the day came to a close.

From the trees, though, another pair of eyes gazed hungrily across the shore. Attracted by the sounds and the scent of the birth, four clawed paws padded silently over the sand to crouch beneath the lowest brush that clung to the base of the palms.

IX

The child started to come just as night reached its fullness, Her Stars appearing one by one like bright witnesses in a dark sky. Tolman could tell. Just as he and Ovan were gathering up the worn-out, dried and dressed children to return them to their parents, the distant groans of discomfort and pain reached a new level. Before long, Grea's suffering howls pierced the quickly cooling air.

"Hush," Ovan told the youngest children clinging to him, patting Foeli's head reassuringly. "You are hearing a miracle. There is nothing to be frightened of."

Tolman nodded in encouragement, and together the two men shepherded the group back into the wagon ring. The children huddled together on the far end of the circle from Agais and Grea's tent, not much comforted. The women, too, seemed nervous. Understandable, considering almost half of them had young ones of their own. No doubt their day's conversation had revolved around their own experiences, and how they thought Grea was doing.

Tolman sat with his back to the space between his wagon and the one shared by Prida, Trina, and Kâtyn. The colorful fire in the center of the circle cast waves of steady heat across the camp, banishing the cold, but it did little to block out the sounds coming from the clanmaster's tent. Tolman had hung up his dagger, but he kept his staff on hand instinctively. Maybe he was jumpy, his nerves set on edge by Grea's continued labor, but the weight of the wood felt comforting in his callused palms.

After a while Jarden reappeared from the Grandmother's canvas hut, checking to see the progress on the night's meal before coming to sit beside Tolman. For several minutes both men sat in silence, feeling out of their element.

"How's the boy?" Tolman asked eventually, more to spark conversation than anything. Forced exchange was preferable to whatever else they might hear tonight.

"I left him to his own devices." Jarden jumped on the opportunity. "The birth was making him nervous. I think he could smell it, oddly enough. Combine that with what he could *hear*, and I guess it's understandable. He's playing with that copper circlet he likes so much."

"You think it was best to leave him alone?"

Jarden shrugged. "I tried bringing him outside at one point, but he didn't seem keen on the idea. Maybe it's best we give him some space. Between the lot of us, he hasn't had any time to himself in the last month."

"I don't think time means much when you're out cold for two weeks," Tolman chuckled. "And outside of that, I don't really know how much space a toddler needs on his own."

Jarden smirked, kicking sand out from between his bare toes. "Young he might be, but I swear the boy has an old mind between those spiny ears. You were already with us when Hannas' and Iriso's whelps were young." He jerked his head at the group of children Ovan was now distracting with exuberant storytelling, his arms swinging upward to hold an invisible sword aloft, depicting some heroic moment. "Slobbering little things, you know what I mean. And the Grandmother says that Raz hasn't yet reached three summers. We think the atherian are beneath us, but that boy does a lot to make me question it. I've never known a human child of *two* capable of making himself understood as well as him, and that's without speaking a word of the common tongue."

"True enough," Tolman acknowledged, "but what if he isn't actually as young as the Grandmother says? What if he's just stunted, or a runt?"

"Ha!" Jarden snorted, grinning. "A winged male, the runt of the atherian breed. Sounds like the start of a bad joke… But I guess it could explain much. Still, I think I'll trust the Grandmother, as should you."

Tolman nodded. Although he sometimes found the rest of the Arros' generally one-sided opinion of the old woman tiresome, he couldn't deny her wisdom. She was never wrong.

"I'd rather put my trust in her being able to get that poor girl through her labor," Tolman muttered, listening to Grea's moans pick up again from across the fire. "How long do you think…?"

But he stopped midsentence. His eyes were fixed on the dark space between Agais' tent and the Grandmother's, open to the desert beyond. It was gone as quickly as it had come, but he'd thought he'd seen something glimmer and blink through the night, catching the light of the cooking fire. Only black stared back now, but nomadic life rarely led a man to brush such things aside so easily.

"What is it?" Jarden asked, dropping his voice, following Tolman's eyes into the dark. Ever the fighter.

"Something's moving out there," the man said steadily, trying to peer into the space from where he sat.

Jarden tensed beside him. "Yes," he hissed. "I see it."

Tolman traced the champion's gaze just in time to see an unnatural shadow flick through the next opening in the caravan ring. As one the two men got up casually, not wanting to alarm the others, and split around the fire. Jarden made for the place he'd seen the motion, Tolman for the space beside it in the direction the shape had been moving. They passed the tents and carts quietly. Ovan's loud storytelling faded as they stepped out, one after the other, into the cool desert night. Their outlines danced across the sand before them, towering figures cast by the flames. Tolman kneeled to look under the closest wagon—Ishmal's—but found nothing. He got to his feet, searching the oasis around him again before glancing back at Jarden, who shook his head, motioning Tolman to circle to the left. He would do the right. Nodding, Tolman made his way around the ring, careful to stay low and quiet.

The Garin was still, the lake a pristine sheet of liquid glass that reflected the Moon above almost perfectly. Crickets sang from the palms as he searched, orchestrating their evening chorus. Reaching the third wagon, Tolman peered beneath it as well.

Still nothing.

Jarden seemed to have taken more time, so Tolman moved on to the fourth cart, his anxiety fading. Likely it had just been a child from a new-come clan, curious to see other families. Or perhaps one of the dogs that some of the nomads kept. He knelt down one last time to examine the three-foot space between the wagon's worn under-bed and the sand. Only darkness looked back at him.

Jarden appeared at that moment, coming from around the ring. He shook his head to indicate he'd found nothing out of the ordinary, and Tolman was about to return the gesture when he froze.

Beneath the cart the shadows twitched.

The man didn't budge, hardly even breathing. Despite the precautions, Jarden saw his body language change and so, it seemed, did the thing under the cart.

There was a faint growl, building throatily as two points of glinting light cut through the black. The sound climaxed in a feral yowl, and the sandcat pounced. Tolman felt wide-set claws dig into his chest, and he was bowled backwards, his staff flying from his grasp. For a brief instant he could see the end of his life sitting atop him as the three-hundred pounds of muscle, bone, and teeth weighed him down. Then the pressure was gone, and he felt the cat spring away, its attention fixed elsewhere.

The camp.

"NO!" he yelled, scrambling to stand. Jarden cursed, already chasing after the animal, sand spraying from beneath his feet. He followed it between the wagons and into the caravan ring. Swearing to himself, Tolman followed, snatching his staff from the ground.

The first thing he heard was the women scream.

The scene was one of instant chaos, the fact that a birth was happening completely forgotten. The great cauldron lay abandoned over the fire, the makeshift cooks scattered. Jarden was pulling a flaming branch from the blaze, sending sparks jetting into the air in a thousand twisting directions. Ovan had somehow managed to get between the sandcat and the children, spreading his arms in an attempt to shield them.

Unsurprisingly, the animal did not seem to take this too kindly.

It was a massive thing, bigger than any Tolman had ever seen. Nearly eight feet long from nose to tail, sinewy muscle bunched under a light-brown coat. It circled the group on flat paws that let it move across even loose sand without leaving tracks. A hand-span of white fur, marking it as a fully matured female, encircled its neck. Tufts of longer white hairs protruded at the tip of each ear, like the smaller wildcats that prowled the North's wild ranges. Yellowish fangs the size and breadth of a man's thumb bared as Ovan kicked sand in its face and yelled, trying to scare it off. The cat snarled, black eyes glinting.

Then, before anyone could so much as yell a warning, it pounced.

Ovan went down, a paw catching him in the side of the head, claws extended. There was a *snap* and the man collapsed, his neck at an odd angle, falling into a heap in the sand. Without pausing the cat twisted, going for the closest child within reach. Mychal—Achtel and Iriso's oldest—screamed as the beast's jaws clamped around his left knee. At once it began shuffling backwards, dragging him kicking and shrieking out toward the edge of camp.

"NO!" Jarden screamed this time, leaping after the animal. It pulled the thrashing boy into the night, circling back around the wagons, heading for the trees. Jarden wielded his flaming branch like a sword, swinging it left and right before Tolman joined him, leaping over Ovan's body in his haste to help. Behind him he heard a woman—Iriso, it must have been—screaming through her sobs.

Together the two men chased after the sandcat as it dragged the boy away, moving quickly despite Mychal's added weight. It was nearly in the darkness of the palms when they finally caught it, and Jarden swung his fiery weapon at the animal's head, intent on freeing the child. He missed, but the threatening blaze and showering sparks were enough to make the cat release its prey and snarl, baring teeth again.

"TOLMAN! GRAB MYCHAL!" Jarden yelled, swinging the branch around once more so that it whooshed through the air. Before Tolman could move to snatch the boy up, though, the cat roared and struck at Jarden, lifting onto its back legs to swipe with both front paws at the man. The first caught the base of the flaming limb, knocking it from his hands. The second caught his shoulder, dragging large black claws down Jarden's left arm as the cat fell back on all fours between Mychal and his would-be rescuers. Jarden screamed in pain, stumbling backwards and falling into the sand, clutching at his mangled arm with his good hand. The cat left him, turning its black eyes instead on Tolman, who stood frozen, all strength sapped from his body. He clutched at the staff in his hands, wondering what good the thin piece of wood could possibly be against a monster such as this.

He could see the cat preparing to leap, see the legs tuck and muscles strain, claws extended. It was practically in midair, in fact, when a dark blur not even half-the animal's size collided with its front shoulder. The sandcat yowled, knocked away from Tolman, twisting and spraying sand everywhere as it leapt to its feet again.

Waiting to meet it, teeth bared and clawed hands splayed in the air in front of him, was Raz.

The lizard-babe hissed, extending his wings to their full capacity so that their bluish skin glowed in the moonlight. His ears were spread, as was the neck-crest, a single pale blade rising behind his head in the night. He hissed again, taking a step forward and rippling his wings.

The effect was beyond frightening.

Through the confused haze of events, Tolman realized with a jolt that the babe had *grown*. Despite his poor health, in the three weeks since they'd found him Raz had sprouted an easy inch, maybe two. He stood taller now, perhaps four feet in all, with a bearing that promised a fight.

Even the sandcat seemed to hesitate, despite its greater size. It tried to circle the atherian, eyes darting between him and the crying form of Mychal, lying just behind Raz's spread wings. The lizard-babe was having none of it. He feigned forward with a squawk, collapsing and extending his crest. Not once did his sunset eyes leave the cat's black ones, even when Tolman scrambled to Jarden's side. The man was still conscious, by the Sun's blessing, watching the two beasts face off with a mixture of pain, anger, and intense relief streaked across his face.

After nearly a minute of testing and pushing, the sandcat seemed to realize the only way past the atherian was through him. With another roar it struck suddenly, launching itself directly at Raz's small form. The boy was just as fast, though, darting forward to collide with the beast.

The fight that ensued was bloody and bone shattering. Like the wild animals they were the two forms writhed and spun in the sand, striking and biting and slashing at each other whenever they got the chance. They thrashed, kicking and clawing, sometimes leaping away only to crash head-on again. Tolman and Jarden could do nothing but watch, useless and faintly aware of others running to meet them. Much of the family came—Achtel supporting a sobbing Iriso, Kosen and his daughters, Prida and Surah. There were other forms, though, people they didn't recognize. A dozen members from the other clans camped nearby, alerted by the screams.

Everyone stopped when they got near, fixed with horrified fascination.

The fight raged as loud as a wartime battle, the two combatants screeching and roaring. At one point the cat managed to sink its teeth into Raz's thigh. Tolman felt a sinking fear until the lizard-babe's other foot caught the animal's exposed neck, forcing it to release his leg as blood coursed through torn fur. In the faint light of the Moon the sand around the two creatures grew steadily darker and wetter, sticking to them and their wounds. Exhaustion seemed impossible for the pair, the fight simply growing wilder and more vicious as a minute passed into two, then three, then four.

And then it ended.

With a twist of his body, Raz slipped beneath the beast, clinging to its neck with both arms. A powerful kick of his good leg crushed one of the cat's shoulders, and as the animal screamed in pain the atherian's teeth found its throat, cutting the sound short. For a few silent heartbeats more the cat flailed and the lizard-babe's torso strained, small muscles popping out of his back and neck. Then, with a sound like ripping parchment, the two fell apart. Ten long seconds the sandcat twisted noiselessly in the sand, blood spilling from the fleshy hole beneath its jaw. For a time after that it twitched, convulsing helplessly.

At long last, though, the beast stilled altogether.

There was a moment's peace, a breath of calm stillness in which all watching registered what had happened. Then it broke, and the gathered Arros erupted into cheer. Over the jubilation, however, several outsiders' yells could be heard.

"IT'S OVER! KILL IT! QUICKLY! KILL IT NOW!"

It was then that Tolman saw the blades bristling from the spectators who were not of the Arro clan. Their neighbors had come armed—with the best intentions, no doubt—and now they advanced as a group on Raz. The boy, battered and bloody as he was, leapt backwards. He landed on all fours in front of a feebly stirring Mychal, baring his fangs protectively, misunderstanding the strangers' approach. His wide wings spread once more, their membranes torn and ripped like the tattered sails of some storm-tossed ship.

"NO!"

Four voices screamed it at once. Tolman's was one, as was Surah's, kneeling beside Jarden's still form, her husband having finally passed out from the pain and loss of blood. Another was Achtel's, waving his hands and yelling, running straight at the armed nomads.

The last was Iriso's.

The woman slipped and tumbled in her scramble to get at her son. She ran toward Raz and Mychal, throwing caution to the wind. At first Raz spun to face her, crest flaring in defiance. When she got closer, however, the babe seemed to recognize her, and he calmed. On his hands and feet he shifted aside, letting the crying mother rush to her son, picking his slender form up and holding him fiercely to her. Then she lifted her tearful eyes to look at Raz.

"Thank you," she whispered. "Thank you."

And, before anyone could think to stop her, she reached out and pulled the atherian into her chest, holding the two children tightly as she started to sob once more.

Where Achtel had been able to do little to dissuade the angry group still trying to get at Raz, his wife's action did everything. Almost to a one the men and women stopped dead, utterly confused, watching the three people huddled together just outside the darkness of the groves. Some of them looked disgusted, others curious, but regardless they all paused. For the first time they began to listen to the words of the man who had ridiculously tried to prevent them from defending their kin. Breathless, Achtel explained as best he could, hoping silently that he wasn't dooming Raz even more by telling the boy's story.

Behind him, though, while he spoke, the rest of the Arros watched in amazement as the unthinkable happened. Raz—whose small, scaly, beaten body had gone instinctively rigid at Iriso's contact—relaxed. Then, incredibly, his infantile arms reached up awkwardly to return the crying woman's hug as best they could, his wings wrapping around all three of them like a blanket. For a long moment they held each other, a faint cocoon of patchy blue, still in the night.

Then the wings fell limp, and Raz collapsed, unconscious, to the desert floor.

It was in that moment, at last, that everyone seemed to regain the ability to move. The other Arros rushed to help the injured, most running to Iriso and the children, Kosen and Trina to Tolman. Together, along with Surah, they managed to lift Jarden out of the sand, blood weeping from the gashes in his arm.

They were about to move him when the desert, quiet for the first time since that morning, was rent apart by a scream, agonizing and colored black with grief. With a creeping sense of horror, Tolman realized that Grea had been silent for some time, her pained cries at an end, and that the shriek, which rang clear from the deepest part of the human soul, was not a woman's.

It was a man's scream.

X

The hours the Arros suffered following that night's events were amongst their darkest. Mychal was safe, thank the Sun, but his left leg was beyond repair, torn and twisted at the knee where the sandcat had gotten its teeth around it. After a rushed deliberation—to which Iriso could only contribute blubbering tears and further denial—the Grandmother accepted the help of four healers come from several of the other clans. A concoction of ganet leaf milk and aramora was drafted, putting Mychal into a sleep from which he wouldn't awaken for days.

Then the women removed the mangled limb, cutting it off just above the knee.

After cleaning the stump and bandaging it carefully, the five moved on to the less injured. Jarden and Raz were laid out on the ground inside the Grandmother's tent, both unconscious, and both torn to shreds. Between them, a haggard Surah, Trina, and Prida had managed to stop most of Jarden's bleeding. They could do nothing, however, for the four long slices that ran from his shoulder to elbow, two of which continued down his forearm. Eventually three of the more experienced menders kneeled around him, and within an hour they'd sewn shut most of the wounds with thin sinew string. Meanwhile the Grandmother and the last healer, a younger woman named Evano Ashani of the Ashani clan, tended to Raz as best they could.

"Her Stars," Evano had whispered when she'd first laid eyes on the atherian, "so *this* is the cat-killer?"

"Raz," the Grandmother reprimanded gently. "And born under the Sun, just as you were. Do not let your assumptions blind you, child. Keep that steady hand still."

The woman nodded, and they'd gone to work, both silently wondering whether the babe would make it through the night even with their care.

If Raz had been a mess when the Arros first found him half-dead in the desert, then there was no word to fairly describe his current state. He was slashed and battered, hardly a part of him left unscathed. Parallel gashes crisscrossed his body. Small ribs shone in the lantern light from several of the cuts, many of which seeped blood through a thick cake of sand. His thigh bled continuously where the cat had sunk its teeth in, and one wrist looked to be badly broken. The claws must have caught him across the face, too, because three lines sliced diagonally down his snout, splitting his right lip completely in several places. His wings were even worse. Shredded in more than one place, there were whole slivers of membrane missing in several spots at the edges. It gave them a tattered look, like the worm-worried clothes of an old corpse. While Evano worked on cleaning and closing the wounds along his body, the Grandmother took on the delicate work of slipping the torn skin of his wings back into place. The flesh was almost all there, and slowly she flipped and flattened everything back together with bloody hands. This done, she smeared ointment over every laceration, hoping against hope that infection wouldn't set in and eat away at the delicate membranes.

Only those involved in helping the wounded hovered around the Grandmother's tent. Trina, Kosen, and Achtel had taken the children to bed, though understandably not a one slept a wink the whole night through. Eara and Zadi accompanied Hannas and her twins to Tolman's hut, donated as a place of mourning to house the souls the Moon had claimed that night until proper burials could be held. There the woman and her children wept over the still form of her husband, clinging to the cold hand that hung from under the white silk sheet covering Ovan's body.

On the other side of the room, set on a small copper table borrowed from a dusty corner of the Grandmother's wagon, was a basket, also covered in white. In it rested the small form of a baby girl, too still and too blue, swaddled in the comforts of an old woven blanket.

Tolman alone had braved entering Agais' tent after the night's events, and then only for a brief minute to whisper his heartfelt sorrow and to inform the clanmaster of the state of his brother and the other injured. Agais, sitting at his wife's side, had only nodded, his eyes red and wet. One hand ran through her pale hair slick with the sweat of a difficult labor, the other resting across his knees where he'd been laying his head. Slipping out again, Tolman didn't feel the tear drip down his dark cheek, clinging to the stubble of his chin.

XI

In the week that followed, little changed in the Arros' small camp. Jarden came to the next morning, though Surah forbade him from leaving his bedroll. It was another three days before Mychal and Raz stirred from their induced slumbers. In that time many people came from other tribes, wanting to see for themselves if the rumors were true. Had the Arros indeed taken in a lizard-boy? Was it truly winged? Could it really have taken on a fully grown sandcat?

Not wanting to stir up trouble, Agais—having finally mastered his own grief—allowed them free entry, only forbidding them from getting too close.

Most who came were little more than politely interested, giving their condolences to the families of the dead and wounded when they heard of that night's tragedies. Some even had their clans tender aid, though Agais gently refused everything except bandages and medicines, thanking every benefactor.

But there were always those who could not understand *why* the Arros would endanger the lives of their family by harboring a "savage reptile." More than once Tolman, Achtel, and Ishmal had had to get between Raz and an angry visitor claiming it was his or her right to finish the job the sandcat had started. One woman of a smaller clan, the Syrros, had gone into hysterics, threatening to come back with her husband and brother if they didn't let her "kill the lizard."

It was Iriso that shut her up.

Stepping between the crazed visitor and the three men guarding Raz, Mychal's mother cracked her across the face with a sound like splitting wood. Iriso then did her own screaming, making it clear that the men of *her* clan could do much more than go after just one of her people. Then she'd grabbed the struggling woman by the hair and thrown her bodily from the tent, stepping out and raising a finger to indicate the sands beyond the caravan.

"Get out," Iriso spat, and watched the beaten woman leave, muttering dark threats under her breath.

The Syrros never came.

Thankfully, by the end of the third day the visitors seemed to have had their fill, and life found some balance once again. Hannas and her twins still grieved, but took solace in the activities needed to survive along the Garin. They soon joined the others in fishing and cooking, all three hardly speaking a word between them.

No one pressed them to talk.

Agais, too, returned to them, thanking Kosen for taking on the clanmaster's responsibilities. He still spent much of his time by Grea's side while the woman recovered, but his eyes were dry. Privately, at dusk as the next Moon rose, he'd taken the basket bearing his daughter's still body into the sunset-lit grove, returning several hours later empty-handed.

Ovan had been buried at the edge of the palms, resting at the shore of the still lake beneath the shade of the trees.

The Grandmother tended to Mychal and Raz, pleased with how both were doing. Mychal's stump healed well, his sutures already sealing, and his father had busied himself fashioning a crutch from some spare wood. Raz was doing even better. His wounds had started to close by morning of the first day. New scars in the form of paler, imperfect scales formed, but even the marks along his snout were barely visible. His silver bangles had been pushed back up his left arm to give space for the wooden splint that secured his broken wrist. Even his wings were doing well, though the old woman doubted whether the frayed edges where the sandcat had managed to rip whole pieces free would ever completely heal.

Midmorning of the fourth day, at long last, the two boys stirred. Mychal awoke first, screaming and crying when he saw his lost leg until his parents came running, their faces tear stricken with mixed grief and relief. The child's cries woke Raz slowly, his eyes flickering for a long time before he came to. He called out as well, stiff and sore and barely able to move. The Grandmother rushed to his side, lifting him into a sitting position.

"You foolish boy," she whispered, offering him a cup of water while the babe cried out weakly in her arms. "You foolish, brave child. What would we have done if you'd gotten yourself killed? What then?"

Raz didn't respond, too intent on his parched throat. He gulped down the water in an instant, spilling less now than he had almost a month ago, and then held the cup out for more.

That night the blaze of the cooking fire was larger than ever, and the clan celebrated the return of the two boys to the world of the living. Even Agais emerged from his tent, returning only briefly to bring his wife a plate of steaming silverfish and seasoned tubers. Then he sat down, taking a place beside Raz, who was staring around in wonder. It was the first time he'd been allowed to eat with the clan, and the fire and crowd mesmerized him.

"They're one stronger because of you, boy," Agais told him, knowing he wouldn't understand. Raz looked up at the man curiously, and Agais pointed at Mychal, huddled between his parents close to the fire. He was wrapped in a rough-spun pale blanket, looking significantly happier than he had that morning. Then Agais placed a hand on Raz's chest, trying to convey what he meant.

"Because of you," he said quietly with a small smile, the first real one he'd managed in days.

The babe still looked confused, glancing down at the clanmaster's hand resting on the scarred, scaly muscles of his breast. Chuckling, Agais gave up, handing the boy a plate of food instead as it came around. Raz dug in at once, not bothering with his hands and instead picking the silverfish meat up with his teeth before tilting his head back and swallowing it whole. Next he nibbled on a tuber curiously, and made a face. Beside him, Jarden—allowed out of his tent for the first time as well—laughed, giving the boy a piece of his fish.

It was gone in an instant.

After dinner came to an end, everyone satisfied and feeling better than they had in days, Jarden pulled out his pipes and started to play a desert jig. It was a rough tune, made awkward considering the man only had one hand to move the wood across his lips, but nevertheless it wasn't long before little Barna had pulled her cousin Kâtyn in the circle to dance. The two girls hooted and yelled, twirling around the cooking fire as the blaze burned purple and green and red. Soon they were joined by Iriso and Achtel, Surah and Ishmal, and a number of other odd couples, laughing and kicking sand in all directions with their twisting feet. Their shadows jumped and dashed across the canvas tents around them, and the music grew louder and faster after Achtel's sons pulled skin drums from their wagon to pound a beat along to the pipes.

It was a celebration worthy of both the living and the dead.

From his place on the perimeter between Agais and Jarden, Raz looked on in wonder. His lips were pulled back and his mouth hung half open in his strange alien smile. Side to side he bobbed his head unevenly to the music. After a time, though, his smile faded, and he looked around. He leaned forward, trying to see past the clanmaster, sniffing the air.

Then he opened his mouth.

"Grrrr... Grrrree...rrrreeraaah... Grreerrrahh...?"

Jarden stopped playing so abruptly the pipes might have burned his lips.

It only took a second for the dancers to stop their furious circling of the fire. When the music died, they looked around curiously.

"Wh-what was that?" Jarden demanded, dumbstruck.

Agais gaped at the boy sitting beside him. Raz turned to the man, nudging his arm with his reptilian snout and looking up questioningly.

"Grreerrrahh?" the lizard-babe asked again.

"Her Stars," Agais whispered in shock. "Grea. He wants to know where Grea is."

In its entirety, down to even Anges, the youngest among them, the clan gawked at Raz. Then not a few amongst them smiled.

Agais stood up, took Raz carefully by the hand, and walked him to the tent where Grea still rested.

When the atherian finally arrived from the Crags a week later, bearing with them carved-bone instruments, dried meat, and shiny stones and gems to trade, the Arros avoided them at all cost.

None among them were about to abandon one of their own to an uncertain future.

XII

"Laor may not be accepted in the hearts of all, but Laor holds all close to his heart. Only the most wicked of men will be kept from returning to earth after death. In this way, the Lifegiver weeds out the vile from the constant cycle of life."

—Eret Ta'hir, High Priest of Cyurgi' Di

Damn these stairs.

The harsh winds of the Veitalis Range pulled at Talo Brahnt's white cloak and fur-lined cowl. Snow whipped into the Priest's face, and he hunched over, one gloved hand tugging the worn fringe of his hood down over his brow. His blue eyes, still sharp despite his forty years, kept a close watch on the treacherous path beneath his feet. The carved-stone stairway stretched upward into the white oblivion that was the storm, disappearing barely a dozen yards above his head.

Still, there it was, a silhouette looming like some great beast against the clouds.

"Nearly home, little one!" he called out, pulling gently on the small hand he had clasped in his free one. Glancing back, he couldn't even see the girl's face, so large was the oversized hood that covered it. Talo had had to hurriedly design a makeshift cloak for her from one of his own spares and—considering she was several times smaller than he—the results were questionable.

Carro, you will always be the better seamstress, Talo thought with a smirk that loosened some of the snow caked in his beard. Shifting his pack more comfortably on his shoulders, the man turned his eyes back upward through the storm.

It wasn't long before the stairs finally reached their finish, flattening out as the mountain itself seemed to plateau. A great semicircular platform of leveled stone gave their aching feet respite, but the child didn't appear relieved. Instead she squeaked and hid behind Talo's leg, her pink eyes wide, taking in the sight before them.

Cyurgi' Di, the High Citadel, was Laor's most northern temple. It towered above the pair, utterly dwarfing their forms, the weathered granite bastions on either side of them soaring into the storm. Nestled in this small nook of the wall that was the temple's only entrance, Talo pulled his hood back, letting fall the long brown ponytail that hung just above his waist. He smiled a little now that the snows abated enough to see by.

The Citadel was a massive structure, carved long winters ago into the side of the mountain, the cut stone mortared and shaped into a massive circular wall that hung partially suspended over the cliffs on two sides. Arrow slits leered down on them like eyes, but it had been centuries since they'd been put to any real use. The Laorin had few restrictions, but the one cardinal rule of their faith insisted that no life could ever be taken by a Priest or Priestess' hand, even in self-defense. The slits now served as little more than a good means of getting fresh air into the halls.

Although it did get a little breezy during the harsher blizzards such as this...

Gently tugging the child along with him, Talo approached the temple gateway, a massive vaulted tunnel that cut through the breadth of the wall. The snow finally ceased altogether when they entered the arched way, their damp footsteps echoing loudly across the dry stone. For a few seconds they were free of the storm, free of the battering winds that had almost knocked them clear from the steps more than once. Too soon, though, they cleared the tunnel, and the flurries kicked at their faces once again, mocking the high walls that rose to encircle them.

"Nearly there, Syrah," Talo promised anew, starting across the wide bailey and cutting a path through the three or four inches of undisturbed powder blanketing the brick. It wasn't long before Talo was banging against the tall temple gates, set in the wall at an angle from the tunnel.

A muffled voice picked up from the other side, barely audible against the wind. Abruptly a small slot in the door slid open just around chest level. A pair of blue eyes similar to Talo's blinked at them for a second, then disappeared, and the clambering from the other side of the gates grew exponentially louder. There was a clang, and with the screech of poorly oiled iron hinges one of the massive timber doors swung inward.

"Talo!" a cheery voice greeted them when they stepped inside. "It's been a long time! Thank the Lifegiver you made it through this horrible weather we're having. Wouldn't have chanced that, not me, no sir. I would have—"

"Hello, Dolt," the Priest said with a smile, cutting off the speaker, a portly young acolyte with a patch of curly brown hair atop his head. Talo ruffled it affectionately. "Missed you too. Is Eret awake?"

"Think so, might be," Dolt Avonair muttered, thumbing his bald chin. "He was just sitting for supper with a few of the elder Priests a half hour ago when my watch came up, so he might still be there. Lamb tonight. Very nice. And the potatoes! Absolutely—Hello, who's this?"

The acolyte bent low, peering around Talo's leg. The girl had peeked out of her hiding place once the door *clanged* shut behind them.

"Our newest addition," the Priest informed him, patting Syrah's head. Passing his pack off to Dolt, he reached down and lifted the girl up, resting her awkwardly on his hip. He was a bear of a man, but this apparently didn't bother the six-year-old too much. She clung to his thick neck and buried her face into his shoulder, her head still covered by the hood, hiding once more.

"Have my things brought to my quarters, please. I've business with the High Priest."

Dolt nodded, and was about to say something more when Talo raised his free hand.

"*Now*, Dolt," he said firmly. The acolyte shut his mouth and bowed, then took off sprinting down the hall, pack in tow. Talo smiled, watching him go before turning and heading in the opposite direction.

A fine boy. Just a little loose of the lips.

The halls of Cyurgi' Di—in sharp contrast to the temple's outside façade—were well lit and warm. Copper pipes in the floors and ceiling channeled fresh air and heated steam from furnaces in the deeper chambers of the temple. Oil lamps glowed from their iron brackets every few paces along the walls, supplemented by torches and tall candles that burned white and blue. Rough-hewn tunnels and corridors branched off the main way, some level, some with stairs or slopes that led up or down. Talo smiled again, remembering the early period of his faith just after his conversion. The Citadel was a veritable labyrinth, and in those first few years he'd gotten lost and turned around more times than he could count.

Now, though, he knew the place as well as any man could know his home.

It wasn't long before more and more people started to appear, crossing paths with him in the hall and nodding, or else looking up from their private studies when he passed by open doors. Priests, Priestesses, acolytes—further into the mountain more and more of them appeared, right up until Cyurgi' Di became a bustling hive of life. As the day closed, many of the Laorin were still about, some on duty, cleaning or patrolling, some taking advantage of the idler hours to pursue private thoughts. Talo even passed one room where a group of first-year Priests and Priestesses were practicing self-defense techniques, twirling about the heavy steel staffs they'd received at their consecrations.

Talo rarely carried his, despite a bad knee that was getting worse with every passing year. Even a staff seemed too much like a weapon and—with his old life a trailing shadow that never seemed to let go—a weapon was the last thing he wanted to be near. The few times he *had* been forced to defend himself, his boulder-like fists and quick reflexes always proved more than enough.

It was nice, sometimes, to know that some parts of a former self could still survive with you.

Soon the smell of hot food wafted through the air, thickening with the approaching clatter of the dining hall. It wasn't long before the Priest and his companion stood at the opening of a massive chamber, tall and broad and big enough to fit a thousand people with room to spare. More lanterns hung from the walls, and hundreds of mismatched candles lit the eight long tables that took up the floor. High above them, lining the apex of the vaulted roof, the two rows of stained-glass clerestory windows were darkened by the storm. In the light of the next clear day, though, they would be bright, illuminating the entire chamber with blues and greens and golds that hung in the dusty air.

A smattering of early diners formed little pockets on the benches as they ate and conversed. There was no head table, no raised platform for the elders. Laor saw all living things as equals, after all. The men ate with the women, the old with the young, the converts with those born into the faith. Even those of highest rank shared tables with the acolytes in their first days of training.

Still, it wasn't hard to pick out the High Priest, with the single thick stripe of black that ran down the back of his cloak. He was sitting with a group of the older Priests, picking at a chunk of bread and listening to their discussion.

Talo started making his way through the tables. Syrah, smelling food, peeked from over his shoulder, her eyes hungry, following each unfinished plate they passed. Her stomach growled, betraying her, and Talo chuckled.

He must have laughed louder than he thought, because the High Priest broke off his listening and looked around. Catching sight of the pair, he got up quickly, or as quickly as a man of his age could manage.

"Talo," he greeted the Priest warmly, spreading his arms wide and stepping over the bench. "My young apprentice, how are you?"

"No longer young, Eret," Talo told the old man with a laugh, accepting the embrace carefully. He was sicker, Talo could tell. Eret's fatherly hug was even weaker this time, and as he pulled away Talo could see the toll the years were having on his former Priest-Mentor. The High Priest's eyes were dimming, the crinkles in his face deeper, and his white hair no longer even hinted of the pale golden-blonde it had been twenty years ago when they'd first met.

"And this must be the young lady you spoke of in your letters?" Eret asked pointedly, turning his attention to the small form that was huddled against the Priest's broad chest.

"Syrah," Talo said with a nod, reaching up and attempting to pull down the hood of the child's oversized coat. Syrah wouldn't let him. She clung to the cowl crossly, hiding her face from view. Eret smiled, amused.

"Come now, child," he said kindly. "There's no need to fear anything here. Are you hungry? Jerrom, my plate, if you would be so kind."

One of the elders got up and brought the High Priest the metal dish with his dinner. The food, Talo noticed worriedly, was nearly untouched. Jerrom seemed to be thinking along the same lines, because he handed Eret the plate almost hopefully, as though thinking the old man might take something for himself.

Accepting the dish, however, the High Priest held it up and passed his free hand over it. There was a bare glimmer of white light, and suddenly the spiced lamb, potatoes, and sprouts steamed with heat. Syrah jumped at the magic, but didn't slacken her grip from the edge of the hood.

"I'm afraid you'll have to let go of that if you want to eat," Eret said with a chuckle, putting the plate back on the table beside them. "Talo, let her down. Lazura child, make room for our newest guest, please."

Talo did as he was told, depositing Syrah gently on the ground and smiling when she immediately clambered onto the bench beside the little blonde girl Eret had addressed. He chuckled as, with barely a pause to roll up the oversized sleeves of her robes, Syrah dug into the plate of food with her bare hands.

"Her family?" Eret inquired quietly after a moment, not taking his eyes off the girl.

"Alive and well, actually," Talo said with a sad smile. "One of the few lucky enough to be. Drangstek was a charred ruin when I passed it on the way to Stullens. Most of the town was burned to the ground."

"How many children did they have?"

"Her parents?" Talo asked, glancing at Eret, who nodded. "Five. Two boys and three girls."

"Too many mouths to feed when there isn't even a roof over your head to shield you from the freeze. They made a wise choice."

"It was that or the orphanage in Stullens," Talo added. "Barely more than an old house filled with children who lost their parents to earlier attacks. The oldest children might have fared decently, but I doubt Syrah would have done so well."

"Your reasons?" Eret asked. In response, Talo reached out carefully, pinching the top of the girl's hood, and slowly pulled it back. She didn't fight this time, more concerned with the food that still steamed on the plate in front of her.

Straight white hair, as white as the snow outside and even whiter than Eret's, fell just past her shoulders. Her skin was pale even for a Northerner, almost chalky. She glanced back at them curiously, and the High Priest got a good look at her eyes, those pink orbs that gazed with a mixture of innocence and old grief.

"Ahhhh," Eret breathed, realizing. "Yes... Children can be cruel, can't they? The orphanage would have been a poor place for this one."

Talo nodded. The old man continued to watch the girl for a time, almost contemplating. Then he moved to sit beside her, leaning against the table, his eyes following the food she was shoveling into her mouth at an imposing rate. After a moment he held up a hand, palm up. There was another glimmer of light, a small flash, and suddenly a tiny glowing white flame danced across the air, coming to a halt and hovering inches above Syrah's plate. The girl stopped eating at last and stared. With wondrous fascination she took in the little bit of fire glimmering like a tiny star barely six inches from her nose. It lit up her face in a wash of light, and her pale eyes shined as she watched the glimmering dance.

"A gift, child," Eret said with a smile, dropping his hand as he, too, watched the tiny flame. "One of many given to us by our creator, Laor, the Lifegiver. I hope you will find some measure of comfort living amongst us, or at least find that our love will fill a little bit of that void you feel now. Welcome to Cyurgi' Di, Syrah. Welcome to the faith."

855 v.S.

I

"… v.S.—or ver Syul—is broadly known as the Common Age, or the Age of Sands here in the South. There are discrepancies as to what marked the start of the period, but general belief is that year 1 v.S. was the first year the sand plains of the southern lands—previously called the Tura i'Syul, or "Land of the Sun" translated from old desert—grew to such proportions that special trade routes had to be developed to cross it safely. The plains were retitled as a desert, and the name was changed to the Cienbal, which has no direct translation that we know of."

—Kosen Arro, concerning the Common Age

The dune scorpion was a vicious thing. Hissing wildly, it spun to and fro, snapping massive pincers at anything that came within reach. Sand flew everywhere, thickening the early end-summer air as the creature scuttled over the desert back and forth in an impatient dance. Worn black carapace shone in the hot Sun while Raz toed a deadly circle around it, poking and prodding with the bronze-tipped whitewood stave he held in one hand, looking for an opening. His wings—all fifteen feet of them—flickered in warning, his crest edging up along the back of his head and neck. The scorpion, too dull a being to realize the danger of its situation, didn't draw back.

Raz dodged another snap of the claws, leaping back then forward again, landing a heavy blow on one of the beast's six legs. It buckled, snapping with a sickening *pop*, and the scorpion shrieked, scurrying backwards slightly lopsided. Raz didn't drop his guard, his amber eyes following the giant arachnid's movements, waiting.

The scorpion didn't retreat too far. A few feet away it stopped, pincers raised and snapping at the air menacingly, the venomous tip of its barbed tail curling like a deadly whip above its head. All eight black eyes glistened, reflecting the Sun and sand and Raz, who stood his ground, crouched in Jarden's favorite defensive position.

There was a pause. The scorpion seemed to be contemplating what to do next. The wagon ring was barely a dozen yards away, the horse it had already stung convulsing at its edge while a half-dozen men and women tried to calm the poor animal. Only the atherian, with his slender stick, stood in the way of nearly a half ton of fresh meat…

Without warning the scorpion lunged forward. It rushed Raz so fast he was nearly caught off guard. Jarden's staff was knocked from his hand when the beast's barb shot toward his chest, but Raz was just as quick. Dodging to the side, his clawed hand moved in a blur, catching the base of the stinger.

His own tail swung in a heavy arch.

Scaled muscle connected with a bony joint, and with a *crack* that made even Raz flinch, the scorpion's tail snapped clean off. The beast shrieked again, but before it could retreat once more Raz leapt on its back, his weight almost pinning it to the ground. Drawing the long dagger from his belt, he rode out the beast's mad turns and bucks, wings high and out of reach. For some time they struggled, the scorpion jerking about, fighting to catch him and pull him off, but to no avail. Eventually the dagger tip found an overlap in the carapace, and the fight ended abruptly as steel slid home.

For a while Raz lay there, breathing hard but not loosening his grip on the scorpion's shell. Only when greenish blood began to ooze convincingly from around the hilt of his dagger did he relent. Wrinkling his snout at the stench, he stood up, pulling the weapon loose and wiping the blade against the side of his baggy cloth shorts before turning around.

The group surrounding the stung horse—now motionless and very clearly dead—had grown. One of the kneeling men looked around when Raz moved toward them, glanced back at the still scorpion, then flashed a grim smile.

"Took you long enough to handle the roach," Jarden joked halfheartedly, getting to his feet.

"There's just something about inch-thick armor, big claws, and a fist-sized stinger I can't seem to get around," Raz responded with a shrug, playing along. Jarden snorted.

In the thirteen years that had passed since the events along the shores of the Garin, a thousand things had changed. The Arros, once only one of the larger nomadic clans to travel the desert routes, had arguably become the leading trade family in the Cienbal. They were thirty-nine strong now and still growing. If the rumors were true, Agais and Grea's attempt at a third child would notch them up to a solid forty within the next year. They already had one newcomer—Ahna, their daughter of eight, and Raz's favorite little companion.

"The horse can be buried."

Agais got to his feet. Still a strong man, the clanmaster was only just starting to show the signs of quickly passing years. He stood tall and looked around, silver chain shining over a thick beard that held only the slightest hints of gray in the bleached white. Squinting—his eyes had been slowly going bad in the last half decade—he frowned at the animal at his feet.

"I'd say save the meat, but the poison won't cook out. Have Samso, Ivas, and Ahsabet help you, Jarden. I have to meet with the Grandmother, but I'll be back to lend a hand."

"It wouldn't bother me!" Raz called out in an amused tone from where he was retrieving his uncle's staff. "And I'm starving!"

Agais and Jarden chuckled while the women in the group made a face.

"Raz i'Syul Arro," Grea warned sternly, standing up beside her husband and glaring, "if I hear even a whisper that you took so much as a *nip* out of this poor beast's hide, I swear by the Twins I'll add your skin to the Grandmother's wagon by nightfall."

Raz shuffled his feet, ducking his reptilian head, webbed ears flattened.

"Yes, Mama," he murmured, abashed. Jarden chuckled again, helpless, until Grea shot him a look too. He snapped to attention, winning a brief smile.

"I'll keep an eye on your boy, don't worry," he told her, relaxing and looking down at the horse. "Damned shame, though. We'll have to buy another animal for Tolman's cart once we get to Karth."

"It's definitely a problem," Tolman himself agreed sadly from the other side of the circle, patting the dead mare he was kneeling beside. Prida—his wife of six years now—stood next to him, one hand on his shoulder, the other hitching their little boy, Aigos, after Agais and Jarden's father, higher on her hip.

"We aren't far," the young woman said. "We'll manage. The least we can do is give the poor creature a proper burial."

Jarden, Agais, and Tolman all nodded, and soon everyone was back about their usual business.

"You'd think a scorpion attack would have flustered them even a little," Asahbet muttered after Jarden sent one of the boys to get the shovels.

Jarden shrugged. "Raz can handle himself," he said, glancing at the atherian behind them now rubbing sand on the stave in an attempt to clean off the greenish blood. "I wasn't worried."

"It was a good fight," Asahbet agreed with a mischievous smile. The skinny boy had developed into a strong, handsome man, filling out and sprouting until even Jarden was looking up to him. His brothers, too, had grown, especially in the time since their father had remarried to Leda, a shy and kindly woman from the fringe city of Cyro. The two had birthed another girl, Giovi, who was nearly eleven summers old now. Izan, Ishmal's oldest, had also married, though any talk of children made the poor boy cringe and his wife, Yahna, giggle and blush.

Still, no matter how big they had gotten, even Asahbet and his brothers had to look up to Raz.

Jarden watched the boy finish polishing the wood clean and stand up, giving his folded wings a thoughtless shake to clear the sand from their frayed edges. Well over six and a half feet tall and at a thought to be sixteen summers of age, Raz was a beast of a man—or that was the common joke amongst the family. His body was long and strong, rippling with lithe muscle beneath dark scaled skin. When he moved toward them it was on the balls of his feet, like the rest of his species, his tail lifted above the sand behind him. His clawed hands, ringed with the silver bangles and wooden bracelet he'd been given when he'd first come to the Arros, were still slightly too big for his body, foretelling yet more growth in future years.

Or months, Jarden thought.

It wasn't just how much he'd grown, though. Raz had changed in truth, in both body and mind. Not only was it the membrane of his wings, ears, and crest, steadily fading as he got older from aquamarine to sky blue, hinting of a sunset at the edges now. Not only was it the slim iron clan-chain that ran from one nostril at the end of his reptilian snout to the base of his right ear. Raz had learned and developed as a child. A human child. He'd taken to the language like he'd been born to it, though he continued to have some trouble with a few pronunciations. Still, he was getting better with each passing year.

And the customs? The beliefs? No one cursed or swore to the Sun and Moon more than Raz i'Syul Arro. And—as he slept less than the rest of his family—he could often be found sitting on the roof of Agais and Grea's hardtop wagon in the earliest hours of the morning, taking in Her Stars, his personal deities.

He wasn't perfect, of course. No child ever was. Raz's imperfections were simply... different. When it came to his responsibilities as a son,

Agais could often be overheard boasting proudly that the boy was a gift. He was strong and fast and loyal, always ready to help. As a man, Raz was developing into one of exceptional character, always to be counted on.

It was just the part of him that was not man, the wedge of his instincts that were animal, that Raz had trouble dealing with on occasion.

He ate nothing but meat and fish, preferring it raw when his mother allowed it. More than once in a fight Raz had lost his grip, finding himself with a mouthful of human or animal flesh that was already halfway down his throat. Though he'd never hurt anyone who'd meant him no harm, Raz had killed to protect his family, just as Jarden had killed to protect them before his strange nephew had come along.

And it hadn't bothered Jarden half as much as it bothered Raz.

"Aw, come on! Just one bite!"

Jarden blinked, turning to watch Raz and Asahbet.

"No." Asahbet smiled, punching his cousin's scaly chest jokingly. "You heard your mother. Grea would have our heads if she found out."

"Not all of them," Jarden cut in, jumping forward and plucking his borrowed staff from Raz's grip. "Just mine. I'm the responsible adult here, after all."

"Right," Ivas interrupted, returning with Samso, one of the Arro's younger newcomers, and all five of the camp's shovels. "And the Grandmother is the Moon herself, while Raz is being named king of the North mountain tribes today."

"So long as they don't tell me I have to be human, that's fine," Raz retorted, sticking his forked tongue out. "I could smell you from across the camp, Ivas. Humans reek—or wait, that might just be you."

Ivas threw a shovel at him. Raz caught it, making that sharp series of odd throaty sounds they all knew to be laughter. Grinning to a one, they got to work, a little ashamed to be so amused over the sad body of the dead horse.

Tucked away in her wagon, the Grandmother sat cross-legged on a cushion at the low circular table that took up the center of the cart floor. The years had been kind to her. They always had. But as blessed as she seemed, even the old woman could feel the weight of time start to pull at her thin frame. Her hair, once more bleached than silver, was a pale sheet of silken gray now, tied in the tight bun she'd always preferred. Her eyes were still good, even better than Agais' in fact, but they strained today to see the bones she tossed across the table for a third time, her frown deepening the wrinkles that lined her aged face.

Always the bird skulls and lizard jaws had turned out favorable signs for the Arros, promising a good year of trade. It was a quick tell, one that needed usually only be thrown once or twice to make the signs clear. But not this year.

This year the bones offered nothing.

Gathering them in her hands once more, the Grandmother tossed for a fourth time, scattering them wide. Sometimes space made the telling clearer, easier to decipher.

After a full minute of staring, though, the old woman frowned again. Nothing.

She was at a loss. Never before had she thrown the bones and not found a single sign. Always there was something. Not necessarily clear enough to tell her anything distinct, but at least enough to offer her some minor glimpse of what she was looking for...

Now, though, it was as though the bones had been scattered aimlessly, like toys a child had forgotten to clean up after play.

The cart was momentarily filled with a flood of bright sunlight. Agais grunted, heaving himself into the narrow space. Replacing the skins carefully behind him, the man stood up, blinking in the sudden shade.

"Anything interesting?" he asked after his eyes adjusted, noticing the bones and crouching down on the other side of the table.

"Not in the least," the old woman replied with a huff, rubbing her temples. "I've nothing for you, Agais. I see no signs."

To her surprise, the man laughed

"You don't find it odd?" she asked. Agais shrugged, looking around at the odd baubles of glass and crystal that hung from the Grandmother's ceiling.

"I suppose I find it odd, but what's the point in concern? We've yet to be led astray following our own path."

The Grandmother didn't reply, looking back at the table.

"Our path... yes..." she said after a moment, frowning. "But our path was always advised..."

"Well, then the telling will come eventually," Agais grunted, standing back up. "For now, though, we're less than four days from Karth, so I doubt the Twins will oppose a visit to the place, even if it is a dump."

He made for the front of the wagon and pulled the flaps aside, bathing the hide walls with light once more.

"Send for me if you find anything," he told the Grandmother, shading his eyes with a hand. "And stop worrying." He smiled. "A little hard work will do this family good after the lazy few years we've had."

As he leapt down and let the flap fall back into place behind him, he heard the Grandmother chuckle.

Moving across the circled wagons, enjoying the give of the sand beneath his feet, Agais made a mental count of everyone he came across. Ovan had been the only loss the Arros had suffered at the hands of an animal attack in thirty years, but the memories of burying the man's broken body hadn't faded in the least over thirteen summers. Agais had formed a habit of making sure everyone was accounted for anytime something similar occurred. Most of the clan had been around the horse while Raz dealt with the scorpion, but the clanmaster knew he wouldn't be satisfied until he'd seen everyone well and whole.

Achtel and Iriso had been at the scene, but their young son Razi had not. The twelve-year-old boy was childishly sly to a fault, much like his namesake growing up, but Raz had been far too young at the birth to realize the honor Iriso was giving him. Sure enough, Agais found Razi under his father's cart, filling the pockets of an unfortunate someone's spare pants with sand.

Chuckling and leaving the boy to his games, Agais moved on, nodding to Karren and her husband Sios, the pair of them helping Tolman shift the yoke of his now one-horse cart. Karren, like so many before and after her, had come to the Arros looking for some measure of protection. In the years after Raz's name became known throughout the clans, more than one wanderer had approached Agais in the hopes of joining his family. Almost all of them he'd turned away at once, insulted upon realizing that a majority of them wished only to be backing the strongest party if civil war ever broke out across the South. It was a sad reality that the loosely united governing bodies of the separate cities were only weakening while the underground grew stronger. Slavery, despite being a banned practice, had always had a blind eye turned on it by the authorities. Now, though, the criminal rings were developing quickly, gaining power in the real sense of the word.

Regardless, Agais wouldn't hear of turning his family into a war pack, not from anyone. Those that didn't leave quietly generally didn't put up much of a fight once Raz and Jarden made themselves known.

Karren, however, had been one of the few exceptions. When the Grandmother ruled her a good-hearted person, Agais had listened to her story. It was a lie—something about her father beating her—but the badly hidden, poorly healed scars on her wrists and ankles told the clanmaster all he needed to know. She lived with Trina and Kâtyn for some time before marrying Sios, a merchant from another caravan who'd joined with the Arros, cart and all. They'd had a child in the following year, but the poor boy died in a wave of fever that claimed the life of old Kosen as well.

"Damn you, ya' blasted, useless, Sun-cursed excuse of a limb."

Agais stopped and poked his head around the corner of the oldest and most worn wagon of the lot. A man was kneeling there, struggling to secure a series of boxes to the wall with rope. He had only one hand, the other cut down to a blunt stump just where his wrist might have been, a fact that wasn't making his task any easier.

"Want some help?" Agais asked, pulling himself into the cart.

"Agais," Sameyl breathed in relief, slumping down and leaning back on his good hand, letting Agais take over the knot tying. "Yes, please. I'm still figurin' the details of how to work with this thing." He waved the stump, then smirked as he watched the clanmaster's fingers tie the boxes down in quick succession. "Advice from a friend? Hold onta' those. They come in mighty handy. Eh? Eh?" He laughed at his own joke .

Agais laughed along. Sameyl, Jenie, and their three children—Samso, Tessa, and Johva—were the other group of outsiders to have been adopted by the Arros. The family had been on the run from slavers, though they'd never been caught, and the story they told Agais was true the first time around. Sameyl, a stone mason by trade, had lost his hand in a work accident, nearly giving up his life in the process. He'd pulled through in the end, but no sane man hires a crippled laborer, so to survive the family had been forced to borrow crowns and food from the worst kinds of people. Eventually the debt had piled up so high they couldn't see over it. When men came to collect, carrying chains and shackles, Sameyl and Samso had killed them, and the rest of the story was one of flight.

"You're a handsome and bless'd man," Sameyl joked in thanks once Agais finished the knots, sitting up to examine the work.

"So my wife tells me often," Agais responded with a snort, and with that he hopped off the back of the cart, heading for the edge of the wagon ring to help Raz and the others finish burying the horse.

II

Karth spread like a faint shadow in the distance, swelling from the rippling line that was the horizon as all fourteen wagons crested the last of the desert's high dunes. Seeing a city wasn't a new experience for any of them. Not even seeing Karth specifically. But, regardless, there was always something about spending any amount of time rolling through the hot sands of the Cienbal that made the prospect of mingling with cultured civilization more than a little enticing.

Especially if it meant you got to mingle in the shade.

"Finally," Grea breathed, shielding her eyes with a hand. "We're late. I doubt we'll manage to circle in anywhere near the markets."

"The walk will do us good," Agais told her with a smile, the crinkling around his eyes deepening. "And between Raz and Jarden, I'm sure we'll make it back and forth safely enough."

"More pressure on him," the woman sighed, glancing back into the cart where Raz sat at the edge of his broad bedroll, long legs and tail trailing over the rear edge of the wagon, slim fingers toying with his panpipes. Jarden had made them for him when he'd turned twelve and, though it had taken a long time for him to learn, Raz played nearly as well as his uncle now. With one hand he moved the instrument across his lips, the music sadly lost to the wind and grinding wheels, his other stroking his little sister's dark hair. Ahna was fast asleep, her back to the front of the cart, small head resting in her brother's lap.

"I don't think he minds," Agais said with a shrug, clucking the horses into a canter once they rolled onto the first truly flat ground they'd seen in months. "Raz will always pull his weight. Besides, I'm getting the feeling he prefers the cities to the sands."

Grea smiled, leaning her head against her husband's shoulder.

"Ahh, so there *is* a way the son differs from the father... Who would have guessed?"

Agais chuckled, listening to the clatter of the wagon, the city growing a little more distinct with every knock of the axles.

"Let him be a city merchant, if that's what he wants. In more ways than one it's a better life than this."

"True, but there's no scorpions to bash around in town."

Agais and Grea both jumped. Raz had climbed to the front, his footsteps masked by the wheel sounds. He crouched behind his parents now, one muscular arm extended to balance himself against the wooden wall of the cart. He was grinning, or doing the best imitation his serpentine face would allow, which mostly involved his higher lip twisting a little at the corners, pulling it up to reveal the gleaming points of slim teeth that had long outgrown their infancy. Faded but still visible, the three parallel scars that ran down the right side of his snout stretched the slightest bit, making them more pronounced. The only true-tell sign that he *was*, in fact, smiling was the minute spread of his orange-tinged, sky-blue ears.

Something only his family noticed.

"How many times have I told you?" Grea laughed, reaching back to smack Raz's knee. "Don't *do* that!"

Raz chuckled. "I heard you talking about me." He eased himself down to sit cross-legged behind them. "Being a shopkeeper would be a bore. There's nothing to do except eat and sleep and yell. I like the towns, but not the dullness of the life."

"There's other things to do," Agais said, twitching the reins. "I don't think there's a captain anywhere who would say no to you joining the city guard."

Raz made a face. "No. Never. I'd run off to the North before I joined the guard. They're corrupt and cruel."

"Only the rare few," his father told him. *Although by now it might just be all of them*, he thought privately.

The truth was that Agais had purposefully held his family back a few days this year. Being able to camp close to the market districts had its advantages, that much was true, but at a cost. The place was one of the central hubs of the city, the heart of trade and economy. It was the sort of environment that attracted hundreds of honest merchants and traders every week, along with thousands of Karth's residents, looking for anything from food to weapons to horses.

Unfortunately, the opportunity to cash in on a healthy flow of coin always drew the attention of a different sort of businessman. The slave rings now controlled most of the desert's intercity commerce, Karth being no exception. Circling in past the slums, closer to the wealthier estates in the east districts, meant a long daily walk carrying the goods to sell, but it also meant security. The Arros wouldn't have to deal with slavers or corrupt law officials telling them that they had to pay a "residential tax" out of their daily revenue.

At least we can hope not, Agais told himself.

"You could apprentice somewhere, when you're older. Jerr's

Hammer might even take you. The smith there is the best in the northern fringe towns. Or with a stonemason, or architect! Or—"

Grea and Raz had continued their discussion, unaware of Agais' wandering mind.

Raz was laughing. "I feel like you're trying to get rid of me, Mama," he told her, swaying, the cart thumping over a lump in the sand. "Angling to sell me off to the highest bidder, maybe?"

There was a moment of silence, and the change happened very suddenly. Raz's face, cheery and smiling one moment, froze, registering what he'd just said. His neck-crest twitched, rising slightly. His mouth opened less than a finger-width. His eyes dimmed, growing vacant, the edge of conscious intelligence ebbing away.

"Raz..." Grea began, concerned and about to reach back to touch his face, but Agais stopped her, his eyes on his son.

Raz jokingly called it "slipping out of humanity," and Agais supposed the phrase fit well enough. There were times, occurring less and less often with every passing year, where something would trip Raz up, ripping his thoughts away from what was going on around him and fixating on what was going on in his head. It was, Agais assumed, the part of him that was atherian. Sometimes the triggers were small things, like some motion in the corner of his eye or the wind battering the wagon sides particularly harshly.

Right now, though, it was something else. Agais watched Raz's hands move together, first rubbing the scars on one wrist, hidden by the silver bangles, then the other, covered by the wooden bracelet.

Atherian had a long memory. "Sell me off" had probably not been the wisest choice of words...

Raz's tongue flicked out from between his teeth, tasting the air. His tail slithered forward along the wagon floor. His split pupils didn't flinch, staring out across the desert, seeing something much farther away than the sands and sky.

"Raz?" a quiet voice asked.

The change was just as sudden this time. Raz relaxed, blinking away the primal look that had taken over his golden eyes. His mouth closed, and his crest flattened down the back of his neck. He looked around, the chain on his face swinging.

Ahna had gotten up and made her way to the front of the wagon. One small hand pressed the wall, helping her balance against the sway of the cart. The other clutched a little cloth doll to her chest. Her dark wavy hair bounced with every bump, and her pretty gray eyes, tinted with just the strangest hint of emerald green, were wide as she looked at her brother.

"You're making scary faces again…"

There was a tense moment, Agais and Grea looking on, letting the horses stray from the path as they wished. Raz, for one, seemed at a loss for words. Then he smiled, grinning ridiculously at Ahna. Abruptly he threw his arms up, falling back onto his folded wings, legs still crossed.

"Don't-cha' know my face always looks like this?" he asked her, grinning and crossing his eyes. On a human it would have looked silly.

On Raz it looked ridiculous.

Ahna giggled, smiling and jumping to sit in her brother's lap once he sat up again. At not quite nine summers old, the top of her head barely reached his neck.

Relaxing, Agais and Grea turned their eyes back to the desert. Karth had bloomed through the heat, towers rising from the richer eastern parts of the city, their thick forms shimmering against the cloudless sky. Somewhere behind them they heard a man, probably Jarden or Tolman, yell "*Hyah!*," trying to maintain a good pace in this closing stretch.

"Maybe the city isn't such a good place for me, Mama…"

Grea looked over her shoulder. Raz was gazing off at the western distances, his eyes on the space just above the horizon. He had one arm wrapped loosely around Ahna just to make sure she didn't step too close to the wagon edge, but apart from that he had the look of a mind carried elsewhere.

This time Grea did reach back. She ran her fingers gently across his cheek, marveling, as she always did, at how smooth the scales were. Once, years and years ago near the Garin, she'd grabbed a viper thinking it was dry wood. She'd been lucky enough not to be bitten, but the feeling lingered in her memory, that cool, lethal softness.

Raz's cheek felt the same.

Cupping the bottom of her son's snout in her hand, Grea pulled his face around to look at her.

"You are a better man than you think," she told him with a smile.

Raz averted his eyes. "The trims don't like me."

"They don't know you," Grea insisted, letting go and patting him under the chin. "I recall Iriso felt the same at first."

Raz's ears perked up. "Aunty?" he asked, perplexed. "She didn't like me?"

Agais snorted, earning a smack on the arm from his wife.

"You could put it that way," he said over his shoulder. "Let's just say you have a talent for getting on people's good sides."

Raz didn't say anything, but he looked a shade happier. If his favorite aunt could learn to fawn over him as much as she did, then maybe others could change as well.

It still bothered him, though.

Raz looked down at his sister, blissfully oblivious to the conversation, jumping her doll from one of his knees to the other. It was troubling, how people could be so prejudiced. The Garin was one thing. Everybody there knew him. Raz felt at home, felt safe. He could go from camp to camp with his family to exchange stories and trade, and only the littlest ones of most clans would stare at him in open awe or fright.

Even then their mothers usually scolded them.

But the cities...

Raz liked the cities. That much was true. He had an easier time remembering his infant years than his cousins or sister, and could still recall the first time the Arros had dared take him into town, a few years after his adoption. Miropa had been their first stop that season, the sprawling "Gem of the South." Built around an oasis only slightly smaller than the Garin, Raz remembered his fascination with the city, his curiosity at the towering, oddly shaped hills and mountains he'd eventually understood to be timber and stone buildings. Unlike the other fringe towns, Miropans paid the price to have better materials than clay and mud shipped to them. Heavy pine and granite came from the North, brick from the factories in the port cities to the west, and glass—the reason Miropa was called the Gem—bought from the Imperium and West Isles across the Emperor's Ocean. Most of the roads—with the exception of the dingy shantytown alleys that were an unavoidable offshoot of any city—were paved with stone from all over the occupied lands, making inner-city travel easier. Topping all this off, though, was the fact that Miropa's governing body was one of the few left relatively untouched by the slavers, meaning it still maintained at least some control over its own civil systems and private workings.

Karth was a hellhole in comparison, but Raz didn't care. Whether it was Miropa or Cyro or Karavyl or any of the smaller fringe towns, they all came with their own individual curiosities and dangers. Cities he loved.

What Raz didn't like were the people.

"Trims," nomads called the city-folk, for the decorative and impractically flashy clothes and robes they wore. Trims were a different breed of men, and Raz hated the way they made him feel. They all knew who he was. Part of the Arros' success was a direct result of people thronging to see the "tamed lizard." He knew his father hadn't liked it but, with the family's wellbeing overriding his own personal sense of right and wrong, Agais had let it happen.

To Raz, at least, it turned out to be the better choice. The initial flame of intrigue that had raced through cities upon the Arros' arrival burned out each time after only a few days, diminishing until finally he was a known anomaly rather than a fascinating curiosity. Raz had been too young to realize the exact nature of the events going on around him, but he acutely remembered the relief he'd felt whenever the throngs died away.

As with everything, sadly, there was a price.

Trims were not an open people. They did not welcome Raz i'Syul Arro in the same way the trading caravans had eventually done. When their thirst for a glimpse was quenched, they fell into the only mindsets that possibly made sense to them.

Dislike. Disgust. Contempt.

Sneers were the most common greeting he received from the locals he dealt with. More often than once the Arros had lost a customer because someone "refused to make deals with a scaly" or "didn't want to touch something the 'lizard' had had his dirty hands all over."

Agais himself had personally threatened several such characters' manhoods if they were ever seen near the Arro's stalls again.

Still, maybe Mama was right, Raz thought, holding on to Ahna a little tighter as the cart jolted over another hump of sand. Maybe trims could be made to see that he wasn't the animal most of them thought him to be.

He ignored the tiny voice of experience whispering in the back of his mind, telling him it wasn't likely.

III

"She will return him to the man he was. She will be his guiding light when he is blind. She will be his anchor to true reason."

—Uhsula, Seer of the Under-Caves

"Don't stare."

Syrah tore her eyes away from the ragged group of men she'd been watching, turning her attention back on the road. It was hard to see much through the thin veil of white silk that covered her face, but without it she was almost blind in the sun.

Damn her eyes…

"It's not like they can see me," she said with false innocence.

Beside her, Talo smiled. "Just because no one can *tell* you're staring doesn't make it any less rude."

He stopped to drop a copper into the wooden bowl of a shrunken beggar. The old man was a pitiful thing, all skin and bone and thin pale hair, with a dirty bandage wrapped around one shin. Syrah watched Talo kneel and pass a hand over the injury. There was a white glimmer, barely distinguishable in the bright sunlight, and the Priest stood up again.

Laorin magic could only do so much to help the natural process of healing, but at least the beggar wouldn't die of infection now.

In the thirteen years that had passed since the Laorin took her in, Syrah's Priest-Mentor hadn't changed much. Talo's trimmed beard still framed his strong chin, though there was now a peppering of silver amongst the coarseness. It streaked through his long ponytail too, striping the waist-length brown with pale gray. His ice-blue eyes, so capable of sharpness and discipline when need be, were warm as he pressed a second copper into the palm of a little boy with two missing fingers and barely any clothes to speak of. Still a head taller than most men, Talo leaned heavily on the steel staff in his left hand, something he'd once only rarely carried, trying to keep off the knee that had recently started bothering him on these longer trips.

Syrah reached into her purse for one of her own coppers. The coins were square, different from the circular gold crowns, silver dukes, and copper barons that were the common coinage this far south. That didn't stop the old woman she held it out to from snatching it up eagerly, though, just as it wouldn't stop her from haggling for bread with it. One of the northernmost desert towns, Karth dealt with the few northern tradesmen almost as much as Miropa to the east. It made the North-come coins a generally accepted form of currency, especially in the slums.

Then again, there wasn't much that wasn't a generally accepted form of currency here…

"Seek Laor," Syrah told the grateful woman gently, "for the Lifegiver welcomes all to his faith."

It was a simple enough message, one meant not to push the Laorin way onto nonbelievers too abruptly. Rather, it would hopefully spark the curiosity of a handful of the beggars they helped today, and in time maybe some of them would find their own way into Laor's embrace.

Syrah heard Talo murmur the same words while they worked, moving down the street. Across the way, Priest Jofrey al'Sen and his acolyte, Reyn Hartlet, were progressing in the same direction. They wore white sleeveless tunics and loose tan pants to help keep them cool in the broiling heat. Turbans of light cloth were wrapped around their heads and the bottom half of their faces, protecting them from the sandy wind that frequently graced the dusty streets. Talo wore similar attire, though the wrapping had been pulled down, freeing his mouth so that his words wouldn't be muffled.

Syrah grimaced. Though all three of the men looked flushed from the heat they weren't accustomed to, she was more than a little jealous of them. Her full-length robes covered her from head to toe, not leaving even a sliver of skin available for the sun to claw at. Her hands were gloved in soft, thin leather, and the veil that covered her face was part of a shawl that wrapped over and around her head and neck. Apart from her gloves and boots, every bit of her clothing was specially tailored from thin silk to trap as little heat as possible, but there was only so much the quality of the fabric could do. Even silk was practically useless when the temperatures were so high the contents of a full water barrel could evaporate in an hour if left to the full effects of the sun.

Syrah grit her teeth, feeling beads of perspiration trickle down the curve of her back. The insides of the gloves were soaked from moist palms, and her eyes stung as salty sweat found its way down her forehead. She had to pause often to drink from the flask on her belt, lifting the veil to gulp down mouthfuls of the unpleasantly warm water.

Each time, even in those few seconds of exposure, she felt the sun stab at the skin along her jaw and cheek.

Still, it was a price she didn't mind paying. There was poverty in the

North, of course. Hundreds who couldn't find food or shelter perished in the winter months every year, starving or dying of exposure when the temperatures plummeted. It was an unavoidable tragedy, one the Laorin fought endlessly to fend off.

But it was nothing—*nothing*—compared to what Syrah saw around her now as she straightened up.

They had ventured deep today, farther than they'd managed in the past week or so. The street they were progressing along was narrow, less than fifteen feet wide, and lined on both sides with rickety hovels and crumbling mud-brick shacks that gave little more than the illusion of shelter. Bloodshot eyes watched them from the shadows beyond open doors, and almost every beggar they handed money to thanked them with a smile yellowed and diseased from ragroot abuse. Syrah felt a measured mix of fear and alertness whenever they trekked into the slums. They'd been attacked once already by a man so desperate he'd jumped them bare handed.

Talo had left him in the shade of an alley, unconscious but relatively unhurt, with a whole silver duke in his pocket for when he came to.

That night at the Ovana, Talo had barely touched his mutton and potato stew. It was only after they'd washed their faces, finished their silent prayers, and blown out the candles that he'd spoken aloud at all.

"These people need more help than the whole of our order could offer them in a hundred years," he'd said, then bid Syrah good night.

The populace in Karth was largely divided into two groups: the inordinately wealthy—those few families and individuals who controlled almost all the coin passing in and out of the city—and the unbelievably poor. Slum towns ringed the city in all directions except directly east, and each area was plagued with its own problems. Murder, rape, and theft were a daily part of these people's lives. Slavers ignored the laws which rarely served to punish them anyways, stealing through the night to rip men, women, and children alike from their beds. Brothels—legal, illegal, and everything in between—could be found on almost any main road. Twice now the male Priests had been approached by emaciated whores offering services none of them had ever heard of, or at least pretended not to for Syrah's sake.

The second girl couldn't have been older than eleven.

These pilgrimages south by the Laorin—rare occurrences already since all involved were volunteers—were the only help some of these people would ever receive from complete strangers.

Syrah looked up from her work, watching a group of children playing in the dust a few yards away. The game was something she'd seen before but had yet to figure out completely. It involved three rocks—two painted red and one white—all passed in a circle while the boys and girls chanted the same verse over and over again:

Little by little they all fade away. Little by little, as does the day.
Little by little Her Stars disappear, taking with them all of our fear.

At that point, whoever was holding the white rock would groan and step out of the circle, and the game would start again. Syrah couldn't even give a guess as to what the red ones did, but it didn't matter.

What mattered was that they were playing in the dirt.

The dirt... These children who should have been having about with wooden swords or laughing over straw-stuffed dolls. Who should at least have had the right to return home to a decent meal. A few didn't even have proper clothes. One tiny girl, a small, twig-like figure so thin Syrah couldn't understand how she could be standing, wasn't wearing anything at all.

But it didn't matter to them. The vulnerability of the girl in her nakedness went by unnoticed. This was what they knew. This was the world they'd been born to and brought up in.

And all she could do was give them a few measly coppers...

"Syrah."

She started, realizing suddenly that her eyes were wet. Even as she turned she felt a tear escape her hard-fought attempt to hold it back, joining with the trails of sweat along her neck. Thank Laor Talo couldn't see her through the silks.

Still, as he looked over her shoulder at the group of children, the fall in her Priest-Mentor's face spoke of knowing her thoughts all too well.

"Come. That's enough for today."

Syrah nodded wordlessly, saddened by her helpless relief when the four of them turned to make their way back toward the busier market streets.

IV

"With each passing year the Cienbal widens its reach. Thankfully, to the north and south, where a majority of civilized desert culture has taken root, this growth is minimal. To the east and west, however, butting heads with the Emperor's Ocean and the Crags along the coast of the Dramion Sea, the sands can eat away leagues of richer earths in less than a decade."

— *"The Cienbal,"* by Adolûs Fenn

"Six dukes? That's a crown and a half! This roll of rags isn't worth a third of that!"

"I'm very sorry, sir, but that's the price. I've already given you a reduction on the Karavyl silk, so it isn't possible for me to—"

"If I'd known you expected me to pay that much for cotton I could find in most refuse piles, I wouldn't have come all the way here to begin with, would I?"

"It's not the cotton, sir, it's the dyes that mark the price. See how they swirl without clashing the colors? It's a new technique developed in—"

"Sun burn you, woman. What makes you think I care where you stole this from in the first place to get it? I'm not paying a baron over two silvers, and you'll sell it to me or—"

"That's *enough.*"

Prida and her customer both turned. From the cover of the tent, Raz watched Jarden step over from his table of spun-glass jewelry.

The Arros' first week in Karth had gone well by any standard. True, the half-hour walks to the markets every day were tedious, especially when they were all loaded down with goods and tables and collapsible overhangs, but it was nothing worth complaining about. Already they'd heard that the "tax" for desert traders holding residence near the markets had been driven up to three crowns a week, half again the previous year's. By circling their caravan in to the east, the Arros not only avoided this extortion but also managed to steer clear of much of the crime that had grown even more prominent since the previous summer. The Eomons, another trade group, had already been robbed of half their stores by street runners.

In general, though, commerce was good. Everything was turning a marginal profit, and they'd had few problems with customers until today.

It was bad for business to have someone yelling about how unfair the prices were at a particular booth. It meant those individuals nearby in the crowded market who'd been contemplating stopping by the table were much less likely to do so.

Still, it was worse to let a trim run you down with his bartering. If it got out that a family was selling at cut-costs, it meant two things. First, while everything would likely be sold in days, it would be sold at almost no profit, and the sellers would have less coin to purchase other goods to resell at the next city. Second, the other families would lose business, and bad blood amongst the clans was never a good thing to enter the grueling summer months with.

Dealing with bullying customers was an essential—if distasteful—part of the life.

"The price is set," Jarden said curtly, his gray eyes on the fat man in question. "Either pay, or find somebody else to buy from. You won't come across cloth this good just anywhere, but you are certainly free to try."

"What's going on?" Mychal asked eagerly, scooting so he, too, could peer out from between the tent flaps. They'd been playing at dice before the shouting started. Ahna sat in the corner, occupying herself as she always did with one of her cloth dolls, unconcerned with things that didn't involve her little make-believe worlds.

"Trim thinks he can cause trouble," Raz answered with a smirk. "Idiot."

"Go take a chunk of him," Mychal laughed, moving back and picking the dice up again. "Day's worth of cleanup says I get double sevens."

"You always get double sevens, you cheat," Raz said with a snort, not looking away from the scene outside.

Mychal laughed again, but didn't say anything back. At twenty-one summers, he had grown into a handsome young man. His dark hair was pulled back into a short ponytail like his father's, and the clean shadow of a beard lined his lower jaw. He was strong, and would have been a great help carrying goods to and from the market if the brown cloth of his left pant leg weren't pinned back behind his thigh, covering the stump of his missing limb. As it was, though, Mychal was far from useless. He had quick hands and a good head for numbers, and Agais had tasked him with keeping track of the family's profits while they were in any city. Every night Mychal stayed up well past sunset, counting and separating and tallying the earnings they'd made.

100

"Damn he's loud," Mychal complained, looking up from his game. Outside the voices had gotten angrier, and even Ahna looked up in alarm, gray eyes suddenly scared.

"Don't tell me how to go about my business, you dune-dulled tanny," the customer spat at Prida, who seemed to be trying to calm him down again. He was short and plump, with a dark-red tunic that spoke of a certain wealth. A wispy black beard curled out from the first of his three chins, carefully combed and styled to a point. Puffing out his chest like a sand toad, he continued haughtily. "Do you know who I am? *I* am Hodrin Evony, of the Evony family, and..."

As the man started to spout his titles and the names of his family and what some cousin in Miropa would do to the Arro's trade if they didn't cut prices for him, Raz saw the signal. The derogatory slight at the nomads' tanned skin had done it. Jarden's right hand curled into a fist, coming to rest on his lower back.

Raz moved quickly, leaving the tent out the back entrance with only a pause to pat his sister's head and give her a comforting wink. He was a known figure in the market, and people moved out of his way without question, a few nodding to him but most either glaring or avoiding his eyes altogether. Ignoring them all, he made a short loop through the crowd until he stood directly behind Hodrin Evony, who was still belting about how he could ruin their family with a word.

"I believe my uncle gave you a choice," Raz said calmly. His natural voice was a deep, dangerous tenor, frightening to those who didn't know him. "Pay or leave, Master Evony. *Now.*"

Hodrin Evony turned furiously, and the angry flush in his pudgy cheeks blanched to chalk. He looked up, tilting his head almost completely back. He took in Raz's sharp teeth, golden eyes, and wicked claws with a terrified glance and stumbled backward, knocking into Prida's table and almost upending the bolts of different-colored cloths that were neatly stacked upon it. The man's eyes lingered on the crest of blue and orange skin arcing along the back of Raz's neck, only slightly raised, and he openly stared at the wings partially extended about a foot to either side of powerful scaled arms.

Then Evony dropped the silk he'd already bought, blubbering incoherent words and stumbling sideways, backside rubbing the table until he was clear of the Arros' stalls. From there he took off running, disappearing into the crowd, which acted like they hadn't noticed a thing.

Raz relaxed, pulling his wings flush to his back again before kneeling down to pick up the Karavyl fabric from the dirt. With a sigh he brushed it off carefully, standing and handing it back to Prida.

"I'd feel bad, but covered in dust we won't be able to sell it again for much anyway."

"I'm just glad you two were the ones around today," Prida smirked, accepting the fabric and looking it over. "Tolman would have fed him his fingers."

"I would have offered to find him a fork," Jarden grunted, moving back to the jewelry table as a young couple started examining a necklace strung with tiny glass stars. "They think they know it all, don't they?"

"They're not all bad," Prida insisted, tucking the dirty bolt under the table so that it wouldn't get the others dusty. "I've met some of the local merchants, and they seem nice enough."

"Oh they're fine, until they realize they're losing business to us," Raz muttered, slipping behind the stall and looking out over the crowd.

Karth's market was a hot myriad of swirling colors. Capes, shawls, turbans, and even the dyed hair of street dancers all swept together to form a dull, undulating rainbow. Down the street to Raz's left there was a roar as a fire-breather blew a jet of flames into the air to the crowd's cheers. To his right, the lumbering form of an elephant plodded its way slowly across the road, towing a massive cart filled with thin yellow and green fruits. All around them people called out to each other and the crowd, some buying, some selling, but all sweating under the brilliant white globe of the Sun high above, framed against a cloudless sky.

Raz felt constricted. He didn't like crowds. It was one of those disadvantages that made city life—while appealing—less than perfect. Being surrounded on all sides, elbow to shoulder, bumping into everyone and getting jostled by the current of the pedestrian traffic—it all made him feel tied down and anxious, like he was stuck with nowhere to go. More than once Raz had suppressed the urge to leap straight up, over everyone's heads, and spread his wings. When he was ringed on all fronts by the pressing throng, it often seemed the only place to go was up.

Too bad he'd never been able to fly a day in his life.

It wasn't for lack of trying, mind you. Once, when he'd been ten summers old, he'd rebroken his wrist jumping off the top of his parent's cart, trying to fly. Mychal had put him up to it, of course. The boy had been a little fiend in his younger years. Still, despite this accident, it had taken a long time before Raz finally gave up. The Grandmother thought it might be that he needed to be taught by one of his own, if any lived.

Tolman had once joked that maybe someone should just shove him off a cliff and see what happened.

Whatever it was that could spark some life into his wings, though, Raz had yet to puzzle it out. He'd adapted, in the end, though his father wasn't always the keenest fan of some of his methods of coping.

The Arros were an earthbound people. Heights were not amongst their chosen interests.

"Prida, I'll take over for a bit." Raz crossed his arms and rested a shoulder against one of the stall's wooden posts. "Mychal wants someone to gamble his chores away to, and I already owe him a week."

"Well he's not conning me into it," the woman said with a laugh. "But yes, thank you. It's getting a little hot for me out here."

Raz nodded, watching her tidy up the arrangement of bolts before disappearing into the tent. Absentmindedly he turned to gaze out over the crowd, taking in the bland mélange of movement and colors, glad to be on his feet for a time.

"Worried Master, his Lordship, and High Ruler of the World might come back?"

Raz looked around at Jarden's question, confused.

"Evony," his uncle finished with a chuckle, striking a haughty pose and stroking an invisible goatee.

"What? Oh. No." Raz shook his head, shifting his attention back to the market. A tall woman in green with thin bangles hanging over her eyes stopped briefly to examine the texture of one of his silks. "I would just rather be standing than seated all cooped up in the tent."

"Don't blame you," Jarden said with a shrug, the long scars on his left arm, blatantly visible in his sleeveless tunic, warping a little with the motion. "It's not fun being stuffed up in a hot little room all day. If I had the choice, I'd just as well not stop for more than a week at a time in any one place. Makes me jittery."

"Eh," Raz said, shrugging. "Doesn't bother me. It's a nice change from the sands. I just don't like not being able to spread my wings."

Jarden laughed. "Not sure I can really relate to that," he said with a smirk, his eyes following a tumbler bedecked in green and yellow making his way down the road, balancing and spinning three colored plates on the ends of thin wooden rods. "I feel I'm lacking the necessary appendages to give you fair advice."

"You know what I mean."

There was a minute before Jarden responded as he greeted a dark-skinned Percian and handed him a set of hammered bracelets reserved the day before.

"I suppose," he finally conceded. Then he grinned mischievously. "Go climb the roofs, then."

Raz gave him a sharp look, and Jarden laughed again.

"Oh, I know all about your little nighttime trips. Don't worry," he cut in when Raz opened his mouth to say something. "Your father's still in the dark about it."

Raz was quiet. "He thinks it's dangerous," he grumbled after a moment. "The last time he caught me up there he yelled for half an hour."

"He's right to think that. You climb higher every time he finds you at it. Not to mention there's people around here who don't want strangers snooping around their business. Especially after dark."

"But I'm not—"

Jarden halted the outburst with a raised hand. "I didn't say you were, but think of how it looks. You running around on the rooftops like some thief, in the middle of a city where there's a half dozen murders every night."

"That's exaggerating."

"Is it really?"

There was a sullen pause.

"I'm careful," Raz said after a time, looking up at the clear sky. "I rarely cross into the deep slums. And I don't let anyone see me. But what else am I supposed to do? Even Ahna sleeps at least eight hours a night. I barely sleep three."

"Take up woodcarving," Jarden said with a shrug, turning back to face his table. "No. I'm kidding. With those big hands of yours you'd be likely to lose a finger fumbling over the blades. Just watch your back. You're not a child anymore."

Raz nodded slowly, watching a breeze catch the loose corners of his goods, ruffling them slightly. "I'll stop. I promise."

Jarden smirked.

"Liar."

V

The citizens of Miropa would say he wore a white cloak not to fend off the heat, but rather to symbolized the blaze of the hateful fires that burned within him always…

— *"Born of the Dahgün Bone,"* author unknown

"It's worth the risk."

"Aye, may'haps, but ain't no need to jump into the snake-pit. There's the men to worry about, and one a' them buggers is bigger than anyone I ever seen."

"They're Laorin, Jerd. They won't kill."

"Even a muzzled dog'll find a way to bite back if'n it get is'self cornered. I heard he managed to put down one a' the runners without a problem."

"He knocked out a half-starved addict. That hardly deserves commendation, you dim-witted oaf."

"Call me a dim-witted anything again, ya' gutless trim, and I'll hang ya' upside down by yer—"

"*Enough.* Ayzenbas says you go, so you go. We've got the time. Keep an eye out, and maybe even you can manage to get her away from that entourage you're so afraid of."

"Ain't afraid of nothin', Farro. Remind yerself a' that once the boss smokes himself into an early grave. You won't have many places to run to after that, will ya'?"

The Ovana was a stifling sweatbox dropped in the middle of the desert purely to fool people into thinking it could be cooler inside than out in the sun.

Or at least that was Syrah's opinion of it.

In reality, the Ovana Inn was a tavern along the east side of the main market street, deliberately built right in the middle of the bustle so as to attract maximum notice. It wasn't the nicest or most expensive place to stay, but the city dwellers they'd asked had sworn that it was the safest, and Talo and Jofrey agreed it to be the best option for the duration of the two months they would be spending in Karth.

It had only been three weeks, and Syrah was already ready to dive headfirst out of their market-facing window.

The heat was unbearable, the air so dry her lips were calloused from constantly cracking and bleeding. The sun never waned during the day, and there seemed to exist no clouds to shield the world from its devilish light. Not that the nights were any better. As a clear moon rose each evening, the temperatures plummeted, falling so quickly and drastically that more than once their little group had been briefly caught out in a cold that could have rivaled a Northern freeze.

And the people...

Ugh... the people...

"You'd think they'd be more giving," Syrah thought out loud, chin in her palm, eyes on the street below. She was watching a particular couple, their heavy frames hung with rich clothes and jewels. Steadily the pair were making their way along the far side of the road, flanked on either side by a manservant toting some ridiculous sort of sunshade. Gaudy apparatuses, made of massive colorful feathers bound together at a long handle, the attendants would alternately use them to shade their masters and fan them. Even as Syrah followed the group, blowing a loose strand of pale hair out of her eyes, they passed at least a half-dozen begging vagrants. Each time the haughty pair would turn their heads to feign interest in the other side of the street, ignoring the dirty outstretched hands. Behind them their servants did the same, not even glancing down at the sad forms curled in whatever shadow they'd managed to snatch.

"Why?"

Syrah turned. Talo sat in the opposite corner, his wide frame filling the room's single chair to capacity. He was thumbing through the book in his hands, *A Comprised History of the North*, with careful deliberation.

"Why?" Syrah echoed, surprised and turning away from the window. "Why *not*? There are people starving all around them, and they sit and do nothing. It's murder."

"I don't disagree," Talo responded, not looking up. "But I ask again: Why? Why should they be more giving? What do they have to gain from handing food and coin to those around them who need it more?"

"What? Well... first off they'd get..." Syrah tripped over her own words. "They'd get..."

She paused, unsure, in truth, of the answer.

"Nothing," Talo finished, closing the book with a *snap*. "They'd get nothing. Or perhaps they'd get the fleeting feeling of self-righteousness, of pride in their own generosity. A man might give away a copper and feel that he did a grand thing, and he would be right if not for the fact that he did it for his own selfish reasoning."

Talo lifted himself out of the chair, walking over to stand beside Syrah so that he, too, could peer down into the street.

"What do you feel when we help these people?"

Syrah blinked, looking up at her Priest-Mentor. Then she looked away.

"Out with it," Talo said, his eyes on the crouched figure of a dirty crone skulking in the stolen shade of a shop overhang. "What do you feel?"

Again, Syrah hesitated.

The other acolytes were often jealous of her, and they had every right to be. Talo was one of the most respected Priests in the faith, a man converted who'd found Laor in the middle of the Azbar gladiator arena, his blades on the very verge of taking yet another life. He was responsible for the banning of such pit fights in much of the North, and from there had only aimed higher with his successes. What few peaceful accords had been reached between the raiding mountain clans and the valley towns they'd plagued for centuries, Talo was largely credited for. These pilgrimages beyond the North were most often organized by him, taking the Priests and Priestesses of Laor as far as the swamps of the Seven Cities and the most distant islands of the Imperium. Even in the heart of the temples the ageing Priest had incited change, adapting and improving the self-defense practices and martial arts all acolytes of the Lifegiver learn from an early age.

Talo Brahnt was a man many would "kill to apprentice under," High Priest Eret Ta'hir had joked when he'd told Syrah that she would be Talo's acolyte.

But while he was a kind and gentle man, sometimes his methods of teaching—if efficient—were less than pleasant. He had a way of making Syrah's own experiences part of the lessons he taught her.

It often made her realize things about herself and others she didn't always like...

"What do you feel?" Talo repeated with a firmness that said it would be the last time he planned on asking.

"I..." she began quietly. "I feel... empty. I feel like I should be doing so much more. We come here and we give and we give and we give, but I still feel like it's nothing. I see these sick people, these starving children, and all I can think about is how the money I hand them will only feed them for a day at most."

"And there you have the difference."

Syrah looked up at Talo, who was smiling at her.

"You give those people a copper, Syrah, and you think about how it will *only* feed them for a day. Most others, when they give that copper, would laugh and gloat to themselves about how they just fed that person for a *day*. Do you see the relation? The difference?"

Syrah paused, then shook her head. Talo sighed, looking sadly back out at the street.

"You asked why those people aren't more generous? It's because they've no need to be. Whether because they were raised in such a manner, or because they are greedy by nature, or because they simply don't care, I couldn't tell you. But where what you give is never enough, people like *that*"—he waved a hand at the extravagant foursome before they disappeared into a perfumery—"are completely at peace with giving less, if anything at all. They've no drive to be more than what they are, and if they *do* do more, it is only because they've found a way to make it improve their own lives."

Syrah's stomach twisted. "What a sick way to live," she breathed angrily.

Talo chuckled beside her. "Is it?" he asked, turning away from the window and limping to the far bed where his steel staff lay across the thick blankets. "I would ask you to think about something, then. Your family gave you to the temple because they loved you. They wanted you to have a better life than the one they might have given you. But what if you'd been born to a different place, Syrah? What if you'd been born into a home that would never have considered giving you to Laor, because you would be warm, wealthy, and content just where you were?"

Staff in hand, he made for the door. "I'm going to meet with Jofrey. Don't leave the inn, and think about what I've said. Would you—would any of us—if that were the case, be any different from the people down in that street?"

And with that he gave her a knowing smile, opened the door, and left.

For a long moment Syrah sat silently in the warm breeze by the sill, contemplating the man's words. Would she? Would she be any different from the couple down in the street? She tried to imagine herself living lavishly, having anything she wanted, *doing* anything she wanted. She smiled a little, thinking of her cool room in Cyurgi' Di. While it was far from petty, with its deerskin rug thrown over the stone floor by the bed and its plentiful bookshelves and candles, it was so much farther from lavish. For a moment she felt some odd sliver of what might have been joy as she thought of having her own marble-cut fireplace, or maybe even an expensive glass-paned door that led out to a private garden, its small pine grove and stream covered in snow. She could eat on a carved cedar bench and watch the water flow, warm under her thick furs, sending for more of anything she happened to finish too quickly.

Abruptly, Syrah stopped smiling.

Would she be able to give that up? If she had those things, would she be able to just throw them all away?

Lying was not a sin to the Laorin. It was frowned upon, and punishment was administered for lies of import, but Laor understood that there was no such thing as flawless character. To be human—even when it came to his followers—was too often to be untruthful.

Still, while she could lie to her instructors about studying for a lesson, or to Talo about where she'd been all night, Syrah couldn't lie to herself. And her conscience was telling her that she didn't know if she would be able to give such wonderful things away as easily as she dispensed of her copper coins…

Syrah felt her cheeks flush with anger at the thought. What kind of person was *she*, then? If she couldn't give away overly extravagant comfort in the name of the Lifegiver, did that make her any better than the wealthy sneering at the pleading faces of the beggars in the street below?

No, she thought bitterly. *It didn't.*

She had to leave, she realized. She had to get out, to clear her head, if only for a little while. Talo had told her not to go anywhere, but even as she stepped away from the window the walls of their wide room seemed to warp, tightening around her. Making a decision, Syrah crossed the floor, lifting her robes off the dull iron hook by the doorframe. Stripping out of her cotton shirt and pants, she tugged the silk over her head, letting it fall to the floor. Grabbing her gloves and veil from the cupboard in the corner, she practically ran out the door, letting it shut behind her with a *bang*.

VI

The North and South are so called because never at any point in recorded history have the two great lands been more than a divided rabble of smaller governing forces individually struggling to consolidate their own power. There are those to this day, in fact, who believe a mistake was made with the eradication of the slave rings in the mid and late 800s. Even now, a hundred years later, some say it would be better to be united under a ring of murderers and thieves than separately ruled by politicians who are weak, greedy, and corrupt...

—*The Cienbal*, by Adolûs Fenn

"—and here's for the nopales. It was a good season, so they shouldn't be more than a baron a dozen, at least if you get them from Jillia. See if you can find kindling, too. We're running low, and I don't want to dig into our reserves for the summer season too soon."

Raz nodded, accepting the handful of coins his father dropped into his palm. It was common enough that he be the one asked to do most of the weekly shopping, but he still leapt on the chance. He was ever keen to get out of the camp and explore the markets. The pickpockets and beggars didn't bother him, or at least hadn't tried to yet, and if he finished early his parents let him wander a little deeper into Karth, near the wealthier quarters of the city. He always loved to see the marble fountains and colored-glass windows, the steel gates enclosing manicured gardens. They, and so many other things, were small marvels that the Cienbal would forever be lacking.

"Nopales, bread wheat, a carving knife, meat, and kindling if I can find it," he repeated the list. "Got it. Anything else?"

"Not that I can think of," Agais said, shaking his head before he and Jarden went back to repairing one of the Grandmother's wagon wheels. Rot had gotten at the old wood, cracking it. "Get yourself something to eat if you're out late. Dinner might be cold by the time you wander back, knowing you."

Raz stuck his tongue out at his father, who laughed. Jarden smirked, reaching under the makeshift table they were working on and pulling out his staff. He threw it to Raz, who caught it in surprise.

"Not that you need it, but it'll keep those wandering hands of yours busy."

Raz snorted. It was a common joke amongst the Arros. Barely a few months after they'd adopted him he'd apparently tried to steal half a dried ham from a neighboring clan's tent, not understanding the concept of barter and trade. He'd been too young to remember the details, but the story went that in the end Agais had to pay for the meat in full and then some just to settle the matter without issue. No one had ever let Raz live it down.

Still, the bleached wood felt good in his hands and—even with the long knife strapped to his thigh—it never hurt to be prepared. He nodded his thanks, pocketing the coins before turning and heading around the small horse corral out of the wagon ring. He wore simple clothes, the white silk mantle around his shoulders serving more of a practical purpose than a pompous one. Just because he was better suited to the heat didn't mean he liked it any more than the next person. The silk was perfect for blocking out the sun without making him feel like he was standing in an oven. It draped behind him a little dramatically but— considering the alternative was walking around in the broiling glare all day—he could suffer it.

It was a twenty-minute walk to the market even not weighed down with a hundred pounds of goods and coin, but Raz didn't mind. He liked this time, this brief privacy. It gave him a moment alone to think and take in the city around him. It was interesting, for example, how there was no steady change in the buildings drawing closer to the slums. The houses were all tall and solid, well maintained and cared for. Most of them were two stories high, unlike the structures beyond and around the market street. A few even had faded murals decorating their walls, or brown tendrils of some Sun-resistant vine hanging from iron-wrought balconies.

But as Raz left these small middle-class parts of the city for the shantytowns and market, it always made him sad to see the line appear right before he reached the busy shopping streets.

The alley was twice as wide there, as though the quarter's architect had aspired to erect a deliberate, tangible barrier between the slum dwellers and the wealthier citizens. On one side were the grander homes, tall and clean—if not so regal as the estates in the eastern parts of the city—and on the other were the shacks and hovels, the decrepit buildings that were only currently falling apart if they were lucky. Most were worn down by the elements or age, and crumbling walls and ceilings were more common than doors. The people were no better off. They were shells, empty husks all starving or sick or both. Even when Raz tossed a baron or two to them, they didn't leap for the coins until after he'd rounded the corner.

The slum dwellers frightened him, in a way. Not because they themselves were threatening, but rather because every year the Arros returned to any particular city the number of beggars lining the streets seemed to double.

His mind elsewhere, the walk to the markets took no time at all. When Raz finally stepped into the busy street, he pulled down his thin hood, welcoming the coolness of the scattered angular shadows from the shops and covered stalls and colored ribbons that overlapped and crossed overhead. He sniffed, making a face at the reek of sweat and unwashed bodies mixed with the smells of food and perfume and fire.

The trouble with Jillia, the vendor the Arros bought most of their supplies from, was that she was always moving around. A nomad from the Ashani family before she'd married a trim, she was superstitious about staying in one spot along the market street for more than a few days, claiming her business eventually waned if she did. Raz always had to stop a few people and ask if they'd seen her before he had any luck, and today was no different. After nearly a quarter hour and a dozen dirty looks, an old woman pointed him in the right direction, offering a rare smile when he thanked her. Turning west down the street, Raz made his way through the crowd, cutting his usual swath, people hurrying to get out of the way. The few he recognized he nodded to, but mostly he just kept his eyes out for Jillia.

He was so preoccupied with his search, in fact, that he almost missed the eccentric figure walking calmly along the left side of the road.

She was a tall woman. Or girl? He couldn't be sure. Her face was covered by a faintly opaque shroud of pale silk, and her robes, their wide hood pulled up over her head, were much like his cape, white and light so as to fend off the Sun. Had he been able to raise an eyebrow he would have, though, when he saw that her hands were gloved and her feet booted in the same bleached leather.

He could only imagine how much she was sweating under there...

Suddenly the girl's face glanced toward him, and he turned away quickly, unsure of whether she was looking at him or not. He thought he saw her stop and watch him pass, but it was at that moment that he caught sight of Jillia's tent a short distance down the street. Keeping his eyes resolutely forward, he kept walking, ignoring the figure in white.

A nun of some kind, probably, dressed like that. Or a madwoman who suspected she might be a Star. Whatever the case, Raz wanted nothing to do with it.

Syrah was feeling much better.

Then again, she'd expected it. This was almost always how it was with Talo's teachings. At first she would be hit with the blunt end of his lesson, and for a while the blow would throb. Then, once she'd calmed down, what Talo had actually been saying would come to the forefront.

Do you see the relation? he had asked her. *The difference?*

No. She hadn't.

But now, her eyes on the ground as she headed back to the Ovana after nearly two hours out on her own, exploring the sprawling market street, she was starting to.

It didn't matter what she could have been if things were different. They could have been. Maybe that was the relation. How Syrah felt now, in the present and in the eyes of her own conscience, *that* was what mattered. How she hated the fact that she couldn't do more. That she prayed every night for the ability to give these starving people what they needed. These were the thoughts that counted, not the false greed of some daydream.

The difference was she was not, in reality, that twisted version of herself.

Smiling slightly, her mind clear again, she lifted her head.

And stopped dead.

Talo had told her more than once not to stare, but this time there was no helping it. Syrah gaped openly at the back of the tall reptilian figure that had passed her with barely a curious glance at her shrouded face. He—for she could only imagine it was a he—moved on without looking back, but Syrah stood her ground, turning to watch him pass. His blunt, tapered snout gleamed in the bright sun, several needlelike teeth protruding randomly from beneath his upper and lower lips. His skin was scaly, black with a hinted tinge of mottled green, and his webbed, spined ears were clear blue with just the faintest suggestion of fiery orange along the base. Some kind of loose crest hung against the back of his head and neck, shining the same color as his ears, as did the leathery membranes of the great wings tucked tight to his back. He wore merchant's clothes, dressed almost like some of the traveling traders that frequently bartered with the city folk along the road, and a long cape of similar white silk as her own robes hung to the heels of his feet. Not only did Syrah see with a shock that he walked on the ball of his clawed feet, but when the mantle shifted she realized that a *tail* extended from the base of the lizard-man's loose trousers, held above the dirt, swaying like a thick snake with each step. He walked with a staff in one hand, the tall piece of white wood looking much shorter than it was in his grasp, and when he stopped to speak to a woman selling all kinds of food from her stall, Syrah saw the simple iron chain that hung from his right ear to right nostril.

So he *was* a nomad?

"Miss? Misses?"

Syrah jumped, turning around. A man was standing behind her, bent over and cowering, seemingly afraid to come any closer. One of his eyes was bandaged and bloody, and he held his right hand close to his chest as though it were hurt.

"Y-yes?" Syrah gasped. Her mind wasn't completely off the fact that a giant walking—and apparently *talking*—lizard was standing not twenty paces down the road.

What other surprises did these southern lands hold?

"You're the one who's been helpin' all the slum folk, ain't ya'?" the man asked hopefully, looking sideways at her with his one good eye. "Miss, please, *please* help. My wife and me—we got jumped by some a' them streeters! She ain't doin' too well, miss. Please help!"

"Oh," Syrah breathed, suddenly concerned. "My Priest-Mentor would be better. I don't know much about healing just yet, I'm only—"

"Tell me where he is and I'll go get him!" the injured man squeaked pleadingly, taking a step forward. "But please! Please come see her! She needs help!"

Syrah was torn. Talo would be mad enough when she got back, since he had undoubtedly realized by now that she wasn't at the inn anymore...

Still, he would probably be madder if she risked a life by running to him first.

"Where is she?" she asked, making up her mind and bending down so she could get a better look at the man through her cowl.

His face brightened. "Follow me!" he positively squealed, turning and hurriedly limping along the edge of the throng, back up the road. Syrah followed, hiking her robes and jogging to keep up, dodging around a lady juggler and the half-dozen spectators that were watching her. They kept to the side of the crowds, people giving them coy glances when they brushed past. It wasn't long before they stopped in front of a decrepit old hut right along the side of the market. Dodging into a narrow alley, the man tugged aside the shredded old rags that served to cover the entrance, holding them open for her. Syrah ducked her head and slipped in, happy to be in the shade and looking around. The house was made up of two small rooms separated by a single wall, with little more than a large hole in it to pass as a door. It was dusty and stale, with the dead air of a place that hadn't been used in years. At once Syrah got the feeling that something wasn't quite right.

Too late.

She only had time to realize that there was no sign of an injured woman on the dirt floor that she could see when a thick arm clamped around her waist and a hand covered her mouth over her shroud. She screamed, the sound muffled, kicking out. In response she was lifted clear off the ground. Several men appeared from the other room, all smiling and a few laughing quietly. The man she'd followed stepped out from behind whoever it was that was holding her captive, no longer stooped. Grinning, he pulled off the bandages to reveal a perfectly healthy second eye.

"You'll be proud to know, no doubt," he said, stepping forward while Syrah continued to struggle, his eyes raking her body, "tha' you're the first fish ta' bite on that bait in a good long while. Most people just give me the boot. Or a copper, if'n I'm real lucky."

Syrah kicked out, trying to catch him in the face and screaming again into the hand that covered her mouth. The man laughed, jumping back out of reach. Then he darted forward and slammed a fist into her gut.

Hard.

All the air whooshed out of Syrah's lungs, and she gagged, almost throwing up. She was struggling to inhale when the silk veil was ripped from her face, revealing it, but before she could take a breath to scream again the hand was back, clamping her jaw shut. Her eyes watered. She struggled to breathe, fighting the arm around her waist.

"Well would'ya look at that, Jerd?" one of the other men asked. "We done gone and caught ourselves a rose, ain't we?"

Even through her tears she could tell that they were still all staring at her, and Syrah fought harder, attempting to open her mouth and bite. The man's fingers were too strong, though, and she only won herself a tighter grip by the arm that pinned her hands to her sides.

"You ever seen a rose, Blith? 'Cause I ain't," the man called Jerd snapped. "This one's got ta' be prettier than a rose, though."

He stepped forward, clearly under the impression that she was subdued because he reached out to touch her face. He wasn't happy, therefore, when she kicked again, catching him in the arm.

He yelped and clutched his forearm with his free hand. "Whore!" he hissed, stepping to the side and backhanding her so hard she saw stars. Then he reached up and ripped at her robes, tearing the seam of her sleeve. "Try that again and I'll strip ya' to skin and drag ya' out of here by yer hair to let the Sun eat ya' alive!"

Syrah glared at him, her pinkish eyes blazing. She felt emotions she'd only ever rarely experienced. Hatred, vengefulness, desperation. She struggled, and the man holding her chuckled.

"Hit 'er again, Jerd. Don't think she's gettin' yer message."

Abruptly Raz stood straight, ears extended, interrupting the friendly bartering over the price of a bag of wheat.

"Raz, what—?" Jillia began, surprised, but he cut her off with a finger to his lips.

He was sure he was the only one on the road who could hear the scuffling. Even he could barely make it out over the thrum of the crowd. Still, his ears pricked when what could only have been a woman's muffled scream wound its way through the market sounds. On instinct he turned, looking for the standout, the most likely to be in trouble.

The white robes had disappeared.

Raz wasn't sure what he felt as he looked over the heads that surrounded him on all sides with false calm, listening harder. The girl was a stranger to him, and her face had been masked. Not to mention she'd been wandering so close to the slums on her own.

And yet... which of those facts meant he didn't have to do something?

Another muffled shout, and Raz's eyes latched on to an old abandoned hutch of a house a ways down the opposite side of the street.

"I'm sorry, Jillia," he said, not looking away from the building, placing the bag of nopales he'd already bought down on the table. "I'll be back for these later."

He stepped into the crowd, breaking a narrow line through the swarming bodies. Jarden's staff gripped tightly in his hand, he didn't make right for the building. Instead he crossed perpendicular, cutting pedestrians and carts off alike, ignoring the smattering of angry shouts and insults thrown his way. He could still discern it, still hear the struggle. That was a good sign. Stepping off the other side of the road, he darted through a group of street lyrists and ducked into the shadow of the alleys.

Then, as soon as he was out of sight of the market, he leapt atop an upturned water barrel and vaulted onto the lowest nearby roof.

His nighttime excursions served him well for once. Ducking low, Raz flitted from building to building, making a small loop over the flat rooftops, not wanting to catch the attention of anyone in the bustle of the bazaar. Within a minute he was where he wanted to be, and with a puff of dried dust he landed catlike and low on the abandoned house.

Sure enough he could hear movement inside, and what sounded like someone gagged and struggling to get loose. The noise was clearer now, floating up through a poorly repaired hole to his right. The opening was about the size of a small person, like some child had fallen through the weak mortar, and had been carelessly patched with thatched straw. Loose bricks were still visible, clinging sadly to the sides of the hole.

"Shut it, bitch!" someone hissed from inside the house, and there was a sharp smack followed by a momentary lapse in the sounds of scuffling. "Ain't nothin' to do but sit still and stop tryin' to hit us! Garrot, keep a hold on her. Roe, pass me some of yer rope and start tyin' up her legs. I'll get her hands."

If Raz's scales could have stood up on end, they would have. The silver bangles around his wrist clinked and shifted as he stiffened. There were two possibilities: either the men were rapists...

... or they were slavers.

It was a moment's decision, and without a second thought Raz darted forward, leaping high. He crashed through the brittle roof of the hut, wings spread, falling in a shower of shattered brick. The remainders of the tattered straw thatching floated downward as he landed on all fours on the dirt floor. The kidnappers caught only a moment's glimpse of white teeth and reptilian eyes before he was on them like a whirlwind, Jarden's staff twisting and slashing through the air expertly in his hands, bruising flesh and breaking bones. The girl, one eye blackened and already swelling, took the opportunity to drive her heel into the crotch of the man holding her by the waist, doubling him over and forcing him to drop her.

Raz's clawed fingers found the collar of his tunic, heaved, and threw him straight through the flimsy mud-brick wall that divided the house.

The explosion of reddish dust as a section of the room collapsed blew in the faces of the three men left standing, and their reflexes cost them their lives. The instant their hands went up to protect their eyes, Raz, unhindered by the dirt, moved with all the speed of his kind, slipping in between them and drawing his knife from his belt. The narrow blade found the exposed back of one, his staff crushed the skull of another, and the last went down with a scream when a sweeping tail knocked his feet out from under him.

Well past the point of self-control, Raz dropped his weapons and fell on him like a starved hound, bare-handed. His jaws found the man's throat in moments, lifting him in the air. There was the sound of tearing flesh, and the slaver jerked once, hitting the ground as Raz dropped the body. Blood pooled around the man's head from his shredded neck, and he twitched only long enough to stare disbelievingly at the atherian towering over him.

Raz watched him die, unblinking.

Slowly the sounds of the surrounding city returned. There were panicked shouts approaching outside, shoppers attracted by the noises, and somewhere close a male voice yelled for the guards.

Raz was struggling with himself, will battling instinct. His nose and ears told him that there were two people left alive in the room apart from him. The man he had thrown through the wall was stirring, groaning, his broken bones protesting every motion. Raz felt himself slide down the incline that was the fight to regain control of himself. He turned, folding his wings and bending to retrieve the staff and his knife from the ground. In the emptiness of his slipping conscience he found himself standing over the battered figure, cocking his head to the side and sizing the man up.

He could taste the blood on the air.

It would be so easy. It would be nothing. To cave his chest with a kick, or break his neck—it would take no effort. Maybe even bite, going for the vulnerable arteries about his throat. Raz liked that, didn't he? He enjoyed it. He could still taste the metallic tartness in his mouth, feel the blood drying on his snout, tongue flicking in and out.

It would be nothing...

So what made him stop?

Because there was certainly *something* holding him back, something pushing him to turn away and let the man go. He might survive. He might not. Raz could care less. But there was no need to kill him, helpless as he was.

But still... so, so easy...

Raz felt himself slip again, and he fought tenfold not to give in to savage instinct. He was losing, though. His control was fading, and he could sense something in the back of his mind being pulled from the deepest parts of his thoughts. It felt like an emptiness, a dark hole into which he could tumble so easily, giving in to the animal part of his soul.

Raz felt himself take a step forward, watching as though through a blurry window a clawed hand—*his* hand—reach down toward the defeated man's battered and bleeding face.

"Don't."

Raz's reality shifted with a snap. He found himself standing in the center of the wrecked hut, coincidently almost directly beneath the wide hole he'd ripped through the brick roof. Above him the desert sky was a clean blue, outlined with the barest hints of wispy cloud. Beneath his clawed feet the earth was packed and solid and sticky with blood.

And behind him the girl stood a mere arm-length away.

Raz stood straight and half turned to look at her. Her thin white robes were dirty and torn, one sleeve hanging by only a few threads, revealing the palest skin he had ever seen. She was flushed from the heat and the struggle, but her pallor was unmistakable. Her one good eye, the other dark and swollen shut now, was a pale, colorless pink, returning Raz's stare evenly.

Albino? That took Raz by surprise. Albinos were rare as it was, but in the heat of the South they rarely survived more than a few years past birth, if they were lucky. This girl, whoever she was, was definitely foreign, likely a Northerner.

Well, that explains the clothes...

"Don't," she said again. "He's had enough."

Raz blinked, looking back at the slaver. The man seemed to have passed out from the pain, the struggle to free himself from the remnants of the wall taxing his broken body to its limits.

"You realize he's liable to come after you again?" Raz asked without looking away. "You could have been raped or killed. And those are the most optimistic of your options."

The girl nodded without saying a word. Raz looked around again, sizing her up. She wasn't the least bit frightened by *him*, that was certain.

He found it almost amusing. Of all the things she could have been worried about in that moment, it was the life of the man who'd had her pinned and gagged.

Then he shrugged, leaning down to wipe his dirty blade clean on the slaver's trousers before sheathing the long knife on his hip and throwing the staff over one shoulder.

"It's your mistake to make, I guess. But I'm not helping him up."

And with that, the girl's composure broke

"No—" she said quickly. "Y-you don't have to—" She slumped, as though letting the weight of the events that had just taken place catch hold of her for the first time. Now that she knew Raz wasn't going to kill the man, she paused, taking a deep breath.

"Thank you."

The last bits of the stern, authoritative bearing she'd held herself with seemed to drain away, and she staggered. Raz was just quick enough to catch her arm gently, helping her stand. The voices outside were getting more insistent, and he thought he could hear horses' hooves nearby. The Karthian guard was on its way.

"We have to leave," he said hurriedly, pulling the wide hood of his white mantle back up over his head. "Can you walk?"

She nodded and took a step closer as she, too, heard the horses. The throng outside was growing, shouting and debating whether to brave an entrance now that the fighting inside seemed to have come to an end.

"This way," Raz told her, grabbing her wrist and pulling her along to the back of the hut. One of the windows, boarded up with wooden planks and nails, led to the back alleys. He couldn't hear anything on the other side, and so with his free hand he tore the boards away, scattering more dirt and splinters over the dusty floor.

"Out," he said. "Hurry."

She had just clambered her way through, Raz right behind her, when he heard the guard rush into the abandoned house. Landing on all fours, Raz didn't hesitate. Sweeping the girl into his arms, he took off, moving away from the noise of the crowd.

He ran for a good five minutes, making twists and turns that led in a wide loop through the slum town. They passed rickety sheds of thin cloth and leather, emaciated children playing in the dusty streets, and a mangy dog missing a back leg. A pair of women in old worn clothes that barely covered their wasted bodies watched them pass with tired eyes.

And then they were back in the market, far from the commotion of the fight, Raz breathing hard as he looked around.

A few people glanced at them in surprise, letting the pair be when they recognized him, though more than one stared openly at the blood that was drying along Raz's snout and hands. He ignored them, scanning the bustling crowd for signs of trouble. Seeing nothing, he finally calmed.

Something tapped against his chest.

"Could you let me down now, please?"

Raz placed the girl carefully on her feet. The Sun beat down incessantly, and he watched her tug her ripped sleeve over her exposed shoulder.

"Here," he said, pulling the silks from his back and draping them over her. "I can live without it."

For a second the girl looked like she would protest. Then she glanced up at the broiling ball of white high in the sky.

"Thank you," she told him again, pulling the hood over her head. The mantle hung on her like a grown man's coat would hang on a small child, dragging along the ground and picking up dirt, but it did the trick. She squinted less from the shade, looking around.

"We need to leave." Raz was still peering over the heads of the crowd. "Where can you go?"

"The Ovana Inn," she said at once, looking up and down the road, unsure of exactly where they were. "My Priest-Mentor and our companions will be there. They might already be looking for me, actually."

"Then you need to get there quickly," Raz said with a nod. He pointed a clawed finger down the east road. "Follow this street. Stick to the middle of the crowd, away from the edges. The Ovana is on the left side, about a half mile down. Find your friends and get out of Karth. If you're lucky, those men weren't slavers, but I wouldn't bet on it. If they were, the ring will be after you. Leave as soon as you can."

"What about you?" she asked him as he stepped back into the alley.

"Don't worry about me."

And then he was climbing up the wall of the alley, the staff between his teeth, his strong arms and legs making short work of the cracks and protruding bricks that littered the two stories. Once he'd pulled himself up onto the flat roof, he peeked over the street-facing edge. It took him less than a second to find the girl in the sea of dark hair and colored robes. She was making her way east like he'd said, as close to the middle of the road as possible, but her going was slow through the crowd. Raz was more than a little nervous, keeping an eye out for trouble in the throng.

He must have handled the group involved, though, because in the ten minutes it took her to find the inn he didn't see anything more suspicious than an old one-eyed beggar lurking in the alley beside a dried-meat shop.

He watched the girl step under the awning of the inn, pulling the silk hood down. Her white shoulder-length hair seemed to melt into her skin as she looked around. Then a man with a long ponytail and dressed in similar robes to her torn ones rushed from out of the Ovana's entrance, embracing her.

"Where have you been?" Raz heard the man demand worriedly over the crowd.

Satisfied, Raz turned away, intent on getting home himself.

"Where have you been?" Talo practically yelled, crushing her with an anxious hug. "I've been worried sick about you! Laor save me, I was about to go looking! What happened? Why is your face like that?"

"I'm fine, Talo," Syrah said with a half-hearted smirk, pushing his examining hand away from her cheek. "I'll tell you everything as soon as I can, but we need to leave. Now."

Talo's brow pinched together, and for a second Syrah thought he would demand an explanation again. But his blue eyes lingered on her injuries for another moment, and he nodded.

"You'll speak as we pack, acolyte," he told her sternly, and Syrah bowed her head in understanding. Then she followed the Priest's raised arm inside.

Once she was safely in the dim common room of the inn, Talo looked across the road, scanning the top of the shop roofs that faced the Ovana with narrowed eyes. There'd been something there, he was sure. A figure, peering over the edge of the low rooftops, watching them.

Whoever it was, though, they were long gone.

VII

*"I only ever saw him once after that day, years later. I don't think he recognized me...
I don't think he recognized much of anything from his old life..."*

—Jillia Ashani

"I don't know whether to call you fool or hero, boy," Jarden grunted, shaking his head. He was leaning against the outside of his wagon, one foot resting on the timber spokes of a wheel. In his hands he toyed nervously with his panpipes. Beside him, the Grandmother frowned.

"Would you have done anything differently?" Her gray eyes met Jarden's.

Raz's uncle looked away and tucked the instrument into its leather pouch at his side. They were all convened beneath the canvas overhang attached to Jarden's wagon on the inside of the caravan ring. It had been another day of hard work, and Agais called everyone off a few hours early to get out of the Sun. Raz had returned home at a run—empty-handed, since he'd completely forgotten the original purpose of his trip—and hurriedly told them the story of what had happened.

"Differently? Probably not," Jarden finally answered with a sigh. "But I might at least have gone for help."

"There wasn't *time* to get help," Raz groaned, annoyed. He'd already gone over the events twice now. "They'd probably have beaten her bloody by the time I got back with anyone, or worse."

"You did the right thing."

Everyone turned to Agais, who sat a few paces from his son. He didn't look up when he spoke, eyes on the twig he was whittling at pointlessly with a narrow dagger. Beside him, Grea was fanning herself with a book, cross-legged on the reed mats.

"I agree," she said with a shrug, looking up at Jarden. "I don't like the idea of Raz going off and fighting any more than you do, Jarden, especially not on his own, but what was the alternative? Warn the guards? They probably had something to do with it, the way things have been looking around here. Leave her to fend for herself? This may not be the Cienbal, but our laws still apply where they can, when they can. Raz did what was best with everything he was given, considering the situation."

Jarden sighed again, his chin falling to his chest. "I suppose so," he muttered, staring at the sandy ground. "That still doesn't change the fact that something needs to be done. There could be more of the group."

"I followed the girl all the way back to her friends," Raz cut in eagerly. "I didn't see anyone who looked like they might have been tailing her. Wouldn't they have sent men if they'd been part of a ring?"

"Probably," Jarden said with a nod, "but you can't be sure." He looked at Agais. "I strongly suggest we get out of Karth. Tomorrow if possible. It would only be a week earlier than we'd planned, and business has been good enough to make up for the time twice over."

"A wise suggestion," the Grandmother agreed. "With any luck the weather will favor us and we'll be in Acrosia within a fortnight. If business is good, we gain a week. If not, we'll at least have a few day's advance at the end of the season to make for the Garin."

Agais took a moment to slice the tip of the twig he'd been working on to a small point. Finishing this, he tossed it aside, sheathed the knife, and got to his feet.

"Start packing your things." His silver clanmaster's chain glinted as he stepped out of the shade and into the Sun. "Grea, go tell the others to do the same. We leave in the morning. With any luck we'll be first out of the city gates."

"Assuming we don't run into trouble," Jarden added, coming to walk by his brother once the others went off with their orders. "Let's pray that your boy's right about those men acting alone, Agais. If we've stirred up something with one of the rings... that spells trouble."

The brothel stank of sweat, sex, and smoldering ragroot. Wisps of grayish smoke curled around Farro as he made his way through the dirty, brightly colored common room. The whores—some clothed, some only partially so—scuttled to make a path for him.

Even the new girls only took a few days to learn which men were customers, and which were there on other business.

Turning into the back hall, one side lined with rickety doors that led to the private rooms, Farro spat on the floor and cursed the tar-colored spittle. He'd kicked his habit over a year ago, but the evidence of his root abuse seemed to be clinging to him more firmly than a starving beggar. Reaching the end of the hall, he pushed aside the silk curtain that separated the larger room beyond it from the rest of the building.

It was a circular chamber, a single story high but nearly twenty paces across. Solid stone pillars held up the shallowly domed ceiling, and red-and-black tapestries and rugs hung from walls and covered the floor. There was no bed or desk or any true furniture to speak of, but the standing lanterns scattered around the room cast strange shadows over the great mountain of colorful plush cushions in its center.

Lounging lazily atop them, a pipe hanging from his lips and a pair of naked girls sleeping at his feet, was Crom Ayzenbas.

Tall and skinny, Ayzenbas was staring up at the stones blankly, his green eyes bloodshot and wet. The spiral tattoos that colored the majority of his wasted body seemed somehow to meld with the tendrils of smoke wafting through the air, and his black goatee was tapered and styled into two sharp points. A thin blanket covered him decently enough, but even so Farro could tell that the man was as naked underneath it as his whores.

Ayzenbas never was one to limit himself of life's little pleasures.

"Boss?... *Boss*," Farro whispered urgently.

Ayzenbas blinked and slowly looked down from the ceiling. He was high, a constant condition nowadays, except maybe in the few hours of sleep he caught each night. Even as Farro watched the man took a long drag from his pipe and exhaled the smoke through his nose.

"Whaaaaat?" Ayzenbas slurred, blinking against the delirium. Farro had to work hard to keep the frustration out of his voice.

"The albino got away. That lizard from one of the tanny families butchered Ros, Gillgy, Blith, and Jerd. Garrot's being looked at by the surgeons, but they don't think he'll make it the night. He's bleeding too much on the inside, they say. Damned scaly put him through a fucking wall... He managed to tell us what happened, though."

Ayzenbas stared at Farro for a long moment. Then, slowly, he looked down at the girls at his feet. It seemed to take him a second to figure out how to use his limbs, but when he did he kicked out, catching one of them—maybe twelve or thirteen years old—in the side. She woke up with a cry of pain, crawling up to the man obediently. Ayzenbas laid her down beside him and began fondling her uncaringly, watching her wince.

"The fuck you want me to do 'bout it?" he mumbled. The words were so quiet that Farro almost didn't realize the man was talking to him, and he grit his teeth at the question.

Crom Ayzenbas had once been a powerful figure. Quick minded and good with his hands, he'd banded together a majority of the loose criminal groups festering in the west and northern slums, uniting them into a single strong circle. For half a decade they'd been feared and respected, supplying the highest quality heads to the slave traders that frequented the city's outskirts on the seventh night of every new month.

That had all ended in a whirl of pungent fumes.

The root had done its work, and now most of the man and his small empire had all but wasted away. Soon Ayzenbas would smoke himself within the Moon's reach, and on that day things would hopefully change.

But, until then, people were still too afraid of the man's reputation to strike out at him directly.

"Let the boys... let 'em have some fun," Ayzenbas said finally, running one hand between the girl's legs and taking another drag from his pipe with the other. "Turn 'em loose, do whatever you want... I'm tireeeeed... get out."

Farro nodded and turned. He looked back as he let the curtain fall into place behind him, watching Ayzenbas tug the blanket off himself and pull the naked girl atop him.

VIII

"The Mahsadën had always underestimated him, even after he'd become one of their most valuable assets. They always assumed—be it his race, history, or morals—that Raz i'Syul could be controlled, could be tamed. In the end this was probably their gravest mistake."

—*Born of the Dahgün Bone*, author unknown

There were only a handful of buildings higher than a single story in and around Karth's markets. Shop owners—at least those with the coin to—preferred to expand their stores outward rather than up, buying out neighboring shops and lots. It was cheaper than having expensive wood shipped southward, and the flimsy mud brick that worked so well against the desert Sun didn't do much to ward off the hot gales and sandstorms that swept north from the Cienbal frequently enough to be a problem. Building high only meant the risk of collapse when the winds came.

It made sense, therefore, that the only nearby places in Karth worth exploring at all were its poorest districts, where such risks were ignored more often than not.

Raz watched his breath mist, standing at the edge of the House of Hands, a brothel in the middle of the worst parts of the city, and the only building four stories tall within a couple square leagues. Night had fallen hours ago, but as usual Raz woke after only a short rest. They were leaving in the morning, as his father and the Grandmother had agreed, and he wanted to take advantage of the city one last time before the sands swallowed them up again.

Up here, warm beneath the layers of fur that protected him from the freezing night air, was the only place within the city limits that Raz could truly breathe easy. It was the only place where he could think straight, unchained from the crowds that crushed around him any other time. Here he could come to terms with the day, the events of which had been thrust to the back of his mind until now.

He'd killed today—again. He'd slaughtered those men, and it had been easier than breathing.

None of that bothered him.

Well, it did, but it was a feeling he'd had before and one he knew he would overcome given time. What was gnawing at Raz's mind wasn't the death. It wasn't even that he'd practically ripped one of the men apart with his bare hands, tearing his throat clean from his neck. He'd been right to do those things, been right to end their lives.

What bothered Raz was the last man, the one who'd been lying helpless, unconscious on the ground, twisted and broken.

What bothered Raz was how close he'd come to butchery...

It was midnight now, and while Karth was far from dead, it was quiet at least. Raz's ears didn't ring with the unending pounding of the city's heart. His head, usually suffering the constant throb that was the bastard child of the rumbling streets and throngs and yelling vendors, felt at ease. He looked up at Her Stars in the dark sky above. He'd tried counting them once, two or three years ago in this very same spot, but gave up when he realized he'd barely covered a fraction of the sky in an hour of sitting still and doing nothing else.

Something skittered along the alley below. Two boys, their faces and exposed arms smudged with dirt and dust, darted around a corner, heading for the market. He listened to the young thieves' footsteps as long as he could, holding a cool breath of night air until they faded into the city distance.

Letting it out, he dropped off the edge of the building with wings spread.

While he couldn't fly, at the very least he could slow his falls. He hit the top of the roof two stories below lightly, crouched with one hand on the ground. Then, so quick any witness might have shrugged him off as a trick of the lantern lights, Raz was gone.

The buildings of the slums were little more than an obstacle course to him by now. Not even Jarden knew how often he came up here, because for the last three weeks it had been almost every night, or every other at the very least. He leapt and twisted over alleys, pulling himself up walls and vaulting over cracked chimneys. Mortar and brick broke beneath his feet. Old wood crunched when he landed on worn thatched roofs. There was no nook he did not know. No loose stone or weak ledge. The best handholds seemed to seek out his fingers, and his clawed toes always found true footing.

The cityscape worked for him as though Raz had crafted every glorious, grimy detail of it himself.

While he moved, Raz let his mind go the slightest bit. The last thrum of the world dissipated, and he let his body take over, freeing it of the manacles that held his fragile humanity in place. Everything was fluid, natural. He didn't have to think, didn't have time to plan or decide.

It was his favorite place to be, curled up away from his own conscience. Everything about his surroundings—the half Moon high above, the faint glow of a large bonfire to the east, the hardness of the brick under his toes—it all became part of nothing more than the obscure reality that surrounded his instincts. *This* felt normal to him. *This* felt right.

It was the mental place where he could learn to never again slip too deep, as he had been so close to doing only hours ago.

Raz made one last bound, hurdling over the edge of a roof one story above and landing on his feet. He stood straight and walked to the far ledge, letting go more and more. He could feel himself consciously easing down the hill toward the place he didn't want to cross, edging closer to the line he wasn't sure he'd be able to bring himself back from. But it was a willful act, this time. He controlled his descent, and as he closed his eyes Raz could almost see himself peering over the edge into the bottomless pit he'd only so recently discovered.

He'd felt it for the first time that day, saving the girl. She was most likely Laorin, the Grandmother had explained to him. An acolyte, a Priestess-in-training of Laor, a deity much more commonly revered in the North. It was their faith's code to never take a life, which explained how she'd acted when Raz had been on the verge of finishing off the injured man, the helpless last survivor.

The verge...

Maybe it was that which he had felt, though he'd only realized it later. An edge, inexplicably tangible in the way the wind was, marking a drop whose depths he had sensed only briefly.

Now, though, he let himself go, releasing his chambered nature little by little. He opened his eyes again and stared blankly off into the distance. For a long time he watched the glowing orange of the bonfire on the horizon, its colors accented by the dozens of flickering dots of hand-held torches and oil lamps that sparkled throughout the city.

It was simple now that he knew what was happening. Like he was descending a ladder he eased his way further down into his unconscious, seeking the emotions he'd had during the fight...

He was there, just there at the edge again, when he heard the scream.

Raz's awareness roared back into place in a blur that left him light-headed. Even as he tripped backwards a step, his eyes stayed straight, gazing off at the growing glow in the distance, clinging to the edge of town.

Something was off. Something wasn't right…

For the second time that day, Raz listened as hard as he could. It was easier this time. The silence of the night didn't offer the cacophony for his ears to overcome that the market had. He willed himself to block out the calls of the crickets and the hoots of an owl that had taken residence nearby. He pushed his senses to their limits, fighting until everything but what he wanted to hear was a dull thrum in the background.

Was that another scream? The ring of metal on metal?

Raz frowned, still watching the distant glow.

A bonfire? Is it…?

And then something gripped Raz's stomach and tugged hard, a feeling he didn't know or like. Ice flushed through every inch of his body, and like an arrow shot from a bow he took off, heading for the distant light.

Raz ran as he had never run before, little more than shadow in the night. He leapt from rooftop to rooftop, sometimes dropping to the alleys below just to haul himself back up again. No matter how fast he moved, his wings flattened tight to his back under his furs, he never took his eyes off that reddish glow in the distance. Within minutes he could smell the smoke and ash.

And the flesh… he could smell burning flesh.

The feeling pulled even harder, and he pushed himself to go faster. The closer he got, the greater its grip tightened. He must have made a mistake. It couldn't be. He was going in the wrong direction…

But it was no mistake, and he knew it. That light, that hateful burning glare that lit up the night, was in the same direction as the Arro camp.

"No."

He didn't feel the burn in his legs, didn't feel the pounding of the mud-brick roofs under his feet or the air whipping around his ears. He was out of the slums in five minutes, and soon the streets below, all but empty only a few blocks in the direction he'd come, started to show signs of life. People appeared, at first running in the same direction as Raz, then joining the throng that bottled up the roads, everyone trying to see what had happened.

Finding himself blocked by an alley too wide to jump, Raz dropped down to the main way, landing among the crowd.

"Out of the way!" he yelled. Shoving people left and right, he fought his way forward, beating himself a reckless path through. "Out of the way! MOVE!"

It was frightening how word seemed to spread ahead of him. Most of the crowd parted like they knew he was coming, and the look in some of their eyes did nothing to settle the feeling of foreboding he had.

"I SAID MO—!" he started to yell, but stopped, finding that he had finally broken through the last line of onlookers.

The scene before him caught a strangle cry in his throat.

The camp was an inferno of twisted wood and metal. Almost every wagon had been tipped over and lit ablaze. The horse corral had been bashed to splinters, and to a one every animal lay still in its own blood, throat slit. Smoke plumed like a terrible beacon high into the sky, any hint of Her Stars swallowed by the light of the flames. Heat rolled in waves from the wreckage, roaring wild from the blaze.

For a stunned second Raz stood frozen, shock and terror washing over him.

And then he dashed forward, leaping clear over the remnants of what he thought had once been Karren and Sios' small cart, landing in the broiling sand in the middle of the fiery ring.

"MAMA!" he screamed into the roar, whirling around and calling out, feet and tail kicking dirt and dust into the air. "FATHER! AHNA! *AHNA!*"

Nothing.

There was only the deafening cacophony of the fire, the cracking of wood and the groan of bending metal as somewhere an axle tore free of its hinges.

"FATHER! JARDEN!"

Nothing.

But then, for a second, there was something. What was that?

"WHERE ARE YOU?" Raz yelled, spinning in the heat as he scanned the ruined camp, trying to find the source of what he'd heard. "WHO'S THERE? WHERE ARE—?"

He stopped. In his frantic search he'd lost his sense of direction, but there was something about the burning wagon in front of him that made him halt, taking in the overturned ruin with wide eyes.

He knew that shape...

"No..." he hissed, stepping forward and automatically reaching out to the blazing silhouette of his parents' cart. As he did, part of the covering fell, sending a wide jet of sparks into the air. Raz stopped dead, transfixed.

A blackened, charred hand reached out of the burning wood, fingers extended and resting against the upturned side floor like they were scratching at the timber, trying to get out. For a second the fire abated just enough for him to see by, and Raz caught a glimpse of a skull-like face and what looked like a line of silver hanging loosely from it. The metal was melted and twisted, and even as he watched the clanmaster's chain fell from Agais' nose, anything it might have been attached to burned away.

"No," Raz breathed again, and the stone in his stomach became a boulder, dragging him helplessly down to his knees.

No. *No.* He'd heard something. He *knew* he had.

Tearing his eyes away from the burning remnants of his home, Raz searched again. This time he heard it clearly. A dull banging, coupled with muffled coughs and pleas. He couldn't tell who the voices belonged to, but it didn't matter. If there was a chance, even just a chance, that someone was alive...

Maybe Mama... Maybe Ahna...

His eyes fell on Tolman's wagon, one of the few that still stood straight. Flames licked at its sides, and with a jolt Raz realized that a number of flat timber beams had been nailed over the front opening, effectively boarding it shut with barely space to see through.

Still, it was enough for him to catch sight of the gray eye that stared out at him between the planks, bulging in panic.

Raz leapt to his feet, ignoring the smaller flames around his ankles to reach the cart. The fire-weakened wood tore off in great chunks in his clawed hands, flying in every direction. In a matter of seconds he'd ripped the entrance almost completely open again. As soon as the space was large enough he reached in, grabbed the first handful of whatever felt human, and pulled.

Mychal emerged, coughing and drenched in sweat. His left arm was badly burned, and his pants had giant singed holes in them, revealing the ugly scarred stump of his missing leg.

"Mychal what happ—?" Raz started.

"Inside!" Mychal cut him off. "Get them out! *Get them out!*"

Unceremoniously Raz shoved his cousin out of the ring, clear of the fire. Then, with a massive kick that blew clear through the last of the planks blocking his way, he stepped into the burning cart.

It was like walking into a vat of boiling water.

The air shimmered around him in waves, forcing Raz to bring a hand up and cover his eyes as he stooped, avoiding the burning roof. Instantly the long hairs of his fur collar blackened and curled. Through the dry heat he blinked away he saw several forms nearby, and he grabbed for the closest one, pulling the person toward him.

Prida.

She fell, coughing and gasping, into his chest, her dark hair singed, her clothes so badly burned they hardly clung to her decently.

"B-behind me!" she wheezed. One of the other forms stood just out of reach, and this one Raz recognized.

"Grandmother!" he yelled, and the woman turned, gazing at him blearily through the heat. She seemed... calm.

From above there was a loud *crack*.

"Grandmother, *hurry!*" Raz exclaimed, dropping his arm from his face to shield Prida as burning splinters rained down on the both of them. It was so hard to breathe. The heat bit at every inch of his body.

The Grandmother stood for another second, then walked forward leisurely, as if she were strolling along in the market. Taking a blind swipe at her, Raz grabbed her shoulder.

And then they were out in the night again, all of them gasping and hacking soot.

As soon as he could see, Raz dragged them out of the ring and dropped them both hurriedly by Mychal, who was shivering in the sand nearby. Several townspeople crowded around him, covering his raw shoulders in a loose blanket to ward off the cold, doing their best to help.

Raz had just turned around, taking a step back toward the cart, when a hand grabbed the hem of his shirt.

"D-don't!" Prida gasped, breathing hard and looking up at him. Someone had thrown a blanket over her as well. "They're gone. Delfry, Eara, A-Aigos..." She choked on her son's name. "They're gone, Raz. I... I saw them... saw it happen. Don't go."

Raz looked down at her, his eyes still stinging. Then he looked at the cart. Even standing there, he knew she was right. There were no more bangs or screams now. Nothing but corpses waited for him inside.

"Prida... Prida what happened?" Raz demanded, falling to one knee beside her and taking her face in his hands. "Tell me *what happened!*"

But the woman wouldn't say any more. She stared back at him, her body shaking, tears streaming from her eyes to cut streaks down her soot-covered face and trail along his thumbs.

"Raiders."

Raz looked at Mychal, who was staring wide-eyed back into the flames.

"Raiders. The slave rings... They came all at once. There must have been fifty of them. I was asleep, but the screaming woke me up. A group of men broke into our wagon and dragged my mother away. Then they..." He started to cry, turning to look at Raz. "They took my father, Raz. Slit his throat and left him and my brother to the fires. They threw me in Tolman's cart while he was fighting one of them. I tried to get out, but they threw everyone else in after me and boarded the entrance up. The screams, Raz... I can hear them scream..."

Raz's body was quaking. The heat of the flames had left him feeling icy in the cooler air beyond it. Still, even to this he was numb. Standing up slowly, he turned to look back over the remains of what had been his home, that imperfect, burning ring.

Dead. They were all dead. Nothing but falling ash and breaking wood moved in the fire. He thought he could see their faces, everyone's faces, screaming out to him from the ruins.

Dead. Everyone...

And then something caught his eye. Something moving slowly, painfully across the ground near the edge of the ring to his left, partially shielded by the billowing smoke and distorting heat.

There was another survivor.

One last figure remained untouched by the flames. A man in chain and leather armor was crawling on his hands and knees between the burning wreckages of the Grandmother's and what was left of Raz's parents' wagons. His left leg dragged uselessly behind him, and Raz saw the handle of a dagger protruding from above his knee.

Tolman's dagger. Thrust in to the hilt.

Raz felt some raw chill flow through him. It wasn't shock this time. It wasn't an icy deluge of pain and denial. This... this was something far different. The chasm he had been toying with ripped upwards from inside him, and he suddenly felt himself suspended over its endless opening.

"Mychal, take Prida and the Grandmother and go. There's an abandoned house three streets down from the butcher's on the west side of the south market road. The one with the hole in the roof. I'll be there soon."

Behind him, Mychal looked up. His eyes were red and puffy against his ash-darkened face. His long bleached hair was seared, and the burns on his arms gleamed in the firelight.

"What are you...?"

But he stopped. Raz's head had shifted a quarter turn, and what gleamed there in the one amber eye he could see scared Mychal so much he choked on the question.

"I said *go*."

Mychal swallowed and nodded. With the help of one of the onlookers he stood up, leaning on Prida in place of his crutch, and helped the Grandmother to her feet. The old woman was shaking now, her eyes focused on something far past what was in front of her as she half smiled at nothing. The look on her face shattered the fragile vestiges of what was left of Mychal's heart.

Her mind was gone.

Fighting the tremors of panic and despair that racked his own body, Mychal gently turned the two women away from the carnage that had been their families. They made their way as instructed, the ringing crowd parting to let them pass.

When they were gone, Raz let go, feeling himself swing even further over the dark depths of whatever this blackness was hiding inside him.

He took a step forward, then another one, leaving clawed footprints in the dust and sand to mix with the hundreds of others. The cold came in full, washing over him completely. It numbed him, crawling upwards toward his head.

When it reached his mind, an icy bane seeping into his thoughts, the world changed.

Red outlined every line and shadow. Like a mist descended it clung to the scene around him, highlighting every motion, every flick of the flames. As Raz walked slowly, deliberately hunting down the man who was doing everything he could to crawl away, the cold changed to cool, then warm, then hot.

And then it was boiling, agonizing rage.

The last few steps, Raz didn't remember. Where he was twenty feet behind the slaver one moment, in the next he was beside him, one foot pressed against his side and shoving.

With a *thump* the man fell over, screaming and yelling, desperately trying to scramble away.

Raz heard none of it.

Pinning him to the ground by his throat, Raz fell to one knee again. He brought their faces inches away from each other, thin white fangs a whisper from flushed skin, staring into the pale brown of his captive's eyes.

"*Why?*"

It was a single word, a long, drawn-out hiss of a question, but the injured man stopped struggling. He was silent, terrified and shivering. When no answer was forthcoming, the clawed hand around the man's neck tightened.

"WHY?"

This time there was a gurgle of a response. Loosening his grip slightly, Raz waited for it to come again.

"T-told us to do whatever we wanted… said you deserved it… w-we don't know—AAH!"

The man screamed suddenly as he was lifted and slammed back into the ground, hard. Along the spine of Raz's neck, the blue-orange crest flared like a drawn blade.

"WHO? WHO SAID WE DESERVED IT?"

Silence again, and this time Raz snapped. With a feral roar that made even the men in the crowd around them step back a pace, Raz lifted the slaver clear off the ground with one hand. The man's good leg kicked, and he grabbed at his captor's wrist, trying to relieve the pressure on his throat. Raz moved forward, coming to a halt at the edge of the inferno that was all that remained of Sameyl's cart. The flames were so close they could both feel the heat eating at them. The blackened forms of Sameyl and his sons leered from beneath the burning wood, dead faces laughing at what they saw.

"Keep an answer from me again," Raz hissed, squeezing so tightly he felt claws puncture skin, "and I swear by the Sun, Moon, and all Her Stars that I will feed you to the flames."

Another gurgle of a reply, and Raz lowered his arm so the man could partially stand.

"Ayzenbas!" the slaver gasped, his face turning purple and his eyes popping. "Crom Ayzenbas! Y-you got in our way! He said you got in our way!"

The agony spiked, as did the rage. For a long moment Raz stood, his thoughts tumbling. He dropped deeper into the dark, the fragile human conscience that had taken so long to build barely holding up a fight.

"Where?" he finally asked. "Tell me where I can find Ayzenbas."

This time the answer was prompt.

"Blue Horizon! A brothel in the west slums! Crom does all his work out of the back rooms! Now, please! Let me go! Please!"

Raz was silent for another moment. He could feel the balance inside him shaking.

"And you?" he breathed, looking past the fires and up at the Star-gone night. Somewhere, in a section buried deep now by the brutal side of his soul that was roaring forth, Raz realized that his deities had abandoned him to the dark. "Who did you butcher?"

"Wha?" the man gasped. "I-I'm paid! It was all business! Don't—!"

"*Who?*"

The question was a deadly hiss, but the slaver was silent, breathing hard and clutching at Raz's wrist.

"*WHO?*"

Another silence, and Raz's world shifted into an even darker shade of red. He took a step forward, ignoring the flames that licked at his furs and feet. The man screamed, the fire biting at his legs, searing the hair off the back of his head instantly.

"I don't know who!" he shrieked. "Some girl who threw a rock at me! An old man! The one who stabbed me in the leg! Please!" the man seemed to sag as he started to sob. "Please... my family... let me go back to my family... please..."

In a single fluid motion, Raz ripped Tolman's dagger out of the man's leg, brought it up, and slashed the slaver's throat wide open. The cut was so vicious Raz felt the blade nick bone, and blood gushed from the wound to flow over his wrist and fingers.

Pulling the twitching form close, he waited until the dying eyes met his.

"My family will have to do," he hissed.

Then Raz drove the blade into the man's chest and shoved him backwards into the fire.

It was a long time before the figure stopped writhing in silent torment. Unable to scream, he thrashed, clutching at his body while the flames tore into him. The smell of burning flesh and hair filled the air once more, and finally he seemed to crumple and lie still. The fires had eaten away his clothes and boiled into his skin, but Raz didn't look away until the face was gone, blackening like those of the family the man was curled beside.

When he did finally pull his eyes from the figure, Raz didn't do it because he'd seen enough. His gaze only faltered as a shine caught his attention, a glimmer of something lying on the ground a ways away, half buried in the ash and sand by the remains of Jarden's home.

Raz moved as though in a dream, only barely aware that he'd made the conscious choice to investigate the curiosity. In the half existence he was suspended in, he found himself standing over the source of the gleam, staring down at it.

The bronze-tipped end of a bleached-wood staff.

The rest of the weapon was still there, too, mostly hidden by the mixed dust that had been kicked over it during the struggle. Reaching down, Raz picked it up carefully, lifting it free. As he did, something else came out of the ashes. Something clinging to the other end of the staff.

The better part of Jarden's left arm fell to the ground with a *thump*.

For a full minute Raz looked down at the limb, his eyes fixed on the fingers that had so shortly before been alive and well. Then his gaze moved up, following the length of the arm. He traced the familiar scars—the two that extended farther down than the others, then the rest of them—as high as he could.

The flesh blackened and ended, cut off by fire.

But still Raz followed the path his eyes had taken, and it was only a second before he found what he was looking for. There, half buried under blackened wooden planks and embers, the charred, beaten skeleton that had been his uncle's body lay spread. In death the man did not seem happy or at peace. The wet sockets of his skull stared straight up into the night sky and his jaw hung loose, fleshless face screaming at the dark and smoke above.

It was even possible to see the pointed nick along his ribs where a sword had thrust in and stolen his life.

With a snap Raz could audibly hear, the slope his mind had been clinging from tipped over, and he plunged into a swirling ocean of rage and fear and pain. Falling to his knees, he dropped the staff and clutched at his face, his entire body shaking as it was bathed in the mixed waves of the night cold and fire's heat. Images flashed through his mind, crashing over and drowning him. His mother and father, Jarden, Tolman and Prida and their child, Sameyl and his family, Ahna…

Ahna.

Raz shuddered and stopped moving, his hands over his face, eyes staring into the fire from between his fingers.

Ahna. Ahna was gone. Her body was there, somewhere, hidden in the flames. His little sister, his favorite person in the world, was dead.

They were all dead.

Raz threw back his head and screamed at the night, claws digging into the back of his skull until he bled. To a one every man, woman, and child in the vicinity who heard it caught their breath, and they watched in horrified fascination through the fires as the terrible black silhouette that was Raz i'Syul Arro rose to its feet, wings spread wide.

And then he was gone, a flickering darkness that disappeared like the smoke curling in the air around them.

IX

"Where once the artisans and merchants of the fringe cities were regarded as noncitizens, in the last century their growing importance to the economic balance of the desert cultures has granted many both wealth and position. The market districts of Miropa and Acrosia, for example, are larger than the upper- and middle-class quarters of either city put together. Sadly, they will remain ever dwarfed by the derelict shacktowns of both..."

—*The Cienbal*, by Adolûs Fenn

The blacksmith's shop was hot and unfamiliar, barely more than a heavy wooden roof held up by thick columns of dark timber. A sign hung from leaden chains over the doorway, swinging in the warm wind, embossed with the name "Jerr's Hammer" in curvy, artistic lettering. The air tasted of soot and sweat and metal, and even at this earliest hour of the day, as the Sun only just began to peek over the horizon to the east, three apprentices were rushing about, feeding the fires and filling cooling barrels with fresh water.

Raz stood in the frame of the entrance, an open space where there might have been a wall that had either been removed or simply never built. He said nothing, Jarden's cracked and beaten staff at his side, eyes following the bustling apprentices until one took notice of him and stopped dead. The boy, maybe ten years old, took in the blood-spattered figure wide-eyed. His gaze lingered on the dried darkness that caked Raz's hands and lined his mouth before glancing down at the staff and the leather satchel hanging from one shoulder.

Then the boy rushed to the far corner of the shop where an older man stood working at a bench, his back to the entrance. He was a hulkish figure, bald with broad shoulders and thick arms tanned from years spent over the forge. He looked up when the apprentice tugged on the hem of his leather apron and pointed, and Raz saw the gray eyes of a born and bred desert dweller shining above a thick black beard. They hardly blinked at the sight of him.

"Sethle, run for the surgeon," Raz heard the smith whisper urgently, and the boy took off at a sprint. The man himself hurried forward.

"Raz i'Syul," he said, wiping his blackened hands on a dirty rag. "Nay a common figure 'round these parts. ya' all right, lad?"

Raz blinked. He looked the man up and down. Despite his size, the smith was still a head shorter than him.

"… Do I know you?" he asked quietly. The man must have heard something in that question, because he halted his approach.

"Nay, boy, but who doesn't know you?" he said cautiously. "But I guess it's rude a' me not to introduce meself. Allihmad Jerr, at your service." He made a fist over his heart and bowed briefly.

Raz nodded slowly, not even following Jerr's movements. Instead he looked up to take in the three forges that burned along the back wall. There was a long moment of silence.

"Er… can I do somethin' for ya'?" Master Jerr asked, scratching at his beard. "What happened? ya' need help?"

The atherian looked demented. Blood streaked and splattered his ripped tunic. His arms were bruised and cut, and he had a nasty gash across his right shoulder that looked like a knife wound.

He didn't even seem to notice. Nor did he seem to care that his claws and teeth were stained reddish-black.

Raz nodded, his gaze not leaving the hot glow of the fires.

"… A weapon… I need a weapon, a proper one. She told me… Mama told me to come here. Said it was the best."

"And she'd be right 'bout that," the smith said, braving another step forward. "But you ain't lookin' like you need a weapon, lad. Ya' look like you need a bed. Just come sit until Sethle gets on back. He's off to get the surgeon and—"

"No."

Jerr started, cut off in the middle of his sentence. Quick as the wind Raz was in front of him, shadow flickering against the roof of the shop, twisting into something demonic.

"But look at yourself, lad. You need…"

"No," Raz said again, his voice no longer halting, the look on his face suddenly clear and sharp. He slung the leather satchel off his shoulder, emptying its contents on the ground. A score of broken sword blades and abandoned knives fell to the floor, and Raz kneeled beside them. With the end of Jarden's staff he scratched an outline in the dirt. When he was done he laid the staff down beside the image and stood up.

"Use these." He gestured to the clutter on the ground. Then he pointed at the picture. "Make me that."

Jerr looked down, studying the objects for a moment, and then the sketch. It was a long moment before he looked up again.

There was a hesitation as the man's eyes traced the bloody lines of

Raz's hands, mouth, and wounds.

But, in the end, he nodded.

"Two weeks," he said, motioning for one of the apprentices to come and collect the objects from the floor. "Come back in a fortnight, and you'll have your blade, boy."

Twin prongs—if you could call them that, each one two hand-lengths long, a hand-width wide—and a hand-length apart. They had a gentle curve about them, a delicate sway in their molding starting from their tips downward, moving out, then in, then out again before joining sharply at the base. Every outside edge was honed to a killing whet, as well as inside the scimitar curve at the top of each blade, but apart from that the inner surfaces of the U-shaped spearhead were dull and wide enough to pin a man's neck against a wall. The metal was a thumb-width thick where it hadn't been folded down to an edge.

It would pierce as well as a lance, parry as efficiently as a sword, and slash as savagely as a battle-ax.

Jarden's staff itself had been modified. Not only at the end, where the antler-like blades were fused to a steel cap, but along the length as well. Black-dyed leather wrappings formed grips along the bleached-white wood. The far end, originally crowned with bronze, was now weighed down by a heavy point, slim but dense and sharp, serving to add both balance and bite to the design.

As a whole the weapon was over seven feet in length from tip to tip. It would rise several inches above Raz's head for now, but that would change in time, he knew.

"I've named it a dviassegai," Jerr said, watching Raz run a claw over the wood and contour the inside of the blades. "It means 'twin-headed' in old desert, apparently."

Raz didn't respond. Instead he gripped the two leather handles farthest from each other and lifted the weapon from the table. It was still top-heavy, despite the hefty pointed counterweight.

He would get used to it.

"Melted down all the stuff you gave us, jus' like ya' wanted," the man continued, standing off to the side as Raz examined the spearheads closer. "There wasn't enough steel there, but the alloys we added'll only make it stronger. The hard part was hollowin' out the stave. We had to take the caps off and borrow one a' them four-foot drills they use for shavin' out long flutes. Almost gave up on tha' more than once, I tell ya'. The center's steel now, though. All soldered together into one piece. I'll stake my shop on the fact tha' you're the only person I'll ever know who could pick it up alone without fallin' over."

Raz nodded, hoisting the weapon up. It was indeed heavy, even for him, but he'd get stronger. He had years to get stronger. Satisfied, he let the weighted tip rest on the floor, pulling the leather pouch from around his back. From it he drew the last thing left inside, a heavy sack of coins he'd taken from what little had been left of Crom Ayzenbas' thin body, and handed it to the smith. Then he returned to examining the bladed end.

"What did you call it?"

They were the first words he'd spoken since arriving at the shop, taking Jerr aback.

"A—a dviassegai," the smith stammered, pulling out a handful of gold crowns from the sack while Raz continued to scrutinize the blades. He stood there, staring at his own disfigured reflection in the steel for a second more. Finally, Raz pulled the empty leather pouch over the spearhead and turned away toward the night outside.

"Oy!" Master Jerr yelled after him, holding up the coin sack from which he'd taken his payment. "You've given me too much, lad!"

But Raz didn't turn around, and the smith watched as the boy pulled the fur-lined hood of his cloak up over his serpentine head. Then he was gone, disappearing into the shadows of an alley, the dviassegai slung across one shoulder.

X

"There is only one absolute law amongst our order, but this law will be followed unconditionally: to kill is to steal away the gift that Laor has granted us. It is not our right as His children to throw back in His face that which is most precious to Him, and that which He has given us. Nor can we knowingly perform an act which directly results in death. Follow these ideals, and you will be welcomed with open arms amongst people of all faiths, not just the Laorin. Do not... and we will Break you."

—Eret Ta'hir, High Priest of Cyurgi' Di

Syrah looked over her shoulder, back along the tree-lined road they'd been following for the last four days. It had been just over two weeks since their flight from Karth, and they'd crossed the marked border between the southern and northern lands only hours ago. Her face had healed well with some help from Talo's gifts, and she'd repaired and cleaned her robes as soon as they were clear of the city.

Memories, though, were not so easily mended.

With each passing day the air was growing cooler, and soon they would have to start wearing the thin fur coats they each had packed away in their satchels. Even so, the feeling of the oppressive desert sun lingered on Syrah's skin. She could sense the hot wind and the blowing sands as though they'd followed her into the evergreen groves of the North.

And she remembered the shadows of the abandoned hut, the figures of the men, and the brief moments of brutal combat that had climaxed her visit to the southern lands.

"Something on your mind?"

Syrah jumped. Talo had dropped back to walk beside her, his blue eyes set before him, one mammoth hand on the strap of the bag slung over his shoulder.

She hesitated. "... Raz i'Syul," she said after a moment.

Talo nodded, his steel staff hitting the dirt path with a dull *thunk* every other step. It hadn't been hard to find out who Syrah's rescuer had been, and where he'd come from. Apparently no other atherian—an odd reptilian people Talo had only ever heard of—had ever become so intricately woven into civilized society.

"They usually just make for good slaves" was the common brush-off he'd gotten when he'd had a moment to ask around.

"The boy will be fine," Talo told her reassuringly, resting a hand on her shoulder. "It's clear he can take care of himself, isn't it?"

Syrah nodded, looking at the ground now and kicking a stone with her booted foot. The sun was less abusive this far north, and clouds weren't so rare. The wide hood and thin veil that had protected her sensitive eyes in the desert had been replaced by a simple leather traveler's cloak hung comfortably over her shoulders.

"The atherian is a capable fighter," Talo told her finally, lengthening his stride to catch up to Jofrey and Reyn, "and he's clearly not stupid if he urged you to get out of Karth. Laor forgive him for the lives cut short by his hand, but praise him for his head and heart. The boy is a survivor, Syrah. Don't go wasting your time in worrying. Wherever he is, whatever he's doing, he'll be all right in the end."

862 v.S.

I

"Let him be our weapon. We have all the knives we need in the dark. Let him be our sword in the light. Raz i'Syul will prune our dead weight and, like the Dramion sea hydras of myth, we will be born again stronger for every head he cuts off."

—Imaneal Evony, Mahsadën šef

Ahna cut through the air in a wide arc. Raz dropped low, spinning and catching one of his opponents right above the knee. The dviassegai's blade split through the man's boiled leather like parchment, biting into bone and flesh. Barely losing momentum, Ahna carried through, severing the limb. Screams echoed in the dark chamber as Raz stood, still turning. Ahna came around with another heavy swipe at a second one of the group. The man ducked, smiling at his own cleverness.

His grin was still frozen on his face when Raz twisted, bringing the dviassegai close, and speared him through the throat with her pointed tip, pinning the man to the wooden column behind him.

Prying the weapon free, Raz let the body fall to the ground with a *thud* and turned to face the three left standing. Two men and a woman, none of them looking very happy with their predicament despite the nice odds.

Maybe it was due to the five already dead, scattered in a ragged circle on the larder floor around Raz's feet.

All three were still armed, their swords held in both hands, eyeing him nervously. Almost uncaringly Raz met their gaze, resting Ahna's point on the ground. The hood of his white robes had fallen back during the fight, and he regarded the three of them calculatingly, the sunset-red skin of his ears spread wide and menacing. The metal armor that encased his left arm gleamed in the light of the oil lamps hanging from the low ceiling. Leather manica wrappings covered his right forearm and right thigh, stretched tight and firm. His left leg was shielded with steel plate mail, extending from the bottom of his hip all the way to his ankle, and his right lower shin was fit with a light iron guard. Heavy gauntlets gloved both hands, each finger tipped with a steel claw Raz had always thought completely unnecessary. His own claws worked just fine for tearing through armor, cloth, and flesh.

Master Jerr had been insistent, though...

"This ain't yer business, scaly."

Raz's eyes shifted to the man who'd spoken. He stood in the middle of the group, and seemed to have plucked courage from somewhere because he was edging forward, sword still held high.

"I'm paid to make it my business," Raz told him coolly, extending his crest so that it rose above his head. All of them glanced up fearfully. "It's simple: you're here, I'm here... you die."

"We can pay ya'!" the woman to the left squeaked. She was shaking from head to toe and couldn't have been more than eighteen or nineteen years old.

The rings are recruiting young, now, Raz thought sadly.

"Thank you for the offer," he said, "but I don't break contracts."

In a flash he leapt forward, dropping Ahna to his side. Her lower point knocked the sword from the middle man's hand, gashing his wrist. Before he could so much as flinch in response, the dviassegai's ax-like blades slashed upwards diagonally, catching him below the jaw.

The greater part of his head spun a fair ways through the air before landing and rolling across the dirty floor.

The swing carried through, and Ahna's head crushed into the wooden ceiling, sinking in. Letting her hang there, Raz dropped again to avoid a desperate two-handed horizontal swing from the girl. Drawing the long gladius from over his shoulder and the short-handled war ax from where it was looped in his belt, he shifted from his crouch and pounced. Knocking the woman to the ground, he felt his sword blade pierce her leather jerkin, slipping between her ribs before severing the arteries above her heart.

"*Don't kill me! Don't kill...* don't... d—"

The words died on her lips in a bubble of blood.

There was a strangled yell. Raz spun to see the last man charging him, sword held high above his head. Letting the blow fall, Raz's hand flicked up at the last second, catching the blade in the crook of the ax and dragging it outward, away from him. The tip of the sword sparked as it clanged against the stone floor, pulling the man off balance. Raz's gladius flashed at the exposed neck, the long razor edge cutting clean.

He watched another head hit the floor, the body flopping beside it, sword clattering away into one of the far corners of the room.

The light of the lamps glimmered. Eerie reflections twitched in the black blood pooled about the eight bodies scattered around the basement. Raz listened, tasting the air and smelling the room, searching every shadow.

Then, satisfied that the fight was over, he flicked the gladius blade clean, spattering blood across the wall, and sheathed it over his shoulder before sliding the ax back into its loop.

"Bayl!" he yelled, grasping Ahna's white handle with one hand and wrenching her loose from the ceiling. With a crunch of splintering wood the dviassegai fell heavily into his grasp. "It's done. Get out here!"

There was a snuffling, then a grunt of exertion. After a moment a stooped, fat rat of a man crawled out from the stack of wine barrels he'd been cowering behind. As he shuffled into the light, Raz's snout wrinkled in distaste.

Bayl Vyzen was the kind of slum runner who didn't take baths even though he could afford them. In his younger days he'd done well dealing in ragroot and other opiates, even managing to put together a small band of street muscle that contracted out as bodyguards and smash-and-grab thieves. All that had since fallen apart, but a little power went a long way in these dingier parts of town. Bayl now worked as a coordinator for one of the few root distributors left in Miropa that wasn't under the control of the Mahsadën.

And—unfortunately—the pungent, sour smell of his history in the industry always seemed to cling to him.

"By the Sun," Bayl wheezed, his beady eyes wide, taking in the room. "If I hadn't seen it myself, Monster… by the Sun…"

"Your problem has been handled, as agreed," Raz said curtly, pulling the leather sack that covered Ahna's blades in public from where he'd tucked it into his belt. "Pay up. And two extra crowns for wanting to witness."

"You only said one extra!" Bayl squawked.

"You only said there'd be six of them."

Bayl swelled, about to protest, but Raz stared him down. Almost at once the man deflated. Grumbling, he opened the drawstring of the fat purse at his side and pulled out a handful of gold coins.

"You charged me extra the first time, too," he mumbled angrily, dropping the money into the leather palm of Raz's gauntlet. "Why I hired you again is beyond me."

"Because you wanted the guarantee," Raz told him simply, counting the gold. Bayl had tried to dupe him the last time, assuming Raz was as dumb as most mercenaries.

He'd been smart enough not to do it again.

Raz dropped the coins into the pouch at his side and pulled the white hood of his thin robes back over his head. He cut a frightening figure, even with the blades of his dviassegai covered and his other weapons sheathed, and Bayl shivered.

"You know where to find me if you've got more work." Raz turned and made for the stairway to the upper floors. Bayl nodded, scratching his head at the bodies he now had to figure out how to dispose of.

By the time he looked up again, the door to the house had closed shut with a *bang* above.

On the stoop of Bayl's home, Raz breathed in the hot air with a mix of masked relief and distaste. He didn't like cramped spaces. They made him feel limited and trapped, although he'd never admit so aloud. On the other hand, it was early summer and—though Miropa's slums were a far reach from the Cienbal—the blistering heat bothered even Raz when he was in full gear.

A hot breeze tugged at the thin fabric of his hood, blowing the cloak around his feet and bare chest. He let his wings relax a little, catching the gust so that it ran through them as he turned and followed the road east. The wind felt good, and he fought the temptation to spread them and let the dark membranes breath. The White Sands, the tavern he'd taken up permanent residence in, wasn't a far walk away, but he lived on a delicate balance. It was no good tipping it in one direction or the other by scaring the few people who saw him on a day-to-day basis.

If you could call these poor souls people...

Raz always looked, always forced himself to see the slummers, the runners and beggars. Too many people ignored them as it was and, while it was generally bad news to catch a slum dweller's eye, most had enough sense to leave him alone. A few were even friendly, or would have been if Raz had let them.

Man just wasn't worth trusting.

But he could still feel a pang for their predicament, all things considered. Over the last seven years the situation in the South had gone from bad to worse to downright ugly. Even Miropa had fallen to the thieves and slavers, and in a few months the world had changed.

And not for the best.

Crime was everywhere, in front of everyone's nose, and there weren't many people who did much about it. The Mahsadën, the unseen society whose grasp over the "official" governing bodies was an open secret, was turning on its history. It had risen from the worst parts of the cities, growing out from the secret brothels and root dens and grimy slums. As the smartest and vilest criminals realized their lives were a hundred times easier if they made truce and consolidated their power, so the trouble began.

Now, though, the Mahsadën seemed to want nothing to do with the trash it had risen from. Whole families were dragged out of their homes by the city guard and arrested on falsified or exaggerated charges before being hauled off to the Cages. Since forced slavery was still technically illegal—the only reason the South wasn't overrun by atherian slaves, like Perce and the Seven Cities—they couldn't be sold outright. Men and women had to willingly accept their "civil repayment," promising servitude as punishment for the crimes they had been found guilty of. More often than not the prisoners fought back, refusing to accept the terms of their "release," spending days screaming their innocence to deaf ears.

But nothing tore at a person's spirit faster than being left in the broiling sunlight for days on end, often without food or water and certainly without privacy. People locked in the Cages weren't even allowed a bucket to shit in, much less a blanket to keep warm when the temperatures dropped below freezing at night.

Raz grit his teeth, eyes on the road, Ahna snug in her habitual resting place over his shoulder. The Mahsadën were the blackest of the black, and he hated the work he did with them. Unfortunately, almost all his contracts came from the society through direct and indirect channels. Personal employers like Bayl were a welcome rarity.

On the other hand, the Mahsadën paid well and were familiar and comfortable with his one limitation, his calling card: "death deserved." The men and women he hunted, the marks he was paid to attend to, had earned their sentence one way or the other. It was a drawn line that was never crossed. One of their less popular šef, the Mahsadën's overseers, had tried to trick him once. Raz had refused any of their work for a year.

But that was only after he'd found and hung the would-be employer by his own entrails from the topmost balcony of his sprawling four-story home.

As far as he knew, none of the Mahsadën had made to fool him again. They were, if nothing else, accepting of his conditions. Why not, after all? It worked well for them. Some no one making claims and boasts they shouldn't in the local pubs? The city guard could handle that. Small-timers trying to get ahead of the truce and make a name for themselves? Common assassins were ten a copper in any alley of the city.

But when a true threat raised its head, the game changed. When a competitor proved themself dangerous, when one of the šef climbed too high and grabbed for too much, when treachery needed to be rooted out within the society itself—well, in those cases the Mahsadën liked to send a message. A kind of blanket statement that said, *We own this city. We own you.*

Raz i'Syul Arro, the atherian sellsword—over seven dark feet of lean muscle, cruel claws, and pale, sharp teeth with a grudge—was exactly the kind of message they liked to send.

It irked Raz to no end that he had to work with the scum. Just thinking about it made him clench Ahna's shaft so tightly his hand hurt. If it were up to him he would have wiped them all out years ago. He loved nothing more than the idea of cutting the shadow government from the heart of the city, thrilling in the act of whittling them one by one till nothing was left.

Sadly, it was an abandoned dream.

The problem was that the rings simply grew too fast for such treatment, working as a pack of separate factions rather than as a single whole. Even if he *could* wipe out the Mahsadën in Miropa, the other cities would survive, and within a month a new ring would be in place, running things as usual.

Raz cursed under his breath.

Still, his uncle had once told him that to rip out the weeds you have to start by kneeling in the dirt.

Raz looked up from the road, the metal claws of his free hand tracing the iron chain that still ran from the bottom of his ear to his nostril. It had been ripped out twice in fights in the last few years, but each time Raz had found someone to replace it.

He would always find someone to replace it.

Abruptly something hard knocked into the side of his foot, and Raz paused to look down. A fist-sized wooden ball lay in the dust, crudely chiseled until it was passable for a sphere. Bending down to pick it up, he turned it over in his hand. There was a sizable crack in it, like it had been bounced off a wall a few too many times, but it still held together well enough. Standing up, Raz looked around.

He found them hiding in the shadows a dozen yards away, a boy and girl, maybe ten or eleven years old. Haggard things with scraggly hair, they looked to be made more out of dirt than flesh and bone. The instant they realized they'd been seen, they vanished, ducking behind the wall they'd been peering around.

Jenza and Iro Zannyz watched the lizard-man with a mixture of fear and excitement. The Monster of Karth was huge, a beast that could probably have touched the sky if he'd wanted to. His giant two-headed spear rested on his shoulder, its evil curved blades hidden under a leather sack. They watched him bend down and pick up the ball that had gotten away from them as they played. For a few seconds he looked at it, rolling the wood in his fearsome metal claws.

Mother had told them to stay away from the sarydâ. The Cienbal mercenaries were supposed to be bad, bad men, men who'd come pouring out of the desert when the nomadic trading clans had fallen apart. They killed for money and for fun, nothing more. She had told them that they didn't have a problem with murdering children either, and that the sarydâ ate little boys and girls that got too close to them.

But the Monster didn't look like he was going to eat them. He looked like he certainly *could*, but not like he necessarily wanted to. Jenza and Iro huddled behind the corner of the hovel, safely hidden. Maybe if they were lucky he would leave their ball when he went. Mercenaries and sellswords couldn't have much use for toys, after all, and it was the only plaything they had left that Mother hadn't had to sell for bread...

And then the Monster's golden eyes looked right at them.

Jenza and Iro both squeaked and dodged back behind the wall. For a full minute they stood there, plastered against the rotting wood of the house, their heartbeats heavy and frantic. They listened for the sound of grinding dirt that meant the sarydâ was coming to eat them.

Nothing. Maybe they were safe after—

Thump.

Both of them jumped as something came rolling past their feet, stopping squarely by Jenza's bare toes. The pair squealed again, stopping suddenly when they realized what it was.

Their ball had come back to them.

Being the older one, Jenza knew she had to be brave. Still, it took her a moment to bend down and pick it up. When she did, though, she realized that it felt heavier than usual.

Then Iro gasped, his eyes on the back of the toy.

Slowly Jenza turned it over in her little hands. There was the crack they'd made playing against the wall of the local whorehouse a few weeks ago. Wedged in it, tight enough so they wouldn't fall out but loose enough to pry free, were a pair of shiny gold crowns.

By the time they peeked back around the corner, the Monster of Karth was little more than a faint blotch of white disappearing down the dust-blown street.

II

The din and chatter that usually reverberated inside the White Sands' common room died swiftly when Raz ducked under the low overhang of the tavern entrance. A few of the regulars gave him polite nods when he passed, making his way across the ale-stained floor toward the staircase at the back of the room. He ignored everyone, eyes set resolutely forward. This was his little haven, as much of a shithole as it was. He didn't like to be bothered in general but—considering this was as close to a home as he'd had in years—Raz always went out of his way to avoid any kind of interaction in and around the inn.

Miropa, though far gone from the city it had been even a short decade ago, was still the wealthiest of the southern municipalities. Its citizens could afford the risk of building up rather than out and, while the White Sands was nothing compared to some of the lumbering marble towers in the center of the city, its three half-timber stories were nothing to scoff at.

Especially bearing in mind its location smack-dab in the middle of one of Miropa's poorest districts.

Raz's room was on the top floor, per his request, and the biggest available. It was two rooms, in fact. There was always one šef or another who didn't appreciate the work he did for the Mahsadën, and a few years back a pair of hired cutthroats had tailed him home from a job. The ensuing fight left the two men in more than thrice as many pieces, and had torn a massive hole through the wall between Raz's and the adjoining room.

The tavern's matron hadn't been happy about it, but when he offered to pay the rent for both rooms *and* front the masonry costs of removing the remainder of the wall, she'd given in. Business was too slim to turn down the crowns of a permanent resident, even if that resident was Raz i'Syul Arro.

As he climbed the stair, Raz couldn't help but smirk at the voices picking up again the moment he was out of sight. He didn't mind the effect he had on people. Being frightening meant he was taken seriously, and only idiots and drunks didn't take Raz seriously.

Sadly, the idiots and drunks more often than not outnumbered the intelligent and sober these days.

At the top of the stairs, Raz reached into the leather pouch at his side, fumbling through the crowns he'd won until his fingers found the room key. Pulling it out, he unlocked his door quickly and stepped inside, locking it again behind him.

Breathing easy for the first time since he'd left that morning, Raz propped Ahna against the wall by the door and looked around.

Even expanded, the room could barely be considered large. About twenty feet long and ten or so wide, it was spacious only because Raz had stripped it of any furnishings he'd deemed impractical. He'd had the beds removed from both rooms. Instead, he'd claimed the most outside corner for a bedroll with a half-dozen books piled next to it, a number of dirty candlesticks partially melted into the wood floor at its head. The dressers he'd kept, one for his clothes and light gear, the other for the armor he commissioned from Master Jerr. There was a table, too, set up beside the door, and Raz drew his gladius, ax, and long-knife, placing them all carefully beside the bowl of water and dirty rag he would clean them with later. His pouch he tossed on his bedroll, pulling the white cape from around his shoulders and moving to the dressers on the far wall by one of the room's three shuttered windows.

Flipping the latch of the first wardrobe, he pulled it open to reveal a half-dozen outfits, mostly plain and inconspicuous, only two richly colored and specially tailored for those rare times he had formal business in the inner parts of the city. Hanging his silk cape, Raz bent down and pulled a thin wooden box from the bottom corner, sliding it across the floor toward his bedroll.

His armor only took minutes to unclasp. Allihmad Jerr's work was always beyond perfect and—as one of the few humans Raz trusted—the man received all of his orders, supplying nearly everything he needed to work with. Opening the second wardrobe, Raz set his mail, gauntlets, and the rest of his plating carefully on the shelves he'd built inside for easy access. Carefully he hung his leather wrappings before shutting the wooden doors and latching them closed again.

With nothing on now but his loose cloth britches, Raz extended all eighteen feet of his wings. The muscles of his back, sore all the time from being taut and folded, pulled and relaxed, and he groaned in relief. As he stretched he pressed up against the flat ceiling he so passionately hated, barely a foot above his head. More than once he'd contemplated asking the matron if he could tear *it* down, too.

"Better," he grunted to no one in particular, crossing the room and rolling his head, wincing as his long neck popped. Jerr's armor was comfortable and efficient, but even a man so talented as the old smith couldn't take the weight out of steel.

Sitting cross-legged on his bedroll, Raz picked up the slim box he'd taken from the dresser and pulled it open. Inside were his grays, a carefully folded shirt, pants, and cowl, all colored the same mottled black and slate, woven from the same thick, form-fitting wool. It wasn't ideal material for its purpose, sadly. It got caught on edges and rough surfaces and itched around the exposed scars on his wrists, but it was the only material that worked. It hadn't been news to Raz that the cold affected him more profoundly than it did men, but only once he'd started having to venture out during the frigid southern nights *without* his usual swath of thick furs and layers did he realize to what extent the icy air got to him. His first contract, long before he'd started accepting jobs from the Mahsadën, had almost been botched for the mere reason that Raz hadn't managed to stay warm. The cold slowed him down, making him sluggish and tired, and it was more luck than skill that had ended the life of the smuggler he'd been hunting that night.

Mychal used to joke that Raz was "a whole new kind of cold-blooded killer."

Raz frowned at the thought of his cousin, but pushed it aside, unfolding the dark clothes and laying them down by the bed. Turning over, one wing unfurled to drape over his body, his tail snaking to curl around him. Needing little sleep was a blessing considering he worked all hours of the day, but it was still a good idea to catch it when he could. He already had another job lined up for the evening, and the Sun would start setting in only a few short hours. Raz closed his eyes, letting the limited light of the room filter in through the dark-red skin of his wing, and willed sleep to come.

Soon after, old habits found him drifting off with one hand around the handle of the throwing knife he kept under the corner of the mat.

A blue half Moon hung in the midnight sky when Raz stepped out of the alley shadows, turning along the brighter streets of the market districts. Behind him the body he dragged scraped and bumped over the cobbled stone, leaving a trail of smeared blood to harden in the cold night air. Ahna wasn't with him, as was usual on jobs like this. She was heavy and cumbersome, problematic considerations when it came to stalking the evening darkness.

Not to mention Raz had never liked the idea of carrying his sister's namesake when he was out with the intent of murder.

Then again, it had been a long time since he'd lost any sleep over simple murder. He'd done his research. He always did before contracting with the Mahsadën. The man trailing behind him, dead eyes staring back at his own blood, was no innocent. Avon Plyth was a lower lieutenant to one of the šefs' stronger competitors, a slavemaster named Kî Orran. Orran had been smart and careful, staying in the shadows as her organization grew. She'd only made herself known recently, once she posed a decent enough threat to force the Mahsadën to take things a step at a time with her.

Killing one of her lesser officers was the first move, an unmistakable warning that Orran would either heed or ignore, at which point the next move would be made.

The hunt had been a hard one, by most standards. The šef had their spies in every corner of Miropa but—as much as the society liked the world to think they were all-seeing and all-knowing—the reality was that in a city of a half-million people it was always possible to lose yourself, at least for a time. Plyth had somehow gotten wind that something was coming for him, and he'd taken measures to vanish almost at once.

Still, it took more than a few friends willing to lie for you to keep the Monster of Karth off your scent.

It barely took Raz two hours to figure out the game. Whereas coin spent on information was generally well worth it, tonight it had been a waste. For most of the evening he'd found himself going in circles between a dozen different brothels, inns, and root dens, with nothing to show for any of it. In the end, he'd changed the rules. Plyth had a brother, Barrus, whom he was well known to be close with. Barrus, having no reason to be afraid of the Mahsadën himself, was wasting his night gambling in a tavern in the east district, the Seven-Sided Dice. Raz had found him and offered a dozen crowns for information on where his brother was hiding. He'd paid up front, all twelve gold pieces, almost half of the bounty he would collect for Avon Plyth dead. Barrus had taken the gold eagerly enough and pointed Raz in the direction of an old abandoned storehouse in the middle of the slums to the west. Raz had thanked him and taken his leave at once, turning west.

Then he'd darted into the side streets and climbed his way up to the rooftop across from the Seven-Sided Dice.

It had only taken minutes for Barrus to appear, hurrying from the tavern, swaddled in furs to ward off the cold. Looking around briefly to make sure no eyes were watching him, the man turned north.

Quiet as death, Raz tailed him roof to roof.

Plyth, it turned out, was hiding in the modest home of a distant cousin the Mahsadën's spies hadn't seemed to have found out. When Barrus rapped out some secret knock on the timber frame of the door, Raz dropped on him from above with gladius drawn. Avon opened the entrance just a crack, expecting to hear news of how the plan to mislead his hunter was turning out. Instead he'd found Raz i'Syul Arro over the twitching corpse of his brother, and he'd barely taken breath to scream before the evening's bounty was fulfilled.

Raz made sure to retrieve his dozen crowns from Barrus' body before dragging Avon out by the bloodied collar of his shirt.

Torchlight crawled around a corner ahead, and Raz flattened himself against the wall of the closest house, shoving the body unceremoniously behind a water barrel. Privately he smiled. He liked these wars the rings waged with each other. They were rare—the Mahsadën did a fair job of lassoing in all the loose ends that were or would be competition—but when they *did* come around every few years it meant one certain thing: lots of work.

Which in this case meant a lot of dead slavers.

Within a minute a half-dozen men in matching yellow and purple tunics rounded the corner, torches held high. Raz didn't even flinch as they moved closer. The city guard were entirely in the Mahsadën's pocket, the exceptions either quickly flipped or their hacked pieces left as meaty fodder for the pig sellers along the market roads. He watched them march, feeling his temper flare with the light of their torches. They were nothing but a ceremonial unit now, a vestigial offshoot of a government that had at one time held its own.

Now, he thought, watching the group yell and halt around the dead man's blood, *you are the perfect symbol of what once was and what is now.*

One of the men—their captain, judging by the triangular gold patch on his left breast—knelt down by the faded trail and followed it to the side. They were only a couple paces away, so to a one the guards all jumped when the torchlight fell on Raz. He could have avoided them, probably even cut them to ribbons before they knew he was there, but it was the little things about his work that made him enjoy it so much.

Like the reactions.

159

He watched them, smirking and imagining the figure he must have cut, casually leaning against the wall with arms crossed, bedecked and hooded in gray and black layers that probably made him hard to see even in the light. The gladius strapped to his back stuck out over his right shoulder, the length of rope around his chest casting twisted shadows like a snake. There was a tense moment, every eye on him.

Then the captain stood up, shifting his torch so that Raz fell into darkness again.

"Forward," he said over his shoulder, and at once the rest of the patrol started moving again, acting as though the crimson splatters at their feet didn't exist. Turning back in Raz's direction, the captain nodded once, then hurried to catch up to his squad.

Reaching down, Raz pulled the body back out into the street, his eyes trailing the men down the road.

Nothing I can do.

He always had to remind himself of that. The world was beyond saving.

Starting off in the opposite direction, Raz lifted the corpse and tossed it over his shoulder, grimacing at the touch of the dead arms flopping against his back. The run-in had put him behind schedule. Picking up the pace, he hurried, making his way toward center district.

Miropa's design was more efficient than that of most cities, especially compared to the likes of Karth. Though it was still cleanly divided by class and wealth, its sectors had a structured shape to them, each centered around an open square with roads radiating outwards in all directions. In the city slums these "squares" were little more than wide patches of dirt the children played in to stay out of their parents' way, but in the market and the wealthier districts they were cobbled and clean.

And huge.

It was five minutes before Raz turned the corner onto a main road, and another ten before he stepped out onto the square itself. Nearly two hundred paces across, the circular plaza had once been a favored spot for trade and exchange. Raz could remember setting up shop with his family not a dozen yards from where he stood, in fact, shouting and waving out into the crowd. Even during the summer the place used to be packed with people out enjoying the days, mixing with vendors publicizing their goods at the top of their lungs.

Now? Now it was all gone, and the monstrosities that replaced the crowds loomed like iron skeletons out of the night.

Spaced evenly near the center of the wide circle, three rectangular pens rose straight from the stony ground, ghostly visible in the Moon's light. About eight feet high, they were ten feet wide and two dozen long, built close together so that the shade of the surrounding buildings never once reached their edges except for the very extremes of dawn and dusk. The slim iron bars, spaced barely a hand-width apart so that not even infants could slip through, were bent and dented where prisoners had attempted desperate escapes.

When they were full, the sobbing screams and pleas from the Cages could be heard from nearly anywhere in the district.

Tonight, mercifully, they were quiet. Two small forms were huddled in the corner of one pen, but even as Raz approached he knew they were too still, too silent. In the quiet of the night he'd have been able to hear their breathing a dozen yards back, but there was nothing. Again he forced himself to look, stepping into the circle. Again he forced himself to bear witness, to remind himself why he did the work he did, why he'd turned into this person he'd become.

A child. One of them was a child no older than ten…

Swallowing back the raging whirlwind of emotions that ripped through his chest at the sight, Raz turned away. There was one less head-trader in the world tonight because of him. Maybe it would mean one less body in this very spot tomorrow.

The Cages were eerie in the dark, torturous hollow enclosures that seemed to emanate fear and pain. Raz clenched his teeth and looked up at the Moon, offering a brief prayer that she would rush the poor souls who'd died miserably here up into Her Stars.

Then he dropped the body and got to work.

Lifting the rope off his shoulder, he moved to the closest of the pens, pulling a key he'd lifted from one of the Cage guard out of his pocket. The lock opened with a *click*, and Raz stepped in, instantly uncomfortable in the confined space. Brushing the feeling aside, he reached up, looped the rope over one of the bars, and pulled the end down. Tying it into a noose, he let it hang there, moving back to drag the body inside.

It was quick work to get the noose around the dead man's neck, and after hauling him up till his head lolled about a foot from the top of the Cage, Raz tied the rope to one of the side bars. For a minute he watched the body spin in a slow circle in the middle of the enclosure, suspended above the ground.

"Sun burn you," he spat before stepping out, not bothering to lock the door behind him. Throwing the key aside, he walked away without looking back. The Cage guard had already been paid off to arrive late to their shift in the morning. The first people to see the body would be locals and traders, and from there word would spread fast. No one would dare cut it down. Everyone knew better than that, and if they didn't they'd best learn damn fast.

The Mahsadën liked to teach by example.

Pulling his hood down, Raz let his ears spread, welcoming the brief breeze that dipped down off the surrounding rooftops and into the street. It was a surprisingly warm night, more cool than frigid. Raz was quiet, walking the wide route he'd mapped out for himself. Stopping by a public water trough, he dipped his hands in, scrubbing the remaining blood from his skin. He watched the dark swirls dissipate in the ripples of his own reflection, brooding.

The Mahsadën had won again.

He couldn't understand his own thought process. He *hated* them, hated every one of them. He'd killed men barely old enough to be called men just for being a *part* of the underground rings. He'd hunted them, cutting them down one after another in the name of the innocents whose lives they'd ruined.

So how did he justify his own actions now?

He was working under different conditions. That was what it always came down to. He was powerless to wipe out the growing beast that was the Mahsadën, powerless to even limit it or tie it down. He'd tried when the rings had first started to bind together. He'd killed more men in a handful of weeks than he could count, drunk on blood and the desperate need to keep the slavers from taking over.

And he'd achieved nothing.

No, he thought, watching Her Stars shimmer across the water's surface. *I achieved something. I got them to notice me.*

At first the rings had treated him like exactly what he was: a threat. They'd sent soldiers and assassins, hired killers and anyone looking to make a crown. They'd even tried to send true sarydâ, he'd heard, but the desert bandits turned mercenaries had been familiar with him and his family long before Raz had become a problem for the underworld.

Each and every one had firmly refused the contract.

It was then, probably, that the Mahsadën—for they'd already become a single group when they approached him—sought him out on different terms. They offered him everything imaginable: money, property, titles, power. They'd even offered him whores, human women, something he'd found abhorrently amusing.

Even if he'd been attracted to them, he'd asked, what was he supposed to do with them?

The Mahsadën messengers all returned to their employers with the same things: a polite decline of all offers, and the hands and heads of the enforcers sent to guard them.

It was then that one of the šef finally recognized what it was that Raz was after, and offered him exactly that.

"Work for us," the man had exclaimed pompously, bravely paying Raz a personal visit, "and we'll *give* you the coin and supplies to hunt whoever you like. Kill whoever you like. *Do* whatever you like. We have common enemies, I think you'll find. An infinite number, in fact. Deal with them, and you'll be getting paid to do what it is you do best."

The next day, small pieces of the man had been sent to each of his colleagues in expensive silk-wrapped gift baskets.

But the offer had stuck in Raz's head, flitting around in his thoughts like an angry fly. A week later the Mahsadën had received Raz's reply, accepting the terms of the arrangement.

And now, after three long years, he was stuck.

"You didn't really think it through, did you?" he asked his now-still reflection with an angry snort. For a second the cold breeze of the desert night picked up again, ruffling the skin of his wings.

No, came the reply, like it had ridden the wind to his ear.

What he'd expected to happen differently, though, Raz wasn't sure. Maybe he'd thrown himself in with the mindset that the accord would bring him closer to the center of the organization. Or maybe he'd just limited his vision to what was happening directly in front of him, refusing to acknowledge the consequences of opening certain doors. When he killed, whenever he killed, he wiped another monster off the map. A murderer dead, a rapist slaughtered, a slaver butchered. One by one they fell.

What he'd always willed himself to be blind to was the beast lumbering in his wake, devouring the piling bodies and growing stronger with every kill he made.

There was nothing Raz could do. He'd entered this vicious circle of his own accord. He'd stoked the fires that were the Mahsadën and watched them grow, watched until the dark flames consumed Miropa.

And now he had to live with it.

Turning away from the water, Raz kept walking, looking up into the sky. Searching, it took a moment to make them out, but he finally caught sight of the three Stars—two bright orbs sitting side by side in the sky with a tiny one resting just below them.

What would the Arros think of what he'd become? What would his mother and father have said? Ahna would have forgiven him, of course, but she'd been only eight when the rings fell on his family like wolves in the night.

She'd be what? Fifteen, sixteen now? Would I have forgiven myself then, if I knew the path I was choosing? Would I have allowed it?

That, he couldn't be so sure of.

Suddenly aware of where he was, Raz stopped again, looking around. He hadn't realized it when he'd mapped the job, but he was so close…

It had been almost a year since he'd seen them. His last visit had left a bad taste in his mouth, and he wasn't sure he could deal with it again.

Still… maybe things had changed.

Making up his mind, Raz ducked into a nearby alley. Leaping high, he caught the wooden ledge of the nearest building's second floor, swinging himself upward. It took a minute to make his way up the wall, hurdling onto the rounded roof and pausing to get his bearings.

Then he leapt over the ten-foot gap to the next building, rolling to his feet smoothly as he started to run.

She hadn't changed in the year that had passed. Her clan-chain was gone, removed not long after they'd arrived in Miropa, but she still had the bronze elder's ring piercing her eyebrow. Her hair was more white than silver, but even so Raz could only see the woman she'd been in his youth.

It made him sad, clinging there to the side of the five-story estate of a wealthy gem trader named Yvin Gors. It had been years since the shell Raz beheld now, sitting at her usual place on the balcony of the three-story home across the street, had been Grandmother Arro.

She hadn't spoken a word since the day he'd pulled her out of the burning wagon with Prida and Mychal. Their few mutual acquaintances, unaware of Raz's relationship to her, called the old woman senile and dead inside, which he was hard-pressed to deny. She always had that little half smile on her face, even in her rare moments of sleep, but her eyes were distant and empty.

There was nothing left behind them. The wise elder she'd been was long gone.

Raz's free hand curled into a fist, his white cape catching the desert wind behind him. Another thing he could do nothing about, although to be fair there was nothing anybody could do about it. When he and Mychal had still been on speaking terms, his cousin had told him he'd taken her to every physician in the city with no success. At the time, Raz hadn't doubted him.

Now, though... He wasn't so sure. The world was a different place, and Mychal was living proof that all things changed.

Raz's eyes shifted to the window directly above where the Grandmother sat looking out across the road. Light outlined the expensive diagonal glass panes, and he could barely make out Mychal's figure seated at his desk, scribbling at a bit of parchment with a feather quill.

So, dear cousin was still toiling away. It wasn't hard to guess who those papers were meant for...

Mychal's change had been progressive at first. He and Raz had had the occasional dispute about money and how the four of them lived. It was Mychal's belief that Raz's actions put them all at risk. He would argue they should be working to find an easier method of survival. They barely made by scrounging on the meager pay he had as a baker's aide and the fees Raz collected from the rare paying client. It hadn't been easy, and they'd been forced to move several times, but Mychal had wanted to look for employment with the local government.

Raz, though, forbade it.

Mychal was older, but Raz had been the one to take things over once he, his cousin, Prida, and the Grandmother had finally been able to escape Karth. He'd gotten them back on their feet, doing his best to take after his father and find them a new life.

And his decision had been final.

"Working for them would be working for the rings, Mychal!" he'd screamed the last time they'd had a bad argument. "I won't let you get that kind of blood on your hands!"

For a while he thought Mychal had forgotten about it, because the subject wasn't brought up again. Then, one day, his cousin came home announcing that he'd received employment as an adjunct accountant in the city treasury.

He'd left that night, taking the Grandmother with him.

For the next two years Raz and Mychal had remained in touch. Raz's rationale had been that he couldn't blame the man for his actions. Mychal didn't frequent the worst of the crowds, the kind of people Raz dealt with every day. He probably wasn't as aware of the reach the Mahsadën had, or the corruption he was employed by.

And then word leaked that Mychal's talent for numbers had been noted, and that his loyalties had shifted from the pseudo-legal systems to a different group altogether...

Raz hadn't spoken to his cousin since, and in the last two years he'd had to bear the whispers of how the man had risen through the ranks like fire took to a dry crop. Eventually he found out Mychal was working as the personal banker of Ergoin Sass, one of the group's most infamous— and therefore powerful—šef. Sass was responsible for the vast majority of assassination contracts that were filtered through the Mahsadën channels.

And Mychal was his right-hand man.

Not only that, but Raz's cousin had even abandoned his real name. Mychal Arro was listed as dead in the city archives, left a corpse of ash, along with the rest of his family, in the caravan fire seven years ago.

Adrion Blaeth had taken his place.

Raz could still remember the day he'd heard the news, when he'd returned to the small house he'd been hiding out in with Prida.

"No," was all the woman had been able to say, repeating it over and over again. For two days she'd refused to sleep or eat anything. Then, on the morning of the third day, she'd finally looked at him again.

"What happened, Raz?" she'd asked quietly. "Where did our family go? Where did they all go?"

With nothing to answer her with, Raz had left for a job. The next morning he'd returned to an empty house, Prida having gone without leaving so much as a note.

He hadn't looked for her.

Letting go of the roof's edge, Raz dropped a floor, catching hold of a windowsill below him. The last two floors he didn't bother stopping himself, leaping out and landing stooped on the stone before looking up. The Grandmother's eyes didn't move, didn't flinch downward from that distant place she always seemed to be looking to. Even though he was standing in the middle of the Moon-lit road, she didn't look.

It was a minute or so before Raz turned and walked away.

III

"While there are a few segregated factions of Laorin Priests and Priestesses who brave the harsh weathers of the North and travel the lands giving aid where it is needed, a majority of the faithful work out of home temples, of which there are dozens. Cyurgi' Di, the High Citadel, is by far the largest, but in total it only harbors a fraction of the faith's numbers."

—*Studying the Lifegiver*, by Carro al'Dor

The trailing line of figures could be followed for nearly half a league, a snaking thread of black against the white and gray of the snowy cliffs. At its head, four men trudged resolutely forward, careful not to tilt the wide litter rested upon their shoulders. No one wanted to disturb the body lying atop it, the man's still form surrounded by gifts of silver and gold trinkets to be carried with him into the beyond.

Talo limped along only a few steps in front of them, murmuring his prayers to Laor and using his free hand to mark the mountainous horizon with an upwards half circle, the sign of the rising sun, the sign of rebirth and new life. He had gloves of black fur to match the dyed cloak around his shoulders, and he leaned heavily on his staff as he walked. For once he ignored the pains in his knee that had gotten so much worse in the last few years. He could barely move around Cyurgi' Di comfortably now, much less make this long trek through the snow along the mountainside without some difficulty. Healing spells and rune binds had helped for a time, but there was only so much the arcane could do for any one body. Carro had offered to aid him to the Giving Grounds, but Talo refused. Carro was a good man, a kind man, with every good meaning at heart. But leading this line was something Talo had to do on his own.

Eret Ta'hir deserved to have someone who could stand on his own two feet at the front of his funeral procession.

Talo's prayers caught in his throat for a moment, but he kept moving, reaching the first of the stone steps leading up to the Grounds. Carefully he moved, glancing over his shoulder to see that Carro, Jofrey al'Sen, Ambrose Finn, and Willem Mayle started the ascent safely. From a few steps up he looked down at Eret's aged face, white hair and beard catching in the cold wind and whipping around his closed eyes. His hands were clasped over his chest, his steel staff nestled into the nook of his left elbow, as was tradition. Talo had to force himself to look away from his old mentor, keeping his gaze on the horizon while they climbed.

It took ten minutes to make it to the top of the mountain. Once he made the first step onto the great circular platform, Talo moved aside to let the litter pass. The bearers treaded carefully, not wanting to disturb the bodies and bones that lay everywhere, scattered over the stone. The Giving Grounds of Cyurgi' Di were high enough that the old Laorin funeral traditions could still be followed. Burials and cremation piers were common enough in the temples closer to the southern borders, but in the reaches of the mountains such practices were never needed. The dead were left to the elements, offered for the wind and rock and rain to take back what they had given, thus preserving Laor's gift of life in its purest form. There were thousands of them, lined in circular rows around the flat Grounds, the oldest at the edges little more than pieces of bone and tattered cloth. Even as he watched, Talo saw the wind dislodge what might have been the remains of some ancient cloak and toss them over the edge of the mountain.

It was a natural process.

But the dead were always to be remembered. In the left-most corner of where each body lay, a steel staff was hammered into the ground like a thousand silver needles pointed at the sky. There were five full rings of them, the fluid circle broken only by the path the procession took through the dead.

Carro and the others placed Eret down in the next open patch of stone, placing him beside the desiccated form of a young convert who had fallen to his death from the cliffs only the summer before. They laid the body to rest, then stepped back, falling into the ranks of mourners who'd made their way into the ring behind them.

For a long moment the Grounds were silent but for the hungry murmur of the wind, whistling through the cliffs.

"For those of you too young to remember," Talo began softly, coming to stand over the old man's body and looking into the crowd, "Eret Ta'hir will first and foremost be remembered as the High Priest of Cyurgi' Di, a great leader who even in his failing years still fought to bring Laor's light to the darkest places of this world. Despite all hardships, this man"—he motioned to Eret's body—"still leapt on the chance to do anything and everything he could, for whoever he could."

There was a general nod from the crowd, and tears ran free on more than one cheek to burn streaks in the icy wind.

"But to the rest of us," Talo continued louder, looking to Carro, who gave him a sad smile, "Eret Ta'hir was even more. He was a man always in his prime, if not physically so. He was a mentor to the most fortunate of us and, to the rest, a master they were proud to learn from. He was the incarnation of Laor's good will, and sought to live and teach by example, modeling his life in the shape of that will. We would all do well to take what we can from his great character, even as his soul is carried into Laor's embrace."

Someone sobbed from the back of the crowd.

"It is for this... for this reason"—Talo couldn't help his voice from cracking, and another muffled wail joined the first—"that I would ask something of you now. I take it upon myself to do so, because I know Eret never would. If there was anything wrong with the man, it is that in life he was too modest. I-I would... I would..."

He paused again, taking a slow breath to steady himself before continuing in a strong voice that rose above the wind.

"I would ask that we all, each and every one of us standing here now, strive to follow our High Priest's actions and words, even though he is no longer with us to provide them. Remember the things he told you in life, that we might pass them on to those who will follow our bodies beyond the boundaries of Laor's gift."

Every head Talo could see nodded resolutely.

"Let us pray."

A few knelt, some on two knees, some on one. There were a couple that prostrated themselves on the flat stone, but most stood or sat, doing whatever was comfortable, as the prayers decreed. Whatever the choice, no one spoke. There were no texts to be read, no phrases to be memorized. The prayers came from the people, Eret had often said. They should be organic, should have life. Let prayer be a fluid thought, not a signed and sealed letter.

Let it be from the heart.

Lifegiver, Talo prayed, gripping his staff with both hands and closing his eyes, feeling the mountain air whisper through his graying hair and beard, *I would ask that you hurry this man into your arms, for he has wanted nothing more for as long as I knew him. If you would treat him half as well as he treated the rest of the world, you would be favoring him above all your other followers. He deserves no less than the highest place of honor in your rebirth.*

Talo opened his eyes, turning to look out over the edge of the Giving Ground.

And please, he continued, *bring Syrah home... I've heard no reply since the beginning of the freeze, and I fear for her. I would ask this boon of you.*

His prayer at an end, Talo looked back to the crowd. Most were opening their eyes, a few already regarding the others, waiting patiently. When Ambrose Finn finally climbed to his feet, Talo held out a hand.

"Jerrom, if you would."

The elder stepped forward, leaning heavily on a younger Priest's arm and a thick wicker cane. The last of his generation to have outlived Eret, Jerrom Eyr was bent and half-blind, his thin frame swathed in thick gray and black pelts. His eyes, though, were red and puffy, tears tracking wet lines across his face.

When he was close to the body, the elder thanked his aide, who stepped away to follow Talo back to the crowd.

It was a long while before Jerrom did anything. For a time he just stood over Eret, sharing a last moment with an old friend.

Then he lifted a hand above his head, and a white light flared along the tips of his shaking fingers.

Slowly, as though pulled by a careful puppeteer, Eret's staff rose from the litter, sliding from under the man's arm. It turned as it did, revolving so that when it finally hung free in the air it was perfectly vertical to the ground.

For another span it hung there, suspended. The mourners looked on, some watching the staff, some watching Jerrom.

And then there was a flash of light, and with a deafening *crack* the staff shot downward, piercing the floor of the Grounds and sending flecks of stone and earth in all directions.

Jerrom sagged, and at once the closest men and women rushed forward to help him. Behind them, the rest of the crowd looked on.

The faintest traces of pale mist hung in the air around the base of the staff, the remnants of the old magic that would seal it there forever. As the wind picked up, the mystic tendrils were whisked away, leaving the steel to shine as a thin pillar, forever marking the final resting spot of Eret Ta'hir, High Priest of Cyurgi' Di.

IV

"The criminal rings were an evolving thing, an organic faction of the South's culture. If they didn't learn and adapt, they would eventually fail, falling either to the limited groups of moral crusaders or to their own kind. The Mahsadën were the pinnacle of this process, rising from the ashes of a weak underworld. They thrived by entwining their lives with the very existence of the 'law,' working the 'honest' government like a marionette."

—*The Cienbal,* by Adolûs Fenn

"Apparently your message wasn't as clear as we would have liked."

Raz paid no heed to the voice behind him, feigning excessive interest in the great bowl of lamb stew that had just been set on his table in the White Sands' common area. Truthfully it was less stew and more a warmed combination of broth and raw meat, but it was just the way he liked it. Raz plunged in uncaringly, ignoring the splatterings that stained his cloth shirt and pants. He didn't bother with the dingy copper forks the matron had brought out with the food, preferring to use his hands to rip at the shank and tip his snout directly into the broth.

"Ahh," the voice continued, coming around to the side before the creak of a chair told Raz he'd been joined at the table, "so it even eats like an animal. How appropriate."

Raz looked up, mouth dripping. The man across from him was attired in dark-blue clothes of rich silk with white trimming, accenting the ice-chip irises of his eyes. He was tanned from his time spent in the South, but despite all those years his skin was still several shades lighter than any true Southerner's. A neatly trimmed, blonde goatee adorned his jaw and chin, and a single pale crystal hung from the lobe of his left ear.

"What do you want, Sass?" Raz demanded, sitting up to wipe his mouth with his sleeve.

Ergoin Sass smiled. He was a handsome man, almost exotically so. In the South his northern upbringing was a rare quality. More than one woman had fallen under the spell of that careless smile, attracted by his looks and flaunted wealth. The fact that he was a šef of the Mahsadën— almost singly responsible for half the murders occurring daily in and around the city—didn't often bother them.

They were a bit more troubled when they found out Sass generally preferred his bedmates *much* younger, and not necessarily female...

"I've got more work for you," Sass said. "Kî Orran didn't go for—"

"Pay."

Sass blinked as Raz went back to his food, ripping at the broth-soaked lamb noisily.

"Pardon?"

"I said *pay*," Raz snarled without looking up. "You owe me twenty-five crowns for the first job. My gold, then we'll talk about whatever else you have for me."

Sass frowned, clearly not appreciating Raz's tone. After a brief pause he leaned back, pulled a small cloth purse from the inside of his shirt, and tossed it across the table. It landed with a heavy *thunk*. Picking it up, Raz tugged the pouch open with a finger and counted quickly. Then he nodded.

"Now, again... What do you want?"

Sass leaned forward. "Kî Orran didn't take as kindly to your gift as we'd hoped she might," he said, not bothered to keep his voice down. The tables around them were all empty, smartly vacated and avoided by every other patron in the room. "She's made a move to take the southern quarter of the slums, and she might succeed if we don't handle it soon. We've hired sarydâ, but my 'colleagues'"—he grimaced at the word—"want you in on it as well."

Raz smirked. The Mahsadën were successful in large part due to the detailed level of structure they managed to wrangle out of an organization that, not long ago, had been a dozen different factions all snapping at each other's throats. Now, half-a-dozen years later, it was a loosely stitched blanket that all but covered the South, a dark cloud clinging to every dank corner it could find.

Still, Raz always found it amusing how the individual šef mistrusted each other no less than they had a decade ago. The feuds might be generally bloodless, but each leader was always vying for a position of higher power within the overall group.

It made for an interesting dynamic...

"But you don't want that, do you, Sass?" Raz asked him, grinning and pushing the bowl out of the way to cross his arms on the wooden table. "You'd rather you handle this yourselves, without bringing in more outside help."

"If you still consider yourself 'outside help,' scaly, you clearly haven't been paying attention to the last few years of your life, have you?" Sass retorted.

Raz's grin fell. His jaw slackened, revealing his half-finger-long needled white teeth.

"If you think you have any measure of control over me," he hissed, his crest lifting just so, "then I suggest you tug on my leash and see if I bite."

Raz could see the muscles in Sass' chiseled cheeks work, but the šef managed to maintain his contemptuous sneer.

"I was *merely* suggesting," he stated forcibly through his strained lips, "that you are better served in other respects. There are jobs I would personally rather you…"

"Sun burn you, you stuck-up trim!" Raz spat, slamming a fist on the table. The remains of the stew jumped. "I don't give a *fuck* what you would 'personally' rather I do. Just tell me what the job is."

Sass licked his lips, glaring across the table, blue eyes reflecting an equal mixture of disdain and loathing. In any other man they would have held a healthy portion of fear there, too, but Ergoin Sass hadn't become the hand pulling the strings of every well-known assassin in the city by being easily frightened.

Mostly he'd managed it by killing off every competitor with his own two hands.

Even so, it was a moment before Sass spoke again, crossing one leg over the other and patting dust off his leather boot.

"Through some of our contacts we've managed to figure out where Kî is hiding out—in a series of tunnels under the home of one of her other officers. The problem is that the house is very near the market square. It's a busy area, and Kî will be on the lookout ever since you pulled the job in the Cages. Not a good place to make our move."

"But?" Raz prodded.

Sass scowled. "Don't interrupt me, you cretin. *But…* Kî moves every few days anyway, and it's not the fact that we know where she is now that's important. It's the fact that we know where she's going next. She's moving to an abandoned grain house along the slum line. Likely tomorrow, maybe the day after. Regardless, it doesn't matter. If we have men in place before she arrives—"

"You'd have the tactical advantage of knowing the place as well as her entourage, not to mention the element of surprise," Raz finished for him, no longer listening, turning the information over in his head.

The šef opened his mouth to snap at being cut off again, but thought better of it. "I've been authorized to offer you forty crowns for the job in advance, and to tell you that there is a direct bounty of another fifty for Kî's head, payable to whoever brings it forward."

Raz blinked. For the first time Sass' words surprised him.

"You want her dead?" he asked. "You don't want to flip her?"

"We're passed that." Sass' sneer shifted into a teasing smile, and he winked at a passing serving girl, making her giggle. As soon as she was gone, his face twisted back into the crooked smirk. "We've offered her everything, with no word back. She's gained too much power as an individual to be allowed to live. Even if she did join us, the manpower she might bring in would—"

"*You*," Raz snarled. "Even if she joined *you*."

Sass waved the comment away with a hand. "As you wish. Even if she joined the society, her followers are too numerous and too loyal. It would be more effort than any of us are willing to offer to have their minds changed. No. Kî's bounty is for her head, and only that."

Raz sat for a moment, thinking. Here he was on the brink of another decision that would drag him farther down the slick hill he was trying so desperately to scale. On the other hand, if he didn't accept he'd potentially be sparking a second war with the most powerful criminal alliance in the South...

That isn't really true, though, he thought. He'd refused work from the Mahsadën before, and it had only led to minor confrontation.

But if he said no this time, wouldn't he be saying no to every time after? If not, what was the point of refusing this particular contract?

And ninety crowns...

He had no doubt that he would be the one to get to Kî first. He wasn't bothered in the least with the idea of cutting down the sarydâ to get to the prize. The Cienbal sellswords—even though many of the city folk wrongly lumped him in with them—were nothing more than bandits and raiders who'd been forced to take up mercenary work when the nomadic trade caravans fell apart. They were cutthroats and marauders. Raz would be almost as happy taking Ahna to them as he would be taking her to the slavers.

And if they got in the way of his bounty, he would.

Ninety crowns...

Raz's temper sparked as he realized he'd made his choice. That kind of money was too much to refuse, even from a man like Ergoin Sass.

"Deal," Raz said, watching Sass' satisfied smirk widen. "I'm assuming you have instructions with you?"

The šef nodded, pulling another—much larger—bag of gold and a folded sheet of paper from the other side of his shirt.

"Want me to read it for you?" he drawled, sliding both across the table. "Or maybe the barmaid can help you with it—"

"Get out," Raz spat, tucking the paper into the pocket of his cloth shorts and weighing the coins in one hand. "Now."

V

"Though there are no clear records regarding the High Citadel before the faith took residence within its resilient stone walls, we are fortunate for the work of Priest Duul Obli. A man of Laor, he made it his life's work in the mid-third century v.S. to piece together the history of Cyurgi' Di. It is, therefore, only through his thorough research that we know some small parts of our home's story. Once a military outpost of great import against the savage tribes of the frozen tundra beyond the Vietalis and Saragrias mountain ranges, Priest Obli's writings tell us that the Citadel seems to have been abandoned during a period of decades of which there are no records. 'I assume,' Obli writes, 'that the winter freezes were particularly brutal for a time, or that some great plague swept through the mountains. After nearly a half century spent empty and hollow, a traveling Laorin—whom I have yet not been able to name—discovered the vast fortress while exploring the ranges. As far as I can tell, this man summoned others to his purpose, becoming the first High Priest of Cyurgi' Di, and its halls have been filled ever since.'"

—*Studying the Lifegiver,* by Carro al'Dor

Damn these stairs!

Syrah Brahnt squinted, grimacing at the long line of carved stone steps twisting and turning their way up the mountain face before her. High, high above, barely a silhouette in the clouds, the paired towers of Cyurgi' Di's great outer gate rose like twin guards to the heavens.

Well, at least I'm definitely moving, she thought with a smirk, shading her eyes.

Three years. Had it truly been three years since she'd been granted her staff? Three years since she'd left the Citadel to follow her own path for a time? It must have. She'd made some headway with the treaties between the western Sigûrth tribe and the great valley cities of Metcaf and Harond, whose provinces the mountain men had been raiding for the last century. Traveling from town to village, she'd helped the people on both sides of the battle line make fortifications to their walls, improve their medicine, and even set up schools of reading and arithmetic for the youngest among them. Need had dissolved old rivalries, and friendships had been forged, both likely and unlikely. Trade routes were formed, and people were brought together in rare opportunity to hammer out the vestiges of a peace that might finally last…

For the first time since she'd been indoctrinated, Syrah had truly felt Laor's gifts at work, could see them flowing from her hands when she healed and helped those who needed her most.

Talo would be so proud.

Syrah smiled as she climbed, thinking of her old mentor, the steel of her staff clinking against the stone. She'd heard little from him in the last year. Not surprising considering the past winter had been one of the most brutal in recent history. The storms, in fact, were the only reason she'd managed to improve the situation with the mountain clans at all, convincing Metcaf and Harond to offer some fraction of their spare resources to the wild men so that they might survive the freeze. The old Kayle, Emhret Grahst, hadn't been happy to accept the handouts. Taking the charity stepped away from his tribe's traditions, turned its back on centuries of ritual pillaging and raiding. Many members of his court and family had been outraged, openly opposing the proposed treaty. One of Grahst's nephews, a brutal man named Gûlraht Baoill, had been particularly outspoken, going so far as to threaten Syrah's life for poisoning his uncle's mind with her tricks and whispers. He hadn't been alone, either, but in the end need had outweighed custom, and the Kayle took Syrah's counsel to heart.

At least it meant that all those others claimed by the cold hadn't died in vain...

Now, though, summer had arrived. Even in the mountains, where the air still held firm to the chill bite of winter, it was more pleasant than uncomfortable. Syrah pulled the hood of her robes back, letting her braided, shoulder-length white hair swing free. It was a clear day, the blue sky that was so much more common now than in the months of the freeze dotted with patches of wispy clouds. Somewhere in the distant cliffs a hawk called out, its screech echoing off the crags. The air was crisp, and Syrah took in a deep breath, feeling her energy leap anew now that she could at least see the end of her travels.

Twenty minutes later she reached the top of the stairway, the roughness of the steps flattening suddenly into the huge semicircular plateau of the outer plaza. The midmorning sun was rising, bathing the eastward entrance of Cyurgi' Di in light, washing over the mottled gray walls. Syrah smiled again, vaguely remembering the first time she'd seen the leviathans. The two towering bastions pierced with arrow slits had hung, brooding, over the tunnel entrance. Like titans from some child's nightmare they'd stood, waiting to devour whoever was fool enough to walk between them. But that was then.

Now the place spoke only of the warmth and the comfort of home.

Hitching her bag higher onto her shoulder, Syrah hurried into a jog, staff at her side. She made her way through the tunnel, shivering when the shade sucked away what little heat the sun could bring. There were voices up ahead, echoing happily along the tunnel walls. As she stepped into the light once more, Syrah slowed and stopped, smiling.

Under the watchful eye of a half-dozen older acolytes, two score or so of children were rushing about, playing and enjoying what must have been one of the first clear days of summer this high up the mountain. Syrah felt the nostalgia swell watching the little ones run, screaming in delight and laughing into the bright sky. She could remember those days, too. How she had hated being cooped up for months, locked in the keep...

"Syrah?"

Syrah turned. A man was rushing toward her, waving. He was tall and fit, his strong jaw clean shaven, blonde hair falling to the base of his neck. It took her a moment to recognize him.

"Reyn!" she exclaimed, dropping her pack and staff to the ground to allow him to scoop her up and hug her so tight she gasped. *"Whoof!"* she exhaled when he put her down, grinning up at him. "Reyn! How are you? You've grown."

"I'm the same height I was when you left, you liar," Reyn Hartlet said with a laugh. His blue eyes glinted with amusement, and he pushed a lock of loose hair behind his ear. "Maybe that southern sun got to your eyes while we were down there after all."

"I didn't necessarily say you'd grown *up*, did I?" Syrah asked playfully, whacking his muscled arm.

Reyn laughed again. "I'm working under Master Brern, now," he told her, reaching down to pick up her bag as she collected her staff from the ground. "It comes with the job of apprenticing with the weapons master."

"Wow." Syrah whistled, impressed. "You're working in the practice chambers? That's amazing! And that means you got your staff! When?"

"About two years ago," Reyn said proudly, throwing her bag over his shoulder and leading the way around the packs of playing children, heading toward the great gate of the keep itself. "I almost managed to do it as fast as you!" He elbowed her teasingly.

"You're a year older than me," she said, rolling her eyes with a smile. "I don't think a year after me is doing it 'as fast as me.'"

"Maybe, but you got here a whole year before I did," he pointed out, knocking on the heavy timber as they reached the gates. "So… we're even."

Syrah laughed. "Fine," she conceded with a nod. There was a *clang*, and the door swung forward.

"Master Hartlet," a tired, resigned voice grumbled through the opening, "I really must insist that you do not keep requesting to come in and out like this. I'm not as young as I once—by the Lifegiver! Syrah Brahnt! Is that you?"

"Hello, Dolt," Syrah said with a shy smile as a tubby middle-aged man with a tuft of graying hair atop his head stepped out and into the light. Dolt Avonair had been one of the gatekeepers since before she or Reyn had come to Cyurgi' Di, and he squinted at her blearily.

Then he smiled.

"It *is!* Blessings, child, I didn't think to see you back for a good while. Have you come to pay your respects? Poor man. We will sorely miss—"

"Talo said to bring any word of you straight to him," Reyn cut in suddenly, smiling pointedly at the gatekeeper. "He'll be happy to see you. Do you know if he's in his quarters, Dolt?"

The man scratched at his bald chin. "I think so… They just finished moving him in yesterday, so he's probably rearranging things. Goodness they're a change from his old chambers. Makes me want to be High Priest just thinking about—"

"Thanks!" Reyn called back, already pulling Syrah along into the halls.

"What was that all about?" Syrah asked him as they walked, twisting and winding their way through the citadel. "Who am I supposed to be paying my respects to?"

The inside of the great temple was unchanged, leaping right out of her memories. Dusty rays of light poured in from the arrow slits along the halls that trailed the outside wall, candles and lanterns lighting the inner ones. The air was warm, the pipes that ran under the stones still working, which meant they hadn't shut down the boilers in the bottom levels for the summer yet. Classrooms and quarters to either side of them had their doors swung open, and she caught more than one glimpse of acolytes and Priests praying and studying.

Beside her, Reyn's face contorted for a moment into what looked like the remnants of grief. It shifted back almost immediately.

"Talo should be the one to tell you," he said hesitantly, ending the conversation.

Syrah frowned, feeling a knot form in her gut. Ignoring it, she looked around. She wasn't familiar with the route they were taking, but it didn't surprise her. There were a dozen different ways to get to any single place within the temple, and everyone had their preferences. It used to be a child's game, in fact. Those with the fastest route were the winners, and got to be King of the Citadel for a day.

But wait... no... She did know this path...

"Is Talo with Eret?" she asked, suddenly excited. She'd thought she recognized this particular hall. It led almost directly to the High Priest's quarters, a place she'd been more than a few times during her acolyte years. Eret Ta'hir had been nearly as important in her life as Talo had been before she'd gained her staff.

The knot in her stomach tightened, though, when she saw Reyn's face. It was a true mask of grief now, contorted and stricken.

"No," he managed to say. "No, Syrah..."

Syrah stopped dead, realization crashing over her. Her staff dropped from her hands, clanging against the stone floor.

"No," she whispered, covering her mouth, taking a step away from the man. "Reyn... no..."

Reyn's body shook, but he clamped his jaw shut resolutely. Then he nodded.

Syrah ran.

Her feet pounded the ground as she rushed down the hall, turning right, left, and right again. Her body made the decisions automatically, plucking the directions of this familiar route straight from her childhood days.

The door was there, as she remembered, ordinary as every other wooden door in the Citadel. There was a moment where she saw it and realized that she wanted to stop, wanted to never open it. She wanted to walk away and never find out what news waited for her inside.

Her hand, though, reached out, lifting the cold iron handle, and the door swung open with a *bang*.

Two men were in the room beyond, both jumping when she rushed in, her eyes wet, looking around frantically. Talo was seated behind the High Priest's desk, a broad L-shaped escritoire set almost directly in the middle of the wide circular chamber. He seemed to have been sitting there with his face in his hands. His eyes were red when he looked up, and Carro, his partner, was standing beside him, one hand on his shoulder as though to comfort him.

"Sy-Syrah?" Talo blurted, stunned.

Then he leapt up and hurriedly limped around the table.

"It *is!* It is you! Syrah! When did you…? How have you…?"

But he stopped, standing helplessly when he saw the tears rolling down her colorless cheeks.

"Talo…?" She *hated* that she was crying, blinking up at him. "Is Eret…? Did he…?"

Talo's face—originally a strangled mixture of surprise, joy, and overbearing sadness—fell just like Reyn's had. He stepped forward, wrapped her completely in his arms, and pulled her close, hushing her and patting her white hair like he'd done when she'd still been a little girl twenty years ago, newly arrived to Cyurgi' Di.

"Shh," he whispered, rocking her side to side. "Shh, child. Eret is returned to His embrace. This is no time for tears. It is a time to remember him and to realize that he has achieved what he has always wanted to. Shh… shh…"

Carro came to stand beside them, eyes glistening.

"Come sit, Syrah," he told her in his fatherly voice, prying her gently from Talo's embrace. Carro al'Dor was nearly as big as his lover, his long blonde hair tied in three thin ponytails behind his head, his beard braided with bone beads and narrow iron rings. His mother had survived an invasion on her village as a young woman, but not unscathed. She'd given birth to him that summer, and hadn't been able to bear the thought of keeping the bastard child of the father that haunted her nightmares. Despite all odds, however, and as much as he looked the part of the mountain tribesman, Carro had grown into a kind and strong man.

He led Syrah to the room's single large bed and seated her on the corner so she could lean against one of the thick canopy bedposts. She rested her shoulder and head against it, body shaking under the stress of trying to hold back the waves of nausea that coursed up and through her.

If Talo was as much a father figure as Syrah could ever remember, so had Eret been her grandfather of sorts. The old man had paid her special attention over the years, personally attending the ceremonies in which she'd been granted her staff and title as a Priestess of Laor. Younger than that, he'd been her confidant, the friend she turned to when she had things she couldn't tell Talo or her class companions.

And now he was gone…

Syrah took a steadying breath. Carro sat down beside her, sinking the

bed with his weight.

"When did he pass?" she asked at last, blinking and looking to Talo, who stood on the other side of her.

"Eight days ago," he responded sadly. "He was sick through the better part of the freeze. I tried getting birds to you, but it seems they didn't make it through the storms."

"The last letter I received was over six months ago," Syrah agreed, shaking her head. "Damn those blizzards. If I'd known—"

"If you'd known, you would have come running at once," Carro interrupted with a sad smile. "And as a result you probably wouldn't have made half the headway you did with the clans over the winter. Oh, we heard," he said with a proud grin at her surprised face. "We may not have been able to stay in touch with you directly, but your work seems to have found its way back to the Citadel somehow. Laor has his plan for all of us, Syrah. If He'd seen fit to warn you of Eret's passing, I'm sure He would have done so."

"Well sometimes I wish He'd bend His rules on occasion," Syrah grumbled, wiping her eyes but laughing a little. "Eight days... if I'd just left a week earlier—"

"You'd probably have run into wolves or a flood or something else that would have ended up delaying you anyway," Talo offered with a chuckle. "Knowing your luck, I'm surprised you managed to get here at all."

"One time," Syrah sighed. "You get ambushed one time in the middle of a strange city in a land you know nothing about, and everyone seems to think you're accident-prone."

Talo and Carro both laughed, and all three of them felt the grief drain away the slightest bit.

"So," Syrah started, grinning mischievously, "High Priest, huh? The Council are either daft, or you're sleeping with someone apart from Carro to make this job, Talo."

"You know," Carro said thoughtfully, playing along, "I never thought of that. You *didn't* trade this position for sexual favors, did you? Because if that's the case..."

"Neither of you think I might have actually deserved the job?" Talo growled feigningly, eyeing them both. "Well, that certainly makes me feel appreciated. The two dearest people in my life, and they think I had to bed a bunch of old Priests to get the position. Wonderful."

"Well we didn't say you bedded *all* of them," Syrah grinned, rubbing her red eyes. "I'm sure some of them would have cast their vote in your favor. What do you say, Carro? Three-fourths? Two-thirds?"

"Hmm... I don't think so. Your old Priest-Mentor is more popular than that. I'd say he only had to sleep with half of them at most."

"Six old men," Syrah surmised, whistling. Then she cringed. "Ugh. Those images aren't going leave me anytime soon."

"Serves you right," Talo said with a snort, turning and returning to the wingback chair behind the High Priest's desk, favoring his good leg. "Syrah, I'll have someone prepare quarters for you. Drop off your things and wash up, then meet us in the mess hall for lunch. We have a great deal of catching up to do."

Syrah groaned, getting up from the bed. "Does that mean I have to eat with the two of you? What will my friends think if they see me sitting with a pair of old nags?"

"I wouldn't be too concerned with that, darling," Carro said with a wink from the bed. "For that to be a problem, you'd have to have friends in the first place."

Syrah stuck her tongue out at the man, then laughed as she moved to leave.

"Syrah."

She turned again. Talo was watching her with a sad smile, leaning back in his chair.

"If Eret had known you'd be here so soon, I'm sure he would have prayed for another few days. Welcome home, child."

VI

"The Mahsadën were organized and methodical to a degree beyond anything the South had ever seen. Corrupted governments were falling one after the other in the mid-800s v.S., and out of the wreckage rose the worst kinds of men and women: the careful, intelligent, and cruel. Witnessing an opportunity unlike any before, they worked to set aside their feuds and grudges, banding together until a net of shadows fell over every city in the South. Miropa was the last to give in, but the Mahsadën—as this group had titled themselves—eventually dug their claws into the dying beast that was the city's spirit."

—*As Death Rose from the Ashes,* by Kohly Grofh

The grain house was as risky a place to hole up as you could find, even for a few days. It was right on the lip of one of the main market fairways, barely two buildings from the thriving road that signified the end of the slum quarters. Its size and location—taking up a majority of the block on the destitute side of the line—attracted beggars and vagabonds who sought shelter from the Sun during the day and any measure of warmth they could find during the night. Members of Kî's entourage had come through to clear them out—she'd probably be arriving that evening, after all—but half the homeless who'd been chased away slunk back into the shadows of the building as soon as the men had gone

Kî must be confident in her secrets if she risks this much attention, Raz thought, huddled in the shade of an alley, watching an old one-legged woman wobble back into the grain house.

He'd been sitting there since morning, suffering the boredom and stiffness of the dirt ground to gauge what he was dealing with. Curled up, knees to his chest and tail tucked out of sight, he was unrecognizable beneath the dirty old rags he'd piled over himself. Even his hands were wrapped, providing a convincing display when Kî's men passed him, dodging his outstretched palm as he begged for crowns in a raspy voice.

They'd probably thought he was a leper, or something worse.

Still, the trouble was worth the wait. He'd watched the group enter and chase away the building's occupants, then leave again in the same direction they'd come. He'd been half tempted to follow them just to see if Sass was right about where Kî was now, but resisted. Waiting ten minutes to ensure no one was coming back, Raz pulled off the disguise, unwrapping his hands and standing up. He winced and groaned, joints popping and stiff muscles straining, unhappy with the combination of an uncomfortable position and the relative coolness of the shade that his body never took well to.

Reaching down, Raz pulled Ahna out from behind the heap of refuse he'd been sitting by and stepped across the alley into the sunlight. At once he felt better, rolling his shoulders as the naked skin of his arms and back tingled in the heat. He wore only a loose pair of cotton shorts, having opted to dress lightly in case he had to make a quick escape, and it felt good to spread his wings a little and stretch them unhindered. He'd gotten accustomed to human clothing a long time ago, even liked it at times, but in the end he was always more comfortable either bare chested or in the armor Jerr specially tailored to offer his limbs free movement.

And, since almost a hundred pounds of steel was less than ideal when it came to quick escapes, bare chested it was.

Raz moved carefully, scanning the grain house. He was sure all four of the men he'd seen were gone, but he'd made the mistake of trusting only what he *saw* enough times to know it paid to be alert. There was no harm in being careful, after all, particularly when one had the time for it.

A band of feral cats yowled and shot away from him when he stepped inside. Raz was pleased with how high the ceiling was. From the outside it looked like the building was two stories, but the end he'd walked into was in fact a vast open space, most likely where they'd kept the grain during years past when there'd been enough to store. The roof was vaulted, and windows pierced the upper part of the high wall, probably to keep the grist dry with fresh air and light.

If he'd been any good with a bow, they would have offered him any number of clear shots come nightfall...

Something to bring up with the saryda, he thought, moving toward the far end of the building, Ahna resting across both shoulders. The air smelled of unwashed bodies and human waste mixed with stale crust and cheap ale. Raz counted no less than a half-dozen forms cowering against the walls, every single gaze fixed, terrified, on him. He ignored them, chuckling at the thought that, if Ki's men were all as careless about their duties, he was going to make easy coin tonight.

He stopped halfway across the floor, just under where the levels split, an open second-story loft extending all the way to the opposite wall. From what he could see, the top level was similar to the space behind him, a flat storage area. Raz ignored it, more interested in what was below, in the area directly before him. Dozens of square-cut timber pillars held up the low ceiling, spaced a body length apart from each other, like a man-made forest. Old crates, broken barrels, and a multitude of different-sized baskets were tucked away against the walls, which had no windows. Cellar storage, he decided, peering into the shadows. The alcohol the owners distilled from the soured grains had to ferment somewhere, after all. Even in the middle of the full day it was gloomy, only partially lit by a single open archway in the left wall.

At night, that would be dark too…

Raz smiled again, turning to leave, his mind at work before he'd taken a single step back out into the Sun.

"I say we let 'im make the kill, then jump 'im after all the dust settles. Saves us the trouble of havin' to get through all of the bitch-woman's bodyguards."

"Yer mad, Davin. ya' double-cross the lizard and the only thing you'll end up with is yer guts in yer hands. He'll tear ya' apart."

"So we gets to 'im before he knows what's goin' on. C'mon Lev, you really think we got a chance at the fifty crowns with him here? That bounty'll make us *rich*."

"I'd rather be alive and livin' off nothin' than dead, mate."

Smart boy, Raz thought with a smirk, hidden in the shadows across from where the two men were whispering. The Sun had set an hour ago, and all that was left to do was wait and keep as warm as they could. Davin and Lev, though, apparently didn't like to wait in silence.

Nor did the pair seem to realize that Raz could hear every word they were saying.

They'd all been huddled in the dark of the grain house's first floor since midafternoon. The vagrants had been chased away hours ago, the crates and baskets and other junk shifted so that the group had adequate places to hide. In short order they'd set up their ambush, then tucked themselves away to wait. Seven in total, they comprised of Raz, four sarydâ who called themselves the Crows, and two brothers with blonde hair, mean eyes, and thick arms that looked good at swinging the matching heavy axes slung over their backs. Raz had taken a liking to the pair. They'd barely spoken a word since meeting up with the rest of the group. The Crows on the other hand—Lev Sayl, Alexy Kone, Basser, and their leader, Davin Goyr—seemed unable to comprehend the concept of silence. Former Cienbal bandits all, they were as boastful and long-winded as every other desert mercenary.

Still… Goyr could have put a deaf man to sleep with all his stories of conquest and riches.

"You might be wantin' to keep yer words down, boss." Another voice—maybe Alexy's—joined Lev's and Goyr's. "I heard the scaly's got hawk's eyes and wolf's ears. If'n he can hear you'ze two goin' at it he's likely to—*ouch!*"

There was a *smack* of a hand hitting face, and the man stopped speaking abruptly.

"You tellin' me what to do now, Lexy?" Davin hissed, and there was another *smack*. "What's it matter if'n i'Syul can hear us? All animal, ain't he? Too dumb to understand what we sayin', probably."

Not so smart boy.

Raz could feel his temper flare, his crest twitching reflexively. He was half tempted to sneak across the floor and give Goyr a good scare just to put the man in his place, but he fought off the impulse. Raz had developed a thick skin over the years, and it would take a lot more than ignorant slander to push him over the edge.

Raz relaxed, forcing himself to stop listening to the Crows' conversation. He rattled the slightest bit, shifting from a sitting position into a crouch, the armor encasing his left arm and leg gleaming in the dark as it caught the limited light of the Moon through the open archway on the opposite wall. The leather wrappings around his right forearm and right thigh were stiff from the cold, and he reached down to loosen them. He was in full gear tonight. He had no delusions the element of surprise would only get them so far in these cramped quarters, and was glad for the white robes he wore under the steel. He'd kept himself moving as much as he could the last hour, but if Kî and her entourage didn't arrive soon he would have to think of something else to keep from stiffening up in the cold. The heat of the day had dissipated in minutes, like every summer night, and even through his cloth layers Raz could feel the coolness of the metal against his skin. His wings were freezing, cramping uncomfortably from being held tight to his back for so many hours already. His gladius was slung diagonally between them, and every few minutes he reached down instinctively to check that his long knife was still strapped to his thigh and the war ax was looped at his waist.

Come on, he thought, eyes on the faint glow of the open front door.

Where are you, you slaving witch?

Expectedly, nothing answered him.

It was almost another quarter hour, in fact, before his ears twitched up, spreading to catch a faint sound in the distance. His first thought was of street runners, already responsible for a few false alarms in the last couple hours, but listening harder he realized the shuffling was getting steadily closer. Grabbing a hard lump of dirt from the ground, Raz tossed it at the dark corner he knew the chattering Crows were crouched, listening to it *thunk* against some piece of the junk they hid behind.

"Shut up," he hissed across the floor. "They're coming."

For what seemed like the first time all night, the Crows stopped their bickering. Raz turned his ears back on the door. He could make out the footsteps almost perfectly now, along with the clinking of armor, growing suddenly louder like the group had turned a corner. In agreement with the thought, the right side of the doorframe was abruptly awash with torchlight, bathing the distant perpendicular wall and casting every other shadowed place inside into even deeper darkness.

Lowering himself so that only his eyes and hood were above the box he crouched behind, Raz reached out and tapped the nearest of the brothers. In unison he heard two axes being unclasped and drawn, and following the example he moved one hand to grasp Ahna's handle and lift her from the floor. By the time he had her ready in his hands the first silhouette of a man appeared in the archway. Stepping in and looking around, the slaver brandished a torch high to illuminate the better part of the empty chamber that made up the first half of the building. His sword was drawn, and he peered into every corner of the immediate space around him, looking for anything that might spell trouble. After a few seconds the man seemed satisfied, and he sheathed the weapon before yelling over his shoulder.

"All's clear!"

Six figures trooped in after him, one pair holding two more torches aloft while the other four dropped several heavy bags to the ground, along with what looked like a folding table. Not long after, yet another body stepped out of the night, lavish in heavy red silks that looked ludicrously misplaced in their surroundings.

Kî Orran was not a beautiful woman, such as the rumors she'd undoubtedly started herself murmured. She was fit, that wasn't in doubt, slim around the waist and legs and wide across the bodice, but those were her only fortunate features. A furry mantle was pulled over bony shoulders to ward off the night chill, and she clutched at it, looking around. The unfortunate frame of her face reminded Raz of some combination of a horse and a pig. It was narrow, her oversized white teeth gleaming from between prominent lips that seemed to rest unnaturally far apart. Her jowls hung like an old woman's, and her long nose was upturned, offset by narrow eyes that took in the building around her with extreme distaste.

Raz watched two of her guards lift and unfold the table, setting it down. Another procured a chair from somewhere. Kî didn't sit, though, instead motioning to one of the men.

"Bring me my writing materials, then have someone check the storage areas." She had an oddly sweet, husky voice that didn't fit her looks. "It *reeks* in here. I wouldn't be surprised if we find some dead slummer tucked in a corner. And tell Dole to bring in the merchandise and start a fire. No use having them die from the cold before morning."

Raz's blood chilled hearing the words. The man Kî had been speaking to nodded and moved back to the door. He leaned around the corner of the entrance, exchanging words with what must have been another guard. At once the clinking sounds Raz had assumed were armor started up again, and another group was led in, wrists shackled, feet strung together by a pair of long chains. Raz felt his body go rigid.

Slaves! Sass didn't say they were actually traveling with slaves!

He watched the dozen individuals herded to the far wall of the building by four men with whips. They were dirty and sleep deprived, their mismatched clothes—undoubtedly the same ones they'd been wearing when they'd been snatched—torn and dusty. Within moments of their entering the room, Raz could smell them, a mixed stench of vomit, sweat, and unwashed bodies.

"Sit down and shut it!" one of the drivers yelled when they reached the left wall, shoving them one by one to the ground. "You be quiet, you eat! You gripe, and ya' get the whip! *Got it?*"

The slaves nodded, some of them crying, some shivering from a mixture of the cold and fear. Raz had to consciously keep himself low, unable to look away. He felt Ahna in his hands, and the sudden image of smashing her into the heads of every one of Kî's entourage was so enticing he almost missed the man ordered to check the rest of the warehouse, torch in hand and looking around. Raz only got down in time because one of the brothers grabbed his shoulder, pulling him low.

"Thanks," he whispered, glancing back at the man before peering over the edge of the boxes again, carefully this time. The guard passed them by, inspecting the spaces between the piled crates and boxes less than meticulously. He hummed a tune and kept moving, the torchlight casting odd webbed shadows across the wall as he ducked his way through the grid of columns. It was after the man passed the stacked barrels behind which the Crows were crouched that Raz had the idea.

They'd all agreed to a flexible plan, considering how little anyone actually knew about the circumstances of Kĭ's move to the grain house. They'd opted against positioning Basser—who claimed to be a dead-shot with a bow—on the roofs outside, just in case Kĭ's men had the same idea. If they could move quickly and maintained some element of surprise, working as a group would be effective enough.

With this in mind, Raz made his decision. Lifting himself from his crouch just enough to move, he eased Ahna gently to the floor.

She wouldn't be needed for this.

"What're you—?" one of the men behind him began in an angry hiss, but his brother clapped a hand over his mouth. Ignoring the pair, Raz snuck forward, edging away from the darting light, tailing the slaver.

Raz was a deadly whisper, slipping fluidly across the floor so as to avoid making any noise—an accomplishment in full gear. He stepped with the shadows until he was perpendicular to the man. There Raz stilled and watched the figure bend over, searching the last corner of the building.

The moment his back was turned, Raz darted forward, uncaring of the noise. He reached up and around, grabbing the man's jaw with one hand and pressing against the back of his neck with the other. Twisting them so viciously the metal claws of his gauntlets cut furrows into the slaver's cheeks, he felt the spine pop and snap.

There was a shout from behind him. Raz let the body fall to the floor, torch rolling from the man's dead hands. Snatching it from the ground, he watched the other ten men that made up Kĭ's guard spin to face him with drawn swords.

Then he flipped the torch over, extinguished it in the dirt, and bolted through the sudden black.

"Distract them!" he hissed in the general direction he knew Goyr and his gang were hiding. Raz had long since memorized every inch of the building. He slipped out the side door, turning and dashing toward the main entrance.

There was a sentry posted out front, arms wrapped around himself and chin tucked to his chest for warmth. He hadn't even noticed someone running silently up beside him when Raz's armored fist collided with his temple, caving in the side of his skull.

Barely slowing down, Raz grabbed the doorway and swung into the building, drawing the gladius and ax. Just as he'd expected, every head was turned toward the back of the first floor, a few scuffles already breaking out in the limited light.

Raz pounced, aiming for the nearest exposed back. The ax's small blade collided with the base of the man's head, crushing bone and cutting sinew, and he fell like a dropped stone. Spinning, Raz whisked his sword up. It caught the face of the second man who'd had just enough time to turn and look, splitting it.

Well trained, Raz thought to himself, mildly impressed when the third guard got his blade up in time to deflect a blow from the gladius, parrying it to the side. Using the momentum to his advantage, Raz struck three quick blows with the ax. One to the ribs, then the wrist, then across the throat. He turned away, leaving the man to stagger back and clutch at his neck with his good hand as blood stained the cotton of his shirt.

The ambush was in full swing now, the Crows and two brothers each engaged in their own battles. Not including Kî—who was yelling orders even as she pressed her back to the wall, trying to get away from Raz—the odds were seven on seven with the five guards dead.

Odds he liked better.

Raz's weapons worked together in fluid motion, blocking and deflecting. They took advantage of every opening, sliding into any flawed defense as he darted across the floor. A thrust glanced off the steel of his plate mail, the blade's owner stumbling past him off balanced. Raz kneed him in the chest, feeling ribs snap. He stepped back, swinging his sword in a vicious backspin that caught another man across the bridge of his nose, sending him howling to the ground, thrashing and grasping at his eyes.

The razor-thin blade of the gladius flashed once, piercing the man's heart. His dying breath seeped out like a sigh.

Raz looked up, searching.

Kî.

With all the men around him dead and caring little that the sarydâ were still fighting, Raz spun around. He found her sliding sideways across the wall toward the door, trying to attract as little notice as possible. Her eyes went wide when she caught sight of him looking at her. She started to sprint, making a break for the night outside.

Sheathing his weapons in a blink, Raz took two steps and leapt, crashing into her back and bearing her to the ground. Pinning her there, he grabbed a handful of hair and forced her face into the dirt. She was screaming, his wings spreading over her like death's red cloak. Raz snarled, bringing his teeth inches from her ear.

"Don't! Please! *Please!*" she shrieked, squirming facedown under him, trying to get free. In response Raz put a knee on her back, making her scream again.

"Tell me what you were going to do with those people!" he roared at her, pointing to the slaves still cowering against the wall behind them. "Where were you taking them?"

"S-southeast edge of the city!" she gasped. His knee ground into her back unforgivingly. "They were sold to some trader from Cyro! They're supposed to be shipped in the morning! You want them? Take them! Tell your šef they're theirs! They're all theirs! Just let me go!"

"Like I would let the Mahsadën have them," Raz hissed, pulling her head back by her hair. He drew his knife and pressed it to her throat. "You can *all* just—!"

"TAKE THEM YOURSELF, THEN!" the woman screamed, sobbing as she struggled under his weight. "IF THAT'S WHY YOU'RE HERE THEN TAKE THEM YOURSELF! I'LL TELL YOU WHERE THEY'RE BEING SOLD! I'LL TELL YOU! YOU CAN…!"

The words hit Raz like a hammer to the head.

He felt numb shock rock through him as he looked down on Kî, watching her continued to thrash under him. She thought *he* wanted the slaves. She thought he was looking for his own niche in the market.

And then, in one moment, every repressed thought and doubt he'd had about what he was doing crashed down on Raz like the roof had caved in. He reeled away from the woman, gasping as he scrambled back, eyes fixed on her stunned face. His metal claws tore at the dirt in his rush to be separated from her, tossing dust in the air. He couldn't breathe. He couldn't *think*. He barely noticed that the sounds of fighting had finally come to an end, barely noticed Kî leap to her feet and run for the door.

He didn't even blink when Davin Goyr stepped between her and freedom, cutting the woman down so viciously her last screech was brought short when the man's blade cleaved through lung.

What am I doing? Raz thought, trapped in a maelstrom of fear and panic. *What am I doing? What is this? What have I done?*

It was like he was drowning in fire, struggling to breathe, his mind reeling. Kî had thought he was there for the slaves! And why shouldn't he have been? For years he'd been working with the Mahsadën, misleading himself the whole time. He'd known that his actions did little to change the situation of those whose captors he killed, but he'd never thought of it like this…

Is this what I am now? Raz thought to himself, watching Goyr bend down and wipe his blade on Kî's silks. *A thug they use to make their takeover that much easier?*

Yes.

Raz shook as the answer ripped at him. The flames that were his memories burned, and he remembered the faces of the men and women he'd killed for what he'd deluded himself into thinking was the greater good. In reality he'd just been clearing a path, making it easier for the Mahsadën to slip their thin fingers into every nook and cranny of Miropa.

They'd played him like a fiddle.

"Oy! Scaly!"

Raz blinked, realizing he'd been staring at Goyr. The man was smirking, eyeing him contemptuously.

"Bounty's mine! Don't even think about tellin' Sass otherwise! I saw what ya' did. What? The little cunt scare you off, Monster?"

Ordinarily, Raz would have torn the Crow's throat out without a second thought, even if money hadn't been involved. Now, though, he did nothing, getting to his feet and looking around numbly. Every one of Kî's guard was dead or dying, scattered where they fell. The other three Crows were moving about, stripping the bodies of anything useful and knifing those still breathing. The two brothers sat in a corner, one helping to wrap a loose bandage around the other's thick arm, gashed by some blade or another. Behind Raz the slaves were cringing, either sobbing or staring at the seven of them with terrified eyes.

"Sass told us to hold the fort until mornin'," Goyr said, coming to stand beside Raz. He, too, looked at the trembling forms. "He'll be comin' with a crew to clean up with, and our pay. You even think abou' tryin' to take the bounty, and I'll gut ya' from—"

"It's yours."

Goyr blinked in surprise at Raz's words. "Oh… Right then."

He scratched his beard, studying the dozen figures before them. He caught sight of a pretty girl near the end, and a nasty smile spread across his face. She was dark haired, with empty gray eyes that said she'd given up every hope.

"If'n that's the case, I'm gonna have me a lil' celebration."

He moved toward the girl hungrily. She hadn't noticed the Crow looking at her, but saw him now and scooted back at his approach, horrified.

"C'mon, girly," Goyr crooned, bending down beside her. Sitting on his heels, he reached out a callused hand to move a hair from her face. "Let's you and me have a tumble, eh?"

The girl sobbed, cowering and turning away, shaking as the man's fingers trailed down her cheek and neck, fondling the hem of her dirty shirt.

It was all it took.

In one instant of terrifying change, Raz felt himself lifted from the boiling pit of realization and dropped into an emptiness he hadn't felt in seven years. The abyss rushed up to meet him, the world falling into faded shades of red and black. What humanity was left, only ever distant in most of the past decade, disappeared altogether.

Raz moved with the speed of a whip, unleashing the animal. His weapons forgotten, he leapt, seizing the back of Goyr's neck and wrenching him to his feet as the man sputtered a surprised yell.

Then, snarling, Raz slammed his face into the rotten planks of the nearest wall.

The brittle timber splintered. Goyr screamed, his cry muffled through broken teeth. Raz's snarl grew into a roar, and he slammed the Crow's face into the wood again, then again, then again. Each time, Goyr's screams died a little more. Each time, the wood came away wetter and redder. Finally, after a dozen crushing blows, the wall gave in completely. Goyr's head went straight through, buried to the shoulder, and at last he was silent. Only then did Raz stop, releasing the back of the man's head to let the body hang there by its throat. The slaves were screaming, the woman he'd saved trying to scramble away from the gore trailing to the floor by her hands.

Raz ignored them all. His vision shimmered. He fought the black, turning to face the room.

Each of the five sarydâ left alive was turned toward him, their faces pale, gaping at Goyr's twitching carcass hanging from the bloody hole in the wall.

"You leave, you live," Raz growled. "Stay, and I will tear you to pieces."

One of the brothers, the uninjured one, narrowed his eyes. Reaching out, he grabbed the handle of his ax from where it leaned against the wall behind him.

Raz struck the man before he could so much as twitch the blade up, one armored hand around the wrist of his wielding arm, pushing the ax out of the way. They hit the ground with a crash. Raz's wings spread to their full extent over the pair of them, his teeth finding flesh.

It only took a moment for the man's throat to become little more than shredded meat.

"SHRYN! NO!"

A heavy booted foot caught Raz in the side, and he felt ribs snap. A second kick knocked him free of the body. The dying man's brother leapt at him, roaring in rage and hefting his ax overhead. Raz dodged out of the way, ignoring the burning pain in his side. He rolled to his feet inches from where the thick blade fell, digging into the dirt. His hands a silver blur, Raz caught the man on either side of the head, fingers piercing skin and flesh. As the mercenary screamed, Raz pulled with all his might, turning and twisting. There was a *pop*, and yet another spine cracked in Raz's hands, the large man flying through the air, spinning like a top before landing with a bone-shattering *crunch* a dozen feet away.

Breathing heavily, Raz spun around, wincing when his throbbing side chose to protest the motion. Drawing the gladius with his good hand, he hissed at the three men remaining, flicking his wings in warning. Alexy, Lev, and Basser all froze.

Three swords fell to the ground in unison.

"N-no trouble, friend," Lev stuttered, raising his hands and stepping back, his companions doing the same. "Bounty's yours. No arguin' here, right boys?"

Alexy and Basser both nodded vigorously, looking terrified.

"GET OUT!" Raz screamed, smashing the gladius' blade against the steel of his other arm. "*OUT!*"

Lev and Alexy actually tripped over each other as all three men sprinted for the door. Raz listened to them go, waiting to hear their footsteps fade into the distance.

Then he sagged, groaning before falling to one knee, his breathing labored through the pain in his side. It had been a couple years since he'd suffered a broken bone, and ribs were the worst. There was nothing really to do except wait and give them the time to heal.

Time he probably didn't have now...

196

Forcing himself back to his feet, Raz ignored the sounds of the slaves behind him. He moved back into the shadows of the storage area, kicking aside the junk in his way. Ahna was there in the dark, right where he'd left her, and he picked the dviassegai up gingerly as his side throbbed. Stepping over bodies, he made his way out from under the lofted floor, chuckling darkly when most of the slaves shrank away from him.

"Stop worrying. You're safe." He groaned, putting his back to the wall and sliding to the ground haltingly. "For the time being, at least. The Mahsadën will be here in the morning, unless they've already been alerted. Can you all walk?"

One of them—the girl Goyr's had been fondling—hesitated before nodding. "We can," she said, her accent surprisingly educated for someone who'd probably been Caged. She paused again, then scooted forward a little. "Are you hurt?"

Raz laughed, then hissed as that turned out to be a horrible decision. Rolling his head on the wall, he looked at her. "I'll be fine. What's your name?"

"Eva," the girl replied quickly.

"Nice to make your acquaintance, Eva. Now. The keys to those chains. Do you know where they are?"

The girl nodded. Raising a hand, she pointed to one of the bodies. Raz followed her finger.

Ki.

Groaning, Raz used Ahna to pull himself back to his feet, limping over to where the dead woman lay spread-eagled in the dirt.

VII

"The name "Mahsadën" was a combination of old desert words—mahar-sadan-adën—and the organization made no secret of the phrase's meaning. Roughly translated, it could be read as: 'Give Life and Spirit, or Have It Taken.'"

—*As Death Rose from the Ashes,* by Kohly Grofh

"They're *WHAT?*"

Adrion Blaeth smirked as his employer's denying shriek rang through the door to his left. He was standing outside Ergoin Sass' office, using the wall and his tailored pine-and-ivory crutch to balance on his one leg, the other severed just above the knee. It wasn't often he heard the man lose his temper like this. Sass was generally the calm sort, the one to keep his cool even when the other šef were bickering and throwing empty threats at each other.

Now, though, whatever had happened seemed to have pushed him over the edge.

"WHAT DO YOU MEAN THEY'RE *GONE?*"

"I mean," said another voice evenly, "that your merchandise wasn't at the granary. Neither were your men. Not alive at least."

Ooh, Adrion thought, listening more closely, *this is going to be good...*

"Dead?" Sass's voice demanded. "Those were the best sellswords money could buy! What happened?"

"Then three of your best seem to have been bested," the other man responded, and Adrion could hear the sneer in his voice. "As for what happened, I'll give you a hint. No, three hints rather: Davin Goyr had his head pushed through a wall, Shryn Or'Tand's throat was ripped out, and his brother Skore's neck was wrenched around so badly he was facing the wrong direction on his body. Whether that happened before or after he was hurled a dozen feet across the room, I couldn't say, but I needn't remind you that he was no small man."

There was a creaking, and Adrion could just imagine the man, whose voice he still couldn't recognize, leaning forward, drinking in every ounce of Sass' rage.

"Now who does that remind you of?"

"Raz i'Syul," Sass breathed angrily. "I *said* it was a bad idea to have him brought into this, Evony. The Monster isn't what you think. If you pull his strings, expect him to bite, not dance."

Adrion's intake of breath hissed as he heard the names. Raz i'Syul Arro, the Monster of Karth... Now *there* was a character he hadn't dealt with in some time. In truth, though, it was the other name that caught Adrion's attention the most: Evony. Though the Mahsadën's highest echelon had no actual form of ranking—theoretically giving each šef equal power—if someone were said to be in control of the underworld in Miropa, it would have been Imaneal Evony. The man had his hands in everything, including the businesses of his colleagues, and he didn't mind flaunting it.

"Regardless," Evony answered Sass' retort, "after the decision was made to use i'Syul, *you* were told to get a group together that could control him if he decided not to cooperate."

"Given the circumstances, I did my best. We wanted a small group to do the job. A large one would have attracted attention. But the reality is that there is no small group that can handle that animal. He's a winged demon, Evony, which you would know if you weren't frightened of meeting him."

There was a silence, and Adrion realized he was staring at the floor so hard he was surprised there wasn't a hole burned through it.

"Call me a coward again, Sass, as underhanded as you think it might be, and it will be the last mistake you ever make. The fact that I haven't ever met the atherian has nothing to do with being afraid of him. It has to do with the reality that such menial tasks as feeding our *pets* are generally passed on to society members of less... importance."

Another silence.

"Get out," Sass' voice spat.

Adrion heard a chuckle and the scrape of a chair, and he hurried to cross the polished floor, not wanting to be caught eavesdropping. Sure enough, within moments of his settling against the opposite wall, the office door swung open, and a tall man in purple and gold robes strode into the marble hall.

Imaneal Evony was the oldest of the šef, nearing his seventieth birthday, but he was fit and strong, his dark eyes sharp and savagely intelligent. He was bald, but his beard was trimmed silver, tapered to a point an inch or so below his chin. When he caught sight of Adrion, he stopped, smirking.

"You keep the company of animals and cripples, Sass," he called over his shoulder, gaze traveling down Adrion's body to the limb that wasn't there. "Small wonder you're losing your edge. They're rubbing off on you."

There was a crash of something being thrown against a wall in the room, and Evony laughed, striding down the corridor before disappearing into a stairwell. When he was gone, Adrion moved to knock on the open door, peering into the office.

Sass had his back to him, leaning against his desk and staring at the wall. He wore a crisp white shirt with frilling at the collar, nicely offset by a set of black pants, boots, and gloves. His blonde hair was stylishly spiked in the front and cut long at the back so that it barely touched his shoulders.

"Come in," he said gruffly, and Adrion closed the door behind him, dodging around the broken remains of the clay vase on the floor.

"What's going on?" Adrion asked, acting the innocent bystander.

Sass looked over his shoulder and raised an eyebrow. "Don't play coy. You know exactly what's going on."

Adrion smirked. "I wouldn't have learned from the best if I didn't," he agreed, crutching to the desk and taking a seat in the chair Evony must have just vacated. "I remember a few of your tricks, believe it or not."

Sass' office was a small marvel. Deep-crimson curtains of thin silk hung over the three windows, and at night there was always a fire burning in the hearth along the right wall. Shelves of black wood lined every spare surface, broken only by a painting directly behind Sass's desk portraying a Cienbal sunset over the roofs of some mud-brick city. Books and trinkets and odd mechanisms were neatly displayed everywhere, Sass' way of proudly showing his talents as a "collector" of fine things. It encouraged his clients to think they were in the absolute best of hands when they paid him a visit.

A few years ago, Adrion hadn't been able to appreciate what his employer did. Slavery, extortion, assassinations… it all went against every moral he'd been raised with, every ethic and belief he'd had since before he could remember. Still, it was a job, and far come from his previous employment as a baker's apprentice. It offered him the means to support himself and the Grandmother luxuriously, something none of his family had ever attempted, much less achieved.

But it had bothered him, nonetheless.

Over time, though, things had changed. He'd grown closer to Ergoin Sass, and found him to be a dangerously charming individual. An individual whose opinions he valued. It hadn't been long before he was seeing a side of the Mahsadën and its dealings he'd never imagined. What else were the people who were thrown in the Cages going to do with their lives? Most were beggars and whores, the scum that clung to the city's underbelly. By forcing them into labor, those people *became* something, became a part of the society by serving and building. They were also taken care of, and Sass had long ago convinced Adrion that a life of servitude was far better than a life of begging and starving. As for the contract killings, a day didn't go by in this city without a half-dozen murders. Why not maintain some control over the proceedings? It was distasteful, yes.

But it was necessary.

"Your cousin is causing trouble for us again, *Mychal*," Sass grunted sarcastically, lifting himself from his desk and sitting down behind it.

"Don't call me that." Adrion bristled. "That name holds no meaning for me anymore, as you well know. And as for Raz, he stopped being family when he put his own needs ahead of the blood he'd promised to protect. He deserves his 'Monster' moniker. He's an animal, incapable of being responsible for anything or anyone but himself."

"I'm glad to hear that," Sass said quietly, "because we need to deal with him."

Adrion clenched his jaw, but said nothing.

"No words? Good, then just listen. You probably caught most of the conversation between me and that stuck-up bastard, so here's the shorthand. I hired the lizard to help deal with our situation regarding Kî Orran. We figured out where she was going to be, along with twelve of the healthiest slaves that have gotten through the Cages all year. Slaves she somehow thieved right out from under us. Each head was worth three-hundred-and-some-odd crowns. i'Syul was part of a group that was supposed to take out Kî, severing her operation at the top, and reclaim the merchandise. The problem is—"

"Wait," Adrion interrupted. "Stop. Did Raz agree to this job, or did you trick him?"

"He agreed."

"And you told him everything?"

"I told him there was a bounty on Kî's head. I figured the rest would come."

"Ah," Adrion said with a smile, leaning back his chair. "And therein lies your problem."

Sass didn't respond.

"I suppose it's fortunate, actually," Adrion continued thoughtfully, thumbing the bone handle of his crutch. "If you'd told Raz you wanted him to recapture heads you'd lost, he'd probably have taken yours then and there. Or at least torn off several limbs. Raz doesn't like our kind, the lawbreakers. He butchers them."

"Which is why he's been such a useful asset."

"Yes, true, but where you went wrong is with your assumption that Raz is willing to do what's wrong to do what's right. I admit it's an understandable expectation. Is he willing to murder to be rid of a murderer? Absolutely. Would he accept money in exchange for his talents? Without a doubt. We've both seen him do it. But Raz will never—and I do mean *never*—knowingly put a person in chains, no matter how much you offer or threaten him. In that respect he is stuck in the mindset of our old family and his own deluded beliefs."

"I thought that was the case as well," Sass cut it, playing with a polished quartz ball he used as a paperweight, rolling it across the desk with his fingers. "But in the years since he joined us he hasn't seemed to have any qualms with taking jobs for me. I thought he'd grown up a bit. You did."

Adrion snorted. "I'm human. Raz is far from, as much as he'd like to think he is. I know enough about the jobs you've given him to point out that you've only ever offered him assassination contracts and used him as a warning. I don't know if that's a coincidence, or if you didn't give him head bounties for some other reason, but it's probably the only thing that kept him in line. Raz will never see himself as part of the Mahsadën. He will kill us all before that happens."

Sass pondered the words, picking the sphere up and examining it, turning it over in his palm. "So where do you think he is now? With the slaves?"

"My best guess?" Adrion asked, leaning back in his chair to think. "You broke him, in a sense. And not in a good one. Up till now we had some measure of control over him, even if it wasn't exactly a leash. Raz kills for crowns. Coin is the only thing that really mattered to him until yesterday, so the fact that he hasn't turned up with Orran's head on a spike isn't a good thing. If he was just bothered by this particular job, he would have let the merchandise go, returned for the bounty, and told you that if you ever sent him to collect your slaves again he would make you eat your limbs one by one."

"But he hasn't..."

"Which means we're back to square one. Raz is no longer an asset,

Sass. His mindset is most likely reverted back to where it was before Master Rafeal convinced him we had some 'similar' goals."

"He ripped Frân Rafeal apart and had his limbs shipped to the šef in baskets!" Sass exclaimed. "I got a foot! I don't know about you, Adrion, but I hardly consider that 'convincing' him."

"Rafeal offered him the deal that he ended up taking," Adrion said with a shrug. "The deal that gave the šef some ability to use him."

"So... what? You think the fact that he didn't fulfill the contract means he wants to start a war with us again? He's broken contracts before when he didn't like the terms. At worst he stopped accepting jobs for a time."

"*But*," Adrion insisted, smoothing the fabric of his pant leg, "in those cases he always informed us of his actions and decisions. This is different."

He sighed, putting his chin in his palm and leaning against the arm of his chair. His gray eyes followed the tiny sliver of window he could see through the space in the curtains to his left, and after a moment he turned to look at his employer.

"You asked me where I thought he was. I don't know. But if you asked me what I thought he was doing, I'd say getting ready to turn on you. I would encourage you to warn the other šef that Raz is no longer playing nice. Whatever he's up to, I would bet my house it has something to do with hunting you and the others down."

The quartz paused in its rolling. Sass was watching the polished surface without seeing it, preoccupied with Adrion's words. It was a long few seconds before he looked up.

"We have to deal with this quickly."

"But quietly," Adrion told him sharply. "I agree, but if we let on that he's gotten to us, you'll find yourself fighting against half the city rather than just one out-of-control animal. Better to take your time and plan it out than rush in and fail. Still, move now. If I know Raz, he'll be a step ahead of us already."

VIII

"The Cages are our greatest source of revenue, but also our greatest source of entertainment. I would be a bored old man, I believe, if not for the view of the market plaza from my balcony window."

—Imaneal Evony, Mahsadën šef

"Ready?"

Raz took a breath. Eva's hands were shaking, which didn't bear much confidence to the situation, but any help was better than none. Closing his eyes, he nodded.

He felt the girl give the binds around his chest a last securing tug, and then twist them sharply.

Pop.

Raz grunted, feeling the last rib slip back into place. His claws dug furrows into the room's dirt floor as agony washed through his chest into every limb. For several seconds he couldn't breathe, feeling the pain weigh on his body like a heavy stone. Then it subsided, seeping away, and he sighed, opening his eyes.

Beside him, Eva smirked, tying one final knot before sitting back to rinse her hands in the bowl of clean water beside the mat.

"And here I thought I'd never see you wince." She double-checked the bandages before helping him into a sitting position against the wall.

"Being used to injury doesn't mean I enjoy it," he retorted with a grimace, spreading his wings so they didn't get pinned against the brick. "And pain is pain. Still, I'm glad you were a surgeon. If I'd done that you'd likely find me curled up in the corner crying like a babe."

"The operative word in that phrase being 'were.' And I was only ever the surgeon's apprentice. Not to mention I'm a bit out of practice ever since... since then."

Eva's eyes fell, and she grew quiet. Picking the bowl up off the floor, she moved to the window and dumped it out.

It had been almost a week since the Kî job went south, and with every guard in the city looking for them it was difficult for the group to make any headway toward getting out of Miropa. Raz hadn't even bothered trying to get back to his room at the White Sands. It would have been the first place the Mahsadën would looked. Eva and a few of the others, on the rare occasions he'd let them run to the market for food and water, returned each time with more stories of how scribed portraits of him were plastered on every shop wall.

Raz wasn't too worried, though. He had a dozen safehouses throughout the city. Most, granted, were set up for him by Ergoin Sass, but there were still two or three he was positive the šef knew nothing about. He'd manage, one way or the other. At the moment they were all stuffed into a tiny hovel in the middle of the northern shantytowns, too deep in the labyrinth of run-down buildings for the guard to come across them by anything but dumb luck.

Nevertheless, Raz had moved them once already, because dumb luck always seemed to come into play at the worst of times.

Some of the others were nervous about hiding in plain sight, but it made the most sense. They all knew the Mahsadën wouldn't risk a public disturbance just yet. Such shows of power tended to shift balances, and if too many Miropans thought the shadows were losing their grip, civil outbreaks might erupt.

Assassins they might send. Raz had picked this particular house just for that reason. All but one of the windows were boarded shut, and the ceiling—usually a point of weakness since mud brick didn't hold up all that well against the elements—was still strong, even reinforced by arched timber beams. The door was never opened unless he did it himself, and together the group had fashioned ragged curtains from dirty cloth they'd salvaged from the abandoned buildings nearby, hanging them over every opening. They took turns posting watch after the Sun set, just in case, but so far nothing hinted that they'd been found out.

So far, Raz repeated to himself, looking around at the ten remaining of the ragtag bunch, all huddled in whatever cramped space they'd been able to grab on the ground.

He was less than pleased with the situation, never a fan of crowds much less a packed sweatbox of a house he couldn't even stand up in. Despite this, Raz was slowly finding that he enjoyed the company, at least for the moment. Especially Eva, the girl he'd ripped from Goyr's grubby hands. A former physician's apprentice, she'd been grabbed three months ago when her employer's business collapsed and he'd arranged to sell his assistants to the Mahsadën in exchange for loan payments. Her skills, rusty as they were, would hopefully set Raz on a quicker path to recovery than he'd anticipated.

At the moment, though, he was stuck, barely able to get up and walk without trouble breathing. Ahna and his other weapons were tucked against the wall within easy reach, but he doubted he could have hefted any of them properly in his current state. There was nothing to do but sit and wait.

Sit and wait and plan.

Raz's eyes shifted over the forms of the runaways. They could scheme and plot all they wanted, but the most immediate problem to be tackled was getting them all out of the city, headed anywhere, the general agreement being northward. They were close enough to the border that they could risk the summer heat, and these couple of months were all that the North could offer for safe travel before the freeze picked up again. Raz had heard the winters there were harsh, and that the previous year's had been particularly devastating.

None of the group wanted to get caught in a storm like that.

Sadly, not everyone would make it. Two of them—a former blacksmith named Abon Grous, and Yuri Avina, a member of the city guard who'd refused to take bribes from the Mahsadën—had opted to risk making a break for it. On their own they'd taken their leave, heading for other cities in the hopes of staying with family until other plans could be made. They'd said their farewells two days ago, and Raz didn't have the heart to tell the group that one of his contacts—via letter hidden in a loaf of bread—had informed him that Yuri had been killed and Abon was back in the Cages.

That had been the day they'd moved. He wasn't about to let that happen to the rest.

"The atherian said he knows someone who can get us out of here within the week," one of the women whispered from the far corner of the room. "Even if they take us as far as the border, we'd have plenty of time."

"You're really going to trust *him?*" a man hissed, jerking his head to indicate Raz, who pretended he couldn't hear. "Why? He's one of *them*, I'm telling you! This 'someone' he's told us about is probably a private buyer that he just wants to up the price on! No. I won't go back. I'd rather find my own way out."

"How?" Eva demanded. She'd finished drying the bowl and moved to sit with the group. "With what means? We have no coin to pay anyone with, the Mahsadën have city patrols searching every caravan coming in and out of the gates, and I don't know many people of the sort to risk their necks smuggling would-be slaves out of Miropa. You're paranoid, Dayle. It might have served you well in the chains, yes, but right now it's going to get you killed."

Dayle grumbled under his breath, folding his arms.

"I'm thinkin' I'm jumpin' in with the ladies," a man Raz was pretty sure was called Tym, a street runner who'd been grabbed while begging outside a tavern, offered. "No hard feelin's, Dayle. I don't much fancy lizards neither, bu' we all done heard the stories about this one, ain't we? The things they done to his family... I'll trust he ain't about to sell me back to the Cages after that. And if'n it means gettin' away from the Mahsadën... Well, Sun take them, he can bleedin' well ship me away with any lad he feels like."

Raz couldn't help it. He smiled.

It felt alien on his face, a strange, unpracticed motion. The last few days had not been easy for him. It wasn't the ribs. Those were the least of his worries. And he was confident that he could get the rest of the group out of Miropa without a problem since he'd called in a favor with Bayl Vyzen, who owed him more than a few.

What bothered Raz was the reflection he saw in the shine of his armor, or in the ripples of his washbasin when he scrubbed his face in the morning. It was the frightened look he still got from several of the group when he caught their eye, the whispers he heard when they all thought he'd dozed off to sleep. Eva was the only one who seemed to believe in him wholeheartedly, for which he was grateful.

He just wasn't sure he deserved it.

The Mahsadën had used him, played him. They'd been the puppeteers behind his actions from the start, manipulating him into thinking he'd managed to stay above their games. He'd fooled himself just as much, truthfully. He'd suppressed the voices of doubt and convinced himself he'd somehow kept his nose clean of their trickery.

And now it was costing him.

Whereas he'd been smart, they'd been smarter, playing on his desires and twisted concepts of justice to forge him into the first blade of their headlong charge. He'd become more than just a sword-for-hire to them. The name Raz i'Syul Arro, the Monster of Karth, had become a face of the system he hated so much. Unconsciously he'd fueled the machine he'd been fighting to tear apart, feeding the Mahsadën its own refuse and only making it stronger. They'd used him, toyed with him. They'd conned him into believing he was working of his own free will when, in reality, he was more like the kites children of the wealthier families would fly in the streets on a cool day. He could move about in any direction with some measured freedom but, in the end, his string was always wrapped around one finger or another.

Thing was, though, it was easy to blame them.

In truth the Mahsadën had only been the catalyst of every decision he'd made in the last few years, merely sparked the events and actions that shaped him into what he was. They'd fed him partial truths, paid him the crowns he'd demanded, given him the work he'd asked for. They'd provided the illusion of willpower, provided him everything he needed to fight the fight he was only too anxious to pursue. They'd pushed him toward the edge every time, nudging him closer and closer.

But on every occasion, without exception, it was *he* who had decided to take the plunge.

Raz's arms knotted, the lithe muscle under his scaly skin flexing as he clenched his fists. His tail snaked over the floor and mat to his left, curling around Ahna's handle.

How many people had he personally put in chains? How many of the faces floating in front of his eyes—those poor distorted masks of pain that were every figure he'd ever seen in the Cages—were in those iron prisons because of him? What had he done to help them? Had he ever in the last few years actually stuck out his hand to pull someone free of the shackles that rubbed their wrists and ankles raw?

No, Raz thought, turning gingerly to steady himself on the loose brick and ease to his feet. *I haven't.*

Leaning heavily against the wall, he limped to the window Eva had just emptied the basin out of, the only one not boarded up. Pulling the curtain aside an inch with one finger, Raz peered out into the deserted street. He stood there for a time, looking at nothing in particular.

What do I do now?

"Atherian?"

Raz looked over his shoulder. Eva was there, her face lined with concern. Behind her the rest of the group still whispered, only a few of them having glanced up when he'd pushed himself to stand.

"Is everything all right?" Eva asked, moving to stand beside him. "Are the bandages too tight?"

Raz chuckled humorlessly and turned to look back out the window. High, high above them, a hawk circled in the blue sky, wings dipping lazily in a great spiral over the city.

"No. Nothing like that."

"Then what is it?"

Raz frowned, thinking of how to answer the question.

"I lost my way," he said after a pause, his eyes still following the bird of prey against the wisps of clouds. "I thought I was doing one thing, and in the end it turns out I was doing nothing. Worse actually. I was the right hand of the kind of people I would like nothing better than to rid the South of."

"The Mahsadën," Eva stated simply, and Raz nodded.

"I'd convinced myself I was above their games, above their schemes and plots." Raz frowned. "But who was I kidding? Annoyances like Kî Orran? If I'd done what I was contracted to do, I would have killed her, gotten paid, and accepted the fact that everything else around me was out of my hands. Do you know what that means, Eva? It means you and the rest of the group would be in chains right now. Again. Probably on your way to a gem mine outside the Seven Cities, or some other awful place."

Eva was quiet, her shoulder against the sill of the window.

"Do you know how many contracts I've taken from them?" Raz hissed, closing his eyes. He leaned his elbow on the side frame of the window and rested his forehead on his wrist. "Because I don't. And the only difference between this job and those is the fact that in this case everything was right under my nose. What if you lot hadn't been with Kî? What if you'd been left at her last safehouse? Sass and his men would have found you and sold you, and I would have been none the wiser. How many times do you think that's happened? Ten, twenty, a hundred? How many people have I had a part in throwing in the Cages?"

"I don't know."

Raz opened his eyes and looked at her. Eva was frowning, watching the others plot away.

"I don't know how many you could have helped, but I do know how many you put in worse situations than they were already in. None."

"Makes no difference," Raz growled, looking back out the window just as the hawk dove, rocketing toward some prey in the streets below. "I should have—"

"It *does* make a difference," Eva cut in, looking up at him. "Yes, perhaps you could have realized all this sooner, done something sooner. But that didn't happen. Instead, you woke up now. You are aware *now*. You know what that means?"

Raz didn't respond, but he looked down at her.

"It means that now you have the knowledge to do something about it. Rest. Heal. Help us out of the city."

She stepped away, moving to rejoin the others. Then she looked back over her shoulder at him.

"And when that's over, you make them *pay*, Monster."

IX

Raz stood alone in the dark beyond the west wall of the city, white hood pulled up to cast his features in shadow. He watched the small bob of light that was the cart's only lantern swing side to side as the driver shouted a distant "Hyah! Hyah!" driving the horses through the night. Raz thought he saw the silhouette of a hand rise and wave in farewell, and he returned the gesture, the wind rustling his robes and tossing sand against the steel of his mail. Ahna rested beside him, the point of her bottom tip sunk into the desert floor.

It was almost ten minutes before the light vanished altogether, marking the disappearance of Eva and the others into the leagues of rolling hills south of the northern border. Even so, well after they'd gone Raz stood staring at the spot where the light had faded away.

Then he looked up into the night sky, taking in the Moon and Her Stars before closing his eyes.

See them safely to new life, he asked in silence. *Watch and protect them, that they may never again know the hopelessness of stolen freedom.*

He opened his eyes, searching the sky until he found a familiar pair of twinkling orbs crowning the smaller one sitting between them.

Help me, Raz prayed. *Give me the strength I would have if you were here. I will need it soon.*

The small gate, one of the city entrances used only by guards and the "diplomats" who were in fact Mahsadën messengers from the other cities, was still ajar. Slipping in, Raz darted into the cover of the nearest buildings. He was in the wealthiest of Miropa's districts, a risk in and of itself. Night patrols circled more frequently here than anywhere else, and the contingents were always veteran soldiers, alert and ever wary. It had been a challenge sneaking ten wanted men and women through the brightly lit streets. In comparison, Raz relaxed. Getting back to the safe house would be less of a problem on his own.

First, though, he ducked into the third alley he came to, kneeling beside a group of figures all but hidden in the dark.

"Wake up," he growled, gripping the chin of the closest one and shaking him. The guard came to at once, grunting as he tried to yell through the cloth gag in his mouth. The sound came out pitifully muffled, and he struggled with the bindings on his wrists and ankles.

"Shout all you want. No one can hear you through that," Raz spat, standing up. The man stilled and grew silent, eyes wide, taking in Raz's towering outline against the lantern light from the road.

"If I'd wanted you dead, you'd be dead, so stop worrying. I have a message. On the other hand, if you don't deliver it—well, your friends will be happy to explain the consequences to you."

He gestured to the other figures lying in the dark past the first guard, who turned to look at them. His muted scream was oddly satisfying, and Raz smirked humorlessly. The man fell over in his haste to scoot away. Blood pooled on the cobbled ground, forming black puddles where each of the rest of the patrol had had their throats slit. Every horrified pair of eyes was wide and staring, some gazing up at the night sky above, some at the walls around them.

Raz had made sure each and every one knew they were going to die.

"Are you listening?" he asked. The man nodded hurriedly, seeming unable to look away from the bodies of his comrades.

"Good. Then tell your šef that Raz i'Syul is coming for them next. Tell them the Monster says they'd best start running, and that they'd best start running *now*."

X

"In the records we have, we find that the Laorin eventually came to call him 'the Warring Son.' 'Violent by nature and content to kill if it served his purpose,' the Priest-author Carro al'Dor wrote, 'it is odd to say that he is the greatest ally our faith has ever come across. Laor bless him for his strong heart and kind soul, but the creature is a conflicted being. Talo always used to remind me that all beasts are of the Lifegiver, but I wonder at Laor's greater plan, and how it might involve this haunted child.'"

—*The Atherian,* by Jûn fi'Surr

"He's a madman, Grandmother," Adrion growled, coming to sit on the balcony chair opposite the woman's, looking out over the city. The Sun hung imperiously at its apex in the sky above, a single bright eye gazing down on the world. "Do you hear me? Your pride and joy, the animal you had brought into our family. In the last week he's decimated three full patrols, assassinated both the captain of the detail responsible for the Cages *and* his replacement, freed two shipments of slaves, and made an attempt on Gaorys' life while he was collecting fees in the market. I'm telling you, the beast's gone insane."

The Grandmother didn't react to his words, her empty gray eyes ever distant. She continued to stare out over the expansive slate rooftops of the houses around them. Her white hair, once neat and always kept in a tight bun, was disheveled and loose, hanging about her face and framing that maddening half smile plastered there. Adrion sighed.

"I'm sorry," he said, leaning back in his chair and rubbing his temples. "I know how much you hate it when I bring up work with you, but this is important. If we don't do something soon, Raz is going to cause a real problem for the society."

The woman didn't budge, the only motion in her entire bearing being the shallow lift and drop of her chest. A breeze picked up, catching a few strands of her loose hair.

Thank the Sun for this weather, Adrion thought, squinting to look up at the sky. The temperature was actually bearable, an exquisite rarity during the summer months even this far from the rolling dunes of the Cienbal.

"I'll tell you what," Adrion grunted, picking himself up out of the chair and grabbing his crutch from the bench beside him, "I'll have Lazura bring you something to eat, shall I? Might do you some good."

Hobbling back inside, he grabbed a silver bell from where it hung on the wall and rang it once. It was a quiet sound, but in moments the door to the study creaked open, and a young woman stepped into the room.

She wore dark robes of black silk so thin they were almost transparent, the color clashing beautifully with her blonde hair and blue eyes. She was tall and slim, and Adrion would have found her attractive were it not for the great X-shaped scar that marred her face, leading from around her right eye and crisscrossing diagonally along her face in two perfectly straight lines.

"You rang, Master Blaeth?" she asked, her sweet, clear voice cutting through the silence of the house.

The woman was a miracle for her ability to get the Grandmother to eat and drink, but even if she hadn't been, Adrion was fairly sure he would have kept her around if only to hear that voice at dinner every night. The one-sided conversation the old woman offered could get lonely, truth be told.

"I did." Adrion moved to the great timber desk in the corner of the room. The study was a spacious chamber, lined with shelves much like Sass' office was, but Adrion rarely had the chance to peruse any of them. Most of his time was spent locked in his office upstairs, going over numbers till the earliest hours of the morning for his employer and the other šef.

He really did need to invest in some oil lamps, considering how many candles he went through in a week…

"Could you see to it that my Grandmother gets fed, Lazura?" he asked, easing himself into the heavy wooden chair behind his desk. He found that he got better results with a kind word rather than a heavy hand, considering the image he cut. "And have the handmaids come and change her, if you would."

"Those poor girls," Lazura giggled, her laugh like a tinkling wind chime. "They won't like that."

"I wouldn't wish it on anyone," Adrion agreed with a smile. "Least of all you or I."

Lazura gave a small curtsy, a motion Adrion had yet to get accustomed to despite the fact that he had five servants employed in his estate, all women with the exception of Bertran, the cook.

The Grandmother required a lot of looking after.

After Lazura took her leave, Adrion rubbed his forehead again, feeling the headache that had built up over the last week throb painfully behind his eyes.

"Drink water. It works better."

Adrion didn't even jump as he looked up. Sass was standing in front of his desk, examining the shelves with an interested eye, flashy orange and black shirt and pants standing out in the shaded room. The šef had appeared out of thin air too many times before to scare his confidant, but it didn't help Adrion's mood in the least.

"You don't ever knock, do you?"

"Not if I can help it," Sass replied without looking around at him, reaching out to pluck a book from its place. "Ah, *The Merchant's Trail*. And a first edition at that! I've been looking for this. Where did you—?"

"What are we going to do about Raz?" Adrion cut in, his temper flaring. "You're standing there, drooling over books I keep for the effect they give the room, while he's out there pulling our roots up one by one."

"A handful of guards and some dozen slaves are 'our roots'?" Sass chuckled, putting the book back and turning to look at Adrion. "I must have missed that part of the meeting."

"He almost took out Gaorys, and would have if the man hadn't been paranoid about going out in the first place. Even surrounded by sarydâ he barely got away with his life, and a half dozen more of our men are dead."

"Calm down, Adrion," Sass said sternly, interlocking his fingers behind his head and leaning against the shelf. "I *know* he's causing problems, and believe me I'm doing everything I can to fix it. We all are. But life goes on, and we have business as usual to deal with." Slipping a hand into his shirt, he pulled out a thin roll of parchment. "I've brought you the figures for the last section's earnings. I need you to launder the coinage and stack the numbers by the end of the week. Can you do that?"

Adrion sighed. "Of course," he replied, reaching to take the parchment. "But you really think this is the time to be focusing on details we can deal with later? Raz is going to be more than a thorn in your side soon, Sass. He—"

"It. Will. Be. Handled." Sass pressed every word in poignantly. "In the grand scheme of things, what can the lizard do to us? He's a pain, I'll admit, but everything he's done and can do is mendable."

"*Don't underestimate him*," Adrion insisted. "You've hired him for more jobs than all the others put together! You should know what he's capable of! And as for me, he was like a brother to me for over fifteen years. I saw him change, Sass, and while he used to be as human as the rest of us, he's not anymore. The man is an animal in truth, pun and all. He won't stop until he's taken us all down. We should do something about it *now*."

"He's not a *man* at all," Sass retorted, turning on his heel and crossing his hands behind his back.

"Fair enough, but he's smarter than your prejudice allows you to see, and it's going to cost you if you don't listen to me!"

Sass stilled for a moment, turning his head to look out the open doors that led to the balcony. The Grandmother still sat there, gazing out into emptiness, the wind ruffling her gray gown. For a second, Adrion thought he had gotten through.

"Run the numbers," Sass said over his shoulder before heading for the door. "I'll be back at the end of the week for the sheets."

And then he was gone.

"Idiot!" Adrion hissed, wincing as the headache throbbed again. Pushing himself up from the chair, he got to his feet, grabbing his crutch and the sealed roll of parchment Sass had brought him.

He was making his way around the desk, turning to head up to his offices, when a shadow fell over the room like a cloud crossing the Sun outside. Before he could turn around, though, something thin and heavy collided with Adrion's back, sending him crashing to the ground.

"You're the idiot, Mychal," a harsh voice breathed while he struggled onto his good knee, winded and gasping. "These dealings of yours are going to get you killed."

Raz stood over his cousin, Ahna held in both hands. He'd used her shaft to knock his cousin to the ground, and now he watched Mychal— *No*, he conceded—Adrion, struggle to breathe.

"You!" the man wheezed when he finally managed to turn around. "How did you get in here? Get out!"

"Not yet." Raz knelt down and reached for something on the ground. "Don't get me wrong, I love these family visits, but this time I came for something more valuable than your silver tongue." He held up the roll of parchment.

Sass' numbers.

"*Bastard!*" Adrion spat, scooting forward and making to swipe it from his cousin's armored fist. "Give it to me!"

"No," Raz replied simply, standing up and stepping back. "If I'm right—and I certainly pay people enough to be right—the Mahsadën only ever keep two financial records of any specific group of transactions. One for use by the šef and their underlings"—he said the word with a sneer—"and one for records keeping, locked away in some secret vault."

"Which means what you hold in your hand is worthless!" Adrion exploded, crawling to the nearest bookshelf and pulling himself up into a standing position. "Give it to me, Raz, or by the Moon I'll—!"

"It's only worthless," Raz interrupted, "if you don't have both."

He pulled a small leather satchel from around his back and flicked it open. Inside were a half-dozen similar rolls of parchment, each sealed shut with a black circle of wax the size of a coin, embossed with a curvy *M*.

Adrion was speechless.

"Your messenger ran into a bit of trouble," Raz explained, closing the bag and tucking it away again. "Don't bother looking for him. I always found it shameful how little they feed the oasis crocodiles."

"NO!" Mychal screamed, throwing himself at Raz, who dodged out of the way. "Sun burn you, Raz! Lazura! *LAZURA!* CALL THE GUARD! HE'S HERE! TELL THEM HE'S...!"

But Raz was already running, ducking his head and darting through the doors onto the balcony. Jumping up, he planted a foot on the balustrade and with a great shove leapt into the air. Spreading his wings, Ahna held in one hand and the satchel secure in the other, he soared.

The fall was magnificent, the air rushing around him like a storm. For the brief few seconds it lasted, Raz remembered the times years ago when he'd spent his nights leaping from roof to roof in every city his family traded in.

Then the memories were gone, and he landed smoothly on the cobbled ground below, right in the middle of the crowded streets. There were gasps and screams as he rolled and leapt to his feet, but Raz ignored them, ducking and pulling his hood up before taking off. He'd never been good at blending in with a moving crowd. His size had its downsides, after all.

Still, if he could stay low enough and not jostle too many people, he might just be able to get to safer roads without much of a—

"STOP! AFTER HIM! STOP!"

Or not, Raz thought, cursing.

It had been a risky plan, breaking into Adrion's house in the middle of the day. But when their messenger didn't show up for records keeping, Raz was sure the Mahsadën would have gotten the second copies under lock and key within an hour. It left him only a small window of time in which to pull off the theft. Still, he'd managed it, and now he had the only two copies of Sass' financial exchanges for the last three months, along with five or six other scrolls he was hoping might contain valuable information.

Assuming he could make it out alive, this would be Raz's most fruitful day yet.

Forgoing his attempt at stealth, Raz ran, dodging through the crowd as best he could and shoving people aside as needed. Catching a break in the throng, he took it, making for the alley that headed south toward the market quarters. Before he took his first step onto the sidewalk, though, two uniformed men cut across his path, swords held high.

Ahna's pointed tip took one of them through the sternum, the other going down under Raz's fist, the gauntlet colliding with his face, splitting his nose and shattering at least a half-dozen teeth.

Bulling over the collapsing pair, Raz made it into the shade of the alley, halting to look left and right. It took a second to figure out exactly where he was, but it was all he needed, and he took off again just before another group of guards poured in behind him. He could take them. He had no doubt about that, but he would be wasting valuable time in which reinforcements would be called. Even he would get swamped if one against five suddenly turned into one against fifty.

He was good, but he wasn't *that* good.

Left. Right. Right. Left. Right. It was a good thing he'd made it an essential part of his self-training in his first years as a sword-for-hire to memorize every inch of the city he could. Using all his speed and cunning, he put distance between himself and the guard, dodging through the maze of alleys and back roads that only in this district would be kept so clean. Another left and he was almost positive it would be... *there!* The narrow space, barely a foot wide, between the guesthouse of one of the estates and Miropa's only bookstore.

Making the corner, Raz turned his body and tucked his wings, shimmying through the opening. He was two-thirds of the way through when the guard caught up, most of them running right past the space before one of the stragglers noticed him.

"OY!" he yelled to his compatriots, slipping in. "HERE! HE'S HERE!"

He was halfway across when Raz's dagger caught him in the throat, accurate as an arrow despite the awkward throw with no room to spare. Raz watched him gurgle and collapse, body held upright by the opposite wall that had been barely two or three inches away from his chest to start with. Smirking, Raz heard the other guards curse when they couldn't get past the body, and he scooted the last few feet to freedom, popping out in a tiny square courtyard surrounded by walls on every side. The stones here had been torn up from the ground, leaving the sandy earth bare, and the careful care and delicate hand of the estate's widowed heiress had turned the place into a tiny garden.

There was even a small tree—oak, someone had told him once—growing in its center.

Sadly, as this wasn't the time to marvel at a rich old woman's use of her crowns, Raz kept moving, aiming for the tree. When he was a few feet from it he jumped and grabbed the lowest branch with his free hand, using his momentum to swing and wrap his legs around the next one. Using his tail as an anchor, he pulled himself up, climbing branch by branch, tugging Ahna free when she got caught and checking every few seconds to make sure the stolen satchel was still closed and safe.

In twenty seconds he was high enough and, gathering his courage, he crouched for one last leap.

Then he jumped, flying through empty air, limbs flailing until he crashed onto the slanted roof of the bookstore.

By the time the guard got through to the garden, Raz had disappeared, leaving nothing but a handful of mottled green leaves to float down around their perplexed heads.

A quarter league away, an old woman caught a glimpse of a figure jumping across her field of vision, leaping from roof to roof, a great two-headed spear in one hand. For the briefest of instants something like a memory pricked at her mind, and the half smile widened the tiniest fraction before she found herself surrounded by limbo once again.

XI

"Since before written memory there were legends and stories of the dahgün, the mountain dragons of the old North. The Laorin claim that the creatures were the Lifegiver's first children, his first Gift, but when Laor discovered that his creations were capable of nothing but chaos and destruction, he grew terribly angry and wiped them from the face of the world. Yet despite the tale, every so often one may come across those who will claim to have seen a great winged beast circling the skies far above the highest peaks of the Saragrias Ranges."

—Legends Beyond the Border, by Zyryl Vahs

Syrah crouched low to the ground, inching her staff down into the grass at her feet so gently her shoulder ached. She had to. Any sudden motion would scare off the doe standing not ten yards from her, ears flicking back and forth while it bent to graze between the trees.

The Arocklen Woods stretched almost half-a-hundred leagues east, west, and south from the base of the wide, winding stairs that led up the mountains to Cyrugi Di'. During the winter it was a harsh place, the pine groves growing so thick and tall that when they were coated with snow the floor of the Woods was almost pitch black and all but impossible to navigate. Wolves hunted in packs in the forested hills, and snow leopards crept along the lowest branches. There was even the occasional news of the great white-and-brown ursalus bears mauling foolhardy travelers to death.

All that, though, was during the freeze.

Now, in high summer, the Arocklen was an utterly different place. Even as Syrah crept forward, careful to stay downwind of the deer, she had to skirt around bright patches of sunlight and be sure not to rustle the thick beds of white mornin'loves that patterned the ground. Birds sang in the branches above her head, and it was warm enough that she'd finally been able to exchange her white robes for a thin sleeveless leather jerkin and comfortable cotton shorts.

Off to her left, Syrah could barely hear Reyn moving on a parallel path forward, trying to catch the deer from two angles.

It was the gathering time, the apex point of summer where the residents of the Citadel capable of doing so took turns making the trip down the mountain every other day to aid in stocking the temple's stores for winter. Carro was somewhere nearby, partnered with Jerrom, Reyn's former Priest-Mentor. Four score others were spread out in the first dozen acres from the base of the stairway, all heeding to their own tasks. Some were foraging, gathering roots and mushrooms and any other edibles they could find. Others were collecting kindling and chopping firewood from the fallen trees that succumbed to the weight of the snow and ice every year.

And others were hunting for meat that would be salted and preserved, hopefully lasting long enough to get them through the ten months of freeze without having to resort to a staple diet of wheat porridge and dried berries.

Ducking silently beneath a pair of low-hanging evergreens, Syrah saw Reyn hunch behind on old stump. Catching his eye, she motioned that she was ready. The man nodded and returned the gesture. Exhaling slowly, Syrah lifted a hand and slowly curled her fingers into a loose fist.

They had no bows and arrows, no slings and certainly no hunting spears. The Laorin had little use for them, and as far as Syrah knew the only weapons in the Citadel were dulled steel imitations Reyn taught with under the weapons master, Audus Brern. There was no need for such things, after all, when other tools could replace their uses…

Feeling the flash and coolness in her palm, Syrah leapt up only seconds after Reyn. She watched as the man hurled a tiny white orb of light, throwing with the same motion he might a javelin. The doe, though, ever on the alert, darted away, leaping aside so that Reyn's bolt zipped harmlessly through the air and hit the underbrush, fizzling out with a tiny *pop*.

Syrah ignored her partner's curses, studying the animal's frantic path through the pines. She watched her target zigzag deeper into the Woods, disappearing behind one tree before appearing again for the briefest of moments on the other side.

Then Syrah saw her chance, and she threw.

The little ball of light shot through the air like an arrow, flying between the trunks. Guided with a skillful hand, it caught the doe in midair just as the animal leapt over a fallen log, striking the unfortunate beast squarely in the front shoulder.

There was another flash of white light, and the deer tumbled to the ground, dead.

"Praise Him for his goodness," Syrah prayed quietly, touching the fingers of her throwing hand to her forehead before looking up again.

Reyn was already crashing through the bushes toward their kill, whooping when he came to a stop over the animal.

"That was incredible!" he yelled back to where Syrah was retrieving her staff before making her way through the trees toward him. "That's the best shot I've seen you make yet! What are they feeding you out there in the world?"

"Baby rabbits, clumps of dirt, and hard stones," she teased with a laugh, hopping over a felled log. "And it was more luck than anything else."

"Luck my ass," Reyn snorted, crouching down. Aside from the dirt and leaves that clung to its body from the fall, the deer looked practically untouched. There was no sign of injury, no wound or blood. To the human eye it was as though the animal had keeled over on its own and died.

Which was pretty much the case, Syrah thought, sticking her staff in the soft ground before unwinding the leather straps she'd had wrapped around her waist and kneeling down.

Laor's gifts were many and great, but the small talent he granted his faithful in the arts of magic were possibly the most potent of all. In their varying years of training the Priests and Priestesses learned to control and manipulate the powers, changing them to suit their needs. Most of their studies were devoted to healing, something Syrah had unfortunately never had a true talent for. On the other hand, these other—less docile— aspects of magic certainly had their uses...

And what Syrah had always had a talent for was fighting.

Maybe it was the fact that she'd practically been raised by a former gladiator. Maybe it was the remnant memories of a thatched mud-brick house, the floor covered in blood and dust and bodies. Regardless, what Syrah lacked in ability for the mending hand she made up twice over with her skills in the field. Even before she'd been granted her staff she'd often been a member of choice for the rare expeditions the Laorin took down the mountains during the freezes. Eret, bless his soul, always knew that she could take care of herself, even within the boundaries of the faith. The cardinal rule of the Laorin still held her firm and—while Syrah had left more than one man bloody and unconscious in her life—she'd never gotten near the edge of killing. It was an experience, even if it had been allowed, she was sure she'd never want to explore.

Taking a life is like falling off a waterfall, Talo once told her on a rare occasion they'd discussed his former life. *There's a moment of exhilaration, a minute where you feel invincible as the red dyes your hands… And then you hit the water below and it rushes over you, flooding into your lungs until you can't breathe.*

No. That wasn't something Syrah ever wanted to experience.

But it wasn't merely the horror of the actual act that stopped her. Murder was an unforgivable sin, and the punishments for a Laorin knowingly taking a life were severe and brutal, even by the kindest standards. Priests, Priestesses, and even acolytes who partook in the knowledgeable death of a person were cast out of the faith, carted to Ystred, the closest of the North's mountain towns, and given enough money for food and shelter for a single night. Then they were left to find their own way in a harsh world many of them had little experience dealing with.

But not before they were Broken.

Even in the summer warmth Syrah shivered, giving the leather straps she'd tied around the deer's feet one final tug. Laorin who were Broken were separated from Laor's gift, had the magic ripped out of them in a ceremony that left them scarred and marked forever as a traitor to the faith. She'd only seen it happen once, to a young Priestess who hadn't been more than three or four years her senior, but Syrah had prayed every day for the next two months that she would never witness such a thing again.

The screaming had been the sort to craft nightmares not quickly forgotten.

"Wait'll Carro and Jerrom get a load of this one! They'll piss themselves, the old tarts!"

Syrah blinked and looked up at Reyn, who was smiling mischievously, already wrapping one of the leather strap's loose ends around his wrist. Getting to her feet, Syrah smirked, doing the same.

"You don't think it's a little early to be gloating?" she asked, pulling her staff from the earth and grunting as they started making their way back through the Woods toward the mountain stairway. "I think you said something like that two days ago, and those two came back with a net-full of fish the size of your body…"

"Yeah, but that day we only caught a couple of hares and a pheasant." He smiled again, pushing aside a pine branch. "This time we've got enough meat to last a whole table the night!"

Syrah rolled her eyes and laughed, watching Reyn smile and tug the deer around a rock with arms toned from years of instruction under Master Brern.

It was good to be home. It was good to see her friends again, and to be free of the responsibilities she'd had working in Metcaf and Harond. The past few years had been hellish, a constant war to forge relations between the mountain clans of the Vietalis—the ranges that capped the west and northwest corner of the North—and every nearby town. She'd been homesick for a majority of it, disliking the feeling of being hundreds of leagues from where she felt safe, and so far hadn't regretted a moment of returning.

But what she *had* been regretting of late were the strong hands of the young night-watch captain she'd been seeing for the better part of the last half year.

Her fair features, despite her pale skin and pink eyes, had always been good at supplying certain comforts…

"It's always the same with you men," she huffed playfully, pushing a lock of her white hair out of her face and tucking it behind an ear. "Size always has to come into play, doesn't it?"

Reyn tripped over a protruding root, almost tumbling to the ground.

"I-I—Wha—? I mean—Who said—?" he stuttered, fumbling over his words.

Syrah smiled, winked, and said no more as they kept moving through the trees, deer in tow. Reyn, for his part, was open mouthed and silent the rest of the walk, lost for words.

The only sound he managed to make for a while, in fact, was a hopeless groan once they arrived back at the stairway.

Carro and Jerrom were waiting for them, smiling knowingly and lounging in the grass beside the bodies of an antlered buck and a boar whose shoulder would have reached a short man's hip.

XII

"I never saw him fight, a fact I will always regret. I heard say he could enter a ring bare-handed and give the crowd a show, plucking the sword from another man's grasp before running him through with it. Even when he didn't kill he was the one the people always thronged to. Above all else, I wish I'd been there just to understand how he could do it, how he could fight and kill so many and yet claim to hate it so much..."

—Xerus Junt, Doctore of the Stullens Arena, c. 865 v.S.

The documents hadn't yielded a fraction of what Raz hoped they might. Barely any of the šef seemed to keep records with anything more than numbers and a few coded words to spare, and those foolish enough to mark down such things as times or places had scrambled to change their plans before Raz could do any real damage. He'd been pleased to hear he'd caused a minor financial crisis for Sass and a few others but, infuriatingly, the biggest coup he'd been able to pull off in the month since was freeing all the Caged prisoners from their confinements two weeks back.

And now the sentries along the market square had been tripled, so even that opportunity was gone.

Raz sat on the dirt floor of the cellar of an abandoned butcher's shop a few blocks west of the east slums. He'd been there for almost a week now, and knew he would have to move again soon. Sharpening his gladius in the sparse light of a few candles, though, he had other things on his mind.

He was losing momentum. Twice now Raz had approached old contacts only to discover they were shocked to see him, informing him the rumor was he'd been killed. He hadn't flung himself into this crusade to give people hope for a better future, but it still somehow irked him that so many thought him dead when in truth the Mahsadën had simply tightened their defenses tenfold. Plans he'd started forming weeks ago were now that much more difficult to pull off. Chances were missed, opportunities snatched away. The whispers said Ergoin Sass was behind it all, urging the other šef to treat Raz as a direct threat after the mess he'd caused.

Thank you for that, cousin, Raz thought bitterly, holding the sword up and examining his reflection in the steel. The amber eyes looked back at him, full of judgment.

Putting the gladius aside, he reached to grasp Ahna's shaft and pulled her across the ground into his lap. The bleached wood of the dviassegai was marred and chipped, evidence of the years of abuse he'd put her through. The leather wrappings Jerr had strung around the shaft were worn and frayed from use. There were nicks and scratches that gave her twin blades a scarred appearance, crisscrossing over the steel and chipping tiny fragments from her honed edges.

Raz reached up and ran a finger over his snout, feeling the three dents of the scars he'd had there for as long as he could remember.

"Figures you'd end up looking like me in the end, huh, sis?" he chuckled, putting Ahna aside again and climbing to his feet. Crossing the cellar, he moved to lean over an old table set up against the far wall, the only other furniture being the sleeping mat he'd rolled out directly in front of the room's door. A pair of candles lit the table's surface, illuminating the array of objects littered across it.

There were the fiscal records, flattened and scattered now, piled around an old brass inkwell and feather quill. Beside them a bone-handled knife doubled as the paperweight for a few sheets of blank parchment and a series of useless correspondences he'd intercepted. The remainders of his last meal, the stripped bone of some raw lamb he'd stolen, sat below one of the candles.

Uninterested in all of these, Raz pushed the scattered papers aside, searching. It took a minute, but eventually he managed to find the bundle of rolled-up scrolls, pulling them free of the mess. Unlooping the twine that held them closed, he spread the thin parchments out across the table.

He'd stolen the maps from Adrion's office half a week ago without his cousin realizing, layouts to a building Raz suspected to be the center of operations for a good many of the Mahsadën's bigger dealings. It had been a desperate move, especially after Sass tasked a half dozen of his hardest enforcers to look over his accountant's house, but Raz hadn't known what else to do. Adrion was his only link to the heart of the Mahsadën. Raz knew of other hideouts and estates where a few of the šef themselves lived, but they were too well guarded to be worth risking his neck for the life of one or two of eight ringleaders. He had to figure out a way to get them all in the same room, or at least closer together.

Looking down at the maps laid out before him, Raz's mind whirred.

Maybe this would be his chance. He would have checked it out more thoroughly, but lack of proof and the recently bolstered measures of the entire organization had pushed him to decide it wasn't worth the risk.

Now, though, risks were all that were left. Sass had been right, in a way: all the things Raz had done, with some exception, were small fish, little more than annoying pokes in the back of the Mahsadën's leg. He could pull off pranks like that for the rest of his life and accomplish nothing at all.

No. He had to make a bigger move. He had to cut at the šef's hold on the city somehow, had to deliver a blow that would actually damage them.

To do that, though, he had to gamble…

Raz picked up the knife and used it to trace the lines in the upper-left quadrant of the first map, lifting the corner up so that the candlelight could shine through the paper. He'd only suspected the building because he'd heard rumors of deals and meetings taking place there, but the fact that Adrion had had these plans must have meant something, right? The man was one of the group's top bookkeepers. They probably trusted him with safekeeping the records they didn't deem important enough to lock away.

Which meant that, even if this building wasn't as significant to the Mahsadën as Raz hoped, maybe it held some clue as to what he should do next.

At worst he would just burn the whole place to the ground.

Making up his mind, Raz let the corner drop to the table, his eyes flying over the papers, trying to memorize every detail. Those things he was sure he would need he copied down. Finishing with one section, he moved on to the next.

After two hours of poring over the parchments, he had everything he needed, and Raz moved back to his mat on the floor. Lifting the edge, he pulled out a thin wooden box from under it. It had been risky, but he'd snuck back to his old rooms in the White Sands and salvaged what he could from the wreckage of his belongings. Most of his possessions had been destroyed or taken by the Mahsadën agents who'd tossed the place, looking for a clue as to where he might be hiding. Some things, though, had been missed or ignored, the box being one of very few items he'd found worth salvaging.

Flipping the catch, he opened it, reaching in to pull out the thin wools of his mottled night gear.

Raz couldn't help but feel sad, swinging himself over the edge of Adrion's balcony. The Grandmother was still there, staring off into the night, layers of thick fur blankets wrapped tightly around her, and a cap pulled over her head. She didn't even notice him crouching beside her, pausing despite his better judgment.

Then he bowed his head respectfully before looking to the wall above.

It was several hours past midnight, the only time he knew his cousin would be asleep. Raz barely had any time to get back to his hole in the ground before day broke, and the last thing he wanted was to be caught in the streets again with only the gladius to defend himself. He wished he'd had more time to plan. He hated rush jobs, and this couldn't really be considered anything but. He needed to get the maps back into Adrion's office before anyone noticed they were gone—if they hadn't already—so he'd be free to see what was *actually* going on without risk of being found out. If the Mahsadën realized one of their operations was compromised in any way, they would pull out within hours, leaving nothing behind.

A gamble again, but he didn't have many other options.

Following the same path he had on his last "visit," Raz crouched and leapt. Catching the windowsill of Adrion's office with one hand, his feet found the top ledge of the balcony doors below him. Hoisting himself up high enough to grab the top of the window frame, he tucked into the narrow foot of space between the glass and the ledge of the sill. When he found his balance, Raz dug claws into the wood of the window and pulled, feeling it move just a little before catching.

Adrion had locked it this time, it seemed.

Drawing a thin knife from his hip, the blade too fragile to be of any use in a fight, Raz slid it carefully into the lower portion of the crack between the window and its wooden frame, moving it upwards slowly. When edge hit latch, he wiggled it, getting the tool snug before tugging upwards smoothly. There was a muffled *clunk*, and the window swung inward the slightest bit.

Moments later Raz dropped into the office, no louder than a ghost as he landed on all fours on the carpeted floor.

Cautiously he studied the room, peering into every dark corner. It was a spacious chamber, an excellent example of the fine tastes Adrion had developed since he'd found his apparent calling in the Mahsadën's ranks. Tapestries and brightly colored paintings covered the walls, offsetting a large mirror with golden engravings depicting the Sun and Moon in each corner. Raz grit his teeth when he saw it.

"If only They would take you, cousin," he grumbled under his breath, standing up. "It would probably make my life a little easier, at least."

He could smell no one else, and his vision was good enough in the dark to notice any motion that spelled a trap. The guards Sass had left must have been downstairs. He was safe for the moment, and Raz hurried to the wide desk set up against the back corner of the room. Tugging the middle drawer open, he dug through the papers and letters carefully until he neared the bottom.

Then, pulling out the maps he'd stowed in his shirt, Raz tucked them exactly where he'd found them, closing the drawer silently.

He was out the window in a minute, using the thin blade to push the latch back down, locking it behind him. Dropping silently to the balcony below, he knelt in front of the Grandmother.

"He's turned traitor," he spoke quietly. "A betrayer to our family and our ways. I hope you hear this, because I would ask you to pray to keep him out of my way. No one else is going to."

And then Raz leapt over the balustrade, dropping to the street below.

If he'd taken a moment to look back up, perhaps just in the vain hope that the Grandmother's eyes had followed his departure, Raz might have noticed the slim figure watching him. Swathed in black, she crouched down, peering over the edge of Adrion's roof, balanced masterfully on its apex.

XIII

"While the rule of the Mahsadën covered only a relatively brief period in the grand scope of history as a whole, it is a well-remembered one. Even now, a century and a half after the fall of the shadow government, unhealed scars mar the faces of most of our cities. Amongst the worst to suffer during those years, the fringe town of Karth never fully recovered, becoming a den for thieves, bandits, and the sarydâ that still travel the desert routes. It is for this reason that, in the 23rd year b.S., the Age of Change, Karth was renamed Tatrê Suav, or Haven of the Traitor."

—*As Death Rose from the Ashes,* by Kohly Grofh

"Our scrolls were back, like you said they'd be," Adrion spoke up from his seat in Sass' office, turned in the chair to watch the man pace.

"Then everything is going smoothly."

"You're assuming a lot. How do you know he'll take the bait?"

"The Monster hasn't been able to make a move in weeks." Sass stopped by the window, pulling the crimson curtains aside with a finger to peer out. "It's a stalemate, and you told me yourself he won't be able to sit around and do nothing."

"Even before everything happened, he was like that," Adrion agreed, nodding thoughtfully. "Picked that up from our uncle. But are you sure he's going to go for it?"

"What else could he do? We've offered him no other opportunity to strike. We're too tightly guarded. If we can maintain that and hold out a few more days, I'd bet any amount of crowns you can think of that he will make a move to see what we're doing there."

"It's an old bathhouse," Adrion said with a smirk. "What does he think he's going to find?"

"Does it matter?"

Adrion shrugged.

"Well, I'm glad *you're* so sure it's going to work. Sun knows we could use some credibility in the eyes of the others."

Sass turned to glare at him, and Adrion smiled disarmingly, raising his hands in a gesture of peace.

"I only mean," he clarified, "that we're not exactly the most popular figures with the society at the moment."

"Which wouldn't be the case if you'd kept your animal of a cousin's filthy claws off those records!" Sass snapped, turning away from the window and taking a seat behind his desk. "Because of you it will be months before we clear up this fiasco!"

"Well, as glad as I am that the other šef finally have some perspective on how essential my numbers are to them, it's far from fair to blame this on me. I told you not five minutes before this 'fiasco' that you were underestimating him, and it takes losing our earning calculations for a whole section to figure out I was right."

Sass was silent, glaring at Adrion, who stared right back levelly.

"On top of that," he continued, "Master Evony should have posted an escort to travel with the messenger. He can be equally blamed, if you like."

At that, Sass laughed dryly.

"Ha! Maybe, but just go try telling him that," he scoffed.

"I'd rather not."

Sass grunted, raising a hand in dismissal.

"I have things to attend to. I'll send for you if I get word from Orture. His guard have a close eye on the bathhouse."

Mychal nodded, setting his crutch on the ground and leveraging himself out of the chair. When he was gone, Sass leaned back with a sigh.

"You would do well to flip him," a voice spoke. "From what I saw, the atherian is as good as me. He would be useful to your organization."

A figure detached itself from the darkest corner of the room, stepping out of the shadows like she were made from them. Dressed in black silk so thin it would make a decent man blush to see her, the woman approached the desk gracefully.

"Don't flatter yourself," Sass began, tilting his head as he looked into her blue eyes, examining the scars that crossed her pale face. "He's better than you, Lazura."

The blonde woman smiled venomously, claiming the chair Adrion had just vacated.

"I don't know about that," she said, crossing her legs, the silk falling open to reveal the smooth skin above her knee, "but you're entitled to your opinion."

Sass raised an eyebrow.

"You forget that your charms don't work here. You're not my type. And as for flipping him, we've been down that road, and it didn't work out well the first time around. I very much doubt it would be any different now. But regardless"—he leaned forward hungrily—"tell me what you know."

Lazura frowned, her expression suddenly businesslike.

"He's holed up in an abandoned shop a short ways off the main fairway into the west slums," she said. "I didn't follow him in, like you said, but if you move quickly you might be able to get at him before he changes locations."

"Not worth the risk," Sass muttered, eyes on his desk as he thought things over. "If he's there, he's holed himself up in a way that would take an army to get to him, maybe in the basement or cellar. Likely he even has another exit you wouldn't be able to see from the surface. Worse, if he's already moved then he'll have eyes on the place. The minute he hears we raided an old hideout he'll drop off the grid again, and it'll be ten times harder to find him."

"Then let *me* go," Lazura said, her smile popping up again. "He has to sleep, right? I can be in and out in minutes and your problem is solved without a—"

"He sleeps less than four hours a night, probably with one eye open, and is faster and stronger than any of the fat old trims I've had you take care of in the past."

"But if I can catch him at the right time—"

"You won't. You can't. I've been working with the lizard longer than anyone. As much as I'd like to think he's nothing but a dumb animal, the reality is that he's smart. Maybe as smart as you, with your northern education."

"You can hardly call it an *education*," Lazura retorted. "A bunch of brainwashing old nags too rooted in old ways to see what their abilities could offer themselves and the world? The Laorin Broke me. Because I wasn't about to let myself turn out like them, they Broke me."

"Well you've certainly put what talents you were left with to good use," Sass said with a nod. "But even with your abilities, you won't get the best of i'Syul."

"Can't know that until we try."

"I said *no*," Sass breathed with lethal finality. "And you will follow my directions, or I will find my accountant a new housekeeper. I know how much you would hate to be taken away from that precious charge of yours. Studying Adrion's grandmother has already brought you so much closer to finding your original gifts again... It would be so sad, don't you think, to be taken away from her?"

Lazura stiffened.

"You wouldn't dare."

"I would dare to do a lot, my dear," Sass said with a shrug, leaning back. "I didn't get to where I am by being slow and cautious. There are other people out there with your skill sets, Lazura, believe it or not. Not many as good as you, I admit, but those that are can be found and hired and those that aren't can be bought and trained. You seem to forget who *taught* you your skills."

"Lifegiver take you, Sass," the woman spat, her eyes narrowed, and for a second Sass thought she might go for the throwing needle she had disguised as a decoration in her blonde hair.

Then she seemed to think better of it.

"Fine," she breathed. "I'll stay away from the atherian."

"Thank you." Sass gave her a patronizing smile. "A wise decision. Now, if you would, I wasn't lying when I told Adrion I have other things to take care of. You may go."

XIV

"There is almost always another way. Take the time to look for it. You will go through life with more friends and less scars. It is not the coward who steers clear of a fight. It is the wiser man."

—Jarden Arro, Champion of the Arro clan

Raz crouched low to press himself against the brick and marble wall, waiting for the guard to pass his narrow alley. They were seven in total, a standard patrol, and on any other night he wouldn't have hesitated to take advantage of their turned backs and relinquish their spirits to the Moon.

Tonight, though, he didn't have the time to waste.

They marched past steadily, torches held high, peering through the dark. In full gear Raz ducked farther back into the shadows, hoping they hadn't caught the glint of steel. He didn't so much as twitch, waiting for the last flickers to fade in the distance before he dared the street again.

It wasn't often he visited this part of the city. The middle class was a relatively small group, larger than the wealthy by far but still barely a fraction the population of the slums. They were a generally honest people, merchants and artisans who practiced their labors rather than steal or slave for their fortune. As a result Raz had only twice before accepted a contract on a local resident, though he'd done a number of private jobs for some of the shopkeepers nearby who'd wanted protection for their goods.

It seemed odd therefore that his investigations would lead him here of all places. He did rare business in these parts, and since the Mahsadën's dealings ran parallel to his own in a sense, he found it strange that they would be using this particular district as a trading front.

It had taken Raz some time to discern what was going on. He'd been watching the place in question—an old bathhouse that appeared to have been recently restored into some sort of local bazaar—for four days now. All had seemed innocent at first—people milling throughout, going in and leaving with fresh fruits or clothes or other merchandise. The bustle and murmur of the bartering had taken him back to years long gone, and for a time he'd been hard-pressed to think of the place as anything but the sort of market he and the Arros might once have set up shop in.

Then Raz had started watching those people he knew weren't locals, men whose countenances seemed too gruff for the decent clothes they wore. Pairs would enter the building with wrapped parcels and depart empty-handed. Three times he'd seen individuals he knew were the right hands of some šef or another enter the bathhouse, only to leave hours later. Adrion had made an appearance once, as had Vyrr Gaorys, the šef responsible for every crown the Mahsadën leached out of Miropa and its citizens. The pudgy man had been surrounded by his usual contingent of burly guards, all of whom seemed impossibly bigger and beefier than the ones Raz had slaughtered trying to get at him a month and a half ago.

Needless to say, there was certainly something going on within those walls…

Turning right, he made his way cautiously down the cobbled street. That last patrol had been the third he'd run across thus far. The Mahsadën seemed to have spared no measure. It was the kind of manpower usually retained for the roads in and around the wealthier estates to the north, and it had taken him by surprise. He was already behind the two-hour schedule he'd drawn up for himself to get there, get in, and figure out what the hell was going on inside. After that he'd have another hour again to make for the new safe house set up at the very edge of the city before the Sun started to rise.

It had already been over an hour, and he was still fifteen minutes from the bathhouse.

The city was dead as Raz moved, inconspicuous in the night. Ahna was thrown over his shoulder, her shaft resting between the crook of his neck and the handle of his gladius, her blades hidden by their leather cover so as not to catch the light of the street lanterns. At one point he thought he heard yet more footsteps in the distance, and he ducked behind a large pile of pine crates. There he waited, but after a full two minutes of listening to nothing but the cold night breeze whistle through the street he got to his feet and started running again, cursing his paranoia.

The bathhouse loomed out of the dark not long after, a large, rectangular one-story structure with brick chimneys once used to clear the steam out of the bathing rooms. There were four doorways, one facing outward from each wall, allowing the separate genders to enter their segregated chambers from one direction and leave in another. Where there'd once likely been open archways, the Mahsadën had hired masons to erect thick double doors with lock-bars that could be dropped from the inside of three, effectively sealing the building every night.

Raz darted across the road. Reaching the wall of the bathhouse by the south-facing entrance, he looked left and right, still keeping an eye out. Satisfied that he was alone for the moment, he knelt down in front of the door and pulled a thick roll of soft leather from the back of his belt. Leaning Ahna against the wall within easy reach, he unrolled the leather sheet over the ground at his feet. Wrapped inside were a series of odd instruments, all designed by Jerr—with the help of some lower-moraled consultants—and most of which Raz had never used. He wasn't good at picking locks. Despite his claws, his fingers did well enough with the delicate work, but he'd always been too strong for his own good, often bending or cracking the fragile mechanisms before he could get them open. Even with the picks and shims tailored to fit him he was a better pickpocket, and getting the key always seemed easier than breaking in. Unfortunately, only one of the doors worked by key, and thieving it hadn't been an option tonight.

Choosing carefully, Raz selected two of the instruments and tested their weight. The first was the odder of the pair, a flattened steel rod with a long braided metal chain at the end, thin but strong. The second was little more than a long, thick needle, its tip bent into the shape of a hook. Taking this one, Raz stood up, pressing it carefully through the slit between the double doors at head height. Finding no resistance, he slid it all the way to the base of its leather handle, then moved the entire instrument down through the crack, inch by inch.

He'd pushed it all the way to his hip before, with a quiet *tink*, it ran into the lock-bar.

Raz knelt down, still holding the hooked instrument in place. He lifted the narrow chained end of the other tool and started pressing it through the doors at his knee. It took more effort, but after about a minute of wiggling and grunting he managed to force it through. With another push the trailing end of the chain disappeared into the door crack. This done he slid the handle upward until it hit the same metal bar about a hand-width below the other instrument.

And now for the fun part, Raz thought sardonically. Grimacing, he turned the hooked tool and tilted it down, working blindly to catch the chains.

It was painstaking work. Again and again he tried, failing with each attempt. It wasn't long before he found himself cursing between grunts of frustration and grumbling threats at various inanimate objects. After five precious minutes wasted away, he was near ready to throw caution to the wind and take Ahna to the door, noise be damned.

Then at long last he felt the hook get a solid catch, and Raz groaned in relief. Drawing it carefully back through the door space, he felt the chain strike against the wood on the other side. Then he pulled, hard.

The hook came out with little resistance, completing the crude metal noose around the lock-bar.

Thanking Her Stars, Raz dropped the first tool back onto the leather roll, grabbing the exposed chain. Using both hands to pull each end of the instrument, he jerked upwards. The bar *thunked* out of its hold, and he cringed as it clattered to the stone floor on the inside of the bathhouse. Even through the thick timber the sound echoed down the silent streets.

Muttering under his breath, Raz rushed to pull the chain back through the crack, wrapping the instruments up again before tucking the kit away. Grabbing Ahna from the wall, he pushed the unlocked door open just wide enough to fit his body through, slipping into the darkness of the room inside.

The air tasted of sweat, new fabric, and the day-old food that was always left scattered after the merchants closed shop for the day. Raz could hear his heartbeat in the silence of the building, listening to the echoing of the door shutting behind him. He stuck an armored hand out, trying to see something. In the absolute lack of light, even he was blind.

He'd anticipated that, though, and as he found the wall to his left he reached up, sliding his fingers across the stone until they came in contact with something metal.

He'd noticed the torches the first day he'd started stalking the property. When night fell, a man would go around to light them so customers could still peruse the wares after sunset. They were replaced when the market closed an hour before midnight, leaving fresh ones for the next day. Raz's hand found the wood through the iron grate, and he pulled the torch free, smelling the oil waft through the air. Leaning Ahna against his cheek, he reached into the pouch hanging from his hip and pulled out the tinder and flint he'd brought for just this reason.

A minute later the torch roared to life, and Raz held it up, squinting into the darkness of the room he stood in.

The building was divided into four large chambers, two for where the men once bathed and two for the women. Originally these sections were separated by a solid wall that diagonally bisected the structure— mostly for the women's sake—but when the building had been converted, parts of the wall had been knocked down and refortified in several places with wood and iron. Now an open path for the foot traffic joined the four rooms, each of which had their own door leading back to the streets.

It was an impressive adaptation, but for Raz it meant only frustration. Now that he was inside, he realized how little space there was to be spared for a secret meeting room, or even a segregated corner where the Mahsadën might make their private dealings. Taking a step forward, Raz raised his torch high, Ahna slung back over his shoulder.

The chamber's floor was rough and dirty, the day's refuse splattered over the tiled ground, dropped by the careless or carefree. There was a wide walkway that encompassed the entirety of the room, wrapping around a flat-bottomed pit about hip deep where the bath had once been. Tables and makeshift tents were set up everywhere, left standing overnight to be claimed by the earliest risers the next day.

None of it was any help as Raz made his way around the room.

Maybe they're doing their business in the open, he thought, peeking behind one of the tables set up along the wall and wrinkling his nose at the soured half slab of meat lying there on the floor.

But no, that didn't make sense. It would be easy for the Mahsadën to make a few underhanded deals directly under the noses of the market goers, true, but Raz had seen more than *a few* suspicious people come and go from this place in the last four days. No, there had to be something going on here, something more elaborate than a handful of minor exchanges. If men like Adrion Blaeth and Vyrr Gaorys were involved, then the place was bound to hold sweeter secrets than it was revealing at first glance.

This is gonna take a while.

Moving quickly, Raz began his search, careful not to leave any trace of his passings. An open door was one thing, easily explained by a careless closer or a poorly set lock, but if he tore the place apart the Mahsadën would know someone had come snooping around, and the night would be a waste. He was hoping whatever he'd find here would lead him further, maybe even where and when the slave shipments came and went from Miropa. If his intentions were discovered, not only would he lose his advantage, but the Mahsadën's defenses would probably increase once again. They might even request aid from the rings in the other fringe cities. None of the other southern metropolises had as great a presence as Miropa, but they also didn't have the Monster of Karth running around wreaking havoc. Dynec, Cyro, Karavyl, even Acrosia or Karth itself had resources to spare, and it was best not to tantalize them into offering support.

In fifteen minutes he'd done a general sweep of every one of the four chambers, looking for signs of hidden doors in the walls or maybe some particularly suspicious tent tucked away in one corner or another. Finding nothing promising, he started over, moving more carefully, making sure to light up every square foot so he could look for anything that might point him in the right direction.

It was frustrating work, especially since Raz didn't know what exactly it was he was looking for. Soon another quarter hour flew by with no results. He was halfway through scrutinizing the second room, his temper spiking every time the firelight revealed nothing but more rotting food and empty shadows, when he stopped.

Were those footsteps outside, muffled by the stone?

Raz's ears perked. He stood up, turning west, in the direction he'd heard the noise. He didn't bother extinguishing his torch, confident the light wouldn't be able to sneak through the windowless walls, but nonetheless he shrank back into the most distant corner of the room, listening hard.

So hard, in fact, he almost jumped out of his skin when his foot hit the floor of the corner with a loud *thunk*.

Elation shot through Raz like lightning, and he looked down, moving the torch to illuminate the ground. There, well hidden under a moth-eaten old rug, was a wooden trapdoor. Kneeling, Raz set Ahna on the ground and reached out, tapping the bit of exposed wood with a steel claw.

It knocked hollow.

That same feeling of anticipation rocked through Raz's core again, and without a moment to waste he flung off the dirty rug, revealing the door in full. Three thick padlocks latched the wood in place, looped around iron hooks bolted to the stone floor on two sides. Raz lifted one of them in his hand and tugged it firmly. The lock held, but it was nothing he couldn't handle. Drawing the leather kit from the back of his belt once more, he leaned the torch carefully against the closest wall. Shapeless jumping figures licked at the floor around him, the flames dancing against the stone.

The picks he chose were simple things, short and slim but flexible. With careful precision one tip went into the narrow keyhole, followed by the other. Three painstaking minutes later, the first lock snapped open.

It took more effort to undo the other two, their mechanisms more complex and heavy. There was much cursing and pointless threatening before Raz finally pulled them off the latches to be tossed aside. His work done, he replaced his picks and grabbed the torch again with one hand, running the other over the door hurriedly. There was no handle, but after a few seconds the metal claws of his gauntlets found a divot between the tiled floor and wood.

Getting a good grip, he heaved and threw the door open.

XV

Beneath the hatch was nothing but reddish, sandy dirt.

There was a hole, about half a foot deep, as if someone had taken a shovel and roughly scooped out a heavy wedge of earth from beneath the tiled floor of the bathhouse. Then a door had been carefully placed over it, and locked tight. A time-consuming decoy. A tantalizing distraction.

A trap.

The thought flicked through Raz's head, and in the instant that it registered he knew it was too late. He could hear them now, the footsteps outside thundering in from all directions, pouring out of the alleys and roads to circle the building. He'd been too distracted, too preoccupied and fixed on his treacherous trapdoor.

Now, though, he could even smell the men and women of the Miropan guard surrounding him.

There must have been two hundred of them, lining up on every front. The drumming of their feet quieted as they came to a stop at different intervals, replaced by the frantic pounding of Raz's heart. He snatched Ahna up from the ground. Muffled orders for silence dulled by the thick walls of the chamber did nothing to hide the vast size of the group. They numbered enough that Raz could still hear the clatter of spear butts hitting the ground, and sword scabbards knocking against hard thighs.

He ignored it all, his mind a violent blur of jumbled thoughts and realizations. An unbidden, wrathful snarl built in his throat, and he looked around, frantically trying to think.

His planning was heavily impeded by the screaming, self-berating wrath that seemed to consume his every idea.

The Mahsadën had made him dance *again*, playing on his strengths to ruse him into a deathtrap. The large room was a double-edged sword; while he'd be able to fight at full advantage, putting Ahna and his tail and wings to perfect use, he would also be surrounded, with no avenue of escape. Even Raz doubted he'd be able to last more than a few seconds ringed by an enemy whose numbers seemed to have reached triple digits. As for making a stand outside, he might be able to get his back against a wall, but he'd still be overrun. Not to mention he had no doubt Ulan Orture, the šef who doubled as head of the city guard, had posted his best archers and crossbowmen on top of the highest properties in range of the bathhouse.

Not even Raz's talents for acrobatics could help him now. Even *if* he could get to the roof, the jump to the next building would be too wide and high to manage.

Cursing his own folly, Raz bared his teeth. He was caught. The Mahsadën had known he would go after Adrion again, given time. They'd planted all the evidence he needed, then had notable men purposely come and go from the market, knowing he'd be watching the place. But there was nothing here.

Nothing.

Stupid. Fucking. Idiot! Raz cursed himself. His eyes darted around the room, assessing his situation. He had no time to rebuke himself. He had to get out. But, even before he could think of escaping, he had to focus on surviving. The guards were still outside, no doubt waiting for a signal to storm the place, and as soon as they did they would be flooding in from three directions: both arched entrances that led to adjacent rooms, and the barred entrance door in the west wall.

It was when his eyes fell on this door that Raz's mind started to click together the details that lay around him. A plan started to form, and he almost laughed out loud at the desperate ideas bouncing around in his head. Looking up, he scrutinized the rafters that supported the ceiling, slightly sloped to avoid catching the Sun all day. The wooden beams crisscrossed in several places, overlapping and webbing, with their foundation timbers in each corner of the room...

Giving in to his own daring, Raz leapt into action.

Jumping down to the pit floor, he pulled the leather pouch free of Ahna's blades and tucked it into his belt, dropping the dviassegai directly in the middle of the room. This done, he ran to the doorway. Stuffing his torch into the nearest wall bracket, Raz didn't wince as the fire caught the tip of the other already hanging there, lighting it with a short-lived *whoosh* of flames. Grabbing the nearest table, he grunted and dragged it to block the door, flipping it over. Repeating this, he grabbed the next table— more of a small stall than anything—and, thankful it wasn't bolted to the ground, heaved it over on top of the first.

In a frenzy Raz worked, tearing down cloth and the thin wooden beams that held up the room's tents, tossing them on top of the pile that was growing wider and higher with every second. Chairs and empty wooden boxes left from the day added to the mess, and Raz was careful to keep spreading it to the left, southward. Within several tumultuous minutes the heap of dirty rags, tipped-over tables, and splintered wood was wide enough that it cut around the corner, blocking the arched opening to the next room. Raz was just heaving a wide bench over to completely bar the path when he heard a distinct shout from outside, and as the timber crashed to the ground he stopped to listen.

"—Arro! Raz i'Syul Arro! By order of Captain-Commander Ulan Orture of the city guard, you are to surrender yourself for arrest!"

Oddly, the call seemed to be coming from all directions, as though several people were yelling at once.

They don't know where I am, Raz realized.

He was torn. Shouting back would lose him what little advantage he might have, but it might also buy him some time. Reaching up to tear down the cloth overhang of a small tent, Raz thought quickly.

Even if they didn't know where he was at the moment, it would be seconds before the guard rampaged in and found him. No, it was better to clue them in and take the risk if it meant he might get so much as another minute to prepare.

"On what charges?" he roared back through the wall, tossing the fabric onto the pile in front of the arch, already grabbing yet another table. Sure enough, over the groan of the heavy wood he could hear the flurry of feet and the not-so-quiet orders of the guard surging in front and around the western room.

"You are to be arrested on charges of disturbing the peace, theft, assault, and multiple counts of murder and attempted murder! Place your weapons on the ground and come out unarmed, and we will escort you to the court keeps where you will receive fair trial!"

Raz snorted. Fair trial only meant one of two things: either the Mahsadën would try to flip him again, or they'd have him assassinated before he could so much as reach his cell. Grabbing a chair in each hand, Raz threw them on top of the mess, stepping back to examine his work.

"And if I don't?" he shouted, not really caring what the man said in return, studying the pile. It satisfyingly blocked both the west door and southern archway, crossing the room's corner in an even L-shape and peaking in the center. Moving back to the wall bracket where he'd hung his torch beside the previously unlit one, Raz reached up and pulled both free. He heard the man outside shout something about "executed on sight" and "strung in the Cages for all Miropa to see."

Raz grinned, inexplicably amused.

Then, taking his flames, he stuck them into the piled heap under every piece of dry cloth he could reach.

Fire roared to life in the fabric instantly. It was only moments before the blaze smoldered throughout the barrage he'd thrown together, growing with each step he took down the line.

"That sounds like fun!" Raz yelled, not taking his eyes off the growing glow. Bright orange and red spread through the dry assemblage faster than he could have hoped. "When do we start?"

There was a silence outside, and then the man yelled again.

"Raz i'Syul, this is your last warning! Come out, unarmed, and we will show you leniency for your crimes against—!"

"SHUT UP AND COME GET ME IF YOU CAN!" Raz roared, hurling his torches across the room at the last few tents he'd left standing.

A little more fire couldn't hurt, after all.

His taunting had the desired effect. As Raz leapt into the bath pit to grab Ahna off the ground, he heard a *crash*. The men outside seemed to have taken a battering ram to the west door, which didn't budge, blockaded by the burning heap.

All around the building though, three more crashes echoed, and in each of the other rooms the doors flew open.

The first thing Raz heard was the panicked shouting and yelling coming from the guards in the southern chamber, their plan falling into confused shambles when they found their way obstructed by a raging fire they couldn't have seen from the outside. Without turning around Raz could hear a few hardy men brave the flames before falling back with cries of pain, their metal armor rapidly superheating.

Then men appeared in the east archway, the only access point left open, and Raz stopped listening, focusing solely on the task at hand.

The first two died together, barely with time to blink away the firelight before a great winged shadow bedecked in white hurdled out of the smoke. Ahna took one head and gashed the other's throat in a single powerful sweep, already crossing back to meet the next group rushing for the archway like a flooding wave.

Choking them through the one entrance, though, Raz had gained back his edge.

Ahna's twin blades were sister scythes, sweeping back and forth and swinging in quick circles like a whirlwind, cutting legs from under bodies, slashing faces, and cleaving through chain mail to leave organs and fluids spilling from open chests. Raz's tail struck out, breaking knees and necks like a lashing great snake as he turned and twisted, dancing back and forth across the archway. Only two managed to slip by, but before either could

244

make use of their position they died, one brutally smashed into the closest wall, the other gasping for life after Raz's metal claws severed the arteries around her throat.

As he fought, though, Raz was careful to keep his wings safely hugged to his back. His plan was insane—there was no doubt about that—but it was the only one he had.

Ahna snuck between the two guards directly in front of him, cutting them down with a quick Z-shaped slash that knocked their bodies sideways into the men on either side of them. The dviassegai spun over Raz's head, slashing vertically with less speed than usual. The line of men and women in front ducked, clearly pleased with their small victory when the blades whizzed harmlessly over their heads.

Their success was short lived, though, as they leapt up, realizing the trap too late to stop Ahna coming full circle for another sweep, unstoppable behind her momentum.

Thump, thump, thump. Three more bodies fell to the floor.

Raz was starting to feel the wear of the fight, though. The first part of his plan was working perfectly, but the wall of guards seemed never ending. The temperature in the room was spiking, and he could see the swarming crowd of bodies through the rippling air. When a jump kept his feet attached to his body, dodging a low blow from a longsword, Raz caught a glimpse of bows at the back of the group.

The archers had been called in.

It didn't worry him. He landed and grabbed the closest man by the arm, throwing him backwards into the fires that were raging throughout the chamber now. In this one-sided fight he'd created, arrows couldn't be let off without a high risk of injury to the rest of the guard. He was safe for the moment, but it wouldn't be long before the officers got smart enough to order a withdrawal, forcing Raz to either follow them into the east room or retreat backwards. If he wasn't fast enough, the archers would get their shots off and—as much as he might wish it at the moment—catching arrows was not in Raz's arsenal of talents.

CRACK.

The sound ripped so sweetly through the roar of the fires, and somewhere behind him Raz heard something fall and crash into the inferno. Sparks spilled in sheets through the air, and he took advantage of the distraction to duck low and sweep the front line of guards with his tail, knocking most of them to the ground. Ahna snaked out in a flash, catching the second line unawares. Two women and a man fell to the floor clutching at the twin stabs that had appeared in their chests as though by magic, the dviassegai spearing each of them in quick succession before being retracted into a defensive position. Parrying a spear thrust with Ahna's pointed tip, Raz struck an arm out at the weapon's owner, catching the man in the side of the head. As the guard was thrown back into the group, the wonderful sound came again, louder this time.

CRACK... CRUNCH.

Something bigger fell, and Raz gave his best guess that it was time to make his move.

Just when he heard the order yelled to fall back, Raz dashed forward. At over seven-feet in length, Ahna's steel-and-wood shaft spanned almost the entire width of the archway, and she caught the front-most soldiers squarely in the chest. With a roar Raz shoved the group back, pushing with all his strength. Unable to stop him, the line toppled over into the men and women behind them, who in turn fell back themselves.

It gave Raz just enough time to leap back, disappearing into the smoke of the room.

A blind arrow ripped through the air to his right, a solid five feet clear of him, but nonetheless Raz threw himself into the bath pit. Crouching low between the fires on every side, he did his best to stay clear of the fumes. The heat was almost unbearable, but with his thick hide meant to withstand the savage beating of the Cienbal's desert Sun, Raz grit his teeth and endured it. The metal of his armor was heating quickly, though. He could feel his steel plating start to sear the scaly skin of his left foreleg and thigh. Hurrying over the tiled floor toward the back corner of the room, it occurred to Raz that if he didn't get out soon he'd be burned alive.

It was at that moment, though, that hell broke free of the sky.

The inferno Raz had set ablaze beneath the foundation rafters had done its job. With a screech of shattering wood and the crunch of tumbling stone, a quarter of the roof caved in right above Raz's head. His reflexes were all that saved him. He threw himself out of the way and rolled across the floor as a wave of flames washed over the tiled ground.

Jumping to his feet, Raz tore off the remnants of his white mantle, the dyed silk aflame. His neck and right shoulder exposed, extending bare from his sleeveless cotton tunic, he felt a chill and looked up.

The night sky, Star-less against the light of the flames, extended infinitely above him.

Raz had never been happier to see it.

There were shouts mixed with a few premature cheers of victory. The guards still posted outside the burning bathhouse were realizing part of the roof had caved in. Grim faced, Raz acted, not having the time to plan his moves. The moment he was spotted the marksmen would sight him out, and then he'd be nothing more than moving target practice. The smoke would cover him for a bit, hopefully.

But "a bit" wasn't long by any standard.

The burning roof ledge was about five feet above his head, easy enough to grab with a jump under regular circumstances, but Raz doubted he could make it weighed down by his armor and Ahna, much less pull himself up without breaking off the charred edge. Instead he ran straight for the burning pile in the very corner of the room, his eyes on the glowing surface of one of the tables that hadn't charred all the way through. Praying to the Sun that the wood wouldn't collapse under his weight, Raz took a running leap. His foot found the surface, pushing off again before the skin had a chance to burn.

He landed shakily on the crumbled stone ledge of the west wall, almost losing his balance and tumbling right over into street below. Steadying himself, Raz held Ahna close and ran along the edge, toward the unburned roof to his left.

He'd just taken his first step onto the slated surface when a crossbow bolt tore a hole through the stone barely six inches from his right foot.

Throwing himself to the side, Raz scrambled up the roof, following the burning edge to take advantage of the smoke. An arrow went wide of him, disappearing into the fires to his left, but now he could hear the shouts of alarm as more and more of the guards spotted him.

He reached the apex of the roof and turned around. Raz could practically feel every sight in the vicinity training on his figure. Even so, he took the briefest of moments to collect himself, drawing a deep breath and watching the pillar of smoke before him disappear into the night.

And then he ran.

Raz could literally hear the doubts screaming in his ears as he shot forward the short way down the slant toward the burning hole. His conscious self was battling with instinct, waging a war to make sure he didn't do exactly what he was planning on doing. The humanity in him shrieked warnings and common sense, begging him not to be a fool.

Drowning it out, though, Raz took the last step before the flaming pillar, spread his wings…

And leapt.

He had some idea of what he was supposed to do. He'd seen desert hawks ride the thermals before, seen them glide gracefully upwards in spiraling circles. Ideally he imagined a serene arc upwards, his wings caught firm in the hot air. He imagined his body lifting high above the ground, shooting off over the rooftops and disappearing into the night before any of the men surrounding him could realize he was gone.

Nothing could have prepared him for what actually happened.

The instant he caught the heat, Raz was jerked upward so violently he nearly dropped Ahna, the broiling heat from the flames below abruptly shooting him a good fifteen feet into the air. He could barely maintain his balance. Muscles in his back he didn't even know he had flexed and strained instinctively, trying to keep him right side up in his tumble skyward. Flaming soot and smoke whirled around him in a fiery storm, blocking his view. The rush crushed against him, filling his lungs with boiling wind. He couldn't breathe, couldn't think. He suddenly realized he was going to black out and plummet earthward to the cobbled road below. He realized he was going to die.

Then, abruptly, it ended.

The heat was gone. Raz was gliding unhindered, suspended by nothing. There was an instant, just a fraction of a second, when the panic disappeared and the city opened up like a map before his eyes. The world below came alive around him, a flat blanket of lights and shapes and lines where lit streets cut across Miropa's dark face. Raz had time for a single gasp, a single moment of unfathomable wonder as he soared.

But the moment didn't last, and with gut-wrenching force Raz felt gravity take him, pulling him down. He floundered desperately to keep his set course, as though the spastic whipping of his legs and free arm would help him through the air. The pull of the earth was cruel, though, aiming him straight at the wall of the three-story building in front of him, the roof he'd so desperately hoped to reach slipping away. He started to fall, losing almost all forward momentum, the solid stone rushing toward him.

And then his wings, extended to their fullest reach on either side of him, strained.

Drawing inward simultaneously, they pushed his body upwards through the air with such force Raz felt the wind whistling through the spaces in his armor. His mouth hung slack in numb realization as he felt his wings beat again with the barest of conscious thought, eyes on the wall slipping by in front of him. The edge of the roof reached his head, then his waist, then his feet, and before long it was ten feet below him.

He was *flying*. Without trying, without thinking or meaning to. The world opened up once more, Miropa suddenly an enchanting puzzle of lanterns and candlelight, a carefully carved floor for his feet to never touch. The rush returned, the air suddenly freer, sweeter.

He was flying…

And it was in that empty second of blooming ecstasy, when all thought was whisked away from his fight for survival, that a skillfully aimed bolt crashed into Raz's side, throwing him forcefully forward while pain like nothing he had ever imagined erupted from his abdomen.

From beneath the overhangs across the street, a pair of blue eyes watched Raz i'Syul's form disappear over the ledge of the high roof. She'd seen the bolt catch him in the back, but her professional experience had outweighed the leap in her breast she'd felt at the sight. The wound would be excruciating, even immobilizing to anyone else since damaging the muscles of the abdomen made it almost impossible to breathe.

But it wouldn't be fatal, and the atherian wasn't anyone else.

Even as Lazura watched a score of the guard sprint for the structure, she knew they wouldn't make it to the roof in time.

"Idiots!" she hissed under her breath, turning away from the flaming bathhouse and sliding into the closest alleyway. They'd had him trapped! Surrounded by half the standing force of Miropa's best!

And they'd let him get away…

Even now the Monster was probably long gone, doubtfully leaving so much as a blood trail to follow.

Sass is going to be livid, Lazura thought, melting into the darkness and making her way to her master's offices.

Especially when he found out the damned lizard had learned to fly…

XVI

Raz shouldered his way into the safehouse basement, nearly knocking the rickety door clear off its hinges in his semiconscious scramble. Ahna fell loosely from his fingers, hitting the dirt floor of the dark room with a dusty clatter.

Raz didn't notice, one hand held tight around his waist, pressing down on the tourniquet he'd made from his shirt and momentarily staunching the blood from flowing freely again. He'd managed to pull the bolt clean through, thank Her mercy, and the wound was far enough from his center to avoid any vital organs. Still, it throbbed like a hot iron pole had been shoved through him, and the bleeding simply refused to stop. Already the cloth beneath his fingers was damp and soaked crimson, and the first free trickle escaped down the skin of his belly while Raz fumbled around the room with his free hand.

In the near dark it took him a moment to find the table. With a grunt he swept it clear, knocking its contents to the floor. The inkwell overturned and splattered. Unlit candles broke and rolled away. Most importantly, though, the stolen scrolls and blank parchments tumbled into a misshapen pile. Raz fell to one knee and felt around for the bag lying in a nearby corner by his bedroll. Finally finding the burlap, he ripped it open.

He'd lost his good flint when he'd abandoned his ruined cloak to the fire. He'd lost his lock-picking set as well, but at the moment that was a minor concern. What *was* important was the little lead box he'd been lucky enough to pack, stuck at the bottom of the travel sack he'd readied for his quick break to the next safehouse.

Finding it at last, Raz tipped it over. A few small scraps of dried paper fell out, nearly lost to the dark, along with two small pieces of flint. Squatting and bending over his knees so that his thighs could hold the tourniquet in place, Raz struck the rocks together over the piled parchments, fumbling as his hands shook.

At last, though, the sparks caught.

Within two minutes a cramped fire burned in the center of the tiny room. Getting up momentarily, Raz lifted the wooden table with one hand and shattered it against the wall, feeding the smallest pieces to the flames, one after the other until they were embers. All the while he turned the night's events over and over in his head.

The ecstasy he'd felt over his escape and momentary flight had far from dissipated, but between the pain in his side and the reality of his situation, Raz fought to focus his mind elsewhere. He had to act fast. The magnitude of the trap the Mahsadën had set for him meant they were getting more than a little serious in their attempts. The silver lining of this gloomy news: such plans were rarely dealt with by middlemen. If he hurried, Raz knew he might have his shot soon, the opportunity to get at more than one or two of the šef. Given that they'd failed to kill him, some—if not all—would convene to plan their next move.

Raz drew his dagger from his side and placed the blade in the flames, wincing at the motion.

He wouldn't be able to follow any of the šef directly. By now word would have reached them of his escape, and in all likelihood each and every one of them would have made for their own secret hideaways. On the other hand, he did know one man who'd had a hand in setting the evening's clever deceptions. One man who did not yet have the wealth and power to afford himself such refuge.

First things first, though, Raz thought, pulling the dagger back out of the flames and grimacing at its white-hot tip.

He had to stop the damn bleeding.

Adrion had set the decoys, planting the false maps in his office. He'd known he was Raz's best opportunity to get to the Mahsadën's highest members. It was obvious now, looking back. The trap had been set, the bait offered, and all the šef had to do was wait and see what would happen, playing on the stalemate Raz had backed them all into.

It was a clever idea, and one that by all rights should have worked.

Once again, though, the society had underestimated him.

And now, Raz thought with a humorless smirk, sneaking a glance over the crenelated edge of Yvin Gors' five-story home across from Adrion Blaeth's, *it's going to come back and bite you in the ass.*

It had been less than two hours since his narrow escape from the middle districts, the Sun barely poking its head over the horizon to the east. Turning to look at it, trying to gauge his time, Raz hissed at the waves of white-hot shock that rippled upward through his right side and neck. Both of the wound's openings were sealed shut, their cauterized flesh forming angry welts that cracked and oozed, but at the very least they weren't bleeding. It had been a desperate measure, one that seemed hardly worth it during the painful rush to reach Adrion's house before morning broke, but Raz hadn't had time to think up anything else.

This might be his only chance. He had to pull it off.

As it was barely dawn and this was one of the wealthiest quarters of the city, the streets below were empty. Raz could even hear Gor's gentle snores emanating from an open window below him. Nothing stirred apart from the swaying of the Grandmother's white hair, the old woman sitting stone still on Adrion's balcony, but for once Raz didn't see her. Instead he watched and listened, inspecting every road and backstreet he could see from his high perch, desperate for a sign that this opportunity would come. If the šef met, and if word was sent to his cousin, then there would be a chance Raz would be able to tail the man...

But that was *if* they were even convening and *if* Adrion was summoned, *if* he was even informed at all.

There were a lot of ifs in this plan of his, Raz realized unhappily.

Still, there wasn't anything he could do about it. He was banking on the fact that a meeting would be called at once, probably in an effort to deal with him before the attempts on his life pushed him to greater lengths in his rebellion. Truthfully there was a good chance Adrion—having the most knowledge of the way Raz worked—would be called on to offer his insight.

Are you important enough, though, cousin? Raz thought, frustrated. If the summons didn't arrive soon and he was forced to follow Adrion in the middle of the day, it would spell trouble. Likely it was going to be difficult enough an endeavor without a thousand people washing through the streets like colored ants.

Raz's ears pricked up. Somewhere nearby, coming from the south, rapid footsteps were approaching. The rustling and clinking of chain mail told him who the group were, and within a minute four guardsmen—three men and a woman—appeared in the street directly below, moving at double pace toward Adrion's home. The first reached the heavy timber door, knocking solidly, and Raz watched the four of them wait, taking in their fidgeting as the seconds dragged on. They clutched at the hilts of their sheathed swords as though wanting to make sure the blades didn't vanish from their sides, alternately looking around into the empty streets.

Whatever their objective was, they were certainly nervous.

There was a quiet *clang* from below, and someone unlocked the door. It opened wide, and a blonde woman dressed in a black nightgown stepped out, her blue eyes considering the unit standing outside with less surprise than Raz would have expected. He barely had time to notice the X-shaped scar that crossed her face, centering around her right eye, when the guard who had knocked spoke.

At the height he was, Raz could barely hear anything, a reality not helped by the fact that the man seemed to be whispering. Still, whether it was luck or the fact that his mind was so focused on the one thing, the words "at once" and "urgent" were amongst the disjointed dozen that he did manage to catch, whispered up to him by the wind.

Anticipation jolted through him. Raz watched carefully as the woman he assumed was one of the housekeepers gave a brief bow and closed the door. Two minutes later it opened again, and this time Adrion himself appeared, his slim form hastily dressed in a light black and gold suit with a white turban that fell down one side of his face. His crutch clicked against the cobbled sidewalk, and he nodded to the guards, who turned and began moving south, back the way they'd come.

Doing his best to ignore the pain in his side, Raz stood, picking Ahna up off the roof where she'd been lying beside him. He'd been unable to get out of his armor—his one attempt ending in the painful realization that he probably wouldn't manage it without help—so while he moved, leaping from building to building and scaling up and down brick and stone walls, he stayed clear of the edges. Every now and then he'd peer over to assert he was keeping with the group of five making their way through the empty streets below.

The going was easier than he'd anticipated. For almost a half hour Adrion and the guards moved as rapidly as they could—surprisingly quick considering the man's handicap—all of them apparently as eager to get to their destination before the morning crowds as Raz was. On the other hand, they seemed to be headed toward the bazaars, a busy place at all times except the darkest hours of the night. It wasn't long before Raz was having to do more stalking than following, darting over narrow alleys and clinging from low overhangs to avoid being seen by the growing number of people milling about. He was positive one woman caught a glimpse of him as she hung her wet laundry out for the dry wind.

He was gone before a double take could tell her it wasn't a trick of the morning light.

For another quarter hour this was the pattern. Raz would check to ensure he was still heading in the right direction, then duck through a window into an empty room or drop onto a hanging balcony before he was spotted. He was just starting to wonder if he'd already been sighted and was being led on a wild chase when finally he stopped, crouching low against the wood-slatted roof beneath him.

Adrion and the guards had come to a halt outside one of the market's dingier buildings. A thick timber-and-brick monolith, it squatted between a tanner's shop and an apothecary famous for medicines that more often than not turned out to be equal parts dirty water and cat piss. It was a surprisingly unassuming structure, far from the grand image Raz had been carrying in his head of where the Mahsadën might hold their most intimate meetings, but it made some sense. The šef wouldn't want to be ostentatious about the business they held behind closed doors. A grand city-palace in the middle of the wealthy districts would have attracted more attention than it was worth. Never a fine idea in their line of work.

Still, Raz was surprised the group had managed to humble themselves to *this* level...

But, inching to the edge of the roof and watching the proceedings below, he grew more and more certain. A pair of men dressed in filthy rags seemed to be loitering pointlessly around the entrance, chatting and kicking small stones back and forth. It was a good act, failed only by the fine sword hilt sticking from the pant loop of one man and the broad-spear poorly hidden in the archway of the entrance door. Those few merchants and customers who moved armed through the marketplaces rarely carried weapons of such quality.

Nor did the guard, for that matter...

Sarydâ, Raz concluded, frowning. He watched Adrion approach the closer of the two men and mutter something in his ear. The mercenary nodded, looking both ways down the street before opening the door and waving Adrion through. Closing it behind him, the man nodded again to the four guardsmen, who dispersed at once for the market.

Within a minute they were gone, and Raz waited. Fighting his impatience, he looked both ways down the narrow street. When the brief moment came where the roads were clear of possible witnesses, Raz opened his wings and dropped, falling silently on the two men below.

They died before either could so much as whisper a breath of warning.

XVII

---

*"They say he's made a' steel and fire, with eyes like a' demon and claws like a' wolf.
He moves quieter than the Moon, and smiles with teeth red from the blood a' bad
children. If'n you don't listen, a silver duke'll buy him for the night, and in the mornin'
you'll be gone, never ta' be seen again…"*

—bedtime fable, c. 860 v.S.

"HOW COULD YOU LET HIM GO? *HOW?* OVER TWO
HUNDRED STRONG, AND ALL WE HAVE TO SHOW FOR IT IS
TWENTY-FIVE DEAD AND ENDLESS QUESTIONS FROM THE
MID-DISTRICTS!"

"Gaorys, you weren't there! My men say i'Syul took a bolt full in the
back! He's likely crawled up in some hole in the slums, bleeding to death.
We've only to wait and—"

"OH, YOU THINK SO, DO YOU?" Vyrr Gaorys spluttered. His
paranoia was clearly getting the better of him. He was purple in the face
from screaming. "AND HOW MUCH ARE YOU WILLING TO BET
ON THAT, HMM? YOUR LIFE? *MINE?* BECAUSE THAT'S WHAT
WE ARE RISKING! WE ARE—!"

"Enough! The both of you!"

Ergoin Sass's words cut through the argument like a whip, and
Gaorys spluttered to a silence mid-sentence. Across the wide circular
table, Ulan Orture caught the retort he'd been about to bellow back.

From his spot against the wall, Adrion watched the proceedings with
feigned boredom, leaning against the arm of his chair with two fingers
pressed to his temple. The meeting had been called in haste, but all came
as summoned. The eight šef had taken their places around the oak table
in the center of the vast window-lit room, their other lieutenants seated
along the wall to Adrion's right.

More than a few of whom were taking in the argument with open
mouths.

"Orture, Gaorys is correct," Sass sighed finally, looking to the
Captain-Commander of the Miropan guard. "I have it on good authority
that the lizard was injured, but most likely not so grievously as to mark an
end to this madness. He'll hide away, but it's only a matter of a week or
two before he—"

"He won't."

Every head in the room turned toward Adrion. Sass shot him a seething look, but Adrion ignored him. It was high time he start making his own voice heard, even if some šef didn't agree.

"Who are you to interrupt us?" Alysya Orture, Ulan's twin sister, demanded sharply. "If he'd wanted your opinion, Ergoin would have—"

"Quiet, Alysya."

The room deadened instantly. Imaneal Evony was watching Adrion with deceptive casualness. The gold and silver rings on his fingers glinted in the light of the morning Sun, and Adrion felt some of his confidence slip away staring into those cruel eyes.

"Speak," Evony ordered coolly, and no other voice rose to oppose the command.

"H-he won't." Adrion tripped over the words, coughed, and continued more strongly. "He won't hide. Raz doesn't have the patience to, and he likely sees this time as our most vulnerable. And is he wrong? We've put all our eggs in one basket and, now that the basket has slipped through our hands, where do we stand? Stalemated again."

"ï'Syul is injured, though." Evony tilted his head. "Of that we are all agreed."

"Short of running him through-and-through, I can't imagine a wound in the world that would slow my cousin down."

Evony nodded slowly, pausing before speaking again.

"And you think... what? That we should expect retaliation today? Tomorrow? When?"

Adrion had just opened his mouth to express his worst fear when there was an abrupt knock on the room's carved double doors.

"What is it?" Sass snarled. He was clearly not happy with the way the conversation was going. "You were told not to disturb us!"

"Urg-urgent message!" a wavering voice called through the wood. "Beggin' yer attention promptly, sirs and madams!"

Sass frowned, looking to Evony, who nodded. Adrion, on the other hand, had heard something else in the messenger's tone. He'd just started crying out a warning when Sass gestured to one of the sentries posted on either side of the door.

"Wait!"

But the sarydâ had already reached down and pulled up the handle.

There was an explosion of wood and dust, and the man was catapulted across the room into the table as the left door was kicked in so violently it ripped free of its top hinge. The second sentry barely had time to loosen his sword from its scabbard when something silver flashed, opening him up from hip to hip. He was on his knees, screaming his last few breaths away, when Raz i'Syul Arro stepped into the room.

In his free hand, held by their hair, swung a half-dozen heads of the sarydâ assigned to guard the stairway outside.

Raz examined the room almost leisurely. Diamond-paned windows cut through the stone of the west wall, casting the floor with bright patches of morning light. Six men and two women leapt to their feet around a circular table in the center of the wide chamber, all turned to look at him with a surprising level of calm. Beyond them, another eleven looked on, clearly much less reserved. Amongst this group, his crutch leaning beside him, was Adrion.

Raz ignored his cousin's glare, tossing Ahna over his shoulder and looking back. The man he'd held at blade point was standing in the doorway, shaking in his boots.

"Why are you still here?" Raz asked him, lacing the question with implication.

The sarydâ ran so fast he tripped and almost fell headfirst down the stairs.

Raz chuckled dourly. Dropping the heads to the floor with staggered *thumps,* he stepped closer to the eight šef. A few flinched when he moved, betraying the fear hidden behind nearly every face, masterfully masked. Even Vyrr Gaorys held his composure, though his hands started to shake when Raz's eyes passed over him.

"Raz i'Syul."

Raz blinked. One of the šef stepped out of the group and walked around the table toward him. He was a tall man, swathed in gold-trimmed lavender robes that swirled with the slightest motion. He looked to be the oldest of them, his head completely bald and chin framed by a pointed goatee. His sharp eyes, though, spoke of wit volumes beyond his age.

A man Raz had never met personally, but knew well by reputation.

"Imaneal Evony," he stated plainly. Evony smiled, coming to a stop a dozen feet away, just outside of Ahna's reach.

Clever old man.

"I see you know me," the šef remarked, gesturing to the other members of the group. "So I assume you know the rest of us, and our confidants." He motioned to the eleven seated against the back wall. Raz's gaze fell back on Adrion for a moment.

"Some better than others," he replied, not taking his eyes off his cousin until the man looked away.

"Excellent!" Evony exclaimed with another smile. "Then there is no need for introduction! Now, tell me… what can we do for you?"

Raz stared at him, and the stillness of the room could almost be tasted on the tongue.

"What do you expect me to say to that?" he asked after a moment. "I'd figured my reasons for being here weren't terribly complex."

"But they are," Evony replied, frowning in false confusion. "We"— he motioned again to the other šef—"are your employers. We have the assets to supply you with whatever it is you need. Work? I'm familiar with your rules, and I can assure you we have plenty of problems you would be interested in handling for us. Money? Not an issue. I'm sure Ergoin and the others haven't been paying you *half* of what you are—"

"*I don't want your money!*" Raz spat, the crest along his neck flaring up. This time a number of the šef cringed. Only Evony and Ergoin Sass, who stood near the far end of the table, didn't budge.

"You're sure?" Evony asked him with a knowing smile. "I don't think you understand. I can offer you rates that are deserving of your skills. And I can offer you other things. Here, Emyl!" One of the men seated at the back leapt up at once. "Draw up documents ceding the Vorshceyer estate to Master i'Syul. They won't be needing it after—"

"I said *NO!*"

The room stilled at Raz's roar. Evony frowned, the flare of his ego winning over his desire to turn Raz in his favor.

"This is your last chance, Monster," the man snarled, glaring with a daring intensity Raz had never seen in a human. "We've given you a place in this society before, and I'm willing to offer it to you again so long as you do *as* I say *when* I say it. You're an animal, and if it weren't for your limited talents I would have had you put down long ago."

Raz's body chilled at the words, and he felt the taunts tear holes in his self-control. His eyes never leaving Evony's, he took a step forward.

"Slaver," he hissed as he moved, staring down the man, who amazingly stood his ground. "Murderer. Thief. Rapist. All of these and more can be applied to every one of you, Evony. Yourself especially, if I've heard right. You kill for personal gain. You take away freedoms so that your own might be improved. You maim and scar and lock people away in places that never see the Sun. You say you know my rules? Then answer me this. This game is at its end. I've done things for you that I will never forgive myself for. So, knowing that, tell me *why* would I *ever* go back to—?"

The whisper of footsteps.

Raz sensed more than saw the motion, leaping to the side in time to evade the curved dagger that would have buried itself into his lower spine. Even so, he couldn't avoid the blow completely, and he snarled when the thin blade caught the membrane of his left wing, slicing a foot-long vertical gash clean through it. Reflexively he twisted, swinging Ahna around like an ax.

Her head caught Sass, who'd taken advantage of Raz's distraction to slip behind him, in the side just below his stomach, ripping him open from end to end.

Raz's body shook from the pain radiating from his wing and the aching crossbow wound. He watched his old handler stumble back, gaining his balance just in time to gape at his own insides slipping through the slash in his gut. Sass dropped the knife and fell to his knees, desperately grabbing at his entrails, scrambling to hold them in place. When he realized it was no use, he looked up at the other šef, his own shock reflected back in each of their faces for a long moment.

Then he collapsed to the ground, eyes open and one side of his face smacking down into the blood pooling around him.

"NO!" someone screamed, and all hell broke loose.

Raz let go, giving in completely to the animal. He turned on the room, his vision slipping into the red-black spectrum of his own bloodlust. Falum Tyle, the head of the Mahsadën's ragroot trade, fell first, braving a bodily lunge at Raz, sword drawn and yelling a warcry before leaping from the table he'd run across.

Ahna speared him out of the air, flinging him through the windows with a *crash*.

Raz was the Moon's reaper, dancing to death's drum, flashing across the room in all different directions. He leapt and twisted, slashed and thrust. Ahna moved through his hands like water, feeling light as air as he twirled her over his head, behind his back, and around his shoulders. She cut through everything she touched like a scythe taken to harvest, and immediately the room was filled with screams. Those few who tried to break for the door found their way somehow barred by Raz, his tail sweeping feet from under bodies and breaking necks. His wings whipped out to join the melee of steel and flesh, shattering bones and throwing people into the table and walls. The šef were struck down one by one, some putting up a fight with daggers and swords, others pleading for their lives. Ahna fell on them like judgment. Krane úl'Syen, master of the local thieves guilds. Vyrr Gaorys, the money handler. Dimonia Gríc, the woman responsible for coordinating and running the black market sex trades. Alysya Orture, a dark-skinned Percian who handled all inter city trade, and her brother, Ulan.

There were others between them, the confidants that had accompanied the group. Raz made no exception, hacking Ahna left and right, up and down, leaving some wounded, some dead, and some hovering in between. Bodies fell, the stone floor of the room growing slick and sticky with blood. One after another they piled up. Throats were cut, bodies mangled, limbs severed, flesh slashed. Raz spun like a whirlwind of vengeance, a gale of steel, teeth, and claws.

After three minutes, it ended.

Raz came to a stop over the last moving figure in the room. Every other body was still, but Imaneal Evony looked up at Raz from his place on the ground. He scrambled back, sliding over the wet floor. One of his eyes was sealed closed by the blood seeping from a cut across his forehead, and his right leg was twisted at an odd angle, broken at the hip where Raz's tail had thrown him across the room.

"I can give you anything!" he screamed. Raz followed him unhurriedly. Ahna at his side, he stepped over the forms scattered across the floor. "ANYTHING! JUST NAME IT!"

Evony's back found the corner of the wall, and he started to shake.

"You can't do this," he breathed, staring up at Raz. "You can't do this! They'll kill you! You think you've won by doing this? YOU'RE WRONG! WE ARE EVERYWHERE! THE OTHERS WILL FIND YOU! THEY'LL FIND YOU AND THEY'LL—!"

Shtunk.

The bottom tip of Ahna's shaft speared his heart, splitting through him, and Evony jerked once. His bald head lolled toward his chest, his forehead resting on the leather of the dviassegai's lowest handle.

For a long time Raz stood over the dead man, watching him, unsure of exactly what he was looking for. He was in control of himself now, he was sure of it. So why did he still have the savage urge to tear Evony apart with his bare hands, along with every other corpse in the room?

He resisted. Placing a foot on the man's shoulder, he pulled Ahna free, letting Evony slide sideways down the wall. The man slumped to the ground, sending short ripples through the thick, pooling blood.

Turning away, Raz listened to the snuffling of the survivors, taking in the moans and keening wails of shock and pain. His eyes moved over the forms of the living and dead alike, and he finally found the one he was looking for shivering near the east wall of the room, curled up on his side by the headless body of Alysya Orture. Moving to stand over the figure, Raz put a foot on his shoulder and shoved him over.

Adrion rolled onto his back, glaring up at Raz and cradling what looked like a broken arm. There was a large gash across his chest, ending just below his collarbone, and red wetness dribbled from a stab in the thigh of his bad leg.

And yet, despite all of it, he still managed a sneer.

"You going to kill me, too, cousin?"

Raz didn't respond at first, looking the man over. He pulled Ahna off his shoulder and gripped her in both hands.

"You don't deserve any better," he said quietly.

"Oh, and you're going to be the judge of that?" Adrion demanded sarcastically, pushing himself up onto his good elbow. "You? Really? Look at yourself sometime, Raz. You turned into you a long time before I turned into me. If anything, you taught me how to sail this ship."

"I'm not you," Raz snapped. "And if you say that I am again, Mychal, I swear by the Sun I'll cleave you open right here and now."

"DON'T CALL ME THAT!" his cousin screamed, striking out at Raz and falling over. "DON'T CALL ME THAT! BASTARD!"

"Fine, *Adrion*," Raz smirked, watching the man struggle to sit up again, his right arm hanging uselessly from his shoulder. "I'll call you whatever you want. I'd rather it, actually. You don't deserve the name your parents gave you."

"MY PARENTS ARE DEAD!"

The room seemed to go quiet, the silence of the dead around them drowning out the cries of the living. Adrion started to laugh.

"Dead!" he chortled, and Raz was shocked to see tears cut through the blood that stained his face. "All dead. Because of you, Raz. My parents, my sister, now my friends. You. Killed. *Everyone*."

"I didn't kill the Arros," Raz hissed.

"You as good as," Adrion chuckled, looking up. "Where were you, Raz? When they came, when those men spilled out of the city like wolves, where were you? You weren't there. You were out playing on the rooftops. And they were there for you."

Abruptly, he stopped laughing. In an instant Adrion's face shifted from maddened amusement to loathing.

"They were there for *you!*" he screamed, throwing himself at Raz. "FOR YOU! I'LL KILL YOU, YOU FUCKING LIZARD! I'LL TEAR YOU APART AND BURN YOUR FUCKING—!"

Raz backhanded the man, sending him sprawling. For a full minute Raz stood over his cousin, heart pounding, feeling Adrion's words rock through his body and tear at old wounds.

Then he calmed himself, resting Ahna's tip on the ground. Using her to help him kneel by Adrion, he found him unconscious but breathing. From a knee Raz stared down at his damaged face, trying to see the boy he remembered from years ago.

He couldn't. Mychal was dead and gone.

"It was my fault," Raz said quietly. "You're not wrong. But at least I fought to make things better, Adrion. You didn't."

Raz got to his feet gingerly and eased Ahna over both shoulders.

"Take care of our Grandmother, cousin."

XVIII

"We're through. You can come out now."

At the driver's words, Raz pushed up on the wooden planks he was lying under, lifting the door to the smuggler's hatch he'd been curled in for the last three hours. Sitting up and groaning at the throbbing of his healing wing and side, he looked out the back of the open cart.

The last twinkling lights of Miropa, the Gem of the South, were fading quickly in the distant night.

Pushing himself to his feet, Raz grasped the cloth covering to steady himself. It had been years since he'd last traveled by cart, and the rumbling, bumpy sensation beneath his feet as he replaced the hatch's cover felt both pleasant and sadly nostalgic. The wagon itself was a lot like his family's had been, in fact, packed with goods and items to trade, pushed to the sides to offer better balance. Somewhere in the mess, Ahna was stowed away, along with his other weapons. His armor was there, too, finally removed with the help of hands greased by a couple of his last gold crowns.

It didn't matter. Money had little value if you couldn't spend it.

Raz moved to the front and knelt beside the old man seated there. It had taken a few days to track down someone willing to sneak him out of the city—not to mention a great deal more coin—since Raz had, in the course of a single morning, become the most wanted fugitive in the South. Still, he'd gotten lucky, though the man had refused to tell him his name.

Raz looked out over the moonlit sands. They'd been traveling for less than an hour, and he already knew he'd never been this far north before.

"S'far as the border," the old man said suddenly, flicking the reins so that the two old mares pulling the cart picked up their pace a little. "I ain't taken' ya' farther than that."

Raz nodded. Looking over his shoulder, his amber eyes fell on Miropa once more.

"It's far enough. Anywhere away from here is far enough."

Adrion was throwing things again. Lazura could hear him screaming profanity from her place on the balcony, grabbing anything within reach of the bed he was stuck in and smashing it against the nearest wall. Night had fallen, and with it came a messenger from the newly appointed Captain-Commander of the city guard.

Apparently, the man hadn't been bearing good news.

"WHAT DO YOU MEAN, 'HE'S GONE'?"

Another crash rang out, and Lazura sighed, lifting a spoonful of soup from the clay bowl in her hand and bringing it to the Grandmother's lips. There was a dull flash, and the old woman coughed, choking on the invisible force that pushed the broth down her throat. A moment later she resumed her statue-like stare.

"Did you hear that, you ancient hag?" Lazura crooned softly, repeating the process. "Your precious pet isn't in the city anymore. He's run off, tail between his legs. Probably heard the other fringe cities are sending their best to get after him, didn't he?"

The Grandmother choked again, inhaling half the soup Lazura was compelling her to swallow, some of it dripping down her chin.

"I can never keep you clean for very long, can I?" Lazura asked with false concern, tsk-tsking. She reached up and dabbed the old woman's lips clean. "Doesn't matter, though, does it? Another year, and I'll have what I need from you."

The Grandmother's eyes never moved, their dull gaze unwavering.

"If only I could hear your thoughts," Lazura laughed, a sound like wind chimes. "If only I knew how you worked. It would be so much *easier*. Look."

Putting the soup down, Lazura held out a hand. There was another dark flash, and a tiny flame appeared, floating above her palm, white like the fine ivories of Perce. She grinned in pleasure at the sight of the arcane fire. The flame grew and spread, building until it crackled around Lazura's entire hand.

Then it sputtered, clung to life for a moment, and died.

Lazura cursed and tried a second time. The flash came, but little more than a spark rose from her palm this time, and she cursed again. Whirling on the Grandmother, she grasped both armrests of the old woman's chair and leaned over until their faces were barely an inch apart, her blue eyes peering into those empty gray ones.

"I will have your secrets," she crooned, searching the still gaze for any sign of motion, any hint that her words were comprehended. "My master is dead. The Mahsadën of Miropa are gone, but only for the moment. And when the other cities replace them, I will have my place there. I will *carry* your pathetic cripple of a grandchild on my back if I have to, but when he is the man I need him to be, my turn to rise will come. And by then, bitch, I will have my strength back. I will have it back, even if I have to cut it from your body with my bare hands!"

"LAZURA!"

Lazura groaned as Adrion's voice rang out from the bedroom. The man had become insufferable since the surgeon ordered him to bed-rest for his injuries three days ago.

"LAZURA! MY TEA! *NOW!*"

Standing up straight and smoothing her black silks, Lazura replaced her charming smile.

"Coming!" she called back sweetly before bending down to pick up the bowl of cold soup. With a last glance at the old woman, she hurried back into the house.

If she'd stayed another minute or so, she might have noticed the movement. If she'd stayed, Lazura might have seen the Grandmother's eyes come back to life, her pupils dilating and focusing.

If she'd stayed, she might have seen those eyes jerk upward, looking pleadingly to the Moon hanging in the sky high above, crowned by Her Stars.

At once a dry wind picked up, whispering through the alleys and open windows of the surrounding buildings. Dust was kicked up in the dark streets. Doors left ajar banged shut. The air rushed back and forth, seemingly moving on no set course until it rushed like a wave over the Grandmother's frail, frozen body, washing through white hair and over mottled skin.

Muscles that had been taut for too many years relaxed. Willful breath rushed into the old woman's lungs, and she partially collapsed in her chair. Gasping and wheezing, the Grandmother grasped the arms of her seat and pushed herself up, barely able to lift her own head. When she did, though, her eyes found the Moon again, and she smiled in content surrender to the call.

Reaching out, the Grandmother grasped the railing of the balcony to her right. It took everything she had to pull herself to her feet. Fragile knees shook under the strain, atrophied muscles struggling mightily to keep her standing.

Another breeze blew, and the woman suddenly found that strength reborn.

Standing tall, the Grandmother looked north. There, between the crowning towers of the two nearby estates, she could see the barest outline of the horizon, marking the land beyond the walls of the city. Her lips cracked open, and words formed gently in a whisper so low they were almost lost to the wind.

"Be safe, my child."

And then the Grandmother tilted herself over the railing, plummeting from the balcony to the cobbled street below.

EPILOGUE

"There is no breaking such a bond."

—from the journals of Carro al'Dor

Syrah awoke so suddenly she jolted up, gasping. She was drenched in sweat, the dark night air digging a chill through her thin gown. She shivered, tugging the quilted furs of her bed to her chest.

Beside her, Reyn groaned groggily.

"Syrah? What... what's wrong?"

"Shhh." She turned to him, kissing his forehead and resting a hand on his cheek. He was warm, whereas her skin might have been ice in comparison. "It's nothing. A bad dream. Go back to sleep."

Reyn nodded, already halfway there. She ran her fingers through his shoulder-length dirty blonde hair until he was breathing deep again, lost to the world.

Sliding out of bed, Syrah stepped into her fur boots before stealing across the room to crack the door, slipping into the lantern-lit hall. Turning right, she started the midnight walk she'd done a hundred times before, but not in years.

For some reason, or perhaps by some strange chance, the terror of old dreams had returned.

She'd visited that house again tonight. That dirty hot hovel of which the memories had only just started to fade. Subconsciously she traced the spot at her side where strong fingers had gripped her, pinning her hands down with a thick arm. The faces of the men she'd finally started to forget returned in vivid detail, leering at her from the dark corners of the hall.

Syrah stopped. Putting her back against the stone, she slid down to sit on the floor, wrapping her arms around her knees. For a long time she stared at the narrow table of lit candles across from her, wishing the faces gone, wishing their wicked smiles and hungry eyes away. Slowly they faded, chased away by the soft light.

The one that took their place, though, most would have called more terrible and frightening.

Syrah had long since removed the black stain of blood from Raz i'Syul's face in her memories. She could picture him, cleansed, amber eyes burning with the same glow of the candles. His strange reptilian features did not seem so harsh these years later. On the contrary, they were comforting, tangible details that were the only things she wanted to remember from that day. For so long she'd prayed to the Lifegiver that she wouldn't forget...

His face was the only thing that ever made the nightmares stay away.

Note From the Author
[aka: The Plight of the Writer]

As a writer, I cannot accurately portray exactly how much your support and enjoyment of this collection means to me, as there are no words grand enough to paint the picture. *Child of the Daystar* is a labor of love, a commitment to the creation of a story that will entertain, enthrall, and inspire, as so many other tales have done for me before. Your appreciation and enjoyment of my writing is a massive portion of the rewards of being an author.

It is with this note that I move on to a more personal plea, a cry for assistance from all of you who got to the end of the volume and were even just a little bit sad it didn't continue on:

Please, *please*, consider rating and reviewing *Child of the Daystar* on one or two major bookselling or book group sites.

Even better, *please* consider supporting me directly on Patreon, and get early access to chapters and books, art, cool stuff, and much more. Find me at:
patreon.com/bryceoconnor

Many people don't know that there are thousands of books published every day, most of those in the USA alone. Over the course of a year, a quarter of a million authors will vie for a small place in the massive world of print and publishing. We fight to get even the tiniest traction, fight to climb upward one inch at a time towards the bright light of bestsellers, publishing contracts, and busy book signings.

Thing is, we need all the help we can get.

Your positive input into that world, whether it's a review, a follow on social media, or financially supporting your favorite authors, makes the climb just a little bit easier. Rating and reviewing books you enjoy and following a writer's journey gives your favorite authors a boost upward.

With that all out of the way, thank you again so much for picking up *Child of the Daystar*. If you'd like to give me feedback directly, have a question about Raz and his adventures, or just want to chat, drop me a message any time on Facebook, or on my website.

It has been a pleasure entertaining you, and I vigorously hope you continue to follow *The Wings of War* series to see what becomes of Raz i'Syul Arro.

Bryce O'Connor

Made in the USA
Columbia, SC
13 July 2020